Brenda Jacks... author of more t... lives in Jackso... between family... at authorbrenda... website at bren...

Sandra Marton is a *USA Today* bestselling author. A four-time finalist for the RITA®, the coveted award given by Romance Writers of America, she's also won eight Romantic Times Reviewers' Choice Awards, the Holt Medallion, and Romantic Times' Career Achievement Award. Sandra's heroes are powerful, sexy, take-charge men who think they have it all – until that one special woman comes along. Stand back, because together they're bound to set the world on fire.

USA Today bestselling author **Heidi Betts** writes sexy, sassy, sensational romance. The recipient of several awards and stellar reviews, Heidi's books combine believable characters with compelling plotlines, and are consistently described as 'delightful,' 'sizzling,' and 'wonderfully witty.'

Scandalous Secrets

Scandalous Secrets:
Secrets
and Lies

BRENDA JACKSON

SANDRA MARTON

HEIDI BETTS

MILLS & BOON

First Published in Great Britain 2021
by Mills & Boon, an imprint of HarperCollins*Publishers* Ltd,
1 London Bridge Street, London, SE1 9GF

www.harpercollins.co.uk

HarperCollins*Publishers*
1st Floor, Watermarque Building,
Ringsend Road, Dublin 4, Ireland

SCANDALOUS SECRETS: SECRETS AND LIES
© 2021 Harlequin Books S.A.

The Secret Affair © 2014 Brenda Streater Jackson
The Real Rio D'Aquila © 2011 Sandra Marton
Secrets, Lies & Lullabies © 2012 Heidi Betts

ISBN: 978-0-263-29911-3

Printed and bound in Spain
by CPI, Barcelona

THE SECRET AFFAIR

BRENDA JACKSON

To the man who will always and
forever be the love of my life,
Gerald Jackson, Sr.

In whom are hid all the treasures
of wisdom and knowledge.
Colossians 2:3 KJV

Prologue

Jillian Novak stared across the table at her sister, not believing what she'd just heard.

Jillian placed the glass of wine she'd been holding on the table, barely keeping the drink from spilling. "What do you mean you aren't going with me? That's crazy, Paige. Need I remind you that you're the one who planned the trip?"

"A reminder isn't needed, Jill, but please understand my dilemma," Paige said in a rueful tone, her dark brown eyes shaded with regret. "Getting a part in a Steven Spielberg movie is a dream come true. You can't imagine what I was feeling—happiness at being chosen one minute, and then disappointment the next, when I found out that shooting starts the same week I was supposed to be on the cruise with you."

"Let me guess, your happiness overpowered your disappointment, right?" Jillian felt a pounding pressure in her head and knew why. She had been looking forward to the Mediterranean cruise—for many reasons—and now it appeared she wouldn't be going.

"I'm sorry, Jill. You've never gone on a cruise and I know it's one of the things on your bucket list."

Paige's apology only made Jillian feel worse. She'd

made her sister feel awful for making a choice Jillian would have made herself if given the chance. Reaching across the table, she grabbed Paige's hand.

"I'm the one who should be apologizing, Paige. I was only thinking of myself. You're right. Getting that part in the movie is a dream come true and you'd be crazy not to take it. I'm truly happy for you. Congratulations."

A bright smile spread across Paige's lips. "Thanks. I wanted so much for us to spend time together on the cruise. It's been ages since me, you, Pam and Nadia have had sister time."

Nadia, a senior in college, was their youngest sister. At twenty-one she was two years younger than Paige and four years younger than Jillian. Pamela, their oldest sister—who Jillian, Nadia and Paige were convinced was the best older sister anyone could ever have—was ten years older than Jillian. A former actress, Pam had given up the glitter of Hollywood to return home to Gamble, Wyoming, and raise them when their father died. Now Pam lived in Denver. She was married, the mother of two and the CEO of two acting schools, one in Denver and the other in Gamble. Paige had followed in Pam's footsteps and pursued an acting career. She lived in Los Angeles.

With Pam's busy schedule, she'd said accompanying them on the cruise would have been close to impossible. Nadia had wanted to go but finals kept her from doing so. Jillian had wanted sister time with at least one of her siblings. And now that she had completed medical school, she needed those two weeks on the cruise as a getaway before starting her residency. But there was another reason she wanted to take that two-week cruise.

Aidan Westmoreland.

It was hard to believe it had been a little over a year since she'd broken things off with him. And every time she remembered the reason she'd done so her heart ached. She needed a distraction from her memories.

"You okay, Jill?"

Jillian glanced up at Paige and forced a smile. "Yes, why do you ask?"

"You zoned out on me just now. I was talking and you appeared to be a million miles away. I noticed you haven't been yourself since I arrived in New Orleans. More than once you've seemed preoccupied about something. Is everything okay?"

Jillian waved off Paige's words. The last thing she wanted was for her sister to start worrying and begin digging. "Yes, everything is okay, Paige."

Paige didn't look convinced. "Um, I don't know. Maybe I should forget about being in that movie and go on that cruise with you after all."

Jillian picked up her wineglass to take a sip. "Don't be silly. You're doing the right thing. Besides, I'm not going on the cruise."

"Why not?"

Jillian was surprised at her sister's question. "Surely you don't expect me to go without you."

"You need a break before starting your residency."

Jillian rolled her eyes. "Get real, Paige. What would I do on a two-week cruise by myself?"

"Rest, relax, enjoy the sights, the ocean, the peace and quiet. And you might luck up and meet some nice single guy."

Jillian shook her head. "Nice single guys don't go on cruises alone. Besides, the last thing I need right now is a man in my life."

Paige laughed. "Jill, you haven't had a guy in your life since you dated Cobb Grindstone in your senior year at Gamble High. I think what's missing in your life is a man."

Jillian bristled at her sister's words. "Not hardly, especially with my busy schedule. And I don't see you with anyone special."

"At least I've been dating over the years. You haven't. Or, if you have, you haven't told me about it."

Jillian schooled her expression into an impassive facade. She'd never told Paige about her affair with Aidan, and considering how it had ended she was glad she hadn't.

"Jill?"

She glanced up at her sister. "Yes?"

A teasing smile spread across Paige's lips. "You aren't keeping secrets, are you?"

Jill knew Paige had given her the perfect opportunity to come clean about her affair with Aidan, but she wasn't ready. Even after a year, the pain was still raw. And the last thing Jillian needed was for Paige to start probing for more information.

"You know the reason I don't have a man in my life is because of time. My focus has been on becoming a doctor and nothing else." Paige didn't have to know that a few years ago Aidan had wiggled his way past that focus without much effort. That had been a mistake that cost her.

"That's why I think you should go on that cruise without me," Paige said. "You've worked hard and need to rest and enjoy yourself for a change. Once you begin your residency you'll have even less time for yourself— or anything else."

"That's true," Jillian said. "But—"

"No buts, Jillian."

Jillian knew that tone. She also knew that whenever Paige called her by her full name she meant business. "If I were to go on that cruise alone I'd be bored stiff. You're talking about two weeks."

Paige gave her a pointed look. "I'm talking about two weeks that I believe you need. And just think of all the fabulous places you'll get to see—Barcelona, France, Rome, Greece and Turkey." Now it was Paige who reached out to take hold of Jillian's hand. "Look, Jill, there *is* something going on with you, I can feel it. Whatever it is, it's tearing you apart. I picked up on it months ago, the last time I came to visit you."

A wry smile touched Paige's lips when she added, "Perhaps you *are* keeping secrets. Maybe there's some doctor in medical school that caught your eye and you're not ready to tell me about him. One who has blown your mind and you don't know how to handle the intensity of such a relationship. If that's the case, I understand. All of us at some time or another have issues we prefer to deal with alone. That's why I believe two weeks on the open seas will be good for you."

Jillian drew in a deep breath. Paige didn't know how close she was to the truth. Her problem *did* center on some doctor, but not one attending medical school with her.

At that moment the waitress returned with their meal, and Jillian appreciated the interruption. She knew Paige would not be happy until Jillian agreed to go on the cruise. She'd heard what Paige had said—Paige knew something was bothering Jillian. It would only be a matter of time before Pam and Nadia knew as well, if they didn't already. Besides, Jillian had already taken those two weeks off. If she didn't go on the cruise, the family would expect her to come home and spend that time with them. She couldn't do that. What if Aidan came home unexpectedly while she was there? He was the last person she wanted to see.

"Jill?"

Jillian drew in another deep breath and met Paige's gaze. "Okay, I'll do it. I'll go cruising alone. Hopefully, I'll enjoy myself."

Paige smiled. "You will. There will be plenty for you to do and on those days when you feel like doing nothing, you can do that, too. Everybody needs to give their mind a rest once in a while."

Jillian nodded. Her mind definitely needed a rest. She would be the first to admit that she had missed Aidan— the steamy hot text messages, the emails that made her adrenaline surge and the late-night phone calls that sent heat sizzling through her entire body.

But that had been before she'd learned the truth. Now all she wanted to do was get over him.

She sighed deeply while thinking that Paige was right. Jillian needed that cruise and the time away it would give her. She would go on the cruise alone.

Dr. Aidan Westmoreland entered his apartment and removed his lab coat. After running a frustrated hand down his face, he glanced at his watch. He'd hoped he would have heard something by now. What if...

The ringing of his cell phone made him pause on his way to the kitchen. It was the call he'd been waiting for. "Paige?"

"Yes, it's me."

"Is she still going?" he asked, not wasting time with chitchat.

There was a slight pause on the other end and in that short space of time knots formed in his stomach. "Yes, she's still going on the cruise, Aidan."

He released the breath he'd been holding as Paige continued, "Jill still has no idea I'm aware that the two of you had an affair."

Aidan hadn't known Paige knew the truth, either, until she'd paid him a surprise visit last month. According to her, she'd figured things out the year Jillian had entered medical school. She'd become suspicious when he'd come home for his cousin Riley's wedding and she'd overheard him call Jillian *Jilly* in an intimate tone. Paige had been concerned this past year when she'd noticed Jillian seemed troubled by something that she wouldn't share with Paige.

Paige had talked to Ivy, Jillian's best friend, who'd also been concerned about Jillian. Ivy had shared everything about the situation with Paige. That prompted Paige to fly to Charlotte and confront him. Until then, he'd been clueless as to the real reason behind his and Jillian's breakup.

When Paige had told him of the cruise she and Jillian had planned and had suggested an idea for getting Jillian on the cruise alone, he'd readily embraced the plan.

I've done my part and the rest is up to you, Aidan. I hope you can convince Jill of the truth.

Moments later he ended the call and continued to the kitchen where he grabbed a beer. Popping the top, he leaned against the counter and took a huge gulp. Two weeks on the open seas with Jillian would be interesting. But he intended to make it more than just interesting. He aimed to make it productive.

A determined smile spread across his lips. By the time the cruise ended there would be no doubt in Jillian's mind that he was the only man for her.

Moments later, he tossed the empty can in the recycle bin before heading for the shower. As he undressed, he couldn't help but recall how his secret affair with Jillian had begun nearly four years ago....

One

"So, how does it feel to be twenty-one?"

Jillian's breath caught in her throat when Aidan Westmoreland's tall frame slid into the seat across from her. It was only then that she noticed everyone had gone inside. She and Aidan were the only ones on the patio that overlooked a beautiful lake.

This birthday party had been a huge surprise and Aidan's attendance even more so since he rarely came home from medical school. She couldn't imagine he'd come home just for her birthday. With her away at college most of the time as well, their paths rarely crossed. She couldn't recall them ever holding what she considered a real conversation during the four years she'd known him.

"It feels the same as yesterday," she said. "Age is just a number. No big deal."

A smile touched the corners of his lips and her stomach clenched. He had a gorgeous smile, one that complemented the rest of him. If there was such a thing as eye candy he was certainly it. She had the hots for him big-time.

Who wouldn't have the hots while sitting across from

this hunk of sexiness? If his lips didn't grab you then his eyes certainly would. They were deep, dark and penetrating. Jillian's heart missed beats just looking into them.

"Just a number?" He chuckled, leaning back in his chair, stretching long legs in front of him. "Women might think that way but men think differently."

He smelled good. When did she start noticing the scent of a man?

"And why is that, Aidan?" she asked, picking up her glass of lemonade to take a sip. It suddenly felt hotter than usual. It had nothing to do with the temperature and everything to do with her body's heated reaction to him.

She watched him lift a brow over those striking dark eyes. A feral smile edged his lips as he leaned forward. "Are you sure I'm Aidan and not Adrian?"

Oh, yes she was sure he was Aidan. She'd heard about the games he and his identical twin would play on unsuspecting souls, those who couldn't tell them apart. "I'm sure."

It was Aidan and not Adrian who stirred her in places she'd rather not think about at the moment.

He leaned in even closer. So close she could see the pupils in his dark eyes. "And how are you so certain?" he asked.

Was she imagining things or had the tone of his voice dropped to a husky murmur? It was rumored that he was a big flirt. She had seen him in action at several Westmoreland weddings. It was also a fact that he and his twin were womanizers and had developed quite a reputation at Harvard. She could certainly see why women were at their beck and call.

"Because I am," she replied. And that's all she intended to say on the matter.

There was no way she would tell him the real reason, that from the moment her brother-in-law Dillon had introduced her to Aidan, before he'd married Pam, she had developed a full-blown crush. She'd been seventeen at the time, a senior in high school. The only problem was the crush hadn't lessened much since.

"Why?"

She glanced back up at Aidan. "Why what?"

"Why are you so certain? You still haven't said."

She inwardly sighed. Why couldn't he leave it alone? She had no intention of telling him. But since she had a feeling he wouldn't let up, she added, "The two of you sound different."

He flashed another sexy smile, showing the dimples in his cheeks. Her hormones, which always acted out of control around him, were erratic now. "Funny you say that. Most people think we sound a lot alike."

"Well, I don't think that."

There was no way she could think that when it was Aidan's voice, and not Adrian's, that stroked her senses. Deciding it was time to take charge of the conversation to keep his questions at bay, she inquired, "So how is medical school going?"

He didn't let on that he suspected her ploy, and as she took another sip of her lemonade, he began telling her what she had to look forward to in another year or so. Becoming a neurosurgeon had been a lifelong dream of hers ever since her mother died of a brain infection when Jillian was seven.

Aidan told her about the dual residency program at hospitals in Portland, Maine, and Charlotte, North Carolina, that he planned to pursue after completing medical school. His dream was to become a cardiologist. He was excited about becoming a doctor and she could hear it in his voice. She was thrilled about becoming a doctor one day as well, but she had another year left before she finished her studies at the University of Wyoming.

While he talked, she nodded as she discreetly gave him a slow, appreciative appraisal. The man was too handsome for words. His voice was smooth as silk, with just enough huskiness to keep her pulse rate on edge. Creamy caramel skin spread across the bridge of a hawkish nose, sharp cheekbones, a perfect sculptured jaw and a mouth so sensual she enjoyed watching it in motion. She could imagine all the things he did with that mouth.

"Have you decided where you're going for medical school, Jillian?"

She blinked. He had asked her a question and was waiting on an answer. And while he waited she saw that sexy mouth ease into another smile. She wondered if he'd known she was checking him out.

"I've always wanted to live in New Orleans so working at a hospital there will be at the top of my list," she said, trying to ignore the eyes staring at her.

"And your second choice?"

She shrugged. "Not sure. I guess one in Florida."

"Why?"

She frowned. Why was he quizzing her? "I've never been to Florida."

He chuckled. "I hope that's not the only reason."

Her frown deepened. "Of course that's not the only reason," she said defensively. "There are good medical schools in Louisiana and Florida."

He nodded. "Yes, there are. How's your grade point average?"

"Good. In fact my GPA is better than good. I'm at the top of my class. In the top ten at least."

Getting there hadn't been easy. She'd made a lot of sacrifices, especially in her social life. She couldn't recall the last time she'd gone out on a date or participated in any school activities. But she was okay with that. Pam was paying a lot of the cost for her education and Jillian wanted to make her sister proud.

"What about the entrance exam—the MCAT—and admission essays? Started on them yet?"

"Too early."

"It's never too early. I suggest you prepare for them during your free time."

Now it was her turn to smile. "Free time? What's that?"

The chuckle that erupted from his throat was smooth and sexy and made her pulse thump. "It's time you should squeeze in regardless of whether you think you can or not. It's essential to know how to manage your time wisely, otherwise you'll get burned-out before you even get started."

She grudgingly wondered what made him an expert. Then she pushed her resentment aside. He *was* giving her sound advice and he had gone where she had yet to go. And from what she'd heard, he was doing pretty well at it. He would graduate from Harvard Medical School at the top of his class and then enter a dual residency program that any medical student would die for. He would get the chance to work with the best cardiologists in the United States.

"Thanks for the advice, Aidan."

"You're welcome. When you get ready to knock them out of the way, let me know. I'll help you."

"You will?"

"Sure. Even if I have to come to you to do it."

She lifted a brow. *He would come to her?* She couldn't imagine him doing such a thing. Harvard was in Boston and that was a long way from her university in Laramie, Wyoming.

"Hand me your phone for a second."

His request jarred her thoughts back into focus. "Why?"

"So I can put my numbers into it."

Jillian drew in a deep breath before standing to pull her cell phone from the back pocket of her jeans. She handed it to him and tried to ignore the tingling sensation that flowed through her when their hands touched. She watched him use deft fingers to key in the numbers. Surgeon's fingers. Long, strong, with precise and swift movements. She wondered how those same fingers would feel stroking her skin. She heated just thinking about it.

Moments later his phone rang, interrupting her thoughts. It was then that she realized he'd called himself to have her number, as well. "There," he said, handing her phone back to her. "You now have my number and I have yours."

Was she jumping to conclusions or did his words hold some significance? "Yes, we have each other's numbers," she agreed softly, shoving the assumption out of her mind.

He stood, glancing at his watch. "Adrian and I are meeting up with Canyon and Stern in town for drinks and to shoot pool, so I best get going. Happy birthday again."

"Thanks, Aidan."

"You're welcome."

He walked away but when he got to the French doors he turned and looked back at her, regarding her through his gorgeous dark eyes. The intensity of his gaze made her stomach quiver and another burst of heat swept through her. She felt something…passion? Sexual chemistry? Lust? All three and more, she decided. She'd thought all the Westmoreland males she'd met since Pam married Dillon were eye candy, but there was something about Aidan that pulled at everything female inside of her.

She cleared her throat. "Is anything wrong?" she asked when the silence began to stretch.

Her question seemed to jar him. He frowned slightly before quickly forcing a smile. "Not sure."

As he opened the French door to go inside, she wondered what he meant by that.

Why, of all the women in the world, have I developed this deep attraction for Jillian Novak?

The first time he'd noticed it was when they'd been introduced four years ago. He'd been twenty-two, and she only seventeen, but still a looker. He'd known then that he would have to keep his distance. Now she was twenty-one and still had the word innocent written all over her. From what he'd heard, she didn't even have a boyfriend, preferring to concentrate on her studies and forgo a love life.

And speaking of life, Aidan was fairly certain he loved every part of his, especially his family. So why was he allowing himself to be attracted to Pam's sister? He didn't want to cause any trouble for Dillon.

Pam Novak was a jewel and just what Dillon needed. Everyone had been shocked when Dillon announced he had met a woman who he intended to marry. That had been the craziest thing Aidan had ever heard.

Dillon, of all people, should have known better. Hadn't his first wife left him when he'd refused to send the youngest four members of the Westmoreland family—namely him, Adrian, Bane and Bailey—to foster care? What had made Dillon think Pam would be different? But it didn't take Aidan, his siblings and cousins long to discover that she *was* different.

As far as Aidan was concerned, she was everything they'd *all* needed; she knew the value of family. And she had proven it when she'd turned her back on a promising acting career to care for her three teenaged sisters when her father passed away.

To say the Westmorelands had undergone a lot of family turmoil of their own was an understatement. It all started when Aidan's parents and uncle and aunt died in a plane crash, leaving his cousin Dillon in charge of the family, along with Aidan's oldest brother, Ramsey, as backup. Dillon and Ramsey had worked hard and made sacrifices to keep the family together—all fifteen of them.

Aidan's parents had had eight children: five boys—Ramsey, Zane, Derringer and the twins, Aidan and Adrian—and three girls—Megan, Gemma and Bailey. Uncle Adam and Aunt Clarisse had had seven sons: Dillon, Micah, Jason, Riley, Canyon, Stern and Brisbane.

It hadn't been easy, especially since he, Adrian, Brisbane and Bailey had been under the age of sixteen. And Aidan would admit the four of them had been the most challenging of the bunch, getting into all sorts of mischief, even to the point that the State of Colorado ordered they be put in foster homes. Dillon had appealed that decision and won. Lucky for the four youngest Westmorelands, Dillon had known their acts of rebellion were their way of handling the grief of losing their parents. Now Aidan was in medical school; Adrian was working on his PhD in engineering; Bane had joined the navy and Bailey was taking classes at a local university while working part-time.

Aidan's thoughts shifted back to Jillian, although he didn't want them to. The birthday party yesterday had been a surprise, and the shocked look on her face had been priceless—adorable and a total turn-on. If he'd had any doubt about just how much he was attracted to her, that doubt had been dispelled when he saw her.

She had walked out onto the patio expecting a going-away party for his sister Gemma, who had married Callum and was moving to Australia. Instead it had been a surprise birthday party for her. After shedding a few happy tears, which he would have loved to lick away, she had hugged Pam and Dillon for thinking of her on her twenty-first birthday. From what he'd heard, it was the first time Jillian had had a party since she was a little kid.

While everyone had rushed over to congratulate her, he had hung back, checking her out. The sundress looked cute on her and it was obvious she wasn't the seventeen-year-old he'd met four years ago. Her face was fuller, her features stunning and her body…

Where had those curves come from? There's no way he would have missed them before. She was short compared with his six-foot-two-inch height. He figured she stood no taller than five feet three inches in bare feet. And speaking of her feet, her polished toes, a flaming red, had been another turn on. Pam might not want to hear it, but her sister was Hot with a capital *H.*

When he realized he had been the only one who hadn't wished her a happy birthday, he was about to do so when his phone rang. He had slipped off the patio to take the call from a friend from college who was trying to fix him up on a blind date for next weekend.

When he returned to the patio after finishing his call, everyone else had gone inside to watch a movie or play cards, and she'd been alone. She would never know how hard it had been for him to sit across from her without touching her. She looked good and smelled good, as well.

Jillian Novak had definitely caught his eye.

But Dillon and Pam would pluck out that same eye if he didn't squash what he was feeling.

Everybody knew how protective Pam was when it came to her sisters. Just like everyone knew Aidan wasn't one to take women seriously. And he didn't plan to change his behavior now. So the best thing for him to do while he was home for the next three days was to keep his distance from Jillian as he'd always done.

So why did I get her phone number and give her mine, for crying out loud?

Okay, he reasoned quickly, it had been a crazy moment, one he now regretted. The good thing was he doubted she would ever call him for help and he would make it a point never to call her.

That was a good plan, one he intended to stick to. Now, if he could only stop thinking about her that would be great. Glancing down at the medical journal he was supposed to be reading, he tried to focus on the words. Within a few minutes he'd read one interesting article and was about to start on another.

"Will you do me a *big* favor?"

Aidan glanced up to stare into the face of his sister Bailey. She used to be the baby in the Denver Westmoreland family but that had changed now that Dillon and Pam had a son, and Aidan's brother Ramsey and his wife, Chloe, had a daughter.

"Depends on what the favor is?"

"I promised Jill that I would go riding with her and show her the section of Westmoreland Country that she hasn't seen yet. Now they've called me to come in to work. I need you to go with Jillian instead."

"Just show her another day," he said, quickly deciding that going horseback riding with Jillian wasn't a smart idea.

"That was my original plan but I can't reach her on her cell phone. We were to meet at Gemma Lake, and you know how bad phone reception is out there. She's already there waiting for me."

He frowned. "Can't you ask someone else?"

"I did but everyone is busy."

His frown deepened. "And I'm not?"

Bailey rolled her eyes. "Not like everyone else. You're just reading a magazine."

He figured there was no use explaining to Bailey that his reading was important. He just so happened to be reading about a medical breakthrough where the use of bionic eyes had been tested as a way to restore sight with good results.

"Well, will you do it?"

He closed the medical journal and placed it aside. "You're positive there's no one else who can do it?"

"Yes, and she really wants to see it. This is her home now and—"

"Her home? She's away at school most of the time," he said.

"And so are you, Adrian, Stern and Canyon, and this is still your home. So what's your point?"

He decided not to argue with her. There were times when his baby sister could read him like an open book and he didn't want her to do that in this instance. It wouldn't take her long to figure out the story written on his pages was all about Jillian.

"Fine. I'll go."

"Act a little enthused, will you? You've been kind of standoffish with Jillian and her sisters since Dillon married Pam."

"I have not."

"You have, too. You should take time to get to know them. They're part of the family now. Besides, you and Jill will both become doctors one day so already you have a common interest."

He hoped like hell that would remain their only common interest. It was up to him to make sure it did. "Whatever," he said, standing and walking toward the door, pausing to grab his Stetson off the hat rack.

"And Aidan?"

He stopped before opening the door and turned around, somewhat annoyed. "What now?"

"Try to be nice. You can act like a grizzly bear at times."

That was her opinion. Deciding not to disagree with her, because you could never win with Bailey, he walked out of the house.

Two

Jillian heard the sound of a rider approaching and turned around, using her hand to shield her eyes from the glare of the sun. Although she couldn't make out the identity of the rider, she knew it wasn't Bailey.

The rider came closer and when her heart began pounding hard in her chest, she knew it was Aidan. What was he doing here? And where was Bailey?

Over breakfast she and Bailey had agreed to go riding after lunch. Because the property was located so far from Denver's city limits and encompassed so much land, the locals referred to it as Westmoreland Country. Although Jillian had seen parts of it, she had yet to see all of it and Bailey had volunteered to show it to her.

Dropping her hand to her side, Jillian drew in a deep breath as Aidan and his horse came closer. She tried not to notice how straight he sat in the saddle or how good he looked sitting astride the horse. And she tried not to gawk at how his Stetson, along with his western shirt, vest, jeans and boots, made him look like a cowboy in the flesh.

When he brought the horse to a stop a few feet from where she stood, she had to tilt her head all the way back to look up at him. "Aidan."

He nodded. "Jillian."

His irritated expression and the cutting sound of his voice made her think he was upset about something. Was she trespassing on a particular part of Westmoreland land where she had no business being?

Thinking she needed to give him an explanation, she said, "I'm waiting for Bailey. We're going riding."

"Yes, those *were* your plans."

She lifted a brow. "Were?"

He nodded. "Bailey tried reaching you but your phone is out of range. She was called in to work and asked that I take her place."

"Take her place?"

"Yes, take her place. She indicated you wanted to tour Westmoreland Country."

"I did, but…"

Penetrating dark eyes held hers. "But what?"

She shoved both hands into the pockets of her jeans. There was no way she could tell him that under no circumstances would she go riding anywhere with him. She could barely be around him for a few minutes without becoming unglued…like she was becoming now.

The reason she had placed her hands in her pockets was because they were already sweaty. And then there was that little ball of fire in her stomach that always seemed to burst into flames whenever he was around. Aidan Westmoreland oozed so much sexiness it was driving her to the edge of madness.

"Jillian?"

She blinked when he said her name. The sound of his voice was like a caress across her skin. "Yes?"

"But what? Do you have a problem with me being Bailey's replacement?"

She drew in a deep breath. She couldn't see him being anyone's replacement. It was easy to see he was his own man, and what a man he was. Even now, the weight of his penetrating gaze caused a heated rush to cross her flesh. So, yes, she had a problem with him being Bailey's replacement, but that was something she definitely wouldn't tell him.

"No, I don't have a problem with it," she lied without even blinking. "However, I would think that you do. I'm sure you have more to do with your time than spend it with me."

He shrugged massive shoulders. "No, in fact I don't, so it's not a problem. Besides, it's time for us to get to know each other better."

Why was her body tingling with awareness at his words? She was sure he didn't mean them the way they sounded, but she thought it best to seek clarification. "Why should we get to know each other better?"

He leaned back in the saddle and she couldn't help noticing the long fingers that held the reins. Why was she imagining those same fingers doing things to her, like stroking her hair, splaying up and down her arms, working their way across her naked body? She tried to downplay the shiver that passed through her.

"Dillon married Pam four years ago, and there's still a lot I don't know about you and your sisters," he said, bringing an end to her fantasizing. "We're all family and the Westmorelands are big on family. I haven't been home to get to know you, Paige and Nadia."

With him naming her sisters his earlier statement felt less personal. It wasn't just about her. She should be grateful for that but for some reason she wasn't. "Because of school I haven't been home much, either, but we can get to know each other another time. It doesn't have to be today," she said.

She doubted she could handle his closeness. Even the masculine scent of him was overpowering.

"Today is just as good a day as any. I'm leaving to go back to Boston tomorrow. There's no telling when our paths will cross again. Probably not until we come home for Christmas or something. We might as well do it now and get it over with."

Why did she get the feeling that getting to know her was something he felt forced to do? She took offense at that. "Don't do me any favors," she all but snapped at him while feeling her pulse pound.

"Excuse me?" He seemed surprised by her remark.

"There's no need to get *anything* over with. It's obvious Bailey roped you into doing something you really don't want to do. I can see the rest of Westmoreland Country on my own," she said, untying her horse and then mounting it.

When she sat astride the mare she glanced back over at him. "I don't need your company, Aidan."

He crossed his arms over his chest and she could tell by the sudden tensing of his jaw that he hadn't liked her comment. She was proven right when he said, with a degree of smoldering intensity that she felt through her clothes, "I hate to tell you this, Jillian Novak, but you have my company whether you want it or not."

Aidan stared hard into Jillian's eyes and couldn't help but feel they were waging a battle. Of what he wasn't sure. Of wills? Of desire? Passion? Lust? He rubbed his hand down his face. He preferred none of those things but he had a feeling all of them were fighting for the number one spot right now.

He all but saw steam coming from her ears and figured Jillian didn't like being ordered around.

"Look," he said. "We're wasting time. You want to see the land and I have nothing better to do. I apologize if I came across a little gruff earlier, but by no means did I want to insinuate that I am being forced into showing you around or getting to know you."

There was no need to tell her that Bailey had asked him to be nice to Jillian and her sisters. He'd always been cordial and as far as he was concerned that was good enough. Getting too close to Jillian wasn't a good idea. But then, he was the one who had suggested she call him if she needed help preparing for medical school. He now saw that offer had been a mistake. A big one.

She studied him for a moment and he felt something deep in his gut. It was a lot stronger than the kick in his groin he'd experienced when he'd watched her swing her leg over the back of the horse to mount it. He'd taken a long, explosive breath while fighting the sexual hunger that had roared to life inside of him. Even now, with those beautiful full lips of hers frowning at him, a smoldering spike of heat consumed him. One way he knew he could put a stop to this madness was to get her out of his system, since she seemed to have gotten under his skin.

But the way he would do that wasn't an option...not if he loved his life.

"You're sure about this?"

Hell no, he wasn't sure about anything concerning her. Maybe the main reason behind his attraction to her, in addition to her striking beauty, was that he truly didn't know her that well. Maybe once he got to know her he'd discover that he didn't like her after all.

"Yes, I'm sure about this, so come on," he said, nudging his horse forward to stand beside hers. "There's a lot to see so I hope you're a fairly good rider."

She gave him a smile that made him appreciate the fullness of her mouth even more. "Yes, I'm a fairly good rider."

And then she took off, easing her horse into a canter. He watched in admiration as she flawlessly jumped the horse over a flowing creek.

He chuckled to himself. She wasn't a fairly good rider; she was an excellent one.

Jillian slowed her pace and glanced over her shoulder to see Aidan make the same jump she had. She couldn't help but be impressed at his skill, but she shouldn't be surprised. She'd heard from Dillon that all his brothers and cousins were excellent horsemen.

In no time, he'd caught up with her. "You're good," he said, bringing his horse alongside hers. The two animals eased into a communal trot.

"Thanks," she said, smiling over at him. "You're not bad yourself."

He threw his head back and laughed. The robust sound not only floated across the countryside, but it floated across her, as well. Although she'd seen him smile before, she'd never seen him amused about anything.

"No, I'm not bad myself. In fact there was a time I wanted to be a bronco rider in the rodeo."

For some reason she wasn't surprised. "Dillon talked you out of it?"

He shook his head, grinning. "No, he wouldn't have

done such a thing. One of Dillon's major rules has been for us to choose our own life goals. At least that was his rule for everyone but Bane."

She'd heard all about Aidan's cousin Brisbane West-moreland, whom everyone called Bane. She'd also heard Dillon had encouraged his baby brother to join the military. He'd said Bane could do that or possibly go to prison for the trouble he'd caused. Bane had chosen the navy. In the four years that Pam had been married to Dillon, Jillian had only seen Bane twice.

"So what changed your mind about the rodeo?" she asked when they slowed the horses to a walk.

"My brother Derringer. He did the rodeo circuit for a couple of summers after high school. Then he got busted up pretty bad. Scared all of us to death and I freaked out. We all did. The thought of losing another family member brought me to my senses and I knew I couldn't put my family through that."

She nodded. She knew about him losing his parents and his aunt and uncle in a plane crash, leaving Dillon— the oldest at the time—to care for all of them. "Derringer and a few of your cousins and brothers own a horse-training business right?"

"Yes and it's doing well. They weren't cut out to work in the family business so after a few years they left to pursue their dreams of working with horses. I try to help them out whenever I come home but they're doing a great job without me. Several of their horses have won important derbies."

"Ramsey resigned as one of the CEOs as well, right?" she asked of his oldest brother.

He glanced over at her. "Yes. Ramsey has a degree in agriculture and economics. He'd always wanted to be a sheep farmer, but when my parents, aunt and uncle died in that plane crash he knew Dillon would need help at Blue Ridge."

Jillian knew that Blue Ridge Land Management was a Fortune 500 company Aidan's father and uncle had started years ago. "But eventually he was able to pursue his dream, right?"

Aidan nodded. "Yes. Once Dillon convinced Ramsey he could handle things at the corporation without him. Ramsey's sheep ranch is doing great."

She nodded. She liked Ramsey. In fact, she liked all the Westmorelands she had gotten to know. When Pam married Dillon, the family had welcomed her and her sisters with open arms. She'd discovered some of them were more outgoing than the others. But the one thing she couldn't help but notice was that they stuck together like glue.

"So how did you learn to ride so well?" he asked.

"My dad. He was the greatest and although I'm sure he wanted at least one son, he ended up with four girls. He felt we should know how to do certain things and handling a horse was one of them," she said, remembering the time she'd spent with her father and how wonderful it had been for her.

"He evidently saw potential in me because he made sacrifices and sent me to riding school. I competed nationally until he got sick. We needed the money to pay for his medicine and doctor bills."

"Do you regret giving it up?" he asked.

She shook her head. "No. I enjoyed it but making sure Dad got the best care meant more to me…more to all of us…than anything." And she meant it. There had been no regrets for any of them about giving up what they'd loved to help their father.

"Here we are."

She looked around at the beauty of the land surrounding her, as far as her eyes could see and beyond. Since Dillon was the oldest, he had inherited the main house along with the three hundred acres it sat on. Everyone else, upon reaching the age of twenty-five, received one hundred acres to call their own. Some parts of this area were cleared and other parts were dense with thick foliage. But what took her breath away was the beautiful waterway that branched off into a huge lake. Gemma Lake. She'd heard it had been named after Aidan's great-grandmother.

"This place is beautiful. Where are we exactly?"

He glanced over at her and smiled. "My land. Aidan's Haven.

Aidan's Haven, she immediately decided, suited him. She could see him building his home on this piece of land one day near this huge waterway. Today he looked like a cowboy, but she could see him transforming into a boat captain.

"Aidan's Haven. That's a nice name. How did you come up with it?"

"I didn't. Bailey did. She came up with all the names for our one-hundred-acre plots. She chose names like Stern's Stronghold, Zane's Hideout, Derringer's Dungeon, Ramsey's Web and Megan's Meadows, just to name a few."

Jillian had visited each of those areas and all the homes that had been built on the land were gorgeous. Some were single-story ranch-style designs, while others were like mansions with several floors. "When do you plan to build?"

"Not for a while yet. After medical school I'll probably work and live somewhere else for a while since I have six years of residency to complete for the cardiology program."

"But this will eventually be your home."

A pensive look appeared on his face. "Yes, Westmoreland Country will always be my home."

She'd always thought she would live in Gamble, Wyoming. Although she knew she would leave for college, she figured she would return one day and work in the hospital there before setting up a practice of her own. After all, she had lived there her entire life; all her friends were there. But after Pam married Dillon things changed for her, Paige and Nadia. They were close to their oldest sister and decided to leave Wyoming and make their homes close to Pam's. It had worked out well for everyone. Nadia was in her last year of high school here in Colorado and Paige was in California attending UCLA.

"What about you? Do you ever plan to return to Gamble, Wyoming, to live, Jillian?"

Again, she wondered why her stomach tightened whenever he said her name. Probably had something to do with that deep, husky voice of his.

"No, I don't plan to return to Gamble. In fact, Nadia and Paige and I talked a few weeks ago and we plan to approach Pam about selling the place. She would have done so already, but she thinks we want to keep it as part of our legacy."

"You don't?"

"Only because we've moved on and think of Denver

as home now. At least Nadia and I do. Paige has made a life for herself in Los Angeles. She's hoping her acting career takes off. We're hoping the same thing for her. Pam has done so much for us already and we don't want her to feel obligated to pay more of our college tuition and expenses, especially when we can use the money from the sale of the house to do so."

He nodded. "Let's take a walk. I want to show you around before we move on to Adrian's Cove."

He dismounted and tied his horse to a nearby tree. Then he turned to help her down. The moment he touched her, awareness of him filled her every pore. From the look in his eyes it was obvious that something similar was happening to him.

This was all new to her. She'd never felt anything like this before. And although her little lovemaking session with Cobb Grindstone on prom night had appeased her curiosity, it had left a lot to be desired.

As soon as her feet touched the ground, she heard a deep moan come from Aidan's throat. Only then did it become obvious that they'd gotten caught up in a carnal attraction that was so sharp it took her breath away.

"Jillian…"

He said her name again and, like all the other times, the deep, husky sound accentuated his sexiness. But before she could respond, the masculine hand planted around her waist nudged her closer and then his mouth lowered to hers.

Three

All sorts of feelings ripped through Aidan, making him totally conscious of the woman whose lips were locked to his. Deep in the center of his being he felt a throb unlike any he'd ever felt before—an intense flare of heat shooting straight to his loins.

He knew he had to stop. This wasn't any woman. This was Jillian Novak, Pam's sister. Dillon's sister-in-law. A woman who was now a part of the Westmoreland family. All that was well and good, but at the moment the only thing his mind could comprehend was that she had desire clawing at his insides and filling his every cell with awareness.

Instead of yielding to common sense, he was captivated by her sweet scent and her incredible taste, and the way her tongue stroked his showed both boldness and innocence. She felt exquisite in his arms, as if she belonged there. He wanted more. He wanted to feel her all over, kiss her all over. Taste her. Tempt her with sinful enticements.

The need for air was the only reason he released her lips, but her flavor made him want to return his mouth to hers and continue what they'd started.

The shocked look in her eyes told him she needed time to comprehend what had just happened between them. She took a step back and he watched as she took a deep breath.

"We should not have done that."

Aidan couldn't believe she had the nerve to say that while sultry heat still radiated off her. He might have thought the same thing seconds ago, but he couldn't agree with her now. Not when his fingers itched to reach out and pull her back into his arms so he could plow her mouth with another kiss. Dammit, why did her pouty lips look so inviting?

"Then why did we do it?" he countered. He might have made the first move but she had definitely been a willing participant. Her response couldn't lie. She had enjoyed the kiss as much as he had.

"I don't know why we did it, but we can't do it again."

That was easy for her to say. "Why not?"

She frowned at him. "You know why not. Your cousin is married to my sister."

"And?"

She placed her hands on her hips giving him a mind-boggling view of her slim waist line. "And we can't do it again. I know all about your womanizing reputation, Aidan."

Her words struck a nerve. "Do you?"

"Yes. And I'm not interested. The only thing I'm interested in is getting into medical school. That's the only thing on my mind."

"And the only thing on mine is getting out of medical school," he countered in a curt tone. "As far as Dillon being married to Pam, it changes nothing. You're still a beautiful woman and I'm a man who happens to notice such things. But since I know how the situation stands between us, I'll make sure it doesn't happen again."

"Thank you."

"You're welcome. Glad we got that cleared up. Now I can continue showing you around."

"I'm not sure that's a good idea."

He watched her and when she pushed a lock of hair away from her face, he again thought how strikingly beautiful she was. "Why not? You don't think you can control yourself around me?" he asked, actually smiling at the possibility of that being true.

Her look of anger should have warned him, but he'd never been one to heed signs. "Trust me, that's definitely not it."

"Then there's no reason for me not to finish showing you around, is there, Jillian? Besides, Bailey will give me hell about it if I don't. There's a lot of land we still have to cover so let's get started."

He began walking along the bank of the river and figured that after cooling off Jillian would eventually catch up.

Jillian watched Aidan walk ahead and decided to hang back a moment to reclaim her common sense. Why had she allowed him to kiss her? And why had she enjoyed it so much?

The man gave French kissing a whole new definition, and she wasn't sure her mouth would ever be the same.

No one had ever kissed her like that before. No one would have dared. To be honest, she doubted anyone she'd ever kissed would know how. Definitely not Cobb. Or that guy in her freshman year at Wyoming University, Les, that she'd dropped really quickly when he wanted to take her to a hotel and spend the night on their first date. He might have been a star on the school's football team, but from the couple of times they had kissed, compared to what she'd just experienced with Aidan, Les had definitely dropped the ball.

But then, regardless of how enjoyable Aidan's kiss had been, she was right in what she'd told him about not repeating it. She had no business getting involved with a guy whose favorite sport was messing around. She knew better. Honestly, she didn't know what had come over her.

However, she knew full well what had come over him. More than once she'd overheard Dillon express his concern to Pam that although the twins were doing well at Harvard, he doubted they would ever settle down into serious relationships since they seemed to enjoy being womanizers. That meant Aidan's interest in her was only because of overactive testosterone. Pam had warned Jillian numerous times about men who would mean her no good, and her oldest sister would be highly disappointed if Jillian fell for the ploy of a man like Aidan. A man who could take away her focus on becoming a doctor just to make her his plaything.

Feeling confident she had her common sense back on track, she began walking. Aidan wasn't too far ahead and it wouldn't take long for her to catch up with him. In the meantime she couldn't help but appreciate his manly physique. His faded jeans emphasized masculine thighs, a rock-solid behind, tight waist and wide shoulders. He didn't just walk, he swaggered, and he did it so blatantly sexily, it increased her heart rate with every step he took.

Moments later he slowed and turned around to stare at her, pinning her with his dark gaze. Had he felt her ogling him? Did he know she had been checking out his rear big-time? She hoped not because his front was just as impressive. She could see why he was in such high demand when it came to women.

"You coming?"

I will be if you don't stop looking at me like that, Jillian thought, getting closer to where he stood. She felt the heat of his gaze on every inch of her. She came to a stop in front of him. She couldn't take looking into his eyes any longer so she glanced around. In addition to the huge lake there were also mountains surrounding the property. "You have a nice mountain view in this spot and can see the lake from here," she said.

"I know. That's why I plan to build my house right here."

She nodded. "Have you designed it yet?"

"No. I don't plan on building for several more years, but I often come here and think about the time when I will. The house will be large enough for me and my family."

She snapped her head around. "You plan on getting married?"

His chuckle was soft but potent. "Yes, one day. That surprises you?"

She decided to be honest. "Yes. You do have a reputation."

He leaned one broad shoulder against a Siberian elm tree. "This is the second time today that you've mentioned something about my reputation. Just what have you heard about me?"

She took a seat across from him on a huge tree stump. "I heard what hellions you, Adrian, Bailey and Bane used to be."

He nodded solemnly. "Yes, we were that. But that was a long time ago, and I can honestly say we regretted our actions. When we grew older and realized the impact we'd had on the family, we apologized to each one of them."

"I'm sure they understood. You were just children and there was a reason you did what you did," she said. She'd heard the full story from Pam. The deaths of their parents, and aunt and uncle, had been the hardest on those youngest four. Everyone had known that their acts of rebellion were their way of handling their grief.

"Sorry I mentioned it," she said, feeling bad that she'd even brought it up.

He shrugged. "No harm done. It is what it is. It seems the four of us got a reputation we've been trying to live down for years. But I'm sure that's not the reputation of mine that you were really referring to."

No, it wasn't. "I understand you like women."

He chuckled. "Most men do."

She raised a brow, not in the least amused. "I mean you really like them, but you don't care about their feelings. You break their hearts without any concern for the pain it might cause."

He studied her for a long moment. "That's what you heard?"

"Yes. And now you want me to believe that you're seriously considering settling down one day, marrying and having a family?"

"Yes. One doesn't have anything to do with the other. What I do now in no way affects any future plans. I need to clarify something. I don't deliberately set out to break any woman's heart. I tell any woman I date the truth up front—my career as a doctor is foremost. However, if she refuses to take me at my word and assumes that she can change my mind, then it's not my fault when she finds out otherwise."

"So in other words…"

"In other words, Jillian, I don't intentionally set up any woman for heartbreak or lead her on," he answered curtly.

She knew she should probably leave well enough alone and stop digging, but for some reason she couldn't help herself. "However, you do admit to dating a *lot* of women."

"Yes, I admit it. And why not? I'm single and don't plan to get into a committed relationship anytime soon. And contrary to what you believe, I don't date as many women as you might think. My time is pretty limited these days because of medical school."

She could imagine. How he managed to date at all while in medical school was beyond her. He was definitely into multitasking. She'd discovered most relationships demanded a lot of work and it was work she didn't have time for. Evidently he made things easy by not getting serious with any woman. At least he'd been honest about it. He dated women for the fun of it and didn't love any of them.

"I have one other question for you, Aidan," she said, after drawing in a deep breath.

"What's your question?"

"If all of what you said is true, about not getting serious with any woman, then why did you kiss me?"

Now that was a good question, one he could answer but really didn't want to. She did deserve an answer, though, especially after the way he had plowed her mouth earlier. She was twenty-one, five years younger than him. And although she'd held her own during their kiss, he knew they were worlds apart when it came to sexual experience. Therefore, before he answered her, he needed to ask a few questions of his own.

"Why did you kiss me back?"

He could tell by her expression that she was surprised by his counterquestion. And, as he'd expected, she tried to avoid giving him an answer. "That's not the issue here."

He couldn't help but smile. Little did she know it *was* the issue, but he would touch on that later. "The reason I kissed you, Jillian, is because I was curious. I think you have a beautiful pair of lips and I wanted to taste them. I wanted to taste you. It's something I've wanted to do for a while."

He saw her jaw drop and had to hold his mouth closed for a second to keep from grinning. She hadn't expected him to answer her question so bluntly or to be so direct. That's something she needed to know about him. He didn't sugarcoat anything. *Straightforward* could be his middle name.

"So now that you know my reason for kissing you, what was your reason for kissing me back?"

She began nibbling on her bottom lip. Watching her made him ache, made him want to take hold of those lips and have his way with them again.

"I—I was…"

When she didn't say anything else, he lifted a brow. "You were what?"

Then she had the nerve to take her tongue and lick those same lips she'd been nibbling on moments ago. "I was curious about you, too."

He smiled. Now they were getting somewhere. "I can

understand that. I guess the reason you asked about the kiss is because I told you I'm not into serious relationships when it comes to women. I hope you don't think a deep kiss constitutes a serious relationship."

From the look on her face, which she quickly wiped off, that's exactly what she'd thought. She was more inexperienced than he'd assumed. He wondered just how inexperienced she was. Most twenty-one-year-old women he knew wore desire, instead of their hearts, on their sleeves.

"Of course I knew that."

If she knew that then why were they having this conversation? If she thought he was looking for something serious just because he'd kissed her then she was so far off the mark it wasn't funny.

"How many boyfriends have you had?"

"Excuse me?"

No, he wouldn't excuse her. There were certain things she needed to know. Things experience had nothing to do with. "I asked how many boyfriends you've had. And before you tell me it's none of my business, I'm asking for a reason."

She lifted her chin in a defiant pose. "I can't imagine what reason you would have for needing to know that."

"So you can protect yourself." He thought she looked both adorable and sexy. From the way her curly hair tumbled down her shoulders to the way the smoothness of her skin shone in the sunlight.

She lifted a brow. "Against men like you?"

"No. Men like me would never mislead you into thinking there was anything serious about a kiss. But there are men who would lead you to think otherwise."

She frowned. "And you don't think I can handle myself?"

He smiled. "Not the way I think you should. For some reason you believe you can avoid kisses until you're in a serious relationship and there are certain kisses that can't be avoided."

He could tell by her expression that she didn't believe him. "Take the kiss we shared earlier. Do you honestly think you could have avoided it once I got started?" he asked her.

Her frown deepened. "Yes, of course I could have."

"Then why didn't you?"

She rolled her eyes. "I told you. The only reason I allowed you to kiss me, and the only reason I participated, is because I was curious."

"Really?"

She rolled her eyes again. "Really. Truly."

"So, you're not curious anymore?"

She shook her head. "Nope, not at all. I wondered what kissing you was like and now I know."

Deciding to prove her wrong and settle the matter once and for all, he moved away from the tree and walked toward her.

Figuring out his intent, she stood with a scowl on her face. "Hold it right there, Aidan Westmoreland. Don't you dare think you're going to kiss me again."

When he reached her, he came to a stop directly in front of her and she refused to back up. Instead she stood her ground. He couldn't help but admire her spunk, although in this case it would be wasted.

"I do dare because I don't just think it, Jillian, I know it. And I also know that you're going to kiss me back. *Again.*"

Four

Jillian doubted she'd ever met a more arrogant man. And what was even worse, he had the nerve to stand in front of her with his Stetson tipped back and his legs braced apart in an overconfident stance. How dare he tell her what she would do? Kiss him back? Did he really believe that? Honestly?

She tilted her head back to glare up at him. He didn't glare back, but he held her gaze in a way that was unnerving. And then his eyes moved, slowly raking over her from head to toe. Was that desire she felt rushing through her body? Where had these emotions inside of her come from? Was she getting turned on from the way he was looking at her? She tried to stiffen at the thought but instead she was drawn even more into the heat of his gaze.

"Stop that!"

He lifted a brow. "Stop what?"

"Whatever you're doing."

He crossed his arms over his chest. "So, you think I'm responsible for the sound of your breathing? For the way your nipples have hardened and are pressing against your shirt? And for the way the tip of your tongue is tingling, eager to connect with mine?"

Every single thing he'd pointed out was actually happening to her, but she refused to admit any of them. She crossed her arms over her own chest. "I have no idea what you're talking about."

"Then I guess we're at a standoff."

"No, we're not," she said, dropping her hands to her sides. "I'm leaving. You can play this silly game with someone else."

She turned to go and when his hand reached out and touched her arm, sharp spikes of blood rushed through her veins, filling her pores, drenching the air she was breathing with heated desire. And what on earth was that hunger throbbing inside of her at the juncture of her thighs? And what were those slow circles he was making on her arm with his index finger? She expelled a long deep breath and fought hard to retain control of her senses.

Jillian wanted to snatch her arm away but found she couldn't. What kind of spell had he cast on her? Every hormone in her body sizzled, hissed and surged with a need she'd never felt before. She couldn't deny the yearning pulsing through her even if she wanted to.

"You feel it, don't you, Jillian? It's crazy, I know, and it's something I can't explain, but I feel it each and every time I'm within a few feet of you. As far as I'm concerned, Pam and Dillon are the least of our worries. Figuring out just what the hell is going on between us should be at the top of the agenda. You can deny it as long as you want, but that won't help. You need to admit it like I have."

She did feel it and a part of her knew there was real danger in admitting such a thing. But another part knew he was right. With some things it was best to admit there was a problem and deal with it. Otherwise, she would lay awake tonight and regret not doing so.

His hand slowly traveled up her arm toward her lips. There he cradled her mouth in the palm of his hands. "And whatever it is has me wanting to taste you and has you wanting to taste me. It has me wanting to lick your mouth dry and you wanting to lick mine in the same way."

He paused a moment and when he released a frustrated breath she knew that whatever this "thing" was between them, he had tried fighting it, as well. But he had given up the fight and was now ready to move to the next level, whatever that was.

"I need to taste you, Jillian," he said.

As much as she wished otherwise, there was a deep craving inside of her to taste him, too. Just one more time. Then she would walk away, mount her horse and ride off like the devil himself was after her. But for now she needed this kiss as much as she needed to breathe.

She saw him lowering his head and she was poised for the exact moment when their mouths would connect. She even parted her lips in anticipation. His mouth was moving. He was whispering something but instead of focusing on what he was saying, her gaze was glued to the erotic movement of his lips. And the moment his mouth touched hers she knew she had no intention of turning back.

Nothing could have prepared Aidan for the pleasure that radiated through his body. How could she arouse him like no other woman could? Instead of getting bogged down in the mystery of it all, he buried his fingers in her hair, holding her in place while his mouth mated hungrily with hers.

And she was following his lead, using her tongue with the same intensity and hunger as he was using his. It was all about tasting, and they were tasting each other with a greed that had every part of his body on fire.

He felt it, was in awe of it. In every pore, in every nerve ending and deep in his pulse, he felt it. Lowering his hand from her hair he gently gripped her around the waist and, with their mouths still locked, he slowly maneuvered her backward toward the tree he'd leaned against earlier. When her back rested against the trunk, her thighs parted and he eased between them, loving the feel of his denim rubbing against hers.

Frissons of fire, hotter than he'd ever encountered, burned a path up his spine and he deepened the kiss as if his life depended on him doing so. Too soon, in his estimation, they had to come up for air and he released her mouth just as quickly as he'd taken it.

He tried not to notice the thoroughly kissed look on her face when she drew in a deep breath. He took a step back so he wouldn't be tempted to kiss her again. The next time he knew he wouldn't stop with a kiss. He wouldn't be satisfied until he had tasted her in other places, as well. And then he would want to make love to her, right here on his land. On the very spot he planned to build his house. Crap! Why was he thinking such a thing? In frustration, he rubbed a hand down his face.

"I think we need to move on."

Her words made him look back at her and an ache settled deep in his stomach. She was beautiful and desire escalated through him all over again. Giving in to what he wanted, he took a step forward and lowered his mouth to hers, taking a sweep of her mouth with his tongue. His groin swelled when she caught his tongue and began sucking on it.

He broke off the kiss and drew in a ragged breath. "Jillian! You're asking for trouble. I'm within two seconds of spreading you on the ground and getting inside of you." The vision of such a thing nearly overpowered his senses.

"I told you we should go. You're the one who kissed me again."

He smiled. "And you kissed me back. Now you understand what I meant when I said there are some kisses that can't be avoided. You didn't want me to kiss you initially, but then you did."

She frowned slightly. "You seduced me. You made me want to kiss you."

His smile widened. "Yes, to both."

"So this was some sort of lesson?"

He shook his head. "Not hardly. I told you I wanted to taste you. I enjoyed doing so."

"This can't become a habit, Aidan."

"And I don't intend to make it one, trust me. My curiosity has more than been satisfied."

She nodded. "So has mine. Are you ready to show me the other parts of Westmoreland Country?"

"Yes. We're headed for Adrian's Cove next and then Bailey's Bay and Bane's Ponderosa."

He backed up to give her space and when she moved around him, he was tempted to reach out and pull her back into his arms, kiss her some more, until he got his fill. But he had a feeling that getting his fill would not be possible and that was something he didn't want to acknowledge.

* * *

"So, how did the tour go with Aidan yesterday?"

Jillian glanced up from her breakfast when Bailey slid into the chair next to her. Pam had shared breakfast with Jillian earlier before leaving for the grocery store, and had asked her the same thing. It had been hard to keep a straight face then and it was harder to do so now.

"It went well. There's a lot of land in Westmoreland Country. I even saw the property you own, Bailey's Bay."

Bailey smiled. "I can't claim ownership until I'm twenty-five so I have a couple years left. But when I do, I plan to build the largest house of them all. It will even be bigger than this one."

Jillian thought that would be an accomplishment because Dillon and Pam's house was huge. Their house was three stories and had eight bedrooms, six bathrooms, a spacious eat-in kitchen, a gigantic living room, a large dining room with a table that could seat over forty people easily, and a seven-car-garage.

"I can't wait to see it when you do." Jillian liked Bailey and had from the first time she'd set foot in Westmoreland Country to attend Pam's engagement party. And since there was only a couple years' difference in their ages, with Bailey being older, they had hit it off immediately. "What happens if you meet and marry a guy who wants to take you away from here?"

"That won't happen because there's not a man alive who can do that. This is where I was born and this is where I'll die."

Jillian thought Bailey sounded sure of that. Hadn't Jillian felt the same way about her home in Wyoming at one time? Although it hadn't been a man that had changed her mind, it had been the thought of how much money Pam would be paying for three sisters in college. Although her older sister had married a very wealthy man, it still would not have been right.

"Besides," Bailey said, cutting into her thoughts. "I plan to stay single forever. Having five bossy brothers and seven even bossier male cousins is enough. I don't need another man in my life trying to tell me what to do."

Jillian smiled. When she'd heard the stories about all the trouble Bailey used to get into when she was younger, Jillian had found it hard to believe. Sitting across from her was a beautiful, self-confident woman who seemed to have it going on. A woman who definitely knew what she wanted.

"I hope Aidan was nice and didn't give you any trouble."

Jillian lifted a brow. "Why would you say that?"

Bailey shrugged. "Aidan has his moods sometimes."

"Does he?"

"Yes, but if you didn't pick up on them then I guess he did okay."

No, she hadn't picked up on any mood, but she had picked up on his sensual side. And he had definitely picked up on hers. She was still in a quandary as to exactly what had happened yesterday. It was as if she'd become another person with him. She'd discovered that being kissed senseless wasn't just a cliché but was something that could really happen. Aidan had proven it. Even after brushing her teeth twice, rinsing out her mouth and eating a great breakfast Pam had prepared, the taste of him was still deeply embedded on her tongue. And what was even crazier was that she liked it.

Knowing Bailey was probably expecting a response,

she said. "Yes, he was okay. I thought he was rather nice."

Bailey nodded. "I'm glad. I told him he needed to get to know you and your sisters better since he's rarely home. And we're all family now."

All family now. Bailey's words were a stark reminder of why what happened yesterday could never be repeated. They weren't just a guy and a girl who'd met with no connections. They had deep connections. Family connections. And family members didn't go around kissing each other. Why of all the guys out there did she have to be attracted to one with the last name Westmoreland?

"So, besides Bailey's Bay where else did he take you?"

To heaven and back. The words nearly slid from Jillian's lips because that's where she felt she'd actually been. Transported there and back by a kiss. Amazing. Pulling her thoughts together, she said, "First, we toured Aidan's Haven."

"Isn't it beautiful? That's the property I originally wanted because of the way it's surrounded by Gemma Lake. But then I realized it would have been too much water to deal with. I think the spot where Aidan plans to build his house is perfect, though, and will provide an excellent view of the lake and mountains, no matter what room of the house you're in."

Jillian agreed and eradicated the thought from her mind that Aidan's wife and kids would one day live there. "I also saw Adrian's Cove. That piece of property is beautiful, as well. I love the way it's surrounded by mountains."

"Me, too."

"And from there we visited Bailey's Bay, Canyon's Bluff and Stern's Stronghold."

"Like the names?"

Jillian smiled. "Yes, and I heard they were all your idea."

"Yes," Bailey said, grinning. "Being the baby in the family has its benefits. Including the opportunity to play musical beds and sleep at whatever place I want. I was living with Dillon full-time, but after he married I decided to spread myself around and check out my brothers', sisters' and cousins' abodes. I like driving them crazy, especially when one of my brothers or cousins brings his girlfriend home."

Jillian couldn't help but laugh. Although she wouldn't trade her sisters for the world, it had to be fun having older brothers and male cousins to annoy.

"What's so funny?"

Jillian's heart skipped a beat upon hearing that voice and knowing who it belonged to. Aidan leaned in the kitchen doorway. Wearing a pair of jeans that rode low on his hips and a muscle shirt, he looked too sexy for her peace of mind. She couldn't help studying his features. It was obvious he'd just gotten out of bed. Those dark eyes that were alert and penetrating yesterday had a drowsy look. And she couldn't miss the dark shadow on his chin indicating he hadn't shaved yet. If he looked like that every morning, she would just love to see it.

"I thought you'd already left to return to Boston," Bailey said, getting up and crossing the room to give him a hug. Jillian watched the interaction and a part of her wished she could do the same.

"I won't be leaving until tomorrow."

"Why did you change your plans?" Bailey asked, surprised. "Normally, you're in a rush to get back."

Yes, why? Jillian wondered as well and couldn't wait for his answer.

"Because I wasn't ready to go back just yet. No big deal."

"Um," Bailey said, eyeing her brother suspiciously, "I get the feeling it is a big deal and probably has to do with some woman. I heard you, Adrian and Stern didn't get in until late last night."

Jillian turned her gaze away from Bailey and Aidan and took a sip of her orange juice. The spark of anger she suddenly felt couldn't be jealousy over what Bailey had just said. Had Aidan kissed Jillian senseless, then gone somewhere last night and kissed someone else the same way? Why did the thought of him doing that bother her?

"You ask too many questions, Bay, and stay out my business," Aidan said. "So, what's so funny, Jillian?"

Jillian drew in a deep breath before turning back to Aidan. "Nothing."

Bailey chuckled. "In other words, Aidan, stay out of *her* business."

Jillian heard his masculine grunt before he crossed the room to the coffeepot. The kitchen was huge, so why did it suddenly feel so small now that he'd walked in? And why did he have to walk around with such a sexy saunter?

"Well, I hate to run but I promised Megan that I would house-sit for a few hours so I'm headed for Megan's Meadows. Gemma is decorating the place before leaving for Australia and is sending her crew over to hang new curtains."

Megan and Gemma were Bailey and Aidan's sisters,

whom Jillian liked tremendously. Megan was a doctor of anesthesiology at one of the local hospitals and Gemma was an interior designer who owned Designs by Gem.

Bailey turned to Jillian. "You're here until tomorrow, right?"

"Yes."

"Then maybe Aidan can show you the parts of Westmoreland Country that you missed yesterday."

Jillian could feel Aidan's gaze on her. "I wouldn't want to put him to any trouble."

"No trouble," Aidan said, "I don't have anything else to do today."

Bailey laughed. "Until it's time for you to go and hook up with the woman who's the reason you're staying around an extra day."

"Goodbye, Bay," Aidan said in what Jillian perceived as an annoyed tone.

Bailey glanced over her shoulder at him while departing. "See you later, Aidan. And you better not leave tomorrow before telling me goodbye." She swept out of the kitchen and Jillian found herself alone with Aidan.

She glanced over at him and saw him leaning back against the counter with a cup of coffee in his hand, staring at her.

She drew in a deep breath when Aidan asked, "How soon can we go riding?"

Five

Aidan couldn't help staring into Jillian's eyes. He thought she had the most beautiful eyes of any woman he'd ever seen. And that included all those women who'd thrown themselves at him last night.

"I'm not going anywhere with you, Aidan. Besides, I'm sure the reason you changed your plans to remain in Denver another day has nothing to do with me."

Boy was she wrong. It had everything to do with her. He had spent three hours in a nightclub last night surrounded by beautiful women and all he could think about was the one he considered the most beautiful of all. Her.

A possibility suddenly hit him. Was she jealous? Did she actually believe that crap Bailey had just spouted about him changing his schedule because of some woman? He didn't know whether to be flattered or annoyed that she, or any woman, thought they mattered enough that they should care about his comings and goings. But in all honesty, what really annoyed him was that she *was* beginning to matter. And the reason he had decided to hang in Denver another day was because of her.

Instead of saying anything right away, for fear he might say the wrong thing, he turned and refilled his coffee cup. Then he crossed the room and slid into the chair across from her. Immediately, he sensed her nervousness.

"I don't bite, Jillian," he said, before taking a sip of coffee.

"I hope not."

He couldn't help but smile as he placed his cup down. He reached out and closed his fingers around her wrist. "Trust me. I prefer kissing you to biting you."

She pulled her hand back and nervously glanced over her shoulder before glaring at him. "Are you crazy? Anyone could walk in here!"

"And?"

"And had they heard what you just said they would have gotten the wrong impression."

He leaned back in his chair. "What do you think is the *right* impression?"

Her hair was pulled back in a ponytail and he was tempted to reach out, release the clasp and watch the waves fall to her shoulders. Then he would run his fingers through the thick, black tresses. He could just imagine the light, gentle strokes on her scalp and the thought sent a sudden jolt of sexual need through him.

"I don't want to make any impression, Aidan. Right or wrong."

Neither did he. At least he didn't think he did. Damn, the woman had him thinking crazy. He rubbed a frustrated hand down his face.

"It was just a kiss, nothing more."

He looked over at her. Why was he getting upset that she thought that way when he should be thinking the same thing. Hadn't he told her as much yesterday?

"Glad you think that way," he said, standing. "So let's go riding."

"Didn't you hear what I said?"

He smiled down at her. "You've said a lot. What part in particular are you asking about?"

She rolled her eyes. "I said I'm not going anywhere with you."

His smile widened. "Sure you are. We're going riding because if we don't, Bailey will think it's because I did something awful and got you mad with me. And if she confronts me about it, I will have to confess and tell her the truth—that the reason you wouldn't go riding with me is because you were afraid I might try to kiss you again. A kiss you can't avoid enjoying."

She narrowed her gaze at him. "You wouldn't."

"Trust me, I would. Confessing my sins will clear my conscience but will they clear yours? I'm not sure they would since you seem so wrapped up in not making any right or wrong impressions."

She just sat there and said nothing. He figured she was at a loss for words and this would be the best time for him to leave her to her thoughts. "Let's meet at the same place where we met yesterday in about an hour," he said, walking off to place his cup in the dishwasher.

Before exiting the kitchen he turned back to her and said, "And just so you know, Jillian, the reason I'm not leaving today to return to Boston has nothing to do with some woman I met at the club last night, but it has everything to do with you."

It has everything to do with you.

Not in her wildest dreams had Jillian thought seven little words could have such a huge impact on her. But they did. So much so that an hour later, she was back in the same place she'd been yesterday, waiting on Aidan.

She began pacing. Had she lost her mind? She wasn't sure what kind of game he was playing but instead of putting her foot down and letting him know she wanted no part of his foolishness, somehow she got caught, hook, line and sinker.

And all because of a kiss.

She would have to admit, it had been more than just a kiss. The fact that he was a gorgeous man, a man she'd had a secret crush on for four years, probably had a lot to do with it. But she'd always been able to separate fact from fiction, reality from fantasy, good from bad. So what was wrong with her now? An association with Aidan would only bring on heartache because not only was she deceiving her sister and brother-in-law, and no doubt the entire Westmoreland family, but she was deceiving herself, as well. Why would she want to become involved with a man known as a womanizer?

But then, she really wasn't involved with him. He was taking her riding, probably he would try to steal a few kisses and then nothing. Tomorrow he would return to Boston and she would return to Wyoming and it would be business as usual. But she knew for her it wouldn't be that simple.

She turned when she heard his approach. Their gazes connected and a luscious shiver ran through her body. He rode just like he had yesterday and looked basically the same. But today something was different. Now she knew he had the mouth of a very sensual man. A mouth he definitely knew how to use.

"I was hoping you would be here," he said, bringing his horse to a stop a few feet from her.

"Did you think I wouldn't after what you threatened to do?"

"I guess not," he said, dismounting.

"And you have no remorse?"

He tipped his Stetson back to gaze at her. "I've heard confession is good for the soul."

"And just what would it have accomplished, Aidan?"

"Putting it out there would have cleared your conscience, since it obviously bothers you that someone might discover I'm attracted to you and that you're attracted to me."

She started to deny what he'd said about her being attracted to him, but decided not to waste her time. It was true and they both knew it. "A true gentleman never kisses and tells."

"You're right. A true gentleman doesn't kiss and tell. But I don't like the thought of you cheapening what happened yesterday, either."

She placed her hands on her hips and leaned in, glaring at him. "How is it cheapening it when the whole thing meant nothing to you anyway?"

Jillian's question stunned Aidan. For a moment he couldn't say anything. She had definitely asked a good question, and it was one he wasn't sure he could answer. The only response he could come up with was that the kisses should not have meant anything to him, but they had. Hell, he had spent the past twenty-four hours thinking about nothing else. And hadn't he changed his plans so that he could stay another day just to spend more time with her?

She was standing there, glaring at him, with her arms crossed over her chest in a way that placed emphasis on a nice pair of breasts. Full and perfectly shaped. He could just imagine running his hands over them, teasing the nipples before drawing them in his mouth to…

"Well?"

She wanted an explanation and all he wanted to do was erase the distance separating them, take her into his arms and kiss that glare right off her face. Unfortunately, he knew he wouldn't stop there. Whether she knew it or not, Jillian Novak's taste only made him want more.

"Let's ride," he said, moving toward his horse. Otherwise, he would be tempted to do something he might later regret.

"Ride?" she hissed. "Is that all you've got to say?"

He glanced back over at her as he mounted his horse. "For now."

"None of this makes any sense, Aidan," she said, mounting her own horse.

She was right about that, he thought. None of it made any sense. Why was she like a magnet pulling him in? And why was he letting her?

They had ridden a few moments side by side in total silence when she finally broke it by asking, "Where are we going?"

"Bane's Ponderosa."

She nodded. "Has he built anything on it?"

"No, because legally it's not his yet. He can't claim it until he's twenty-five."

"Like Bailey. She told me about the age requirement."

"Yes, like Bailey."

He wished they could go back to not talking. He needed the silence to figure out what in the hell was happening to him. She must have deciphered that he was not in a talkative mood because she went silent again.

Aidan glanced over at her, admiring how well she handled a horse. He couldn't help admiring other things, as well. Such as how she looked today in her jeans and western shirt, and how the breasts he had fantasized about earlier moved erotically in rhythm with the horse's prance.

"There is a building here," Jillian said, bringing her horse to a stop.

He forced his eyes off her breasts to follow her gaze to the wooden cabin. He brought his horse to a stop, as well. "If you want to call it that, then yes. Bane built it a while back. It became his and Crystal's secret lovers' hideaway."

"Crystal?"

"Yes. Crystal Newsome. Bane's one and only."

Jillian nodded. "She's the reason he had to leave and join the navy, right?"

Aidan shrugged. "I guess you could say that, although I wouldn't place the blame squarely on Crystal's shoulders. Bane was as much into Crystal as Crystal was into Bane. They were both sticks of dynamite waiting to explode."

"Where is she now?"

"Don't know. I'm not sure if Bane even knows. He never says and I prefer not to ask," Aidan said, getting off his horse and tying it to the rail in front of the cabin.

He moved to assist her from her horse and braced himself for the onslaught of emotions he knew he would feel when he did so.

"You don't have to help me down, Aidan. I can manage."

"I'm sure you can but I'm offering my assistance anyway," he said, reaching his arms up to her.

For a minute he thought she would refuse his offer, but then she slid into his embrace. And as expected the moment they touched, fire shot through him. He actually felt his erection throb. He didn't say anything as he stared into her face. How could she arouse him to this degree?

"You can let go of me now, Aidan."

He blinked, realizing her feet were on the ground yet his arms were still around her waist. He tried to drop his arms but couldn't. It was as if they had a mind of their own.

Then, in a surprise move, she reached up and placed her arms around his neck. "This is crazy," she whispered in a quiet tone. "I shouldn't want this but I'm not thinking straight."

He shouldn't want it, either, but at that moment nothing could stop him. "We're leaving tomorrow. When we get back to our respective territories we can think straight then."

"What about right now?" she asked, staring deep into his gaze.

"Right now all I want to do is taste you again, Jillian. So damn bad."

She lifted her chin. "Then do it."

He doubted she knew what she was saying because her lips weren't the only thing he wanted to taste. He lowered his mouth to hers, thinking that she would find that out soon enough.

At that particular moment, Jillian couldn't deny herself the enjoyment of this kiss even if her life had depended on it.

She was getting what she wanted in full force—Aidan Westmoreland–style.

She stood with her arms wrapped around his neck and their lips locked, mesmerized, totally captivated, completely enthralled. How his tongue worked around in her mouth was truly remarkable. Every bone, every pore and every nerve ending responded to the way she was being thoroughly kissed. When had she become capable of such an intense yearning like this, where every lick and suck of Aidan's tongue could send electrical waves through her?

"Let's go inside," he whispered, pulling back from the kiss while tonguing her lips.

"Inside?" She could barely get the question past the feeling of burning from the inside out.

"Yes. We don't need to be out here in the open."

No they didn't. She had gotten so caught up in his kiss that she'd forgotten where they were. But instead of saying they shouldn't even be kissing, in the open or behind closed doors, she didn't resist him when he took her hand and tugged her toward the cabin.

Once the door closed behind them she looked around and was surprised at how tidy the place was. Definitely not what she'd expected. It was a one-room cabin with an iron bed. The colorful bedspread matched the curtains and coordinated with the huge area rug.

She turned to Aidan. "This is nice. Who keeps this place up?"

"Gemma promised Bane that she would and of course she had to put her signature on it. Now that she's getting married and moving to Australia, Bailey will take over. This place is important to Bane. He spends time here whenever he comes home."

Jillian nodded. "How's he doing?"

Aidan shrugged. "Okay now. It was hard for him to buckle down and follow authority, but he has no other choice if he wants to be a SEAL."

She'd heard that was Bane Westmoreland's goal. "So no one usually comes out this way?" She needed to know. There would be no turning back after today and she needed to make sure they didn't get caught.

"Rarely, although Ramsey uses this land on occasion for his sheep. But you don't have to worry about anyone showing up if that's what you're worried about."

She turned to face him. "I don't know why I'm doing this."

He touched her chin and tilted her head back to meet his gaze. "Do you want me to tell you?"

"Think you got it all figured out?"

He nodded. "Yes, I think I do."

"Okay then, let's hear it," she said, backing up to sit on the edge of the bed.

He moved to sit down on a nearby stool. "We're attracted to each other."

She chuckled slightly. "Tell me something I don't know, Aidan."

"What if I say that we've sort of gotten obsessed with each other?"

She frowned. "*Obsessed* is too strong a word, I think. We've only kissed twice."

"Actually three times. And I'm dying for the fourth. Aren't you?"

She knew she had to be honest with him and stop denying the obvious. "Yes, but I don't understand why."

He got up from the stool and stood. "Maybe it's not for us to understand, Jillian."

"How can you say that? How do you think our family would react if they knew we were carrying on like this behind their backs?"

He slowly crossed the room to stand in front of where she sat. "We won't know how they'd react because you're determined to keep this a secret, aren't you?"

She tilted her head to look up at him. "Yes. I couldn't hurt Pam that way. She expects me to stay focused on school. And if I did get involved with a guy, I'm sure she wouldn't want that guy to be you."

He frowned. "And what is so bad about getting involved with me?"

"I think you know the answer to that. She thinks of us as one big family. And there's your reputation. But, like you said, we'll be leaving tomorrow and going our separate ways. What's happening between us is curiosity taking its toll on our common sense."

"That's what you think?" he asked, reaching out and taking a lock of her hair between his fingers.

"Yes, that's what I think." She noticed something in the depths of his eyes that gave her pause—but only for a second. That's all the time it took for her gaze to lower from his eyes to his mouth.

She watched as he swept the tip of his tongue across his lips. "I can still taste you, you know," he said in a low, husky tone.

She nodded slowly. "Yes, I know." Deciding to be honest, she said, "And the reason I know is because I can still taste you, as well."

Six

Aidan wished Jillian hadn't said that. After their first kiss, he'd concluded she had enjoyed it as much as he had. When they'd gone another round he'd been sure of it. Just like he was sure that, although her experience with kissing had been at a minimum, she was a fast learner. She had kept up with him, stroke for stroke. And now, for her to confess that she could still taste him, the same way he could still taste her, sent his testosterone level soaring.

He took a step closer, gently pulled her to her feet and wrapped his arms around her waist. He truly didn't understand why the desire between them was so intense but he accepted that it was. The thought of Dillon and Pam's ire didn't appeal to him any more than it did to her, but unlike her, he refused to believe his cousin and cousin-in-law would be dead set against something developing between him and Jillian.

But he didn't have to worry because *nothing* was developing between them. They were attracted to each other; there was nothing serious about that. He'd been attracted to women before, although never to this degree, he would admit. But after today it would be a while before they saw each other again since he rarely came home. This would be a one-and-done fling. He knew for certain that Pam and Dillon would definitely *not* like the thought of that. They would think he'd taken advantage of her. So he agreed they did not need to know.

"I won't sleep with you, Aidan."

Her words interrupted his thoughts. He met her gaze. "You won't?"

"No. I think we should get that straight right now."

He nodded slowly. "All right. So what did you have in mind for us to do in here?" To say he was anxious to hear her answer was an understatement.

"Kiss some more. A lot more."

Evidently she didn't think an intense kissing match could lead to other things, with a loss of control topping the list. "You think it will be that simple?"

She shrugged. "No. But I figure if we both use a reasonable degree of self-control we'll manage."

A reasonable degree of self control? Jillian had more confidence in their abilities than he did. Just being here with her was causing a hard pounding in his crotch. If only she knew just how enticing she looked standing in front of him in a pair of jeans and a white button-up blouse that he would love to peel off her. Her hair was pinned up on her head, but a few locks…like the one he'd played with earlier…had escaped confinement.

"Is there a problem, Aidan?"

He lifted a brow. "Problem?"

"Yes. You're stalling and I'm ready now."

He fought to hide his grin. Was this the same woman who only yesterday swore they would never kiss again? The same woman who just that morning had refused to go riding with him? Her enthusiasm caused something within him to stir, making it hard to keep his control in check. His body wouldn't cooperate mainly because her scent alone was increasing his desire for her.

And she thought all they would do was some heavy-duty kissing?

Deciding not to keep her waiting any longer, he slanted his mouth over hers.

When had she needed a man's kiss this much? No, *this* much, she thought, leaning up on her toes to become enmeshed in Aidan's kiss even more. Jillian felt his arms move from around her waist to her backside, urging her closer to the fit of him, making her feel his hard erection pressing against her middle. She shouldn't like how it felt but she did.

The tips of her nipples seemed sensitized against his solid chest. When had she become this hot mass of sexual desire?

When he intensified the kiss even more, she actually heard herself moan. Really moan. He was actually tasting her. Using his mouth to absorb hers as if she was a delectable treat he had to consume. She was losing all that control she'd told him they had to keep and she was losing it in a way she couldn't define.

When he groaned deep in his throat and deepened the kiss even more, it took all she had to remain standing and not melt in a puddle on the floor. Why at twenty-one was she just experiencing kisses like these? And why was she allowing her mind to be sacked with emotions and sensations that made it almost impossible to breathe, to think, to do anything but reciprocate? Their tongues tangled greedily, dueling and plowing each other's mouths with a yearning that was unrelenting.

When she noticed his hands were no longer on her

backside but had worked their way to the zipper of her jeans, she gasped and broke off the kiss, only to be swept off her feet into Aidan's strong arms.

Before she could ask what he was doing, he tumbled them both onto the huge bed. She looked up into his dark eyes as he moved his body over hers. Any words she'd wanted to say died in her throat. All she could do was stare at him as intense heat simmered through her veins. He leaned back on his haunches and then in one quick movement, grasped her hips and peeled the jeans down to her knees.

"What—what are you doing?" she managed to ask, while liquid fire sizzled down her spine. She was lying there with only bikini panties covering her.

He met her gaze. "I'm filling my entire mouth with the taste of you." And then he eased her panties down her legs before lifting her hips and lowering his head between her thighs.

The touch of his tongue had her moaning and lifting her hips off the bed. He was relentless, and he used his mouth in a way that should be outlawed. She wanted to push his head away, but instead she used her arms to hold him in place.

And then she felt a series of intense spasms spread through her entire body. Suddenly, he did something wicked with his tongue, driving her wild. She screamed as a flood of sensations claimed her, tossing her into an earth-shaking orgasm. Her very first. It was more powerful than anything she could have imagined.

And he continued to lap her up, not letting go. His actions filled her with more emotions, more wanting, more longing. Her senses were tossed to smithereens. It took a while before she had enough energy to breathe through her lungs to release a slow, steady breath. She wondered if she had enough energy to even mount her horse, much less ride away from here.

Aidan lifted his head and slowly licked his lips, as if savoring her taste, while meeting her eyes. "Mmm, delicious."

His words were as erotic as she felt. "Why? Why did you do that?" she asked, barely able to get the words out. She felt exhausted, totally drained. Yet completely and utterly satisfied.

Instead of giving her an answer, he touched her chin with the tip of his thumb before lowering his lips to hers in an open-mouth kiss that had fire stirring deep in her stomach. Tasting herself on his lips made her quiver.

When he finally released her lips, he eased back on his haunches and gazed down at her. "I did it because you have a flavor that's uniquely you and I wanted to sample it."

She lifted her hips off the bed when he pulled her jeans back up. Then he shifted his body to pull her into his lap. She tilted her head back to look at him. "What about when we leave here tomorrow?"

"When we leave tomorrow we will remember this time with fondness and enjoyment. I'm sure when you wake up in your bed in Wyoming and I wake up in mine in Boston, we will be out of each other's systems."

She nodded. "You think so?"

"Yes, I'm pretty sure of it. And don't feel guilty about anything because we haven't hurt anyone. All we did was appease our curiosity in a very delectable way."

Yes, it had been most delectable. And technically, they hadn't slept together so they hadn't crossed any lines. She pulled away from him to finish fixing her clothing, tucking her shirt back into her jeans.

"Um, a missed opportunity."

She glanced over at him. "What?"

"Your breasts. I had planned to devour them."

At that moment, as if on cue, her breasts began to ache. Her nipples felt tight, sensitive, pulsing. And it didn't help matters when an image of him doing that very thing trickled through her mind.

"We need to go," she said quickly, knowing if they remained any longer it would only lead to trouble.

"Do we?"

He wasn't helping matters by asking her that. "Yes. It's getting late and we might be missed." When he made no attempt to move, she headed for the door. "I can find my way back."

"Wait up, Jillian."

She stopped and turned back to him. "We don't have to go back together, Aidan."

"Yes, we do. Pam knows of our plans to go riding together."

Color drained from Jillian's face. "Who told her?"

"I ran into her when I was headed to the barn and she asked where I was headed. I told her the truth."

At the accusation in her expression, he placed his hands in the back pockets of his jeans. "Had I told her I was going someplace else and she discovered differently, Jillian, she would have wondered why I had lied."

Jillian nodded slowly upon realizing what he said made sense. "What did she say about it?"

"Nothing. In fact I don't think she thought much about it at all. However, she did say she was glad you were about to start medical school and she would appreciate any advice I could give you."

Jillian swallowed tightly. He'd given her more than advice. Thanks to him, she had experienced her first orgasm today. "Okay, we'll ride back together. I'll just wait outside."

She quickly walked out the door. He'd claimed what they'd done today would get them out of each other's systems. She definitely hoped so.

When the door closed behind Jillian, Aidan rubbed a hand down his face in frustration. He couldn't leave Denver soon enough. The best thing to do was put as much distance between him and Jillian as possible. She felt uncomfortable with the situation and now he was beginning to feel the same. However, his uneasiness had nothing to do with Dillon and Pam finding out what they'd been up to, and everything to do with his intense attraction to Jillian.

Even now he wanted to go outside, throw her over his shoulders and bring her back inside. He wanted to kiss her into submission and taste her some more before making nonstop love to her. How crazy was that?

He'd never felt this much desire for any woman, and knowing she was off-limits only seemed to heighten his desire for her. And now that he'd gotten an intimate taste of her, getting her out of his system might not be as easy as he'd claimed earlier. Her taste hadn't just electrified his taste buds, it had done something to him that was unheard of—he was no longer lingering on the edge of wanting to make love to her but had fallen off big-time.

Every time his tongue explored her mouth, his emotions heated up and began smoldering. And when he lapped her up, he was tempted to do other things to her, as well. Things he doubted she was ready for.

Drawing in a deep breath, he straightened up the bed-covers before heading for the door. Upon stepping out-side, he breathed in deeply to calm his racing heart. She stood there stroking his horse and a part of him wished she would stroke him the same way. He got hard just imagining such a thing.

He didn't say anything for a long moment. He just stood there watching her. When his erection pressed uncomfortably against his zipper, he finally spoke up. "I'm ready to ride."

She glanced over at him and actually smiled when she said, "You have a beautiful horse, Aidan."

"Thanks," he said, walking down the steps. "Charger is a fourth-generation Westmoreland stallion."

She turned to stroke the horse again and didn't look up when he came to stand next to her. "I've heard all about Charger. I was warned by Dillon to never try to ride him because only a few people could. It's obvious you're one of those people."

Aidan nodded. "Yes, Charger and I have an under-standing."

She stopped stroking Charger to look at him. "What about you and me, Aidan? Do we have an understand-ing?"

He met her gaze, nor sure how he should answer that. Just when he thought he had everything figured out about them, something would happen to make his brains turn to mush. "I assume you're referring to the incidents that have taken place between us over the past two days."

"I am."

"Then, yes, we have an understanding. After today, no more kissing, no more touching—"

"Or tasting," she interjected.

Saying he would never again taste her was a hard one, but for her peace of mind and for his own, he would say it. "Yes, tasting."

"Good. We're in agreement."

He wouldn't exactly say that, but for now he would hold his tongue—that same tongue that enjoyed dueling with hers. "I guess we need to head back."

"Okay, and I don't need your help mounting my horse."

In other words, she didn't want him to touch her. "You sure?"

"Positive."

He nodded and then watched her move away from his horse to get on hers. As usual, it was a total turn-on watching her. "I want to thank you, Aidan."

He took his gaze away from the sight of her legs straddling the horse to look into her face. "Thank me for what?"

"For introducing me to a few things during this visit home."

For some reason that made him smile. "It was my pleasure." And he meant every word.

Seven

"You're still not going home, Jillian?"

Jillian looked up from eating her breakfast to see her roommate, Ivy Rollins. They had met in her sophomore year when Jillian knew she didn't want to live in the dorm any longer. She had wanted an apartment off campus and someone to share the cost with her. Ivy, who had plans to attend law school, had answered the ad Jillian placed in the campus newspaper. They'd hit it off the first time they'd met and had been the best of friends since. Jillian couldn't ask for a better roommate.

"I was home last month," she reminded Ivy.

"Yes, but that was a couple of days for your birthday. Next week is spring break."

Jillian didn't want to be reminded. Pam had called yesterday to see if Jillian would be coming home since Nadia had made plans to do so. Paige, who was attending UCLA, had gotten a small part in a play on campus and needed to remain in Los Angeles. Guilt was still riding Jillian over what she and Aidan had done. She hated deceiving her sister about anything. "I explained to Pam that I need to start studying for the MCAT. She understood."

"I hate leaving you, but—"

"But you will," Jillian said, smiling. "And that's fine. I know how homesick you get." That was an understatement. Ivy's family lived in Oregon. Her parents, both chefs, owned a huge restaurant there. Her two older brothers were chefs as well and assisted her parents. Ivy had decided on a different profession than her parents and siblings, but she loved going home every chance she got to help out.

"Yes, I will," Ivy said, returning her smile. "In fact I leave in two days. Sure you'll be okay?"

"Yes, I'll be fine. I've got enough to keep me busy since I'm sitting for the MCAT in two months. And I need to start working on my essays."

"It's a bummer you'll be doing something other than enjoying yourself next week," Ivy said.

"It's okay. Getting into medical school is the most important thing to me right now."

A few hours later Jillian sat at the computer desk in her bedroom searching the internet. She had tossed around the idea of joining a study group for the MCAT and there appeared to be several. Normally, she preferred studying solo but for some reason she couldn't concentrate. She pushed away from the computer and leaned back in her chair knowing the reason.

Aidan.

It had been a little over a month since she'd gone home for her birthday, and Aidan had been wrong. She hadn't woken up in her bed in Wyoming not thinking of him. In fact she thought of him even more. All the time. Thoughts of him had begun interfering with her studies.

She got up and moved to the kitchen to grab a soda from the refrigerator. He should have been out of her system by now, but he wasn't. Memories of him put her to sleep at night and woke her up in the morning. And then in the wee hours of the night, she recalled in vivid detail his kisses, especially the ones between her legs.

Remembering that particular kiss sent a tingling sensation through her womanly core, which wasn't good. In fact, nothing about what she was going through was good. Sexual withdrawal. And she hadn't even had sex with Aidan, but she hadn't needed sex to get an orgasm. That in itself showed the magnitude of his abilities.

Returning to her bedroom she pushed thoughts of him from her mind. Sitting back down at her desk, she resumed surfing the net. She bet he hadn't even given her a thought. He probably wasn't missing any sleep thinking of her, and he had probably woken up his first day back in Boston with some woman in his bed. Why did that thought bother her?

She had been tempted to ask Pam if she'd heard from Aidan, but hadn't for fear her sister would wonder why Jillian was inquiring about Aidan when she hadn't before.

Jillian turned around when she heard a knock on her bedroom door. "Come in."

Ivy walked into the room, smiling. "I know you have a lot to do but you've been in here long enough. Come grab a bite to eat at the Wild Duck. My treat."

Ivy wasn't playing fair. She knew the Wild Duck was one of Jillian's favorite eating places. They had the best hamburgers and fries. "You've twisted my arm," she said, pushing away from the desk.

Ivy chuckled. "Yeah. Right."

Jillian stood, thinking she did need a break. And maybe she could get Aidan off her mind.

* * *

"How are you doing, Dr. Westmoreland?"

Aidan smiled over at the doctor who'd transferred in to the medical school during the weekend that he'd gone home. He really should ask her out. Lynette Bowes was attractive, she had a nice figure, and she seemed friendly enough. At times almost too friendly. She enjoyed flirting with him and she'd gone so far as to make a few bold innuendos, which meant getting her into his bed probably would be easy. So what was he waiting on?

"I'm fine, Dr. Bowes, and how are you?"

She leaned over to hand him a patient's chart, intentionally brushing her breasts against his arm. "I would be a lot a better if you dropped by my apartment tonight," she whispered.

Another invite. Why was he stalling? Why wasn't he on top of his game as usual? And why was he thinking that the intimate caress she'd purposely initiated just now had nothing on the caresses he'd experienced with Jillian?

"Thanks, but I have plans for tonight," he lied.

"Then maybe another night?"

"I'll let you know." He appreciated his cell phone going off at that moment. "I'll see you later." He made a quick escape.

Later that night while at home doing nothing but flipping TV channels, he couldn't help wondering what the hell was wrong with him. Although he'd asked himself that question, he knew the answer without thinking.

Jillian.

He'd assumed once he was back in Boston and waking up in his own bed that he would eradicate her from his mind. Unfortunately, he'd found out that wasn't the case. He thought about her every free moment, and he even went to bed thinking about her. And the dreams he had of her were double X-rated. His desire for her was so bad that he hadn't thought twice about wanting anyone else.

And it hadn't helped matters when he'd called home earlier in the week and Dillon mentioned that Jillian wasn't coming home for spring break. She told Pam she had registered to take the MCAT and needed the time to study and work on her admissions essays. He applauded her decision to make sacrifices to reach her goal, but he was disappointed she hadn't reached out to him liked he'd suggested. He'd made a pretty high score on the MCAT and could give her some study pointers. He'd even keyed his contact information into her phone.

Yet she hadn't called to ask him a single question about anything. That could only mean she didn't want his help and had probably pushed what happened between them to the back of her mind. Good for her, but he didn't like the fact that she remained in the center of his.

Tossing the remote aside he reached for his cell phone to pull up her number. When her name appeared he put the phone down. They'd had an agreement, so to speak. An understanding. They would put that time in Denver behind them. It had been enjoyable but was something that could not and would not be repeated. No more kissing, touching...or tasting.

Hell, evidently that was easy for her to do, but it was proving to be downright difficult for him. There were nights he woke up wanting her with a passion, hungering to kiss her, touch her and taste her.

The memories of them going riding together, especially that day spent in Bane's cabin...every moment of that time was etched in Aidan's mind, making his brain cells overload.

Like now.

When he'd pulled down her jeans, followed by her panties, and had buried his head between her legs and tasted her…the memory made his groin tighten. Need for Jillian clawed at him in a way that made it difficult to breathe.

Aidan stood and began pacing the floor in his apartment, trying to wear down his erection. He paused when an idea entered his mind. He had time he could take off and he might as well do it now. He'd only been to Laramie, Wyoming, a couple of times, and maybe he should visit there again. He would take in the sights and check out a few good restaurants. And there was no reason for him not to drop in on Jillian to see how she was doing while he was there.

No reason at all.

Three days later, Jillian sat at the kitchen table staring at the huge study guide in front of her. It had to be at least five hundred pages thick and filled with information to prepare her for the MCAT. The recommendation was that students take three months to study, but since she was enrolled in only one class this semester she figured she would have more time to cram and could get it done in two months. That meant she needed to stay focused. No exceptions. And she meant none.

But her mind was not in agreement, especially when she could lick her lips and imagine Aidan doing that very same thing. And why—after one month, nine days and twenty minutes—could she still do that? Why hadn't she been able to forget about his kisses and move on? Especially now when she needed to focus.

The apartment was empty and felt lonely without Ivy. It was quiet and just what she needed to get some serious studying done. She had eaten a nice breakfast and had taken a walk outside to get her brain and body stimulated. But now her mind wanted to remember another type of stimulation. One that even now sent tingles through her lower stomach.

She was about to take a sip of her coffee when the doorbell sounded. She frowned. Most of her neighbors were college students like her, and the majority of them had gone home for spring break. She'd noticed how vacant the parking lot had looked while out walking earlier.

Getting up from the kitchen table she moved toward the front door. She glanced through her peephole and her breath caught. Standing on the other side of her door was the one man she'd been trying not to think about.

Shocked to the core, she quickly removed the security chain and unlocked the door. Opening it, she tried to ignore the way her heart pounded and how her stomach muscles trembled. "Aidan? What are you doing here?"

Instead of answering, he leaned down and kissed her. Another shock rammed right into the first. She should have pushed him away the moment their mouths connected. But instead she melded her body right to his and his arms reached out to hold her around the waist. As soon as she was reacquainted with his taste, her tongue latched onto his and began a sensuous duel that had her moaning.

In all her attempts at logical thinking over the past month, not until now could she admit how much she'd missed him. How much she'd missed this. How could a man engrain himself inside a woman's senses so deeply and thoroughly, and so quickly? And how could any woman resist this particular man doing so?

She heard the door click and knew he'd maneuvered her into her apartment and closed the door behind him. Noticing that, she almost pulled back, and she would have had he not at that moment deepened the kiss.

This had to be a dream. Is that why the room felt as if it was spinning? There was no way Aidan was in Laramie, at her apartment and kissing her. But if this was a dream she wasn't ready to wake up. She needed to get her fill of his taste before her fantasy faded. Before she realized in horror that she was actually kissing the short and bald mailman instead of Aidan. Had her fascination with him finally gotten the best of her?

The thought had her breaking off the kiss and opening her eyes. The man standing across from her with lips damp from their kiss was definitely Aidan.

She drew in a deep breath, trying to slow the beat of her heart and regain control of her senses.

As if he'd known just what she was thinking, he said, "It's really me, Jillian. And I'm here to help you study for your MCAT this week."

She blinked. *Help her study?* He had to be kidding.

Aidan wanted nothing more than to kiss the shocked look off Jillian's face. But he knew that before he could even think about kissing her again he had a lot of explaining to do since he'd gone back on their agreement.

"I talked to Dillon a few days ago and he mentioned you wouldn't be coming home for spring break and the reason why. So I figured I could help by giving you a good study boost."

She shook her head as if doing so would clear her mind. Looking back at him, she said, "There's no way you could have thought that. And what was that kiss about? I thought we had an understanding."

"We did. We still do. However, based on the way you responded to my kiss just now, I think we might need to modify a few things."

She lifted her chin. "There's nothing for us to modify."

That response irritated him to the core. "Do you think I want to be here, Jillian? I have a life in Boston, a life I was enjoying until recently. Ever since the kisses we shared on your birthday, I've done nothing but think about you, want you, miss you."

"That's not my fault," she snapped.

"It is when you're not being honest with yourself. Can you look me in the eyes and tell me that you haven't thought of me? That you haven't been wanting me? And be honest for once because if you deny it then you need to tell me why your kiss just now said otherwise."

He watched as she nervously licked her tongue across her lips and his gut clenched. "Tell me, Jillian," he said in a softer tone. "For once be honest with me and with yourself."

She drew in a long breath as they stared at each other. After several tense moments passed between them, she said, "Okay, I have been thinking of you, missing you, wanting you. And I hated myself for doing so. You're a weakness I can't afford to have right now. It's crazy. I know a lot of guys around campus. But why you? Why do I want the one guy I can't have?"

Her words softened his ire. She was just as confused

and frustrated as he was. "And why do you think you can't have me?"

She frowned. "You know why, Aidan. Pam and Dillon would be against it. In their eyes, we're family. And even if you were a guy she would approve of, she would try to convince me not to get involved with you and to stay focused on becoming a doctor."

"You don't know for certain that's how she would feel, Jillian."

"I do know. When Pam was in college pursuing her dream of becoming an actress, I asked her why she didn't date. She told me that a woman should never sacrifice her dream for any man."

"I'm not asking you to sacrifice your dream."

"No, but you want an involvement during a time when I should be more focused than ever on becoming a doctor."

"I want to help you, not hinder you," he stressed again.

"How do you think you can do that?"

At least she was willing to listen. "By using this week to introduce you to study techniques that will help you remember those things you need to remember."

She nervously licked her tongue across her lips again. "It won't work. I won't be able to think straight with you around."

"I'll make sure you do. I'm not asking to stay here, Jillian. I've already checked into a hotel a mile or so from here. I'll arrive every morning and we'll study until evening, taking short breaks in between. Then we'll grab something to eat and enjoy the evening. Afterward, I'll bring you back here and then leave. Before going to bed you should review what was covered that day, making sure you get eight hours of sleep."

She looked at him as if he was crazy. "I can't take time from studying to enjoy the evening. I'll need to study morning, noon and night."

"Not with me helping you. Besides, too much studying will make you burned out, and you don't want to do that. What good is studying if that happens?"

When she didn't say anything, he pushed harder. "Try my way for a couple of days and if it doesn't work, if you feel I'm more of a hindrance than a help, I'll leave Laramie and let you do things your way."

As she stared at him, not saying anything, he could feel blood throb through his veins. As usual she looked serious. Beautiful. Tempting. He wanted her. Being around her would be hard and leaving her every night after dinner would be harder. He would want to stay and make love to her all through the night. But that wasn't possible. No matter how hard it would be, he needed to keep his self-control.

"Okay," she finally said. "We'll try it for a couple of days. And if it doesn't work I intend for you to keep your word about leaving."

"I will." He had no intention of leaving because he intended for his plan to work. He had aced the MCAT the first time around, with flying colors. Once he'd gotten his act together as a teenager, he'd discovered he was an excellent test taker, something Adrian was not. Determined not to leave his twin behind, he'd often tutored Adrian, sharing his study tips and techniques with his brother. Aidan had also done the same with Bailey once she was in college. Unfortunately, he'd never gotten the chance to share his techniques with Bane since his cousin hadn't been interested in anything or anyone but Crystal.

"Now let's seal our agreement," he said.

When she extended her hand, he glanced at it before pulling her into his arms again.

He was taking advantage again, Jillian thought. But she only thought that for a second. That was all the time it took for her to begin returning his kiss with the same hunger he seemed to feel. This was crazy. It was insane. It was also what she needed. What she'd been wanting since leaving Denver and returning to Laramie.

Kissing was something they enjoyed doing with each other and the unhurried mating of their mouths definitely should be ruled illegal. But for now she could handle this—in the safety of her living room, in the arms of a man she thoroughly enjoyed kissing—as long as it went no further.

But what if it did? He'd already shown her that his definition of kissing included any part of her body. What if he decided he wanted more than her mouth this time? Her hormones were going haywire just thinking of the possibility.

He suddenly broke off the kiss and she fought back a groan of disappointment. She stared up at him. "Okay, where's the study guide?" he asked her.

She blinked. Her mind was slow in functioning after such a blazing kiss. It had jarred her senses. "Study guide?"

He smiled and caressed her cheek. "Yes, the MCAT study guide."

"On my kitchen table. I was studying when you showed up."

"Good. And you'll study some more. Lead the way."

* * *

Aidan leaned back in his chair and glanced over at Jillian. "Any questions?"

She shook her head. "No, but you make it seem simple."

He smiled. "Trust me, it's not. The key is to remember that you're the one in control of your brain and the knowledge that's stored inside of it. Don't let retrieving that information during test time psych you out."

She chuckled. "That's easy for you to say."

"And it will be easy for you, as well. I've been there, and when time allows I tutor premed students like yourself. You did well on the practice exam, which covers basically everything you need to know. Now you need to concentrate on those areas you're not so sure about."

"Which is a lot."

"All of them are things you know," he countered. He believed the only reason she lacked confidence in her abilities was because the idea of failing was freaking her out. "You don't have to pass on the first go-round. A lot of people don't. That's why it's suggested you plan to take it at least twice."

She lifted her chin. "I want to ace it on the first try."

"Then do it."

Aidan got up from his chair and went over to the coffeepot sitting on her kitchen counter. He needed something stronger than caffeine, but coffee would have to do. He'd been here for five hours already and they hadn't stopped for lunch. The key was to take frequent short breaks instead of one or two long ones.

She had taken the online practice exam on verbal reasoning and he thought she'd done well for her first time. He'd given her study tips for multiple-choice exams and gone over the questions she had missed. Personally, he thought she would do fine, although he thought taking the test in two months was pushing it. He would have suggested three months instead of two.

"Want some coffee?" he asked, pouring himself a cup.

"No, I'm okay."

Yes, she definitely was. He couldn't attest to her mental state with all that she'd crammed into that brain of hers today, but he could definitely attest to her physical one. She looked amazing, even with her hair tied back in a ponytail and a cute pair of reading glasses perched on her nose. He was used to seeing her without makeup and preferred her that way. She had natural beauty with her flawless creamy brown skin. And she looked cute in her jeans and top.

He glanced at his watch. "Jillian?"

She glanced up from the computer and looked over at him. "Yes?"

"It's time to call it a day."

She seemed baffled by his statement. "Call it a day? I haven't covered everything I wanted to do today."

"You covered a lot and you don't want to overload your brain."

She stared at him for a moment and then nodded and began shutting down her computer. "Maybe you're right. Thanks to you, I did cover a lot. Definitely a lot more than I would have if you hadn't been here. You're a great tutor."

"And you're a good student." He glanced at his watch again. "What eating places do you have around here?"

"Depends on what you have a taste for."

He had a taste for her, but knew he had to keep his promise and not push her into anything. "A juicy steak."

"Then you're in luck," she said, standing. "There's a great steak place a few blocks from here. Give me a few minutes to change."

"Okay." He watched her hurry off toward her bedroom.

When she closed the door behind her, he rubbed a hand down his face. Jillian was temptation even when she wasn't trying to be. When he'd asked about her roommate she'd told him that Ivy had gone home for spring break. That meant…

Nothing. Unless she made the first move or issued an invitation. Until then, he would spend his nights alone at the hotel.

Eight

Jillian glanced across the table at Aidan. It was day three and still hard to believe that he was in Laramie, that he had come to give her a kick-start in her studying. Day one had been frustrating. He'd pushed her beyond what she thought she was ready for. But going to dinner with him that night had smoothed her ruffled feathers.

Dinner had been fun. She'd discovered he enjoyed eating his steaks medium rare and he loved baked potatoes loaded with sour cream, bacon bits and cheddar cheese. He also loved unsweetened tea and when it came to anything with chocolate, he could overdose if he wasn't careful.

He was also a great conversationalist. He engaged her in discussions about everything—but he deemed the topic of medical school to be off-limits. They talked about the economy, recent elections, movies they had enjoyed, and about Adrian's plans to travel the world a few years after getting his PhD in engineering.

And Aidan got her talking. She told him about Ivy, who she thought was the roommate from heaven; about Jillian's decision two years ago to move out of the dorm; and about her first experience with a pushy car salesman. She told him about all the places she wanted to visit one day and that the one thing she wanted to do and hadn't done yet was go on a cruise.

It occurred to her later that it had been the first time she and Aidan had shared a meal together alone, and she had enjoyed it. It had made her even more aware of him as a man. She'd had the time to look beyond his handsome features and she'd discovered he was a thoughtful and kind person. He had been pleasant, treating everyone with respect, including the waitress and servers. And each time he smiled at her, her stomach clenched. Then he would take a sip of his drink, and she would actually envy his straw.

After dinner they returned to her apartment. He made her promise that she would only review what they'd covered that day and not stay up past nine, then he left. But not before taking her into his arms and giving her a kiss that rendered her weak and senseless—to the point where she was tempted to ask him to stay longer. But she fought back the temptation. Knowing she would see him again the next day had made falling asleep quick and easy. For the first time in a long time, she had slept through the night, though he'd dominated her dreams.

He arrived early the next morning with breakfast, which she appreciated. Then it was back to studying again. The second day had been more intense than the first. Knowing they couldn't cover every aspect of the study guide in one week, he had encouraged her to hit the areas she felt were her weakest. He gave her hints on how to handle multiple-choice questions and introduced her to key words to use when completing her essays.

For dinner they had gone to the Wild Duck. She had been eager to introduce him to her favorite place. A dinner of hamburgers, French fries and milk shakes had been wonderful. Afterward they went to Harold's Game Hall to shoot pool, something she had learned to do in high school.

When he'd brought her home, like the night before, he took her in his arms and kissed her before he left, giving her the same instructions about reviewing what they'd covered that morning and getting eight hours of sleep. Again, she'd slept like a baby with him dominating her dreams.

She enjoyed having him as a study coach. Most of the time she stayed focused. But there were a few times when she felt heat simmering between them, something both of them tried to ignore. They managed it most of the time but today was harder than the two days before.

Aidan was tense. She could tell. He had arrived that morning, like yesterday, with breakfast in hand. Since he believed she should study on a full stomach and not try eating while studying, they had taken their meal outside to her patio. It had been pleasant, but more than once she'd caught him staring at her with a look in his eyes that she felt in the pit of her stomach.

He wasn't as talkative today as he'd been the past two days, and, taking a cue from his mood, she hadn't said much, either. On those occasions when their hands had accidentally touched while he'd been handing her papers or turning a page, she wasn't sure who sizzled more, her or him.

That's why she'd made up her mind about how today would end. She wanted him and he wanted her and there was no reason for them to suffer with their desires any longer. She'd fallen in love with him. After this time together, she could admit that now. That little crush she'd had on him for years had become something more. Something deeper and more profound.

The thought of Pam and Dillon finding out was still an issue that plagued her. However, since Aidan didn't feel the same way about her that she felt about him, she was certain she would be able to convince him to keep whatever they did a secret. He was doing that now anyway. He'd told her that neither Pam nor Dillon knew where he was spending this week. That meant Jillian and Aidan were already keeping secrets from their family, and she would continue to do so if it meant spending more time with him.

That night they went to a restaurant she had never visited because of its pricey menu. The signature dishes had been delicious and the service excellent. But the restaurant's setting spoke of not only elegance but also romance. Rustic wood ceilings with high beams, a huge brick fireplace and a natural stone floor. Beautiful candles adorned the tables and even in the dim light, each time she glanced over at Aidan he was looking back at her.

Getting through dinner hadn't been easy. They conversed but not as much as they had the previous two nights. Was she imagining things or did his voice sound deeper, huskier than usual? His smiles weren't full ones but half smiles, and just as sexy.

Like he'd done the previous two nights, he walked through her apartment, checking to make sure everything was okay. Then he gave her orders to only review what she'd studied that morning and get into bed before nine because at least eight hours of sleep were essential.

And then, as had become his habit, he pulled her into his arms to kiss her goodbye. This is what she had anticipated all day. She was ready for Aidan's kiss. Standing on tiptoe she tilted her open mouth toward him, her tongue ready. He closed his full mouth over hers and their tongues tangled, almost bringing her to her knees.

The kiss lasted for a long, delectable moment. It was different than any they'd shared before and she'd known it the moment their mouths fused. It was hot, heavy and hungry. He wasn't letting up or backing down—and neither was she.

Jillian felt herself being lifted off her feet and she immediately wrapped her legs around his waist while he continued to ravish her mouth in a way that overwhelmed her and overloaded her senses. His hunger was sexual and greedy. She could tell he was fighting hard to hold it together, to stay in control, to keep his sanity in check. But she wasn't. In fact, she was deliberately trying to tempt him every way that she could.

She felt the wall at her back and knew he'd maneuvered them over to it. He broke off the kiss and stared at her, impaling her with the flaming fire in his eyes. "Tell me to stop, Jillian," he said. "Because if you don't do it now, I won't be able to stop later. I want to tongue you all over. Lick every inch of your body. Taste you. Make love to you. Hard. Long. Deep. So tell me to stop now."

Her pulse jumped. Every single cell in her body sizzled with his words. Hot, sparks of passion glowed in his gaze and when a powerful burst of primal need slammed through her she didn't want to escape.

"Tell me to stop."

His plea made the already hot sexual tension between them blaze, and she knew of only one way to put out the fire.

"Stop, Aidan!"

His body went still. The only thing that moved was the pulse throbbing in his throat. He held her gaze and she was convinced she could hear blood rushing through both of their veins.

When she felt him about to untangle her legs from around his waist and lower her feet to the floor, she said, "Stop talking and do all those things you claim you're going to do."

She saw the impact of her words reflected in his eyes. While he seemed incapable of speaking, she released her arms from around his neck and tugged at his shirt, working her hands beneath to touch his bare chest. She heard the groan from deep in his throat.

"If you don't take me, Aidan Westmoreland, then I'll be forced to take you."

That was the last thing Aidan had expected her to say. But hearing her say it intensified the throbbing need within him. His crotch pounded fiercely and he knew of only one way to remedy that. But first...

He lowered her to her feet as a smile tugged at his lips. Only for a moment, he gazed down at her shirt, noticing the curve of her breasts beneath the cotton. In an instant, he tugged the shirt over her head and tossed it aside.

He drew in a deep breath when his eyes settled on her chest, specifically her skin-tone colored bra. Eager beyond belief, he touched her breasts through the lace material. When his fingers released the front clasp, causing the twin globes to spring free, the breath was snatched from his lungs.

Mercy. He eased the bra straps from her shoulders to remove it completely from her body and his mouth watered. Her breasts were one area that he hadn't tasted yet, and he planned on remedying that soon.

Deciding he wanted to see more naked flesh, he lowered to his knees and slid his fingers beneath the elastic waistband of her skirt to ease it down her legs. She stepped out of it and he tossed it aside to join her shirt and bra. His gaze raked the full length of her body, now only covered by a pair of light blue bikini panties. His hands actually trembled when he ran them down her legs. He felt as if he were unveiling a precious treasure.

She stepped out of them as she'd done her skirt and she stood in front of him totally naked. He leaned back on his haunches while his gaze raked her up and down, coming back to her center. He was tempted to start right there, but he knew if he did that, he wouldn't get to taste her breasts this time, either, and he refused to miss the chance again.

Standing back on his feet, Aidan leaned and lowered his head. He captured a nipple between his lips, loving how the tip hardened in his mouth as his tongue traced circles around the rigid bud. She purred his name as she cradled the back of his head to hold his mouth right there.

He continued to taste her breasts, leaving one and moving to the other, enjoying every single lick and suck. Her moans fueled his desire to possess her. To make love to her. And what he loved more than anything else was the sound of her moaning his name.

Aidan eased his lips from her breasts and moved his mouth slowly downward, tasting her skin. As he crouched, his mouth traced a greedy path over her stomach, loving the way her muscles tightened beneath his lips.

A slow throbbing ache took hold of his erection as he eased down to his knees. This was what he'd gone to bed craving ever since he'd first tasted her between her thighs. He'd fallen asleep several nights licking his lips at the memory. Her feminine scent was unique, so irresistibly Jillian, that his tongue thickened in anticipation.

Knowing she watched him, he ran his hands up and down the insides of her legs, massaged her thighs and caressed the area between them. His name was a whisper on her lips when he slid a finger inside of her. He loved the feel of her juices wetting him. He stroked her.

Hungry for her taste, he withdrew his finger and licked it. He smiled before using his hands to spread her feminine core to ready her for an open-mouth kiss.

Jillian released a deep, toe-curling moan the moment Aidan latched his hot tongue onto her. She grabbed his head to push him away, but he held tight to her legs while his tongue went deep, thrusting hard. Then she pressed herself toward his mouth.

She closed her eyes and chanted his name as spasms ripped through her, making her thighs tremble. He refused to let go, refused to lift his mouth, as sensations overtook her. Her body throbbed in unexpected places as an orgasm shook her.

When the last spasm speared through her, she felt herself being lifted into strong arms. When she opened her eyes, Aidan was entering her bedroom. He placed her on the bed, leaned down and kissed her, sending rekindled desire spiking through her.

When he ended the kiss and eased off the bed, she watched as he quickly removed his clothes. She could only lie there and admire his nakedness. He was a fine specimen of a man, both in and out of clothes. Just as he'd appeared in her dreams. Thick thighs, muscular legs and a huge erection nested in a patch of thick, curly black hair.

How will I handle that? she asked herself when he pulled a condom packet from his wallet and quickly sheathed himself. He took his time and she figured it was because he knew she was watching his every move with keen interest.

"You have done this before right?" he asked her.

"What? Put on a condom? No. One wouldn't fit me."

He grinned over at her. "Funny. You know what I'm asking."

Yes, she knew what he was asking. "Um, sort of."

He lifted a brow. "Sort of?"

She shrugged slightly. "I'm not a virgin, if that's what you're asking," she said softly. "Technically not. But…"

"But what?"

"I was in high school and neither of us knew what we were doing. That was my one and only time."

He just stood there totally naked staring at her. She wondered why he wasn't saying anything. What was he thinking? As if he'd read her mind, he slowly moved toward her, placed his knee on the bed and leaned toward her. "What you missed out on before, you will definitely get tonight. And Jillian?"

She swallowed. He'd spoken with absolute certainty and all she could do was stare back at him. "Yes?"

"This will not be your only time with me."

Her body reacted to his words and liquid heat traveled through her body. He hadn't spoken any words of love but he'd let her know this wasn't a one-time deal with them.

She didn't have time to dwell on what he'd said. He pulled her into his arms and kissed her. She closed her eyes and let herself be liquefied by the kiss. Like all the other times he'd used his expertise to make everything around her fade into oblivion, the kiss was the only thing her mind and body could comprehend. His hands were all over her, touching her everywhere. She released a deep moan when she felt his knees spreading her legs.

"Open your eyes and look at me Jillian."

She slowly opened her eyes to look up at the man whose body was poised above hers. He lifted her hips and his enlarged sex slid between her wet feminine folds. He thrust forward and her body stretched to accommodate his size. Instinctively, she wrapped her legs around him and when he began to move, she did so, as well.

She continued to hold his gaze while he thrust in and out of her. Over and over he would take her to the edge just to snatch her back. Her inner muscles clamped down on him, squeezing and tightening around him.

As she felt new spasms rip through her, he threw his head back and let out a roar that shook the room. She was glad most of her neighbors had gone away for spring break; otherwise they would know what she was doing tonight.

But right now, all she cared about was the man she loved, and how he was making her feel things she'd never felt before.

He kissed her again. Their tongues dueled in another erotic kiss and she couldn't help but remember the words he'd spoken earlier.

This will not be your only time with me.

She knew men said words they didn't mean to women

they were about to sleep with, and she had no reason to believe it was any different with Aidan.

Besides, considering that she needed to stay focused on her studies, it was a good thing he wasn't serious.

Aidan watched the naked woman sleeping in his arms and let out a frustrated sigh. This was not supposed to happen.

He wasn't talking about making love because there was no way such a thing could have been avoided. The sexual tension between them had been on overload since the day he'd arrived at her apartment and neither of them could have lasted another day.

What was *not* supposed to happen was feeling all these unexpected emotions. They had wrapped around his mind and wouldn't let go. And what bothered him more than anything else was that he knew he was not confusing his emotions with what had definitely been off-the-charts sex. If he hadn't known before that there was a difference in what he felt for Jillian, he definitely knew it now.

He had fallen in love with her.

When? How? Why? He wasn't sure. All he knew, without a doubt, was that it had happened. The promise of great sex hadn't made him take a week's vacation and travel more than fifteen hundred miles across five states to spend time with her. Sex hadn't made him become her personal test coach, suffering the pains of being close to her while maintaining boundaries and limits. And sex definitely had nothing to do with the way he felt right now and how it was nearly impossible for him to think straight.

When she purred softly in her sleep and then wiggled

her backside snugly against his groin he closed his eyes and groaned. It had been great sex but it had been more than that. She had reached a part of him no woman had reached before.

He'd realized it before they'd made love. He'd known it the minute she told him she'd only made love once before. As far as he was concerned that one time didn't count because the guy had definitely done a piss-poor job. The only orgasm she'd ever experienced had been with Aidan.

But in the days he'd spent studying with her he'd gotten to know a lot about her. She was a fighter, determined to reach whatever goals she established for herself. And she was thoughtful enough to care that Pam not bear the burden of the cost of sending Jillian to medical school. She was even willing to sell her family home.

And he liked being with her, which posed a problem since they lived more than a thousand miles apart. He'd heard long-distance affairs could sometimes be brutal. But he and Jillian could make it work if they wanted to do so. He knew how he felt about her but he had no idea how she felt about him. As far as he knew, she wasn't operating on emotion but out of a sense of curiosity. She'd said as much.

However, the biggest problem of all, one he knew would pose the most challenge to the possibility of anything ever developing between them was her insistence on Pam and Dillon not knowing about them.

Aidan didn't feel the same way and now that he loved her, he really didn't want to keep it a secret. He knew Dillon well enough to know that if Aidan were to go to his cousin and come clean, tell Dillon Aidan had fallen in love with Jillian, Dillon would be okay with it. Although

Aidan couldn't say with certainty how Pam would feel, he'd always considered her a fair person. He believed she would eventually give her blessing…but only if she thought Jillian was truly in love with him and that he would make Jillian happy.

There were so many unknowns. The one thing he did know was that he and Jillian had to talk. He'd given her fair warning that what they'd shared would not be one and done. There was no way he would allow her to believe that her involvement with him meant nothing, that she was just another woman to him. She was more than that and he wanted her to know it.

She stirred, shifted in bed and then slowly opened her eyes to stare at him. She blinked a few times as if bringing him into focus—or as if she was trying to figure out if he was really here in her bed.

Aidan let her know she wasn't seeing things. "Good morning." He gently caressed her cheek before glancing over at the digital clock on her nightstand. "You woke up early. It's barely six o'clock."

"A habit I can't break," she said, still staring at him. "You didn't leave."

"Was I supposed to?"

She shrugged bare shoulders. "I thought that's the way it worked."

She had a lot to learn about him. He wouldn't claim he'd never left a woman's bed in the middle of the night, but Jillian was different.

"Not for us, Jillian." He paused. "We need to talk."

She broke eye contact as she pulled up in bed, holding the covers in place to shield her nakedness. Aidan thought the gesture amusing considering all they'd done last night. "I know what you're going to say, Aidan. Although I've never heard it before, Ivy has and she told me how this plays out."

She'd made him curious. "And how does it play out?"

"The guy lets the woman know it was just a one-night stand. Nothing personal and definitely nothing serious."

He hadn't used that particular line before, but he'd used similar ones. He decided not to tell her that. "You weren't a one-night stand, Jillian."

She nodded. "I do recall you mentioning that last night wouldn't be your only time with me."

He tightened his arms around her. "And why do you think I said that?"

"Because you're a man and most men enjoy sex."

He smiled. "A lot of women enjoy it, as well. Didn't you?"

"Yes. There's no need to lie about it. I definitely enjoyed it."

A grin tugged at Aidan's lips. His ego appreciated her honesty. "I enjoyed it, as well." He kissed her, needing the taste of her.

It was a brief kiss and when he lifted his lips from hers, she seemed stunned by what he'd done. He found that strange considering the number of times they had kissed before.

"So, if you don't want to say last night was a one-night stand, what is it you want to talk about?" she asked.

He decided to be just as honest as she had been, and got straight to the point. "I want to talk about me. And you. Together."

She raised a brow. "Together?"

"Yes. I've fallen in love with you."

Nine

Jillian was out of the bed in a flash, taking half the blankets with her. She speared Aidan with an angry look. "Are you crazy? You can't be in love with me. It won't work, especially when I'm in love with you, too."

Too late she'd realized what she'd said. From the look on Aidan's face, he had heard her admission. "If I love you and you love me, Jillian, then what's the problem?"

She lifted her chin. "The problem is that we can't be together the way you would want us to be. I was okay with it when it was one-sided and I just loved you and didn't think you could possibly return the feelings, but now—"

"Hold up," Aidan said, and her eyes widened when he got off the bed to stand in front of her without a stitch of clothes on. "Let me get this straight. You think it's okay for me to sleep with you and not be in love with you?"

She tossed her hair back from her face. "Why not? I'm sure it's done all the time. Men sleep with women they don't love and vice versa. Are you saying you love every woman you sleep with?"

"No."

"Okay then."

"It's not okay because you're not any woman. You're the one that I *have* fallen in love with."

Why was he making things difficult? Downright complicated? She had to make him understand. "I could deal with this a lot better if you didn't love me, mainly because I would have known it wasn't serious on your end."

"And that would not have bothered you?"

"Not in the least. I need to stay focused on my studies and I can't stay focused if I know you feel the same way about me that I feel about you. That only complicates things."

He stared at her as if he thought she was crazy. In a way she couldn't very much blame him. Most women would prefer falling in love with a man who loved them, and if things were different she would want that, too. But the time wasn't right. Men in love made demands. They expected a woman's time. Her attention. All her energy. And being in love required that a woman give her man what he wanted. Well, she didn't have the time to do that. She was in medical school. She wanted to be a doctor.

And worse than anything, an Aidan who thought he loved her would cause problems. He wouldn't want to keep their relationship a secret. He was not a man to be kept in the closet or denied his right to be seen with her. He would want everyone to know they were together and that was something she couldn't accept.

"I still can't understand why you think me loving you complicates things," Aidan said, interrupting her thoughts.

"Because you wouldn't want to keep our affair a secret. You'll want to tell everyone. Take me out anyplace you want. You wouldn't like the thought of us sneaking around."

"No, I wouldn't." He gently pulled her into his arms. She would have pushed him away if he hadn't at that moment tugged the bedcovers from her hands leaving her as naked as he was. The moment their bodies touched, arousal hit her in the core. She was suddenly reminded of what they'd done last night and how they'd done it. From the way his eyes darkened, she knew he was reliving those same sizzling memories.

"Jillian."

"Aidan."

He drew her closer and closed his mouth over hers. She was lost. For a long while, all she could do was stand there feeling his body plastered to hers, feeling his erection pressed against her, feeling the tips of her nipples poking into his chest while he kissed her. Frissons of fire raced up her spine.

And when she felt herself being maneuvered toward the bed, she was too caught up in desire to do anything about it. The same urgency to mate that had taken hold of him had fused itself to her. As soon as her back touched the mattress she slid from beneath him and pushed him back. She had flipped them and was now on top of him. He stared up at her with surprise in his eyes.

She intended to play out one of her fantasies, one of the ways they'd made love in her dreams—with her on top. But first she needed him to know something. "I take the Pill...to regulate my periods. And I'm safe," she whispered.

"So am I."

She maneuvered her middle over his engorged shaft, which stood straight up. Every hormone inside her body sizzled as she eased down onto him, taking him inside inch by inch. He was big, but like last night her body stretched to accommodate his size.

"Look at me, Jillian." Obeying his command, she held his gaze.

"I love you, whether you want me to or not and it's too late for you to do anything about it."

She drew in a deep breath and continued to ease him inside of her, not wanting to dwell on the problems love could cause. They would talk again later. But for now, this is what she wanted. This is what she needed. And when she had taken him to the hilt, she moved, riding him the way she'd been taught to ride years ago. From the look reflected in the depths of his eyes, she was giving him a ride he would remember for a long time.

She liked the view from up here. Staring down at him, seeing his expression change each time she shoved downward, taking him deeper. His nostrils flared. His breathing was choppy. Was that a little sweat breaking through on his brow?

Riding him felt good. Exhilarating. He definitely had the perfect body to be ridden. Hard, masculine and solid. She had her knees locked on each side of his strong thighs. Her inner muscles clenched, gripping him in a hold that had him groaning deep in his throat.

She loved the sound. Loved being in control. Loved him. The last thought sent her senses spiraling, and when he shouted her named and bucked his entire body upward, she felt his massive explosion. He drenched her insides with thick semen. And she used her muscles to squeeze out more.

Perspiration soaked her head, her face, their bodies... but she kept on riding. When another explosion hit him,

BRENDA JACKSON   113

she nearly jerked them both off the bed when she screamed in pleasure.

He held her tight and she held him and she wished she never had to let him go.

Aidan pushed a damp curl out of Jillian's eyes. She was sprawled on top of him, breathing deeply. He figured she had earned the right to be exhausted. He'd never experienced anything so invigorating or stimulating in his entire life.

"Don't ask me not to love you, Jillian," he finally found the strength to say softly, and the words came straight from his heart. For the first time in his life, he'd told a woman he loved her and the woman wished that he didn't.

When he felt her tears fall on his arm, he shifted their bodies so he could look at her. "Is me loving you that bad?"

She shook her head. "No. I know it should be what I want but the timing... There is so much I still have to do."

"And you think I'd stop you from doing them?"

"No, but I'd stop myself. I'd lose focus. You would want to be with me and I would want to be with you. In the open. I know you don't understand why I can't do that, but I can't."

She was right, he didn't understand. He believed she was all wrong about how Dillon and Pam, or the entire Westmoreland family, would handle them hooking up. He doubted it would be a big deal. But it didn't matter what he thought. She thought otherwise and that's what mattered.

"What if I agree to do what we're doing now? I mean, keeping things between us a secret."

She lifted her head. "You would agree to that, Aidan? I'm not talking about a few weeks or a few months. I'm talking about until I finish medical school. Could you really wait that long?"

That was a good question. Could he? Could he be around Jillian at family gatherings and pretend nothing was going on between them? And what about the physical distance between them? She wasn't even sure what medical school she would attend. Her two top choices were Florida and New Orleans, both hundreds of miles away from Boston, Maine or North Carolina.

And what about his family and friends? Like Adrian, Aidan had quite a reputation around Harvard. What would his friends think when he suddenly stopped pursuing women? They would think he'd lost his ever-loving mind. But he didn't care what anyone thought.

It didn't matter. Wherever Jillian was, he would get to her, spend time with her and give her the support she needed to be the doctor she wanted to be.

What Jillian needed now more than anything was for him not to place any pressure on her. Her focus should be on completing the MCAT and not on anything else. Somehow he would handle the distance, he would handle his family and friends and their perceptions.

He held her gaze. "Yes, I can wait. No matter how long it takes, Jillian. Because you're worth waiting for."

Then he tugged her mouth down to his for another one of their ultrapassionate, mind-blowing kisses.

Ten

"This is Captain Stewart Marcellus," a deep voice boomed through the intercom in Jillian's cabin. "My crew and I would like to welcome you aboard the Princess Grandeur. For the next fourteen days we'll cruise the Grand Mediterranean for your enjoyment. In an hour we'll depart Barcelona for full days in Monte Carlo and Florence and two days in Rome. From there we'll sail to Greece and Turkey. I invite you to join me tonight at the welcome party, which kicks off two weeks of fun."

Jillian glanced around her cabin. *A suite.* This was something she definitely hadn't paid for. She and Paige had planned to share a standard stateroom, definitely nothing as luxurious and spacious as what she'd been given. When she'd contacted the customer service desk to tell them about the mistake, she was told no mistake had been made and the suite was hers to enjoy.

No sooner had she ended the call than she'd received a delivery—a bouquet of beautiful mixed flowers and a bottle of chilled wine with a card that read, "Congratulations on finishing medical school. We are proud of you. Enjoy the cruise. You deserve it. Your family, The Westmorelands."

Jillian eased down to sit on the side of the bed. *Her family.* She wondered what the Westmorelands would think if they knew the truth about her and Aidan. About the affair the two of them had carried on right under their noses for three years.

As she stood to shower and get dressed for tonight's festivities, she couldn't help remembering what that affair had been like after they'd confessed their love for each other. Aidan had understood and agreed that it was to be their secret. No one else was supposed to know— unless the two of them thought it was absolutely necessary.

The first year had been wonderful, in spite of how hard it had been to engage in a long-distance love affair. Even with Aidan's busy schedule juggling dual residencies, he'd managed to fly to Laramie whenever he had a free weekend. And because their time together was scarce, he'd make it special. They would go out to dinner, see a movie, or if it was a weekend she needed to study, they would do that, too. There was no way she would have passed the MCAT the first time around without his help. She had applied to various medical schools and when she was notified of her acceptance into the one she wanted in New Orleans, Aidan had been the first person with whom she'd shared her good news. They had celebrated the next time he'd come to Laramie.

It was during that first year that they agreed to bring Ivy in on their secret. Otherwise, her roommate would have been worried when Jillian went missing because she was staying with Aidan at the hotel.

Jillian had fallen more and more in love with Aidan

during that time. Although she'd had a lot to keep her busy, she missed him when they were apart. But he'd made up for it when he came to town. And even though they'd spent a lot of time in bed making love, their relationship wasn't just about sex. However, she would have to say that the sex was off the chain, and the sexual tension between them was still so thick you could cut it with a knife. Ivy could attest to that and had teased Jillian about it all the time.

It was also during that first year that their control had been tested whenever they went home for holidays, weddings or baby christenings. She would be the first to admit she had felt jealous more than a few times when Aidan's single male cousins, who assumed he was still a player on the prowl, would try setting him up with other women.

Everything had gone well between them as they moved into their second year together. Aidan had helped her relocate to New Orleans after she bid a teary goodbye to Ivy. Jillian leased a one-bedroom efficiency apartment not far from the hospital where she would be working. It was perfect for her needs, but lonely.

It was during the third year that it became harder for Aidan to get away. The hospitals demanded more of his time. And her telephone conversations with him had been reduced from nightly to three times a week. She could tell he was frustrated with the situation. More than once he'd commented that he wished she would have applied to a medical school closer to Maine or North Carolina.

Jillian tried to ignore his attitude but found that difficult to do. Although Aidan didn't say so, deep down she knew the secrecy surrounding their affair was getting to him. It had begun to get to her, as well. And when it seemed Aidan was becoming distant, she knew she had to do something.

When Ivy came to visit Jillian in New Orleans one weekend, she talked to her best friend about the situation. Even now Jillian could remember that time as if it was yesterday…

"So, how is Aidan?" Ivy asked, after placing her order with their waitress.

Jillian had to fight back tears. "Not sure. We haven't talked in a few days and the last time we did, we had an argument."

Ivy raised a brow. "Another one?"

"Yes." She'd told Ivy about their last argument. He'd wanted her to fly to Maine for the weekend for his birthday. She had been excited about doing so until she'd checked her calendar and discovered that was the same weekend of her clinicals. Something she could not miss. Instead of understanding, he'd gotten upset with her and because of his lack of understanding, she'd gotten upset with him. Their most recent argument had started because he told her his twin now knew about them. He'd gotten angry when she'd accused him of breaking his promise and telling Adrian. He'd explained that he didn't have to tell his brother anything. He and his twin could detect each other's moods and feelings sometimes.

"I'm tired of arguing with him, Ivy, and a part of me knows the reason our relationship is getting so strained."

Ivy nodded. "Long-distance romances are hard to maintain, Jillian, and I'm sure the secrecy surrounding your affair isn't helping."

"Yes, I know, which is why I've made a few decisions."

Ivy lifted a brow. "About what?"

Jillian drew in a deep breath. "I've decided to tell
Pam about us. The secrecy has gone on long enough.
I believe my sister will accept the fact that I'm now an
adult and old enough to decide what I want to do in my
life and the person I want in it."

"Good for you."

"Thanks. I know she's been concerned about Aidan's womanizing reputation, but once she realizes that
I love him and he loves me, I believe she will give us
her blessing."

Jillian took a sip of her drink and continued, "But
before I tell Pam, I'm flying to Maine to see Aidan. Next
weekend is his birthday and I've decided to be there to
help him celebrate."

"What about your clinicals?"

Jillian smiled. "I went to my professor and told her
I desperately needed that weekend off. She agreed to
work with me and arrange for me to do a makeup the
following weekend."

"That was nice of her."

"Yes, it was. She said I was a good student, the first
to volunteer for projects and my overall attendance is
great. So now I'm set to go."

Ivy grinned. "Did you tell Aidan?"

"No. I'm going to surprise him. He mentioned that
since I wouldn't be there to celebrate with him that he
would sign up to work that day and then hang around
his place, watch TV and go to bed early."

"On his birthday? That's a bummer."

"Yes, and that's why I plan to fly there to help him celebrate."

"You're doing the right thing by being there. I think it's wonderful that you're finally letting your sister know about you and Aidan. When she sees how much he adores you she will be happy for the two of you."

A huge smile touched Jillian's lips. "I believe so, too."

Jillian stepped out on the balcony to look at the ocean as she recalled what happened after that. She had been excited when she'd boarded the plane for Portland, Maine. She couldn't wait to tell Aidan of her decision to end the secrecy surrounding their affair and to celebrate his birthday with him.

Due to stormy weather in Atlanta, her connecting flight had been delayed five solid hours and she didn't arrive in Portland until six that evening. It had been another hour before she'd arrived at his apartment complex, anxious to use the door key he'd given her a year ago for the first time.

The moment she'd stepped off the elevator onto his floor she knew a party was going on in one of the apartments. Loud music blasted and boisterous voices made her ears ache. She hadn't known all the noise was coming from Aidan's apartment until she'd reached the door, which she didn't have to unlock since it was slightly ajar.

Jillian walked in and looked around. The place was crowded and there were more women in attendance than men. The women were wearing outfits that probably wouldn't be allowed out on the streets.

Jillian wondered what had happened to Aidan's decision to come home from work, watch TV and go to bed. It seemed he'd decided to throw a party instead and it was in full swing. In the center of the room Aidan sat in a recliner while some scantily dressed woman gave him a lap dance. And from the look on his face, he was enjoying every single minute of it. Some of the guys on the sidelines, who she figured must be Aidan's friends, were egging on both him and the woman, which prompted the woman to make the dance even more erotic.

When the woman began stripping off her clothes, starting with the barely-there strap of material covering her breasts, Jillian was shocked. She knew she'd seen enough when the woman's breasts all but smothered Aidan's face while she wiggled out of her panties.

Not able to watch any longer, a shaken Jillian had left, grateful Aidan hadn't even noticed her presence. What hurt more than anything was that he'd appeared to be enjoying every single minute of the dance. Aidan Westmoreland had seemed in his element. She couldn't help wondering if they had stopped with the dance or if he and the woman had ended up doing other things later.

When he'd called her a few days later he hadn't mentioned anything about the party at his apartment and she hadn't said anything about being there to witness what had gone on. And when she asked how he'd spent his birthday, he angered her even more when he gave her a smart aleck answer, asking, "Why do you care when you didn't care enough to spend it with me?"

He was wrong. She had cared enough. But he hadn't cared enough to tell her the truth. It was then that she'd made the decision to end things between them, since it was apparent that he missed his life as a womanizer. When he called later in the week and made another excuse for not flying to New Orleans to see her as he'd planned, she decided that would be a good time to break things off with him. She would give him his freedom, let him go back to the life he missed.

Deciding the less drama the better, she told him the secrecy of their affair was weighing her down, making her lose focus and she couldn't handle it any longer. She didn't tell him the true reason she'd wanted to end things.

Her declaration led to a huge argument between them. When he told her he was flying to New Orleans to talk to her, she told him she didn't want to see him. Then she ended the conversation.

He had called several times to talk to her but she'd refused to answer and eventually blocked his number. She knew that was the reason for the angry looks he'd given her when she'd attended the last couple of Westmoreland weddings. The last time she'd seen him was a few months ago at Stern's ceremony.

There had been no reason to tell Pam about the affair that had been a secret for so long, so she hadn't. The last thing Jillian needed was for her sister to remind her that just like a tiger couldn't change its stripes neither could a womanizer change his ways.

It had been a year since their breakup. At times she felt she had moved on, but other times she felt she had not. It was so disappointing and painful to think about the future they could have been planning together now that she'd finished medical school, if only things had worked out the way she'd hoped they would.

Jillian wiped the tears from her eyes, refusing to shed any more for Aidan. She was on this cruise to have fun and enjoy herself, and she intended to do just that.

"Yes, Adrian?"

"I'm glad I was able to reach you before ship left port.

I just want to wish you the best. I hope everything works out the way you want with Jill."

Aidan hoped things worked out the way he wanted, as well. "Thanks."

Like Paige, Adrian and Aidan's cousin Stern had figured out something was going on between him and Jillian a couple of years ago. "I will do whatever I have to do to get her back. When this ship returns to port, my goal is to have convinced Jillian to give me another chance."

"Well, Trinity and I are cheering for you."

"Thanks, bro." Trinity was Adrian's fiancée and the two would be getting married in a couple of months.

After ending his phone call with Adrian, Aidan crossed the suite to step out on the balcony. Barcelona was beautiful. He had arrived three days ago and taken a tour of what was considered one of the busiest ports in the Mediterranean. He had eaten at the finest restaurants, some in magnificent buildings etched deep with history. He had walked through the crowded streets wishing Jillian had been by his side. Hopefully when they returned to this port in fourteen days she would be.

He could just imagine what Jillian had assumed when she'd seen that woman giving him a lap dance last year. He had worked that day, as he'd told her he would, but he hadn't known about the surprise birthday party a few of his fraternity brothers had thrown for him.

And he definitely hadn't known about the lap dancer or the other strippers they'd invited until the women arrived. He couldn't get mad at his frat brothers for wanting to make his birthday kind of wild. All they knew was that for the past few years, the man who'd once been one of the biggest womanizers in Boston had taken a sabbatical from women. They'd had no idea that the reason for his seemingly boring lifestyle was because he was involved in a secret affair with Jillian.

So, thinking he'd been working too hard for too long and hadn't gotten in any play time, they thought they were doing him a favor. He would admit that after a few drinks he'd loosened up. But at no time had he forgotten he was in love with Jillian. The lap dance had been just for fun, and after the party all the women had left.

Yes, he'd made a mistake by not mentioning the party to Jillian. And he would be the first to admit his attitude had been less than desirable for the last year of their relationship. But he knew why. He'd had the best of intentions when he thought he could keep their secret without any problems, but as time went on, he'd become impatient. While she hadn't wanted anyone to know about them, he had wanted to shout the truth from the highest mountain.

It hadn't helped matters when some of his siblings and cousins began falling in love and getting married. It seemed as if an epidemic had hit Westmoreland Country when five of his relatives got married in a two-year period. And some had been relatives he'd thought would never marry. It had been hard being around his happily married kinfolk without wanting to have some of that happiness for himself. He would admit he'd spent too many months angry with himself, with Jillian, with the world. But at no time did he doubt his love for her.

Nothing had changed his feelings. He was still in love with her, which was why he was here. To right a wrong and convince her that she was the only woman he wanted.

He knew he had his work cut out for him. But he

intended to stay the course and not fail in his task. She wouldn't appreciate seeing him and she probably wouldn't like it when she found out about Paige's involvement. Or Ivy's for that matter. If Ivy hadn't told Paige the truth, he would still be angry, thinking the reason Jillian had broken up with him was because they were at odds regarding the secret of their affair.

He went back inside when he heard the cabin phone ring. He picked it up. "Yes?"

"I hope you find your quarters satisfactory."

Aidan smiled. That was an understatement. "It's more than satisfactory, Dominic."

This ship was just one of many in a fleet owned by Dominic Saxon. Dominic was married to the former Taylor Steele, whose sister Cheyenne was married to Aidan's cousin, Quade Westmoreland. Once Aidan discovered Jillian had booked her cruise on one of Dominic's ships, his friend had been all too eager to assist Aidan in getting back the woman he loved. Years ago Dominic had found himself in a similar situation.

"Taylor sends her love and we're all rooting for you. I know how misunderstandings can threaten even the most solid relationships, and I think you're doing the right thing by going after her," Dominic said. "I'm going to give you the same advice a very smart woman—my mother—gave me when I was going through my troubles with Taylor. *Let love guide you to do the right thing.* I hope the two of you enjoy the cruise."

"Thanks for the advice, and as for enjoying the cruise, I intend to make sure that we do."

After ending his call with Dominic, Aidan glanced around the cabin. Thanks to Dominic, Aidan had been given the owner's suite. It was spacious with a double balcony. There were also separate sleeping quarters with a king-size bed and a seventy-inch flat-screen television and a second wall-to-wall balcony. The sitting area contained a sofa that could convert into a double bed, another wall television and a dining area that overlooked yet another balcony. Other amenities he appreciated were the refrigerator, wet bar and huge walk-in closet. The bathroom was bigger than the one he had in his apartment, with both a Jacuzzi tub and a walk-in shower. He could just imagine him and Jillian using that shower together.

He walked back out on the balcony to see that people had gathered on the docks to watch the ship sail, waving flags that represented all the countries they would visit on the cruise. He expected Jillian to attend the welcome party tonight and so would he. Aidan couldn't wait to see Jillian's face when she discovered he was on board with her and would be for the next fourteen days.

He headed for the bathroom to shower.

Tonight couldn't get here fast enough.

"Welcome, senorita, may we assist with your mask?"

Jillian lifted a brow. "Mask?"

The tall crewman dressed in a crisp white uniform smiled down at her. "*Si.* Tonight's theme is a Spanish masquerade ball," he said, offering a red feathered mask to her.

She took it and slid it across her face. It was a perfect fit. "Thanks."

"Your name?" he asked.

"Jillian Novak."

"Senorita Novak, dinner will be served in a half hour

in the Madrid Room; someone will come escort you to your table."

"Thanks."

She entered the huge lounge that had beautiful rosettes hanging from the ceiling and several masquerade props in the corners of the room for picture taking. Flamenco dancers encouraged participation in the middle of the floor and several men dressed as dashing bullfighters walked around as servers. When a woman wearing a gorgeous *quinceañera* gown offered her a beautiful lace fan, Jillian smiled and took it.

"Would the senorita like a glass of rioja?"

"Yes, thanks," she responded to one of the servers.

Jillian took a sip and immediately liked the taste. It wasn't too tart or tangy but was an excellent blend of fruits. As she sipped her wine she looked around the room. It was crowded and most of the individuals were coupled off. Immediately, she felt like a loner crashing a party, but forced the feeling away. So what if there were a lot of couples and she had no one? She'd known it would be like this but had made the decision to come anyway.

"Excuse me, senorita, but someone asked me to give you this," the woman wearing the *quinceañera* gown said, while handing her a single red rose.

"Who?" Jillian asked, curiously glancing around.

The woman smiled. "A *very* handsome man." And then she walked off.

Jillian felt uneasy. What kind of *very* handsome man would come cruising alone? She'd seen a movie once where a serial killer had come on a cruise ship and stalked single women. No one had known just how many women he'd killed and thrown overboard until the end of the cruise. For crying out loud, why was she re-membering that particular movie now?

She drew in a deep breath knowing she was letting her imagination get the best of her. The man was prob-ably someone who'd seen her alone and wanted to state his interest by giving her a rose. Romantic but a total waste of his time. Even the woman's claim that he was *very* handsome did nothing for Jillian since she wasn't ready to get involved with anyone. Even after a full year, she compared every man to Aidan. That was the main reason she hadn't dated anyone since him. On the other hand, she would bet any amount of money Aidan was dating someone and probably hadn't wasted any time doing so.

She drew in a deep breath, refusing to let her mind go there. Why should she care in the least what Aidan was doing or who he was doing it with? Deciding not to think of an answer for that one, she glanced around the room, curiosity getting the best of her. She tried to find any single men but all she saw were the bullfight-ers serving drinks.

Jillian glanced at her watch. She'd deliberately ar-rived a little late so she wouldn't have long to wait for dinner. She'd grabbed breakfast on the run to catch her plane and because she'd come straight from the Barce-lona airport to the ship, she had missed lunch altogether.

After taking another sip of her wine, she was about to check her watch again when suddenly her skin heated. Was that desire floating in her stomach. Why? And for who? This was definitely odd.

Jillian searched the room in earnest as a quiver inched up her spine. Declining a server's offer of another drink, she nearly dismissed what was happening as a figment of her imagination when she saw him. A man wearing a teal feathered mask stood alone on the other side of the room, watching her. So she watched back, letting her gaze roam over him. Was he the one who'd given her the rose? Who was he? Why was she reacting to him this way?

As she studied him she found him oddly familiar. Was she comparing the man to Aidan to the point where everything about him reminded her of her ex? His height? His build? The low cut of his hair?

She shook her head. She was losing it. She needed another drink after all. That's when the man began walking toward her. She wasn't going crazy. She didn't know the when, how or why of it, but there was no doubt in her mind that the man walking toward her—mask or no mask—was Aidan. No other man had a walk like he did. And those broad shoulders…

He was sex appeal on legs and he walked the part. It was a stroll of self-confidence and sinful eroticism. How could he have this effect on her after a full year? She drew in a deep breath. That's not the question she should be asking. What she wanted to know was why he was on the same cruise with her? She refused to believe it was a coincidence.

Her spine stiffened when he came to a stop in front of her. Her nostrils had picked up his scent from five feet away and now her entire body was responding. Sharp, crackling energy stirred to life between them. And from the look in his eyes he felt it, as well. Hot. Raw. Primal.

She didn't want it. Nor did she need that sort of sexual attraction to him again. She blew out a frustrated breath. "Aidan, what are you doing here?"

* * *

Aidan wasn't surprised that she had recognized him
with the mask on. After all, they'd shared a bed for three
solid years so she should know him inside out, clothes
or not…just like he knew her. Case in point, he knew
exactly what she was wearing beneath that clingy black
dress. As little as possible, which meant only a bra and
thong. And more than likely both were made of lace. She
had the figure to handle just about anything she put on—
or nothing at all. Frankly, he preferred nothing at all.

"I asked you what you're doing here."

He noted her voice had tightened in anger and he
figured it best to answer. "I've always wanted to take a
Mediterranean cruise."

She rolled her eyes. "And you want me to believe you
being here is a coincidence? That you had no idea I was
here on this cruise ship?"

"That's not what I'm saying."

"Then what *are* you saying, Aidan?"

He placed his half-empty wineglass on the tray of a
passing waiter, just in case Jillian was tempted to douse
him with it. "I'll tell you after dinner."

"After dinner? No, you will tell me *now.*"

Her voice had risen and several people glanced over
at them. "I think we need to step outside to finish our
discussion."

She frowned. "I think not. You can tell me what I want
to know right here."

In anger, she walked into the scant space separating them and leaned in close, her lips almost brushing
his. That was too close. His bottom lip tingled and his
heart beat like crazy when he remembered her taste. A

taste he'd become addicted to. A taste he'd gone a year without.

"I wouldn't bring my mouth any closer if I were you," he warned in a rough whisper.

She blinked as if realizing how close they were. Heeding his warning, she quickly took a step back. "I still want answers, Aidan. What are you doing here?"

He decided to be totally honest with her. Give her the naked truth and let her deal with it. "I came on this cruise, Jillian, with the full intention of winning you back."

Eleven

Jillian stared at Aidan as his words sank in. That's when she decided it would be best for them to take this discussion to a more private area after all. She removed her mask. "I think we need to step outside the room, Aidan."

When they stepped into a vacant hallway, she turned to him. "How dare you assume all you had to do was follow me on this cruise to win me back?"

He pulled off his mask and she fought back a jolt of desire when she looked into his face. How could any man get more handsome in a year's time? Yes, she'd seen him a couple of times since their break-up, but she had avoided getting this close to him. He appeared to have gotten an inch or so taller, his frame was even more muscular and his looks were twice as gorgeous.

"I have given it some thought," he said, leaning back against a railing.

"Evidently, not enough," she countered, not liking how her gaze, with a mind of its own, was traveling over him. He was wearing a dark suit, and he looked like a male model getting ready for a photo shoot—immaculate with nothing out of place.

"Evidently, you've forgotten one major thing about me," she said.

"What? Just how stubborn you are?" he asked, smiling, as if trying to make light of her anger, which irritated her even more.

"That, too, but also that once I make up my mind about something, that's it. And I made up my mind that my life can sail a lot more calmly without you." She watched his expression to see if her words had any effect, but she couldn't tell if they had.

He studied her in silence before saying, "Sorry you feel that way, Jillian. But I intend to prove you wrong."

She lifted a brow. "Excuse me?"

"Over the next fourteen days I intend to prove that your life can't sail more calmly without me. In fact, I intend to show you that you don't even like calm. You need turbulence, furor and even a little mayhem."

She shook her head. "If you believe that then you truly don't know me at all."

"I know you. I also know the real reason you broke things off with me. Why didn't you tell me what you *thought* you saw in my apartment the night of my birthday party?"

She wondered how he'd found out about that. It really didn't matter at this point. "It's not what I *thought* I saw, Aidan. It's what I saw. A woman giving you a lap dance, which you seemed to enjoy, before she began stripping off her clothes." Saying it made the memory flash in her mind and roused her anger that much more.

"She was a paid entertainer, Jillian. All the ladies there that night were. Several of my frat brothers thought I'd been living a boring and dull life and decided to add some excitement into it. I admit they might have gone a little overboard."

"And you enjoyed every minute of it."

He shrugged. "I had a few drinks and—"

"You don't know what all you did, do you?"

He frowned. "I remember fine. Other than the lap dance and her strip act...and a couple other women stripping...nothing else happened."

"Wasn't that enough?" she asked, irritated that he thought several naked women on display in his apartment were of little significance. "And why didn't you tell me about the party? You led me to believe you'd done just as you said you were going to do—watch TV and go to bed."

He released a deep breath. "Okay, I admit I should have told you and I was wrong for not doing so. But I was angry with you. It was my birthday and I wanted to spend it with you. I felt you could have sacrificed a little that weekend to be with me. I hadn't known you changed your mind and flew to Portland."

He paused a moment and then continued, "I realized after we'd broken up just how unpleasant my attitude had been and I do apologize for that. I was getting frustrated with the secrecy surrounding our affair, with my work and how little time I could get off to fly to New Orleans to spend with you."

As far as Jillian was concerned, his attitude had been more than unpleasant; it had become downright unacceptable. He wasn't the only one who'd been frustrated with their situation. She had, too, which was the reason she had decided to confess all to Pam.

"Now that you're finished with medical school, there's no reason to keep our secret any longer anyway," he said, interrupting her thoughts.

She frowned. "And I see no reason to reveal it. Ever," she said. "Especially in light of one very important fact."

"And what fact is that?"

"The fact that we aren't together and we won't ever be together again."

If she figured that then she was wrong.

They *would* be together again. He was counting on it. It was the reason he'd come on the cruise. The one thing she had not said was that she no longer loved him. And as long as she had feelings for him then he could accomplish anything. At this point, even if she claimed she didn't love him, he would have to prove her wrong because he believed she loved him just as much as he loved her. Their relationship was just going through a few hiccups, which he felt they could resolve.

"If you truly believe that then you have nothing to worry about," he said.

She frowned. "Meaning what?"

"Meaning my presence on this ship shouldn't bother you."

She lifted her chin. "It won't unless you become a nuisance."

A smile spread across his face. "Nuisance? I think not. But I do intend to win you back, like I said. Then we can move on with our lives. I see marriage and babies in our future."

She laughed. "You've got to be kidding. Didn't you hear what I said? We won't be getting back together, so we don't have a future."

"And you're willing to throw away the last three years?"

"What I've done is make it easy for you."

He lifted a brow. "To do what?"

"Go back to your womanizing ways. You seemed to

be enjoying yourself so much at your birthday party I wouldn't think of denying you the opportunity."

He crossed his arms over his chest. "I gave up my so-called womanizing ways when I fell in love with you."

"Could have fooled me with your lap dancer and all those strippers waiting their turn."

"Like I said, I didn't invite them."

"But you could have asked them to leave."

He shrugged. "Yes, I could have. But you're going to have to learn to trust me, Jillian. I can see where my attitude leading up to that night might have been less than desirable, but at no time have I betrayed you with another woman. Do you intend to punish me forever for one night of a little fun?"

"I'm not punishing you, Aidan. I'm not doing anything to you. I didn't invite you on this cruise. You took it upon yourself to…"

Her words trailed off and she gazed at him suspiciously before saying, "Paige and I were supposed to go on this cruise together and she had to back out when she had a conflict, which is why I came alone. Please tell me you had nothing to do with that."

He'd known she would eventually figure things out but he had hoped it wouldn't be this soon. "Okay, I won't tell you."

She was back in his face again. "You told Paige about us? Now she knows I was duped by a womanizer."

Her lips were mere inches from his again. Evidently, she'd forgotten his earlier warning. "I am not a womanizer, and I didn't tell her anything about us. She figured things out on her own. Ivy told Paige about the lap dance and Paige told me. And I appreciate her doing so."

From Jill's expression he could tell that although he

might appreciate it, she didn't. "I am so upset with you, right now, Aidan. You are—"

Suddenly he pulled her into his arms. "You were warned."

Then he captured her mouth with his.

Push him away. Push him away. Push him away, a voice inside of Jillian's head chanted.

But her body would not obey. Instead of pushing him away, she leaned in closer, wrapping her arms around his neck.

Had it been a year since she had enjoyed this? A year since she'd had the taste of his tongue inside her mouth? Doing all those crazy things in every nook and cranny? Making liquid heat she'd held at bay shoot straight to the area between her legs?

How could any woman deal with a master kisser like him? She would admit that during the past year she had gone to bed dreaming of this but the real thing surpassed any dream she'd ever had.

The sound of voices made them pull apart. She drew in a deep breath, turning her back to him so she could lick her lips without him seeing her do so. That had been one hell of a kiss. Her lips were still electrified.

She turned back around and caught him tracing his tongue across his own lips. Her stomach clenched. "I think you have it all wrong, Aidan," she managed to say.

"After that kiss, I'd say I got it all right."

"Think whatever you like," she said, walking away.

"Hey, where're you going? The Madrid Room is this way."

She stopped and turned. "I'll order room service."

Jillian continued walking, feeling the heat of his gaze on her back.

Aidan watched her walk away, appreciating the sway of her hips. He drew in a deep breath. He loved the woman. If there was any doubt in her mind of that—which there seemed to be—he would wipe it out.

Turning, he headed toward his own cabin, thinking room service sounded pretty good. Besides, he had shocked Jillian's senses enough for today. Tomorrow he planned to lay it on even thicker. She had warned him not to be a nuisance. He smiled at the thought. He wouldn't be a nuisance, just totally effective.

Tonight they had talked, although he seemed to annoy her and he'd found her somewhat infuriating. But at least they knew where they both stood. She knew he was aware of the real reason she'd ended things between them. He had to convince her that his life as a womanizer was definitely behind him, that he had no desire to return to that life again.

He would admit getting rid of the lap dancer that night hadn't been easy. Somehow she'd figured it would be okay to hang around after the party was over. She'd been quick to let him know there wouldn't be an overtime charge. He had countered, letting her know he wasn't interested.

When Aidan reached his suite, he saw the elephant made of hand towels on his bed. Cute. But not as cute as the woman he intended to have back in his arms.

Jillian checked the time as she made a call to Paige. It was around ten in the morning in L.A., so there was no reason her sister shouldn't answer the phone. Paige was definitely going to get an earful from her.

"Why are you calling me? Aren't rates higher on the high seas?" Paige asked, answering on the fourth ring.

Jillian frowned. "Don't worry about the cost of the rates. Why didn't you tell me you knew about me and Aidan?"

"Why hadn't you told *me* so I wouldn't have to tell you? And don't say because it was supposed to be a secret."

"Well, it was. How did you figure it out?"

"Wasn't hard to do. Both of you started getting sloppy with it. Aidan slipped and called you Jilly a couple of times, and I caught you almost drooling whenever he walked into the room."

"I did not."

"You did, too. Besides, I knew you had a crush on him that first time we met the Westmoreland family at Pam's engagement party. You kept me up all night asking, 'Isn't Aidan cute, Paige? Isn't he cute?'"

Jillian smiled as she remembered. She had been so taken with Aidan. Although he and Adrian were identical twins it had been Aidan who pushed her buttons.

"Well, no thanks to you he's here and he wants me back."

"Do you want him to get you back?"

"No. You didn't see that lap dance. I did."

"Didn't have to see it because I've seen one before. I know they can get rather raunchy. But it was a birthday party. His. Thrown by his friends and the lap dancer and the strippers were entertainment."

"Some entertainment," she mumbled. "He enjoyed it. You should have seen the look on his face when the woman shoved her girls at him."

"Pleeze. He's a man. They enjoy seeing a pair of

breasts. Anytime or anyplace. Will it make you feel better if I get the Chippendales dancers for your next birthday party?"

"This isn't funny, Paige."

"You don't hear me laughing. If anything, you should hear me moaning. Can you imagine a lap dance from one of those guys? If you can't, I can. And my imagination is running pretty wild right now."

Jillian shook her head. "Before I let you go, there's one more thing. Did you really get a part in a Spielberg movie?"

"No."

"So you lied."

"I was acting, and I evidently did a great job. It sounds like you have some serious decisions to make about Aidan. But don't rush. You have fourteen days. In the meantime, enjoy the cruise. Enjoy life. Enjoy Aidan. He plans on getting you back. I'd like to be there to watch him try. I've got my money on him, by the way."

"Sounds like you have money to lose. Goodbye, Paige." Jillian clicked off the phone, refusing to let her sister get in the last word, especially if it would be a word she really didn't want to hear.

Regardless of what Paige said, her sister hadn't been there to witness that lap dance. She hadn't seen that salacious grin on Aidan's face while looking up at the half-naked woman sprawled all over him. There was no doubt in Jillian's mind that he'd enjoyed every minute of it. He had wanted those women there; otherwise, he would have asked them and his friends to leave. And although he claimed otherwise, how could she be certain one of those women didn't spend the night with him; especially since he didn't tell Jillian anything about the party, even when she had asked? She of all people knew what a healthy sexual appetite Aidan had, and they hadn't seen each other in more than three months. And at the time, that had been the longest amount of time they'd been apart.

Before getting in bed later that night, Jillian checked the ship's agenda. Tomorrow was a full day at sea and she refused to stay locked in her cabin. This was a big ship and chances were she might not run into Aidan. She knew the odds of that were slim; especially when he admitted his only reason for coming on the cruise was to win her back. Well, he could certainly try.

She could not deny it had felt good to be kissed by him tonight. Pretty damn good. But there was more to any relationship than kisses. Even the hot, raw, carnal kind that Aidan gave. And when he took a mind to kiss her all over...

She drew in a deep breath, refusing to let her thoughts go there. He would probably try using his sexual wiles to win her back. And she intended to be ready to disappoint him.

Twelve

"Good morning, Jillian."

Jillian glanced up from the book she was reading to watch Aidan slide onto the lounger beside her. She was on the upper deck near the pool. Why had she thought he would never find her here?

"Good morning," she grumbled and went back to her reading. Although she had gone to bed fairly early, she hadn't gotten a good night's sleep. The man stretched on the lounger beside her had invaded her dreams not once or twice, but all through the night.

"Had breakfast yet?"

She glanced away from her book to look over at him. "Yes." She remembered the pancakes and syrup she'd enjoyed. "It was tasty."

"Um, bet it wasn't tasty as you. Want to go back to my cabin and be my breakfast?"

His question caused a spark of heat to settle between her thighs. Something she definitely didn't need after all those erotic dreams she'd had. "You shouldn't say something like that to me."

"You prefer I say it to someone else?"

She narrowed her gaze. "Do whatever you want. At breakfast I happened to notice a group of women on the cruise. All appeared single. I think I overheard one say they're part of some book club."

"You want me to go check out other women?"

"Won't matter to me. Need I remind you that we aren't together?"

"And need I remind you that I'm working on that? And by the way, I have a proposition for you."

"Whatever it is, the answer is no."

He chuckled. "You haven't heard it."

"Doesn't matter."

"You certain?"

"Positive."

He smiled over at her. "Okay then. I'm glad. In fact, you've made my day by not accepting it. I'm happy that you turned it down."

She stared over at him and frowned. "Really? And just what was this proposition?"

In a warm, teasing tone, he said. "I thought you didn't want to hear it."

"I've changed my mind."

He nodded. "I guess I can allow you to do that." He shifted and sat up. She tried not to notice the khaki shorts he wore and how well they fit the lower half of his body. Or how his muscle shirt covered perfect abs.

He took her hand, easing her into the same sitting position he was in, as if what he had to say was something he didn't want others around them to overhear.

"Well?" she asked, trying to ignore the tingling sensation in the hand he touched.

"You're aware the only reason I came on this cruise was to get you back, right?"

She shrugged. "So you say."

A smile touched the corners of his lips. "Well, I

thought about a few of the things you said last night and I wanted to offer you a chance to make some decisions."

She lifted a brow. "Like what?"

"Like whether or not I should even pursue you at all. I don't want to be that nuisance you insinuated I could be. So my proposition was that I just leave you alone and wait patiently for you to come to me. I hope you know what that means since you just turned it down."

She would not have turned it down had she heard him out, and he knew it. Unfortunately, she could guess what the consequences would be and she had a feeling she wasn't going to like it. "What does that mean, Aidan?"

He leaned in closer to whisper in her ear. His warm breath felt like a soft, sensuous lick across her skin. "I want you so bad, Jillian, that I ache. And that means I'm not giving up until you're back in my bed."

She immediately felt a pounding pulse at the tips of her breasts. She leaned back to stare at him and the razor-sharp sensuality openly displayed in his gaze almost made her moan.

"And before you ask, Jillian, the answer is no. It isn't just about sex with me," he murmured in a low, husky tone. "It's about me wanting the woman I love both mentally and physically. You're constantly in my mind but physically, it's been over a year."

She drew in a deep breath and felt the essence of what he'd said in every single nerve ending in her body. It had been over a year. With Aidan she'd had a pretty active sex life, and although there were periods of time when they were apart, they always made up for any time lost whenever they were together.

"Your needing sex is not my problem," she finally said.

"Isn't it?" he countered. "Can you look me in the eyes

and say that you don't want me as much as I want you? That you didn't dream about us making love last night? Me being inside you. You riding me? Hard. My tongue inside your mouth…and inside a lot of other places on your body?"

She silently stared at him but her entire body flared in response to the vivid pictures he'd painted in her mind. Unlike Paige, Jillian wasn't an actress and couldn't lie worth a damn. But on that same note she would never admit anything to him. That would give him too much power. "I won't admit to anything, Aidan."

"You don't have to," he said, with a serious smile on his face. "And it's not about me needing sex but me needing you." He paused a moment as if giving his words time to sink in. "But this leads to another proposition I'd like to make."

She'd set herself up for this one. "And what is the proposition this time?"

He leaned in closer. "That for the remainder of the cruise you let your guard down. Believe in me. Believe in yourself. And believe in us. I want you to see I'm still the man who loves you. The man who will always love you. But that's something you have to believe, Jillian. However, at the end of the cruise, if for whatever reason, you still don't believe it or feel that the two of us can make a lifetime commitment, then when we dock back in Barcelona, we'll agree to go our separate ways."

She broke eye contact with him to glance out at the ocean. Today was a rather calm day outside but inside she was in a state of turmoil. He was asking a lot of her and he knew it. His proposition meant forgetting the very reason she broke up with him. That would definitely be easy on him if she did. Was that why he'd come up with this latest proposition?

Jillian turned her gaze back to him. "You want me to just forget everything that's happened, Aidan? Especially the incident that caused our breakup?"

"No, I don't want you to forget a single thing."

His answer surprised her. "Why?"

"Because it's important that the two of us learn from any mistakes we've made, and we can't do that if we safely tuck them away just because doing so will be convenient. We should talk about them openly and honestly. Hopefully, we'll be able to build something positive out of the discussions. You're always harping a lot on the things I did. What about you, Jillian? Do you think you were completely blameless?"

"No, but—"

"I don't want to get into all that now, but have you ever noticed that with you there's always a *but* in there somewhere?"

She frowned at him. "No, I never noticed but obviously you have." Was it really that way with her? As far as sharing the blame, she could do that. But she hadn't been the one getting a lap dance.

"My proposition is still on the table," he said. "I've been completely honest with you on this cruise, Jillian. I've been up-front with my intentions, my wants and my desires."

Yes, he had. Every opportunity he got. And she knew that he would have her on her back in a flash if she were to let him. Jillian inclined her head to look deeper into his eyes. "And you promise that at the end of the cruise if things don't work out the way we think they should that you will go your way and I'll go mine?"

He nodded slowly. "It would be difficult, but yes. I want you to be happy and if being happy for you means not having me in your life then that's the way it will be. It will be your decision and I would like to have that decision the night before we return to Barcelona."

She digested what Aidan said. He'd laid things out, with no fluff. She knew what, and who, she would be dealing with. But she also knew that even if she decided she didn't want him in her life romantically, he could never be fully out of it; their families were connected. How could they manage that?

"What about the family?" she asked. "Paige, Stern and Adrian know our secret. If things don't work out between us it might have an effect on them."

"We will deal with that if it happens. Together. Even if we're no longer lovers, there's no reason we can't remain friends. Besides, are you sure there aren't others in the family besides those three who know? It's my guess others might suspect something even if they haven't said anything."

She shrugged. "Doesn't matter who knows now. I had planned on telling Pam anyway."

Surprise flashed in his eyes. "You had?"

"Yes."

"When?"

"After I talked to you about it, which I had planned to do when I flew into Portland for your birthday."

"Oh."

She released a sigh. Evidently the one thing he hadn't found out was that she'd intended to release him from their secret. "Afterward, when things didn't work out between us, I saw no need for me to tell Pam anything.

In fact, I felt the less she knew about the situation, the better."

Aidan didn't say anything for a moment and neither did Jillian. She figured he was thinking how that one weekend had changed things for them. He finally broke the silence by asking, "So, what's your answer to my proposition?"

Jillian nibbled at her bottom lip. Why couldn't she just turn him down, walk away and keep walking? She knew one of the reasons was that her mind was filled with fond memories of the good times they'd shared. It hadn't been all bad.

Would it be so dreadful if she were to give his proposition a try? What did she have to lose? She'd already experienced heartbreak with him. And a year of separation hadn't been easy. Besides, she couldn't deny that it would feel good to be with him out in the open, without any kind of secrecy shrouding them. Whenever he'd come to Laramie, she'd always been on guard, looking over her shoulder in case she ran into someone who knew Pam. And he did have a good point about the remaining days on the cruise testing the strength of a relationship between them.

She met his gaze. "Yes. I accept your proposition and I will hold you to your word, Aidan."

Later that night, as Aidan changed for dinner, he couldn't help remembering Jillian's words.

"Fine, baby, hold me to my word," he murmured to himself as he tucked his white dress shirt into his pants. "That's the way it should be. And that's the way it will be."

Today had gone just the way he'd wanted. After she'd

agreed to his proposition he'd been able to talk her into going with him to the Terelle Deck so he could grab breakfast. She'd sat across from him while he ate a hefty portion of the pancakes and syrup she'd recommended. They had chosen a table with a beautiful view of the ocean, and he liked the way the cool morning breeze stirred her hair. More than once he'd been tempted to reach across the table and run his fingers through it.

After breakfast he had talked her into joining him in the Venus Lounge where a massive bingo game was under way. They had found a table in the back and she'd worked five bingo cards while he worked three. In the end, neither of them had won anything but the game had been fun.

Later they had gone to the art gallery to check out the paintings on display and after that they'd enjoyed a delicious lunch in the Coppeneria Room. After she mentioned her plans to visit the spa, he'd taken a stroll around the ship. The layout was awesome and the entire ship was gorgeous. Tomorrow morning before daybreak they would arrive in Monte Carlo, France, and from there, Florence, Italy. He'd never been to France or Italy before but Adrian had, and according to his twin both countries were beautiful. Aidan couldn't wait to see them for himself.

He smiled as he put on his cuff links. Being around Jillian today had reminded him of how much she liked having her way. In the past he had indulged her. But not this time. While on this cruise he had no intention of letting her have her way. In fact, he planned to teach her the art of compromising. That was the main reason he had suggested she drop by his cabin to grab him for dinner instead of the other way around. Although she hadn't said anything, he could tell she hadn't liked the idea.

He turned from the mirror at the sound of a knock on his door. She was a little early but he had no problem with that. Moving across the suite, he opened the door, and then stood there, finding it impossible to speak. All he could do was stare at Jillian. Dressed in a red floor-length gown that hugged every curve, her hair wrapped on top of her head with a few curls dangling toward her beautiful face, she looked breathtaking. His gaze scanned the length of her—head to toe.

Pulling himself together, he stepped aside. "Come in. You look very nice."

"Thank you," she said, entering his suite. "I'm a little early. The cabin steward arrived and I didn't want to get in his way."

"No problem. I just need to put on my tie."

"This suite is fantastic. I thought my suite was large but this one is triple mine in size."

He smiled over at her. "It's the owner's personal suite whenever he cruises."

"Really? And how did you get so lucky?"

"He's a friend. You remember my cousin Quade who lives in North Carolina, right?"

"The one who has the triplets?"

"Yes, he's the one. Quade and the ship's owner, Dominic Saxon, are brothers-in-law, married to sisters—the former Steeles, Cheyenne and Taylor.

Jillian nodded. "I remember meeting Cheyenne at Dillon and Pam's wedding. The triplets were adorable. I don't recall ever meeting Taylor."

"I'll make sure you meet Taylor and Dominic if you ever come to visit me in Charlotte." He'd deliberately chosen his words to make sure she understood that if a meeting took place, it would be her decision.

After putting on his tie, he turned to her, trying not to stare again. "I'm all set. Ready?"

"Whenever you are."

He was tempted to kiss her but held back. Knowing him like she did, she would probably expect such a move. But tonight he planned to keep her on her toes. In other words, he would be full of surprises.

"Hi, Aidan!"

Jillian figured it would be one of those nights when the group of women sharing their table chorused the greeting to Aidan. It was the book-club group. She should have known they would find him. Or, for all she knew, he'd found them.

"I take it you've met them," she whispered when he pulled out her chair.

"Yes, earlier today, while taking my stroll when you were at the spa."

"Evening, ladies. How's everyone doing?" Aidan asked the group with familiarity, taking his seat.

"Fine," they responded simultaneously. Jillian noticed some were smiling so hard it made her wonder how any-one's lips could stretch that wide.

"I want you all to meet someone," Aidan was saying. "This is Jillian Novak. My significant other."

"Oh."

Was that disappointment she heard in the voices of the six women? And what happened to those huge smiles? Well, she would just have to show them how it was done. She smiled brightly and then said, "Hello, everyone."

Only a few returned her greeting, but she didn't care because she was reflecting on Aidan's introduction.

My significant other.

Before their breakup they had been together for three years and this was the first time he'd introduced her to anyone because of their secret. It made her realize that, other than Ivy, she'd never introduced him to anyone, either.

The waiter came to take their order but not before giving them a run-down of all the delectable meals on the menu tonight. Jillian chose a seafood dinner and Aidan selected steak.

She discreetly checked out the six women engaging in conversation with Aidan. All beautiful. Gorgeously dressed. Articulate. Professional. Single.

"So, how long have the two of you been together?" asked one of the women who'd introduced herself earlier as Wanda.

Since it appeared the woman had directed the question to Aidan, Jillian let him answer. "Four years," he said, spreading butter on his bread. Jillian decided not to remind him that one of those years they hadn't been together.

"Four years? Really?" a woman by the name of Sandra asked, extending her lips into what Jillian could tell was a plastered-on smile.

"Yes, *really,*" Jillian responded, knowing just what the chick was getting at. After four years Jillian should have a ring on her finger. In other words, she should be a wife and not a significant other.

"Then I guess the two of you will probably be tying the knot pretty soon." It was obvious Wanda was digging for information. The others' ears were perked up as if they, too, couldn't wait to hear the response.

Jillian tried not to show her surprise when Aidan reached across the table and placed his hand over hers. "Sooner rather than later, if I had my way. But I'll be joining the Cardiology Department at Johns Hopkins in the fall, and Jillian's just finished medical school, so we haven't set dates yet."

"You're both doctors?" Sandra asked, smiling.

"Yes," both Aidan and Jillian answered at the same time.

"That's great. So are we," Sandra said, pointing to herself and the others. "Faye and Sherri and I just finished Meharry Medical School a couple of months ago, and Wanda, Joy and Virginia just completed pharmacy school at Florida A&M."

"Congratulations, everyone," Jillian said, giving all six women a genuine smile. After having completed medical school she knew the hard work and dedication that was required for any medical field. And the six had definitely attended excellent schools.

"And congratulations to you, too," the women said simultaneously.

Jillian's smile widened. "Thanks."

Aidan glanced down at the woman walking beside him as they left the jazz lounge where several musicians had performed. Jillian had been pretty quiet since dinner. He couldn't help wondering what she was thinking.

"Did you enjoy dinner?" he asked.

She glanced up at him. "Yes, what about you?"

He shrugged. "It was nice."

"Just nice? You were the only male seated at a table

with several females, all gorgeous, so how was it just nice?"

"Because it was," he said, wondering if this conversation would start a discussion he'd rather not have with her. But then, maybe they should have it now. They *had* agreed to talk things out. "So what did you think of the ladies at our table tonight?"

She stopped walking to lean against a rail and look at him. "Maybe I should be asking what you thought of them."

He joined her at the rail, standing a scant foot in front of her. "Pretty. All seven of them. But the prettiest of them all was the one wearing the red dress. The one named Jillian Novak. Now, she was a total knockout. She put the *s* in sexy."

Jillian smiled and shook her head, sending those dangling curls swinging. "Laying it on rather thick, aren't you, Aidan?"

"Not as long as you get the picture."

"And what picture is that?"

"That you're the only woman I want. The only one who can get blood rushing through my veins."

She chuckled. "Sounds serious, Dr. Westmoreland."

"It is." He didn't say anything for a minute as he stared at her. "Do you realize that this is the first time you've ever referred to me as Dr. Westmoreland?"

She nodded. "Yes, I know. Just like I realized tonight at dinner that it was the first time you'd ever introduced me during the time we were together."

"Yes. There were times when I wished I could have."

But you couldn't, she thought. *Because of the secret I made you keep.*

"But I did tonight."

"Yes, you did fib a little. Twice in fact," she pointed out.

He lifted a brow. "When?"

"When you said I was your significant other."

"I didn't fib. You are. There's no one more significant in my life than you," he said softly.

Jillian couldn't say anything after that. How could she? And when the silence between them lengthened, she wondered if he was expecting her to respond. What *could* she say? That she believed him? Did she really?

"And what was the other?" he asked, finally breaking the silence.

"What other?" she asked him.

"Fib. You said there were two."

"Oh. The one about the amount of time we've been together. You said four years and it was three," she said as they began walking again.

"No, it was four. Although we spent a year apart it meant nothing to me, other than frustration and anger. Nevertheless, you were still here," he said, touching his heart. "During every waking moment and in all my dreams."

She glanced away from him as they continued walking only to glance back moments later. "That sounds unfair to the others."

"What others?"

"Any woman you dated that year."

He stopped walking, took her hand and pulled her to the side, back over to the rail. He frowned down at her. "What are you talking about? I didn't date any women last year."

She searched his face and somehow saw the truth

in his words. "But why? I thought you would. Figured you had."

"Why?" Before she could respond he went on in a mocking tone, "Ah, that's right. Because I'm a womanizer."

Jillian heard the anger in his voice, but yes, that was the reason she'd thought he'd dated. Wasn't that the reason she had ended things between them as well, so he would have the freedom to return to his old ways? She drew in a deep breath. "Aidan, I—"

"No, don't say it." He stiffened his chin. "Whatever it is you're going to say, Jillian, don't." He glanced down at his watch and then his gaze moved back to her face. "I know you prefer turning in early, so I'll see you back to your cabin. I think I'll hang out a while in one of the bars."

She didn't say anything for a moment. "Want some company?"

"No," he said softly. "Not right now."

Suddenly, she felt a deep ache in her chest. "Okay. Don't worry about seeing me to my cabin. You can go on."

"You sure?"

She forced a smile. "Yes, I'm sure. I know the way."

"All right. I'll come get you for breakfast around eight."

If you can still stand my company, she thought. "Okay. I'll see you in the morning at eight."

He nodded and, with the hurt she'd brought on herself eating away at her, she watched Aidan walk away.

Thirteen

Aidan forced his eyes open when he heard banging coming from the sitting area.

"What the hell?" He closed his eyes as sharp pain slammed through his head. It was then that he remembered last night. Every single detail.

He had stopped at the bar, noticed it was extremely crowded and had gone to his room instead. He'd ordered room service, a bottle of his favorite Scotch. He'd sat on the balcony, looking out over the ocean beneath the night sky and drinking alone, nursing a bruised heart. He didn't finish off the entire bottle but he'd downed enough to give him the mother of all headaches this morning. What time was it anyway?

He forced his eyes back open to look at the clock on the nightstand. Ten? It was ten in the morning? Crap! He'd promised Jillian to take her to breakfast at eight. He could only imagine what she'd thought when he was a no-show. Pulling himself up on the side of the bed he drew in a deep breath. Honestly, did he care anymore? She had him pegged as a player in that untrusting mind of hers, so what did the truth matter?

"Mr. Aidan," called the cabin steward, "do you want me to clean your bedroom now or come back later?"

"Come back later, Rowan."

When Aidan heard the door close, he dropped back in bed. He knew he should call Jillian, but chances were she'd gotten tired of waiting around and had gone to breakfast without him. He could imagine her sitting there eating pancakes while all kinds of insane ideas flowed through her head. All about him. Hell, he might as well get up, get dressed and search the ship for her to put those crazy ideas to rest.

He was about to get out of bed when he heard a knock at the door. He figured it was probably the guy coming around to pick up laundry, so he slipped into his pajama bottoms to tell the person to come back later.

He snatched open the door but instead of the laundry guy, Jillian stood there carrying a tray of food. "Jillian? What are you doing here?"

She stared at him for a moment. "You look like crap."

"I feel like crap," he muttered, moving aside to let her in. She placed the tray on his dining table. His head still pounded somewhat, but not as hard as the way his erection throbbed while staring at her. She was wearing a cute and sexy shorts set that showed what a gorgeous pair of legs she had. And her hair, which had been pinned atop her head last night, flowed down her shoulders while gold hoop earrings dangled from her ears. Damn, he couldn't handle this much sexiness in the morning.

She turned around. "To answer your question as to why I'm here, you missed breakfast so I thought I'd bring you something to eat."

He closed the door and leaned against it. "And what else?"

She lifted a brow. "And what else?"

"Yes. What other reason do you have for coming here? Let me guess. You figured I brought a woman here last night and you wanted to catch me in the act? Right? Go ahead, Jillian, search my bedroom if you like. The bathroom, too, if that suits your fancy. Oh, and don't forget to check the balconies in case I've hidden her out there until after you leave."

Jillian didn't say anything for a long minute. "I guess I deserved that. But—"

He held his hand to interrupt her. "Please. No buts, Jillian. I'm tired of them coming from you. Let me ask you something. How many men did you sleep with during the year we weren't together since you think I didn't leave a single woman standing?"

She narrowed her gaze at him. "Not a single one."

He crossed his arms over his chest. "Why?"

She lifted a chin. "Because I didn't want to."

"Why didn't you want to? You had broken things off with me and we weren't together. Why didn't you sleep with another man?"

Jillian knew she'd screwed up badly last night and she could hardly wait until morning to see Aidan so she could apologize. When he didn't show up at eight as he'd promised, she would admit that for a quick second she'd thought he might have been mad enough to spend the night with someone else. But all it had taken to erase that thought was for her to remember how he'd looked last night when he told her the reason why he'd introduced her as his significant other.

There's no one more significant in my life than you.

And she believed him. His reason for not sleeping

with another woman during the year they'd been apart was the same reason she hadn't slept with another man.

"Jillian?"

She met his gaze. He wanted an answer and she would give him one. The truth and nothing but the truth.

"Sleeping with another man never crossed my mind, Aidan," she said softly. "Because I still loved you. And no matter what I saw or imagined you did with that lap dancer, I still loved you. My body has your imprint all over it and the thought of another man touching it sickens me."

She paused and then added, "You're wrong. I didn't come here thinking I'd find another woman. I came to apologize. I figured the reason you didn't come take me to breakfast was because you were still mad at me. And after last night I knew that I deserved your anger."

"Why do you think you deserve my anger?"

"Because everything is my fault. You only kept our affair a secret because I asked you to, begged you to. Last night when I got to my room, I sat out on the balcony and thought about everything. I forced myself to see the situation through someone else's eyes other than my own. And you know what I saw, Aidan?"

"No, what did you see, Jillian?"

She fought back tears. "I saw a man who loved me enough to take a lot of crap. I never thought about what all the secrecy would mean. And then the long distance and the sacrifices you made to come see me whenever you could. The money you spent for airplane fare, your time. I wasn't the only one with the goal of becoming a doctor. It's not like you didn't have a life, trying to handle the pressure of your dual residency."

She paused. "And I can just imagine what your

friends thought when all of a sudden you became a saint for no reason. You couldn't tell them about me, so I can understand them wanting to help get your life back on track with those women. That was the Aidan they knew. And unfortunately that was the Aidan I wanted to think you missed being. That night I showed up at the party, I should have realized that you were just having the fun you deserved. Fun you'd denied yourself since your involvement with me. I should have loved you enough and trusted you enough to believe that no matter what, you wouldn't betray me. That I meant more to you than any lap dancer with silicone boobs."

He uncrossed his arms. "You're right. You do mean more to me than any lap dancer, stripper, book-club member or any other woman out there, Jillian," he said in a soft tone. "And you were wrong to think I missed my old life. What I miss is being with you. I think we handled things okay that first year, but during those second and third years, because of trying to make that dual residency program work and still keep you at the top of the list, things became difficult for me. Then in the third year, I was the one with focusing issues. It became harder and harder to keep our long-distance affair afloat and stay focused at work. And the secrecy only added more stress. But I knew if I complained to you about it, that it would only stress you out and make you lose focus on what you needed to do.

"You were young when we started our affair. Only twenty-one. And you hadn't dated much. In all honesty, probably not at all, because I refuse to count that dude you dated in high school. So deep down I knew you weren't quite ready for the type of relationship I wanted. But I loved you and I wanted you and I figured everything would work out. I knew how challenging medical school could be and I wanted to make your life as calm as possible. I didn't want to be the one to add to your stress."

He paused. "But it looks like I did anyway. I tried to make the best of it, but unfortunately sometimes when we talked, I was in one of my foul moods because of stress. I would get an attitude with you instead of talking to you about it. At no time should I have made you feel that you deserved my anger. I apologize. I regret doing that."

"It's okay," Jillian said, pulling out a chair. "Come sit down and eat. Your food is getting cold."

She watched him move away from the door. When he reached the table, she skirted back so he could sit down. When he sat, he reached out, grabbed her around the waist and brought her down to his lap.

"Aidan! What do you think you're doing?"

He wrapped both arms around her so she wouldn't go anywhere. "What I should have done last night. Brought you back here and put you in my lap, wrapped my arms around you and convinced you that I meant everything I said about your value to me. Instead I got upset and walked away."

She pressed her forehead to his and whispered, "Sorry I made you upset with me last night."

"I love you so much, Jillian, and when I think you don't believe just how much I love you, how much you mean to me, I get frustrated and wonder just what else I have to do. I'm not a perfect man. I'm human. I'm going to make mistakes. We both are. But the one thing I won't do is betray your love with another woman. Those days are over for me. You're all the woman I'll ever need."

She leaned back from him to look in his eyes. "I believe you, Aidan. I won't lie and say I'll never get jealous, but I can say it'll be because I'm questioning the woman's motives, not yours."

And she really meant that. When he hadn't come down for breakfast she had gone into the Terelle Dining Room to eat alone. She ran into the book-club ladies and ended up eating breakfast with them and enjoying herself. Once Aidan had made it clear last night that he was not available, they had put a lid on their man-hunter instincts. Jillian and the six women had a lot in common, since they were all recent medical-school graduates, and they enjoyed sharing their experiences over breakfast. They invited her to join them for shopping at some point during their two days in Rome and she agreed to do that.

She shifted in Aidan's lap to find a more comfortable position.

"I wouldn't do that too many times if I were you," he warned in a husky whisper.

A hot wave of desire washed over her. He was looking at her with those dark, penetrating eyes of eyes. The same ones that could arouse her as no man ever had... or would. "Why not?"

If he was going to give her a warning, she wanted him to explain himself, although she knew what he meant.

"Because if you keep it up, *you* might become my breakfast."

The thought of that happening had the muscles between her legs tightening, and she was aware that every hormone in her body was downright sizzling. "But you like pancakes and syrup," she said innocently.

A smile spread across his lips. "But I like your taste better."

"Do you?" she asked, intentionally shifting again to lean forward so that she could bury her face in the hollow of his throat. He was shirtless and she loved getting close to him, drinking in his scent.

"You did it again."

She leaned back and met his gaze. "Did I?"

"Yes."

She intentionally shifted in his lap when she lowered her head to lick the upper part of his chest. She loved the salty taste of his flesh and loved even more the moan she heard from his lips.

"It's been a year, Jillian. If I get you in my bed today it will be a long time before I let you out."

"And miss touring Monte Carlo? The ship has already docked."

"We have time." He suddenly stood, with her in his arms, and she quickly grabbed him around the neck and held on. He chuckled. "Trust me. I'm not going to let you fall." He headed for the bedroom.

"Now to enjoy breakfast, the Aidan Westmoreland way," he said, easing her down on the bed. He stood back and stared at her for a long moment. "I want you so much I ache. I desire you so much I throb. And I will always love you, even after drawing my last breath."

For the second time that day, she fought back tears. "Oh, Aidan. I want, desire and love you, too. Just as much."

He leaned down and removed her shoes before removing every stitch of her clothing with a skill only he had perfected. When she lay there naked before him, he slid his pj's down his legs. "Lie still for a minute. There's something I want to do," he instructed in a throaty tone.

That's when Jillian saw the bottle of syrup he'd

brought into the bedroom with them. She looked at the bottle and then looked up at him. "You are kidding, right?"

"Do I look like I'm kidding?" he asked, removing the top.

She swallowed. No, he definitely didn't look as if he was kidding. In fact he looked totally serious. Too serious. "But I'm going to be all sticky," she reasoned. All she could think about was how glad she was for the bikini wax she'd gotten at the spa yesterday.

"You won't be sticky for long. I plan to lick it all off you and then we'll shower together."

"Aidan!" She squealed when she felt the thick liquid touch her skin. Aidan made good on his word. He dripped it all over her chest, making sure there was a lot covering her breasts, around her navel and lower still. He laid it on thick between her legs, drenching her womanly core.

And then he used his tongue to drive her insane with pleasure while taking his time to lick off all the syrup. The flick of his tongue sent sensuous shivers down her spine, and all she could do was lie there and moan while encased in a cloud of sensations.

He used his mouth as a bearer of pleasure as he laved her breasts, drawing the nipples between his lips and sucking on the turgid buds with a greed that made her womb contract. She wasn't sure how much more she could take when his mouth lowered to her stomach. She reached down and buried her fingers in his scalp as his mouth traced a hungry path around her navel.

Moments later he lifted his head to stare at her, deliberately licking his lips. They both knew where he was headed next. The look on his face said he wanted her to know he intended to go for the gusto.

And he did.

Jillian screamed his name the moment his tongue entered her, sending shockwaves of a gigantic orgasm through her body. His hot and greedy tongue had desire clawing at her insides, heightening her pulse. And when she felt another orgasm coming on the heels of the first, she knew it was time she took control. Otherwise, Aidan would lick her crazy.

With all the strength she could muster she tried to shift their bodies, which was hard to do since his mouth was on her while his hands held tight to her hips. When she saw there was no way she could make Aidan budge until he got his fill, she gave in to another scream when a second orgasm hit.

He finally lifted his head, smiled at her while licking his lips and then eased his body over hers. "I told you I was going to lick it all off you, baby."

Yes, he had. Then his engorged erection slid inside of her. All she recalled after that was her brain taking a holiday as passion overtook her, driving her over the edge, bringing her back, then driving her to the edge again.

He thrust hard, all the way to the hilt and then some. He lifted her hips and set the pace. The bed springs were tested to their maximum and so was she. She released a deep moan when he pounded into her, making her use muscles she hadn't used in a year. And then he slowed and without disconnecting their bodies, eased to his knees. He lifted her legs all the way to his shoulders and continued thrusting.

"Aidan!"

He answered with a deep growl when the same explosion that tore through her ripped through him, as well. She could feel his hot, molten liquid rush through her body, bathing her womb. But he didn't stop. He kept going, enlarging inside her all over again.

She saw arousal coiling in the depth of his eyes. They were in it for the long haul, right now and forever. And when his wet, slick body finally eased down, he pulled her into his arms, wrapped the strength of his legs over hers and held her close. She breathed in his scent. This was where she wanted to be. Always.

Hours later, Jillian stirred in Aidan's arms and eased over to whisper in his ear. "Remind me never to let you go without me for a full year again."

He grinned as he opened his eyes. "One year, two months and four days. But I wasn't counting or anything, mind you."

She smiled. "I'll take your word for it." She eased up to glance over at the clock. Had they been in bed five hours already? "We need to shower."

"Again?"

She laughed out. "The last time doesn't count."

"Why?"

She playfully glared over at him. "You know why."

He'd taken her into the shower to wash off any lingering stickiness from the syrup. Instead he ended up making love to her again. Then he'd dried them both off and had taken her to the bed and made love to her again several times, before they'd both drifted off to sleep.

"I guess we do need to get up, shower and dress if we want to see any of Monte Carlo."

"Yes, and I want to see Monte Carlo."

"I want to see you," he said, easing back and raking

his gaze over her naked body. "Do you know how much I missed this? Missed you?"

"The same way I missed you?"

"More," he said, running his hand over her body.

She couldn't ignore the delicious heat of the fingers touching her. "I doubt that, Dr. Westmoreland."

"Trust me."

She did trust him. And she loved him so much she wanted everyone to know it. "I can't wait until we return to Denver for Adrian's wedding."

He looked down at her. "Why?"

"So we can tell Pam and Dillon."

He studied her expression. "Are you ready for that?"

"More than ready. Do you think they already know?"

"It wouldn't surprise me if they did. Dillon isn't a dummy. Neither is Pam."

"Then why haven't they said anything?"

He shrugged. "Probably waiting for us to tell them."

She thought about what he'd said and figured he might be right. "Doesn't matter now. They will find out soon enough. Are you ready?"

"For another round?"

"No, not for another round. Are you ready to take a shower so we can get off this ship for a while?"

He pulled her into his arms. "Um, maybe. After another round." And then he lowered his mouth to hers.

Fourteen

"I hope you're not punishing me for what happened the last two days, Jillian."

Jillian glanced up at Aidan and smiled. "Why would I do that?" she asked as they walked the streets of Rome, Italy. She'd never visited a city more drenched in history. They would be here for two days and she doubted she could visit all the places she wanted to see in that time. She would have to make plans to come back one day.

"Because it was late when we finally got off the ship to tour Monte Carlo, and the same thing happened yesterday when we toured Florence. I have a feeling you blame me for both."

She chuckled. "Who else should I blame? Every time I mentioned it was time for us to get up, shower and get off the ship, you had other ideas."

He smiled as if remembering several of those ideas. "But we did do the tours. We just got a late start."

Yes, they had done the tours. For barely three hours in Monte Carlo. They had seen all they could in a cab ride around the city. Then yesterday, at least they had ridden up the most scenic road in Florence to reach Piazzale Michelangelo. From there they toured several palaces and museums before it was time to get back to the ship.

She had made sure they had gotten up, dressed and were off the ship at a reasonable time this morning for their tour of Rome. Already they had walked a lot, which was probably the reason Aidan was whining.

"What's the complaint, Aidan? You're in great shape." She of all people should know. He hadn't wasted time having her belongings moved into his suite where she had spent the night…and got very little sleep until dawn. But somehow she still felt energized.

"You think I'm punishing you by suggesting that we walk instead of taking a taxi-tour?" she asked as they crossed one of the busy streets.

"No. I think you're punishing me because you talked me out of renting that red Ferrari. Just think of all the places I could have taken you while driving it."

She chuckled. "Yes, but I would have wanted to get there in one piece and without an accelerated heart rate."

He placed his arms around her shoulders. "Have you forgotten that one day I intend to be one of the most sought-after cardiologists in the world?"

"How could I forget?" she said, smiling. She was really proud of him and his accomplishments. Going through that dual residency program was what had opened the door for him to continue his specialty training at Johns Hopkins, one of the most renowned research hospitals in the country.

Last night, in between making love, they had talked about their future goals. He knew she would start her residency at a hospital in Orlando, Florida, in the fall. The good thing was that after a year of internship, she could transfer to another hospital. Because he would be working for at least three years at John Hopkins, she would try to relocate to the Washington, D.C., or Maryland area.

A few hours later they had toured a number of places, including the Colosseum, St. Peter's Basilica, the Trevi Fountain and the Catacombs. While standing in front of the Spanish Steps, waiting for Aidan to return from retrieving the lace fan she'd left behind in the church of Trinità dei Monti, she blinked when she saw a familiar man pass by.

Riley Westmoreland? What was Aidan's cousin doing in Rome?

"Riley!" she yelled out. When the man didn't look her way, she figured he must not have heard her. Taking the steps almost two at a time, she hurriedly raced after him.

When she caught up with him she grabbed his arm. "Riley, wait up! I didn't know you—"

She stopped in midsentence when the man turned around. It wasn't Riley. But he looked enough like him to be a twin. "I'm so sorry. I thought you were someone else."

The man smiled and she blinked. He even had Riley's smile. Or more specifically, one of those Westmoreland smiles. All the men in the family had dimples. And like all the Westmoreland men, he was extremely handsome.

"No problem, signorina."

She smiled. "You're Italian?" she asked.

"No. American. I'm here on business. And you?"

"American. Here vacationing." She extended her hand. "I'm Jillian Novak."

He nodded as he took her hand. "Garth Outlaw."

"Nice meeting you, Garth, and again I'm sorry that I mistook you for someone else, but you and Riley West-moreland could almost be twins."

He chuckled. "A woman as beautiful as you can do whatever you like, signorina. No need to apologize." He grasped her hand and lifted it to his lips. "Have a good day, beautiful Jillian Novak, and enjoy the rest of your time in Rome."

"And you do the same."

He turned and walked away. She stood there for a minute, thinking. He was even a flirt like those Westmorelands before they'd married. And the man even had that Westmoreland sexy walk. How crazy was that?

"Jillian?" She turned when she heard Aidan call her name.

"I thought you were going to wait for me on the steps," he said when he reached her.

"I did but then I thought I saw Riley and—"

"Riley? Trust me, Riley would not be in Rome, especially not with Alpha expecting their baby any day now."

"I know, but this guy looked so much like Riley that I raced after him. He could have been Riley's twin. I apologized for my mistake and he was nice about it. He was an American, here on business. Said his name was Garth Outlaw. And he really did favor Riley."

Aidan frowned. "Outlaw?"

"Yes."

"Um, that's interesting. The last time we had our family meeting about the investigation Rico is handling, I think he said something about tracing a branch of the Westmoreland roots to a family who goes by the last name of Outlaw."

"Really?"

"That's what I recall, but Dillon would know for sure. I'll mention it to him when we return home. That information might help Rico," Aidan said as they walked back toward the Spanish Steps.

Rico Claiborne, a private investigator, was married

to Aidan's sister Megan. Jillian was aware that Rico's PI firm had been investigating the connection of four women to Aidan's great-grandfather, Raphel West-moreland. It had been discovered during a genealogy search that before marrying Aidan's great-grandmother Gemma, Raphel had been connected to four other women who'd been listed as former wives. Rico's investigation had confirmed that Raphel hadn't married any of the women, but that one of them had given birth to a son that Raphel had never known about. Evidently, Jillian thought, at some point Rico had traced that son to the Outlaw family.

"Ready to head back to the ship?" Aidan asked, interrupting her thoughts.

She glanced back at her watch. "Yes, it's getting kind of late. You can join me and the book-club ladies when we go shopping tomorrow if you'd like."

He shook his head. "No thanks. Although it's a beautiful city, I've seen enough of Rome for now. But I will bring you back."

She lifted a brow. "You will?"

"Yes."

"When?"

"For our honeymoon. I hope." Aidan then got down on one knee and took her hand in his. "I love you, Jillian. Will you marry me?"

Jillian stared at him in shock. It was only when he tugged at her hand did she notice the ring he'd placed there. Her eyes widened. "Oh, my God!" Never had she seen anything so beautiful.

"Well?" Aidan asked, grinning. "People are standing around. We've gotten their attention. Are you going to embarrass me or what?"

She saw that people had stopped to stare. They had heard his proposal and, like Aidan, they were waiting for her answer. She could not believe that here in the beautiful city of Rome, on the Spanish Steps, Aidan had asked her to marry him. She would remember this day for as long as she lived.

"Yes. Yes!" she said, filled with happiness. "Yes, I will marry you."

"Thank you," he said, getting back to his feet and pulling her into his arms. "For a minute there you had me worried."

The people around them cheered and clapped while a smiling Aidan pulled Jillian into his arms and kissed her.

Aidan walked down the long corridor to his suite. Jillian had sent him away an hour ago with instructions not to return until now because she would have a surprise waiting for him when he got back. He smiled thinking she had probably planned a candlelit dinner for their last day on the cruise.

It was hard to believe their two weeks were up. Tomorrow they would return to Barcelona. After two days in Rome they had spent two days at sea before touring Athens, Greece. While there they had taken part in a wine-tasting excursion and visited several museums. From there they had toured Turkey, Mykonos and Malta. Now they were headed back to Barcelona and would arrive before daybreak.

He couldn't help the feeling of happiness that puffed out his chest when he thought of being an engaged man. Although they hadn't set a date, the most important thing was that he had asked and she had said yes. They talked every day about their future, and although they still had at least another year before she could join him in Maryland, they were okay with it because they knew the day would come when they would be together.

They decided not to wait until they went home for Adrian's wedding to tell the family their news. Some would be shocked, while others who knew about their affair would be relieved that their secret wasn't a secret any longer. They would head straight to Denver tomorrow when the ship docked.

He chuckled when he thought about Jillian's excitement over her engagement ring. The book-club ladies had definitely been impressed as well, ahhing and ooing every night at dinner. Jewelry by Zion was the rave since Zion was the First Lady's personal jeweler. Jillian hadn't known that he knew Zion personally because of Aidan's friendship with the Steele family, who were close personal friends of Zion. Zion had designed most of his signature custom jewelry collection while living in Rome for the past ten years. Thanks to Dominic, Aidan had met with Zion privately on board the ship in the wee hours of the morning while Jillian slept, when they first docked in a port near Rome. Zion had brought an attaché case filled with beautiful rings—all originals hand-crafted by Zion. When Aidan had seen this one particular ring, he'd known it was the one he wanted to put on Jillian's finger.

When Aidan reached his suite's door, he knocked, to let her know he had returned.

"Come in."

Using his passkey, he opened the door and smiled upon seeing the lit candles around the room. His bride-to-be had set the mood for a romantic dinner, he thought, when he saw how beautifully the table was set.

Closing the door behind him he glanced around the dimly lit suite but didn't see Jillian anywhere. Was she in the bedroom waiting on him? He moved in that direction and then felt a hand on his shoulder. He turned around and his breath caught. Jillian wore a provocative black lace teddy that showed a lot of flesh. Attached to the teddy were matching lace garters and she wore a pair of stilettoes on her feet. He thought he hadn't seen anyone as sexy in his entire life and he couldn't help groaning in appreciation.

She leaned close, swirled the tip of her tongue around his ear and whispered, "I'm about to give you the lap dance of your life, Aidan Westmoreland."

The next thing he knew he was gently shoved in a chair. "And remember no touching, so put your hands behind your back."

He followed her instructions, mesmerized beyond belief. Her sensual persona stirred his desire. His pulse kicked up a notch, followed immediately by a deep throbbing in his erection. "And just what do you want me to do?" he asked in a low voice.

She smiled at him. "Just enjoy. I plan to do all the work. But by the time I finish, you will be too exhausted to move."

Really? Him? Too exhausted to move? And she would be the one doing all the work? He couldn't wait for that experience. "Now will you keep your hands to yourself or do I need to handcuff you?" she asked him.

He couldn't help smiling at the thought of that. Did she really have handcuffs? Would she be that daring? He decided to find out. "I can't make any promises, so you might want to handcuff me."

"No problem."

The next thing he knew she'd whipped out a pair of handcuffs slapped them on his wrists and locked them with a click to the chair. *Damn.* While he was taking all this in, he suddenly heard music coming from the sound system in the room. He didn't recognize the artist, but the song had a sensual beat.

While sitting there handcuffed to the chair, he watched as Jillian responded to the music, her movements slow, graceful and seductive. She rolled her stomach and then shimmied her hips and backside in a sinfully erotic way. He sat there awestruck, fascinated, staring at her as she moved in front of him. He felt the rapid beat of his heart and the sweet pull of desire as his erection continued to pulsate.

Although he couldn't touch her, she was definitely touching him—rubbing her hands over his shirt, underneath it, through the hair on his chest, before taking her time unbuttoning his shirt and easing it from his shoulders.

"Have I ever told you how much I love your chest, Aidan?" she asked him in a sultry tone.

"No," he answered huskily. "You never have."

"Well, I'm telling you now. In fact, I want to show you just how much I like it."

Then she crouched over him and used her tongue to lick his shoulder blades before moving slowly across the span of his chest. He would have come out of his chair had he not been handcuffed to it. She used her tongue in ways she hadn't before and he heard himself groaning out loud.

"You like that?" she asked, leaning close to his mouth, and licking there, as well. "Want more? Want to see what else you've taught me to do with my tongue?"

He swallowed. Oh, yes, he wanted more. He wanted to see just what he'd taught her. Instead of answering, he nodded.

She smiled as she bent down to remove his shoes. Reaching up, she unzipped his pants and he raised his hips as she slid both his pants and briefs down his legs. She smiled at him again.

"You once licked me all over, Aidan, and you seemed to have enjoyed it. Now I'm going to do the same to you and I intend to enjoy myself, as well."

Moistening her lips with a delicious-looking sweep of her tongue, she got down on her knees before him and spread his legs. Then she lowered her head between his thighs and took him into her mouth.

As soon as she touched him, blood rushed through his veins, sexual hunger curled his stomach and desire stroked his gut. Her mouth widened to accommodate his size and she used her tongue to show that with this, she was definitely in control. He watched in a sensual daze as her head bobbed up and down while she fanned the blaze of his desire.

He wanted to grab hold of her hair, stroke her back, caress her shoulders but he couldn't. He felt defenseless, totally under her control but he loved every single minute of it. When he couldn't take any more, his body jerked in one hell of an explosion and she still wouldn't let go.

"Jillian!"

He wanted her with an intensity that terrified him. And when she lifted her head and smiled at him, he knew what it meant to love someone with every part of your heart, your entire being and your soul.

While the music continued to play, she straightened and began stripping for him, removing each piece of clothing slowly, and teasing his nostrils before tossing it aside. Sexual excitement filled his inner core as he inhaled her scent. When she was totally naked, she began dancing again, touching herself and touching him. He'd never seen anything so erotic in his entire life.

When she curled into his lap and continued to dance, the feel of her soft curves had him growling, had his erection throbbing again, harder. "Set me free," he begged. He needed to touch her now. He wanted his hands in her hair and his fingers inside her.

"Not yet," she whispered in a purr that made even more need wash over him. Then she twisted her body around so her back was plastered to his chest then she eased down onto his manhood and rode him.

Never had she ridden him this hard and when she shifted so they faced each other, the feel of her breasts hitting his chest sent all kinds of sensations through him.

"Jillian!"

He screamed her name as an orgasm hit him again, deep, and he pulled the scent of her sex through his nostrils. He leaned forward. Although he couldn't touch her, he could lick her. He used his tongue to touch her earlobe and her face. "Uncuff me baby. Please. Uncuff me now."

She reached behind him and he heard the click that released him. When his hands were free he stood, with her in his arms, and quickly moved toward the bedroom.

"You're the one who was supposed to be exhausted," she mumbled into his chest.

"Sorry, it doesn't quite work that way, baby." And then he stretched her out on the bed.

He straddled her, eased inside her and thrust, stroking her, wanting her to feel his love in every movement. This was erotic pleasure beyond compare and her inner muscles clenched him, held him tight and tempted him to beg again.

His thrusts became harder, her moans louder and the desire he felt for her more relentless than ever. And when he finally exploded, he took her along with him as an earth-shattering climax claimed them both. They were blasted into the heavens. Jillian Novak had delivered the kind of mindless pleasure every man should experience at least once in his lifetime. And he was glad that he had.

Moments later, he eased off her and pulled her into his arms, entwining her legs with his. He kissed the side of her face while she fell into a deep sleep.

Their secret affair was not a secret any longer and he couldn't wait to tell the world that he'd found his mate for life. And he would cherish her forever.

Epilogue

"So, you thought you were keeping a secret from us," Pam said, smiling, sitting beside her husband on the sofa as they met with Aidan and Jillian.

"But we didn't?" Jillian asked, grinning and holding Aidan's hand.

"For a little while, maybe," Dillon replied. But when you fall in love with someone, it's hard to keep something like that hidden, especially in *this* family."

Jillian knew exactly what Dillon meant. It seemed the bigger secret had been that she and Aidan had wanted to keep their relationship a secret. No one in the family knew who else knew, so everyone kept their suspicions to themselves.

"Well, I'm glad we don't have to hide things anymore," Aidan said, standing, pulling Jillian up with him and then wrapping his arms around her shoulders.

"You mean you don't have to *try* and hide things," Pam corrected. "Neither of you were doing such a good job of pretending. And when the two of you had that rift, Dillon and I were tempted to intervene. But we figured if it was meant for the two of you to be together, you would be, without our help."

Jillian looked down at her ring. "Yes, we were able to get our act together, although I will have to give Paige some credit for bailing out of the cruise. Aidan and I needed that time together to work things out."

"And I guess from that ring on your finger, the two of you managed to do that," Dillon said.

Aidan nodded as he smiled down at Jillian. "Yes, we did. The thought of a year-long engagement doesn't bother us. After Jillian's first year at that hospital in Orlando, Florida, she'll be able to transfer to one near me. That's when we plan to tie the knot."

"Besides," Pam said, smiling. "The year gives me plenty of time to plan for the wedding without feeling rushed. These Westmoreland weddings are coming around fast, but trust me, I'm not complaining."

Dillon reached out and hugged his wife. "Please don't complain. I'm elated with each one. After Adrian gets hitched next month and Aidan is married in a year, all we'll have to be concerned with is Bailey and Bane."

The room got quiet as everyone thought about that. Only two Westmorelands were left single, and those two were known to be the most headstrong of them all.

"Bay says she's never getting married," Aidan said, grinning.

"So did you and Adrian," Dillon reminded him. "In fact, I don't think there's a single Westmoreland who hasn't made that claim at some point in time, including me. But all it takes is for one of us to find that special person who's our soul mate, and we start singing a different tune."

"But can you see Bay singing a different tune?" Aidan asked.

Dillon thought about the question for a minute, drew in a deep breath and then shook his head. "No."

Everyone laughed. When their laughter subsided Pam smiled and said, "There's someone for everyone, including Bailey. She just hasn't met him yet. In other words, Bailey hasn't met her match. But one day, I believe that she will."

The following month

"Adrian Westmoreland, you may kiss your bride."

Aidan, serving as best man, smiled as he watched his twin brother take the woman he loved, Dr. Trinity Matthews Westmoreland, into his arms to seal their marriage vows with one hell of a kiss. Aidan spotted Jillian in the audience sitting with her sisters and winked at her. Their day would be coming and he couldn't wait.

A short while later, Aidan stole his twin away for a few minutes. The wedding had been held in Trinity's hometown of Bunnell, Florida, at the same church where their cousin Thorn had married Trinity's sister Tara. The weather had been beautiful and it seemed everyone in the little town had been invited to the wedding, which accounted for the packed church of more than eight hundred guests. The reception was held in the ballroom of a beautiful hotel overlooking the Atlantic Ocean.

"Great job, Dr. Westmoreland," he said, grinning at Adrian.

Adrian chuckled. "I intend to say the same to you

a year from now, Dr. Westmoreland, when you tie the knot. I'm glad the cruise helped, and that you and Jillian were able to work things out."

"So am I. That had to be the worst year of my life when we were apart."

Adrian nodded. "I know. Remember I felt your pain whenever you let out any strong emotions."

Yes, Aidan did remember. "So where are you headed for your honeymoon?"

"Sydney, Australia. I've always wanted to go back, and I look forward to taking Trinity there with me."

"Well, the two of you deserve a lifetime of happiness," Aidan said, taking a sip of his champagne.

"You and Jillian do, as well. I'm so glad the secret is a secret no longer."

Aidan's smile widened. "So am I. And on that note, I'm going to go claim my fiancée so you can go claim your bride."

Aidan crossed the span of the ball room to where Jillian stood with her sisters Paige and Nadia, and his sister Bailey. He and Jillian would leave Bunnell in the morning and take the hour-long drive to Orlando. Together they would look for an apartment for her close to the hospital where she would be working as an intern. He had checked and discovered that flights from the D.C. area into Orlando were pretty frequent. He was glad about that because he intended to pay his woman plenty of visits.

Aidan had told Dillon about Jillian's chance meeting with a man by the name of Garth Outlaw while in Rome and how she'd originally thought he was Riley.

Dillon wasn't surprised that any kin out there would have the Westmoreland look due to dominant genes. He had passed the information on to Rico. The family was hoping something resulted from Jillian's encounter.

"Sorry, ladies, I need to grab Jillian for a minute," he said, snagging her hand.

"Where are we going?" Jillian asked as he led her toward the exit.

"To walk on the beach."

"Okay."

Holding hands, they crossed the boardwalk and went down the steps. Pausing briefly, they removed their shoes. Jillian moaned when her feet touched the sand.

"What are you thinking about, baby?" Aidan asked her.

"I'm thinking about how wonderful I feel right now. Walking in the sand, being around the people I love, not having to hide my feelings for you. And what a lucky woman I am to have such a loving family and such a gorgeous and loving fiancé."

He glanced down at her. "You think I'm gorgeous?"

"Yes."

"You think I'm loving?"

"Definitely."

"Will that qualify me for another lap dance tonight?"

Jillian threw her head back and laughed, causing the wind to send hair flying across her face. Aidan pushed her hair back and she smiled up at him.

"Dr. Westmoreland, you can get a lap dance out of me anytime. Just say the word."

"Lap dance."

She leaned up on tip toes. "You got it."

Aidan then pulled her into his arms and kissed her. Life couldn't get any better than this.

* * * * *

THE REAL
RIO D'AQUILA

SANDRA MARTON

CHAPTER ONE

Rio D'Aquila was known for many things.

He was wealthy beyond most people's measure, feared by those who had reason to fear him and as ruggedly good-looking as any man could hope to be.

Not that Rio gave a damn about his looks.

Who he was or, rather, who he had become, was what mattered.

He had been born to poverty, not in Brazil, despite his name, but on the meanest possible streets of Naples, Italy.

At seventeen, he'd stowed away on a rusting Brazilian freighter. The crew had dubbed him "Rio" because that was the ship's destination; they'd tagged on the "Aquila" because he'd responded with the fierceness of an eagle to their taunting.

The name had suited him much more than Matteo Rossi, which was what the sisters at the orphanage where he'd been raised had called him. "Rossi" was pretty much the Italian equivalent of "Smith." "Matteo," they'd said with gentle piety, meant a gift from God.

Rio had always known he was hardly that, so he took the name Rio D'Aquila and made it his own.

He was thirty-two now, and the boy he'd been was a distant memory.

Rio inhabited a world in which money and power were the

lingua franca, and often as not handed down as an absolute right from father to son.

Rio's father, or maybe his mother, had given him nothing but midnight-black hair, dark blue eyes, a handsome if rugged face and a leanly muscled, six-foot-three-inch body.

Everything else he owned—the homes, the cars, the planes, the corporate giant known as Eagle Enterprises—he had acquired for himself.

There was nothing wrong with that. Starting life without any baggage, getting to the top on your own, was all the sweeter. If there was one drawback, it was that his kind of success attracted attention.

At first, he'd enjoyed it. Picking up the *Times* in the morning, seeing his name or his photo in the financial section had made him feel, well, successful.

Inevitably, he'd not only wearied of it, he'd realized how meaningless it was.

The simple truth was that a man who ranked in the top ten on the *Forbes* list made news just by existing. And when that man was a bachelor inevitably described as "eligible," meaning he had not yet been snared by some calculating female who wanted his name, his status and his money…

When that happened, a man lost all privacy.

Rio valued his privacy as much as he despised being a topic of conversation.

Not that Rio cared much what people said, whether it was that he was brilliant and tough. Or brilliant and heartless. He was who he was, and all that mattered was his adherence to his own code of ethics.

He believed in honesty, determination, intensity of focus, logic—and emotional control. Emotional control was everything.

Still, on this hot August afternoon, cicadas droning in the fields behind him, the hiss of the surf beating against the shore, he was ready to admit that logic and control were fast slipping from his grasp.

He was, to put it bluntly, angry as hell.

In Manhattan, when a business deal drove him to the point of rage, he headed for his gym and the ring in its center for a couple of rounds with a sparring partner, but he wasn't in New York. He was as far east of the city as a man could get without putting his feet in the Atlantic.

He was in the town of Southampton, on Long Island's exclusive South Shore. He was here in search of that increasingly elusive thing called privacy and, goddamnit, he was not going to let some fool named Izzy Orsini spoil the day for him.

For the past hour, Rio had taken his temper out on a shovel.

If any of his business associates could have seen him now, they'd have been stunned. Rio D'Aquila, dressed in jeans, a T-shirt and work boots? Rio D'Aquila, standing in a trench and shoveling dirt?

Impossible.

But Rio had dug ditches before, not that anyone in his world knew it. And though he sure as hell hadn't expected to be doing any digging today, it was better than standing around and getting more ticked off by the minute.

Especially when, until a couple of hours ago, he'd had a damned good day.

He'd flown in early, piloting his own plane to the small airport at Easthampton where he'd picked up the black Chevy Silverado his property manager had left for him. Then he'd driven the short distance to Southampton.

The town was small, picturesque and quiet early on a Friday morning. Rio had parked, gone into a small café where he'd had breakfast with the guy who was putting in the infinity pool at the house he'd recently had built. The pool would extend over the dunes from the second floor terrace, and they'd talked about its size and the view he'd have. The conversation had been pleasant, almost as pleasant as being able to sit in a restaurant without being the unwilling center of attention.

That was part of the reason he'd decided to build a week-end home here, on six outrageously expensive acres of land that overlooked the ocean.

For the most part—and there were always exceptions to the rule, of course—nobody bothered celebrities in these small eastern Long Island villages. And Rio, God help him, was a celebrity, according to the crazy media.

Here, he could be himself. Have a meal. Take a walk. It was like an unwritten code. Build here, become, for the most part, invisible.

For a man who sometimes had to travel with a phalanx of bodyguards or with a limo crawling along at the curb so he could duck into it, fast, and be whisked away, it was a minor miracle.

So Rio had enjoyed his bacon and eggs, strolled the streets for a while, even checked the hardware store as if he really were going to need to buy hammers and saws.

In fact, there'd been a time he'd owned such tools and used them to earn his daily bread. A little wistfully, he thought about maybe putting in some shelves in his new house, if he could find a place in it that needed them. He wasn't foolish enough to believe that working with your hands gave you special moral status but there was something to be said about leading a simpler life.

At midmorning, he met with the security specialist who'd installed an ultrasophisticated system in and around the house. They sat at a table on the flagstone patio of a little ice cream shop, the sun blocked by a big blue umbrella.

Rio tried to remember the last time he'd had a strawberry ice cream sundae and couldn't.

He felt…what? Lazy. Content. He almost had to force himself to pay attention to the conversation.

There was a malfunction of the security system at the gate. The intercom wasn't working right. His caretaker had told him voices coming over the intercom were almost indecipherably drowned in static, and the gate's locking mechanism didn't always work.

The area was pleasant, there was nothing but a discreet plaque on the gate that said Eagle's Nest, but Rio wasn't a fool. A man like him needed security.

"Not to worry," the security guy assured him. "I'll come out Monday morning and deal with it, first thing."

At noon, Rio had driven to his house. The long driveway had not yet been finished and the tires bounced along over small stones and deep ruts but nothing could dim the pleasure he already took in the place.

The house was just as he'd wanted it. Light wood. Lots of glass. It would be his retreat from the dog-eat-dog world he inhabited 24/7.

The guy he'd hired as his contractor was waiting. They had some things to discuss, nothing major, and then, together, they'd interview three applicants for the job of landscaping the rear terrace and two decks.

No. Not three applicants. Four. Damned if he didn't keep forgetting that. Rio had some definite ideas about what he wanted. Whomever he hired would have to understand that he'd be an active participant in the plans he drew up, just as he'd been an active participant in the design of the house.

The caretaker was there, too, but just leaving. He told Rio he'd taken the liberty of filling the freezer and fridge with a few things.

"Breakfast stuff. You know, eggs, bacon, bread. And steaks, some local corn and tomatoes, even a couple of bottles of wine. Just in case you decide to spend the night."

Rio thanked him, though he had no plans to spend the night. As it was, he'd canceled a couple of meetings so he could get here but it had turned out to be the only chance for all three landscaping candidates to show up for interviews on the same day.

Four. Four candidates. How come he couldn't keep that in his head?

Probably because he wasn't hot on interviewing that fourth one, he thought, and gave a mental sigh. It was never a good idea to mix friendship and business, but when one of your pals asked you to at least talk to his cousin or uncle, or whatever in hell somebody named Izzy Orsini was to Dante Orsini, well, you bent the rules and did it.

After a few minutes, Rio took a picnic hamper from the Silverado's cab. His housekeeper in Manhattan had packed lunch at his request. It turned out to be an elegant one. Thinly sliced cold roast beef on French baguettes, a chunk of properly aged Vermont cheddar, a bottle of chilled *prosecco,* fresh strawberries and tiny butter pastries.

Plus, of course, linen napkins, stemware and china mugs.

Rio and the contractor grinned at each other. They were both wearing jeans, sitting on a pair of overturned buckets on the unfinished terrace, their meal arranged on a plank laid over a sawhorse.

Cold beer and a couple of ham and cheese on rye might have been more in keeping with things, but the lunch was good and they finished every mouthful.

The landscapers started arriving not long after that. They showed up one at a time, exactly as scheduled, Rio buzzing them in through the gate, which seemed to be working perfectly. They were local men, each efficient and businesslike and politely eager to win what would be a substantial contract.

All of them came equipped with glossy folders filled with

computerized designs, suggested layouts, sketches, photos of prior projects and spreadsheets of mind-numbing detail.

Each listened carefully as Rio explained what they already knew. He wanted the perimeter of the terrace planted in as natural a manner as possible. The decks, as well. Greenery. Shrubs. Flowers, maybe. Or flowering shrubs. Rio was willing to admit what he knew about gardening could fit into a teaspoon with room left over, but he made it clear that he knew the overall effect he was going for.

"What I want," he told each applicant, "is to have the terrace seem to flow out of the fields behind the house. Does that make sense to you?"

Each man nodded earnestly; each roughed out some quick ideas on a sketchpad and though none of the sketches had been exactly what Rio intended, he'd known instantly that he could choose any of the three guys and, ultimately, be satisfied.

Three excellent landscapers.

But, of course, there was a fourth.

The contractor said he understood. A friend of a friend. He knew how that was. The friend of a friend was late but the two men settled in to wait.

And wait.

After a while, Rio frowned.

"The guy should know better than to be late," he said.

The contractor agreed. "Maybe he had a flat. Or something."

"Or something," Rio said.

Another ten minutes went by. Damnit, Rio thought, if only he hadn't gone to that party, he wouldn't be waiting to interview another landscaper at all.

The party had taken place a few weeks ago. Dante Orsini and his wife, Gabriella, had invited some people to their penthouse for a charity bash. Rio had gone with a date, a woman he'd been seeing for a couple of months.

She went off to the powder room.

The "little girls' room" she'd called it, and Dante had rolled his eyes at Rio, put a drink in his hand and led him out to the terrace, where it was quieter and less crowded.

"The little girls' room, huh?"

Rio had grinned. "All good things come to an end," he'd answered, and Dante had grinned, too, because he still remembered his bachelor days.

The friends had touched glasses, drunk some of their bourbon. Then, Dante had cleared his throat.

"So, we hear you're building a place in the Hamptons."

Rio had nodded. Word got around. Nothing new to that. New York was a big city but people like he and Dante moved in relatively small circles.

"Southampton," he'd said. "I visited a friend there one weekend last summer. Lucas Viera. You know him? Anyway, Viera has a house on the beach. Very private, very quiet. I liked what I saw, and now—"

"And now," Gabriella Orsini had said, smiling as she joined the men and slipped her arm through her husband's, "you need a landscaper." Her smile broadened. "You do, don't you?"

Rio had shrugged. "Well, sure, but—"

"We just happen to know a very good one."

To Rio's amazement, Dante had blushed.

"Izzy," Gabriella had said. She'd nodded toward the lush plantings along the borders of the terrace. "That's Izzy's work. Spectacular, don't you think?"

Rio had looked at the plantings. Not spectacular, but nice. Natural-looking, which could not have been easy to accomplish when the setting was a three-level penthouse in the sky.

"Uh," Dante had said, "see, Izzy is sort of trying to branch out, and—"

"And," Gabriella had said sweetly, "we're not above a bit of nepotism. Are we, darling?"

The penny had finally dropped.

His friend, actually, his friend's wife, was hustling the work of one of her husband's relatives. A cousin, maybe an uncle, because there were only four Orsini brothers. Rio had met them all and not one was named Izzy.

Whatever, it didn't matter.

The terrace plantings had looked good. And, what the hell, Rio liked Dante and Gabriella, who happened to have been born in Brazil, his adopted country. So when it came time to deal with the landscaping, Rio gave Izzy Orsini's name and email address to his contractor, who'd made the contact and set up the time and date of the meeting.

A meeting for which Izzy Orsini had not showed.

Time had passed, with the contractor trying hard not to look at his watch until, finally, Rio had thought, *basta*. Enough. He'd told the contractor he was free to leave.

"I'm sure you have better things to do than wait around for some guy who's going to be a no-show."

"You sure, Mr. D'Aquila? 'Cause if you want, I can—"

"It's Rio, remember? And it's not a problem. I'll hang around for a while, just in case."

Which, Rio thought grimly as he dug the shovel into the soil in the trench, brought things straight to the present.

To two bloody hours, waiting for Izzy Orsini to put in an appearance.

"Merda," he muttered, and stabbed the shovel blade into the earth again.

His temper was rising in inverse proportion to the depth of the trench which would ultimately be the foundation for a low stone wall but at the rate he was going, he was liable to dig his way to China.

He'd run out of excuses for Dante's cousin.

Rio leaned on the shovel handle, wiped sweat from his eyes with a tightly muscled forearm.

Maybe Orsini got the time wrong. Maybe he'd had a flat. Maybe his great-aunt had come down with an attack of ague, or whatever it was great-aunts came down with, assuming he had a great-aunt at all.

Any of those things could have been explained by a phone call, but Orsini had not called.

Rio's lips thinned.

Okay. He'd wasted enough time on this. It would be sticky, telling Dante and Gabriella what had happened, but he'd had it.

A shadow passed overhead. Rio looked up, tilted his head back, watched a squadron of pelicans soar overhead, aiming for the ocean. The cool, refreshing ocean.

That did it.

He yanked the shovel free of the soil and put it back where he'd found it.

He'd bought this place as somewhere he could relax. Well, he damned well wasn't relaxing now. Thinking about an idiot who'd let a chance at a job like this slip through his fingers made his blood boil.

Back when he was just starting out, he'd never have let something so important get away. He'd have walked, crawled, done whatever it took to snag even a chance at a job that would pay well and could lead to something even better.

No wonder Gabriella was hustling this Orsini jerk. The fool couldn't do anything on his own.

Rio stretched and rotated his shoulders. His muscles ached. He'd skinned a couple of knuckles and there was dirt under his usually well-manicured fingernails.

The truth was, he'd enjoyed a couple of hours of work. Real work, physical work just as he enjoyed being in the ring at his gym. But enough was enough.

Sweat dripped off the end of his nose. He yanked his T-shirt over his head and used it to mop his face.

The sun was starting to drop lower in the sky. The day was coming to an end. He hated to leave. The city would be hot and noisy...

Rio made a quick decision.

He'd take that swim. Then, instead of flying back to Manhattan, he'd spend the night here. Hell, why not? Most of the furniture he'd ordered was in. Thanks to his property manager, he had steaks, fresh corn, even wine. The more he thought about it, the better it—

Bzzzz.

What the hell was that? A bee? A wasp? No. It was the intercom at the gate.

He wasn't expecting anyone...

Bzzzz. Bzzzz. Bzzzz.

Orsini. It had to be. The fool had shown up after all, except he was three hours late.

Rio almost laughed. The guy had *cojones,* he had to give him that, but that was all he had. No way was he going to buzz him in. The business of the day was over. This was his own time. His quiet time. His—

Bzzzz. Bzzzz. Bzzzz. Bzzzz.

Rio folded his arms. Stood his ground.

The damned thing buzzed again.

Cristo! What would it take to get rid of the guy?

More buzzing. Rio narrowed his eyes, marched to the intercom and depressed the button.

"What?" he snarled.

A blast of static roared from the speaker.

Rio cursed, slapped the button. No good. Orsini had to be leaning on the button at his end, or maybe the freaking thing wasn't working again. Nothing but static was coming through.

Bzzzz. Bzzzz. Bzzzz. Bzzzz.

His jaw tightened. If Orsini wanted in, then "in" and a lesson on courtesy and punctuality was what he'd get. And he was in the mood to give it to him.

Rio balled up his T-shirt and tossed it aside, yanked open the glass French doors that led into the great room, marched through the house to the entry foyer, his work boots leaving muddy prints on the Carrara marble floors.

"Damnit," he roared, as he flung open the front door—

And stopped.

A figure was coming toward him, hurrying up the long, unfinished driveway. Trying to hurry, at any rate, but how fast could a person go on that uneven, pitted, rocky surface in—in—

Were those stiletto heels?

His visitor was not Izzy Orsini.

It was a woman.

Damn the malfunctioning intercom and gate!

He'd been this route one time before. A woman had decided he was her true love. He'd never talked to her, never heard her name, never seen her in his life but he'd turned out to be a fixture in her mental landscape. She'd sent him letters. Emails. She'd sent him gifts and cards. She'd stalked him without letup, settled in on the corner near his Manhattan condo, which was when he'd finally, if reluctantly, pressed charges.

Was this her again?

No. His stalker had been fiftyish, short and rotund. This woman was young. Mid-twenties. Tall and slender, and dressed as if she were on her way to a board meeting: the stilettos, a white blouse showing under the suit jacket, dark hair pulled severely back from her face. She didn't look like a crazy stalker or like a nosy reporter, though in Rio's book, the two could easily be one and the same, but who gave a damn?

She had no business here and that was all that mattered.

"Hold it right there," Rio barked, but his command didn't stop her and he trotted down the steps, eyes narrowed. "I said—"

"Mr. D'Aquila expects me."

Not a reporter or a crazy, at least not one looking for him if she didn't recognize him, even shirtless, in jeans and work boots, but clearly a liar with an agenda all her own.

Rio gave a thin smile.

"I assure you, madam, that would be news to him."

There were only a couple of feet between them now. Close up, he could see that there was a rip in her skirt, dirt on those stiletto heels and a smudge on her blouse. Her hair wasn't quite as neatly drawn back as he'd at first thought; tendrils of it, dark and curling, were coming loose around her face.

It was an interesting face. Triangular. High cheekbones. Big green eyes. Feline, he thought.

Not that it mattered, but if she'd been in some kind of accident he supposed he could, at least, offer to—

"It is your attitude that would be news to him," Isabella Orsini said, hoping her voice would not tremble because everything inside her was bouncing around like an unset bowl of gelatin and after all she'd gone through today, there wasn't a way in hell she was going to permit this half-naked, good-looking-if-you-were-foolish-enough-to-like-the-type flunky of a too rich, too powerful, too full-of-himself ape to stop her now.

There was a moment's silence. Then Mr. Half-Naked raised one dark eyebrow.

"Really."

His tone was soft but it made Izzy's heart thump. To hell with thumping hearts, she thought, and lifted her chin.

"Really," she said, with all the hauteur she could muster.

Mr. Half-Naked gave another of those thin smiles and motioned toward the door.

"In that case," he said, in a voice that was almost a purr, "you had better come in."

CHAPTER TWO

A NAKED man.

A house in the middle of nowhere.

An open door, and an invitation to step through it.

Izzy swallowed hard.

Did she truly want to do that? She was not into taking risks. Everyone knew that about her, even her father, who didn't actually know anything about any of his children.

I have heard that you are considering taking on a new client, Isabella, Cesare Orsini had said during one of the inevitable Sunday command performance dinners at the Orsini mansion. *But you will not.*

"Excuse me?" Izzy had said.

Her father had given her what she'd always thought of as one of his "I am the head of this family" glares except, of course, his glares as *don* of the East Coast's most powerful *famiglia* had more impact on those who feared him than they did on his sons and daughters.

To them, he was not the head of anything. He was just a shame to be borne for the sake of their mother.

"Do I not speak English as well as you? I said, you are not to work for Rio D'Aquila."

"And you say this because...?"

"I know of him and I do not like what I know. Therefore,

accepting a position that will make you his servant is out of the question."

Isabella would have laughed had her father's view of what she did for a living not been such an old argument.

"I am not a servant, Father, I am a horticulturist with a degree from the University of Connecticut."

"You are a gardener."

"I certainly am. And what if I were what you call a servant? There's nothing dishonorable in being a maid or a cook."

"Orsinis do not bow their heads or bend their knees to anyone, Isabella. Is that clear?"

Nothing had been clear, starting with how her father had learned she'd been invited to bid on a job for a billionaire she'd never even heard of until a couple of weeks ago, going straight through to how Cesare could have imagined she would take orders from him.

If anything, his certainty that she would click her heels and obey him was what had convinced her to give serious consideration to the offer, something she really had not intended until then.

Now here she was, in Southampton, a place that might as well have been Mars for all she knew about it, hours late for an important interview, her car in a ditch, her suit and her shoes absolute disasters.

No. She was not going to think about that now. It would be self-defeating...and hadn't she had enough of that?

It was enough to wonder at the crazed logic of moving past an all-but-naked man, a gorgeous all-but-naked man, to step inside a house that was, conservatively speaking, the size of an airplane hangar.

"Well? Are you coming inside, or have you changed your mind about Mr. D'Aquila expecting you?"

Izzy blinked. The caretaker, or whatever he was, was

watching her with amusement. Forget amusement. That expression on his face was a smirk.

How lovely to be the day's entertainment, Isabella thought, and drew herself to her full five foot seven.

"I am not in the habit of changing my mind about anything," she said, and almost winced.

Such a stupid thing to say.

Too late.

She'd said it and now her feet, which seemingly had only a tenuous connection to her brain, propelled her past him, up a set of wide steps, through a massive door and into the house. She jumped as the door slammed shut behind her.

She wanted to think it was with the sound of doom but the truth was, it was the sound of a door slamming, nothing more, nothing less...

And ohmygod, the entry foyer was so big! It was huge!

"Yes. It is, isn't it?"

She spun around. Mr. Half-Naked was standing right in back of her, arms folded across his chest. A very impressive chest, all muscle and golden skin and dark curls.

Her gaze skimmed lower.

A six-pack, she thought, sucking in her breath. Those bands of muscle really did exist, neatly bisected by silky-looking hair that arrowed down and down and...

"The foyer," he said, his voice not just amused but smoky. Her gaze flew to his. "You were thinking it was big. Huge, in fact." A smile tilted the corner of his lips. "That was what you were referring to, wasn't it?"

She felt her face heat. Had she spoken aloud? She must have, but she'd certainly never meant to infer...

Isabella narrowed her eyes. Damn the man!

He was playing games at her expense.

Still, she could hardly blame him.

He might be only half-dressed but she—

She was a mess.

Everything she had on was stained, torn or smudged. A few hours ago, she'd looked perfect. Well, as perfect as she could ever look. She'd taken more time preparing for this meeting than she'd ever prepared for anything in her life.

Actually, she hadn't done a thing.

Anna had done it all.

A suit instead of her usual jeans. A wool suit, hot as blazes on a day like this but, Anna had said, The Proper Thing for such an important interview. A silk blouse instead of a T-shirt. Shoes rather than sandals, and with heels so ridiculously high she could hardly walk in them, especially the million miles she'd had to plod after that rabbit had somehow materialized in the middle of the road and her car had taken a nosedive into that miserable ditch.

All of it was Anna's, of course. The suit, the blouse, the shoes.

The car.

Oh, God, the car!

Forget that for now.

She had to concentrate on what lay ahead, the all-important chance to transform Growing Wild from a shoe-box operation in a cheap storefront on what was most definitely not a trendy street near the Gowanus Canal to an elegant shop—an elegant *shoppe,* Anna had joked—in SoHo. Or in the Village. Or on the Upper East Side.

No.

She'd never go that far.

The truth was, she liked the neighborhood she was in, seedy as it was, but she had to admit the growth of her little landscaping business was dependent on location and on landing a couple of really important clients. Aside from the admitted pleasure of defying her father, that was why she'd

agreed to the interview with Rio D'Aquila, a man the papers
called a removed, cold, heartless multibillionaire.

Heaven knew she was familiar enough with the type.

Izzy's work was skilled and imaginative; she used only the
most beautiful flowers and greenery. That made her services
costly. It made them the province of the very rich.

And dealing with them was sometimes unpleasant. It was
sometimes downright horrible. The very rich could be totally
self-serving, completely selfish, uncaring of others…

"They're not all like that," Anna had said.

Well, no. Her brothers were very rich. So was Anna's husband. But—

"But," Anna had said, with incontrovertible logic, "if
you're going to have to like a person before you take him as
a client, Isabella, you're never going to make Growing Wild
a success."

True enough. And when you coupled that simple wisdom
with the fact that the offer was important enough for Anna
to refer to her as Isabella…

Well, that had convinced her.

Unfortunately, Izzy was here, not Anna.

Sophisticated Anna would have known how to handle the
situation. She would not have gotten lost or crashed the car.
She certainly would not have turned up hours late for this
appointment.

And she absolutely would not have let a man like this
intimidate her. She'd have known how to handle the half-
dressed muscleman who was having such fun at her expense.

That smirk was still on his face.

It infuriated her. After the day she'd had, Izzy was in no
mood to be laughed at, certainly not by him.

She knew his type.

Good-looking. Glib-tongued. Full of himself, especially
when it came to women, because women, the silly fools, un-

doubtedly threw themselves at his feet with all the grace of—
of salmon throwing themselves upstream.

Okay, a bad metaphor. The point was, she was not a woman
to be intimidated by an empty-headed stud. She was a self-
sufficient businesswoman, never mind that she wasn't self-
sufficient enough to be wearing her own clothes or driving
her own car.

All that mattered was that she was here. And time was
wasting. The sun would set soon, and then what?

Then what, indeed?

The caretaker was leaning against a table, hands tucked
into the back pockets of his jeans. She had a choice of views.
His incredible face. His incredible chest. The tight fit of those
faded jeans—

Stop it, she told herself sternly, and set her gaze squarely
on his chin.

"Look," she said, "I really don't have time for this."

"For what?"

Was the man dense?

"Where is your boss?"

That won her a shrug. "He's around."

The answer, the lazy lift of those shoulders, those amazingly broad shoulders, infuriated her. All that macho. That
attitude. That testosterone.

That naked chest.

Damnit, she was back to that and it was his fault. She'd
have bet it was deliberate.

Izzy narrowed her eyes.

"Do you think you could possibly muster up enough am-
bition to find him and tell him I'm here?"

Mr. Half-Naked didn't move. Not a muscle. Well, that
wasn't true. He did move a muscle; one corner of his mouth
lifted, either in question or in another bout of hilarity at her
expense.

Could you actually feel your blood pressure rising?

"One problem," he said lazily. "I'm still waiting for you to tell me why you're here."

The simplest thing would be to do exactly that. Just say, *I'm here to meet with Mr. D'Aquila and talk about landscaping this property.*

It was certainly not a secret.

The problem was, she didn't like Mr. All Brawn and No Brains's attitude.

Okay. That wasn't fair.

Just because he looked like he'd stepped off one of those calendars her roommate used to drool over in her college-dorm days didn't mean he was stupid.

It only meant he was so beautiful that looking at him made her heart do a little two-step, and that was surely ridiculous, almost as ridiculous as this silly power game they were playing.

Who cared if it was silly? She was entitled to win at something today!

"What are you?" she said sarcastically. "His appointment secretary?"

One dark eyebrow rose again. "Maybe I'm his butler."

She stared at him for a long minute. Then she laughed.

Rio grinned.

He was really getting to her. Good. Fine. It was a lot more rewarding to take his pent-up irritation out on the woman, whoever she was, than on a trench.

"His butler, huh?" Her chin went up. "One thing's for sure, mister. I guarantee you're going to be looking for another job two minutes after I meet your employer."

Rio folded his arms over his chest.

The lady was losing her temper. Let her lose it. Let her get ticked off. Let her see how it felt to be frustrated enough to want Izzy Orsini to finally show up if only so that he could deck the jerk. If that was unfair—

Hey, life was unfair. Besides, the lady wasn't exactly behaving like a lady.

Well, yeah, she was.

Her clothes were a mess, but they were expensive.

So was her attitude.

He was the peasant, she was the princess. Only one problem in that little scenario.

The princess had no idea he held all the cards.

Well, not quite all. He still didn't know what had brought her here. The only certainty was that her presence could not possibly have anything to do with him.

Maybe she sold magazines door to door.

Maybe Southampton had designated her its Fruitcake of the Month.

Whoever she was, whatever she was, she was a welcome diversion. This little farce was fast becoming the best part of his long and irritating afternoon.

She was also very easy on the eyes, now that he'd had the chance to get a longer look at her.

The made-for-midwinter suit was rumpled, torn and a little dirty, but he was pretty sure it hid a made-for-midsummer-bikini body. Wool or no wool, he could make out the thrust of high breasts, the indentation of a feminine waist, the curve of rounded hips.

Rio frowned.

What the hell had put that into his head?

She was a woman, and women were not on his current agenda. He'd just ended an affair—women called them "relationships" but men knew better—and, as always, getting out of it had been a lot more difficult than getting in. Women were creatures of baffling complexity and despite what they all said, they inevitably ended up wanting something he could not, would not, give.

Commitment. Marriage.

Chains.

Rio moved fast. He intended to keep moving fast, to climb to the absolute top of every mountain that caught his interest. Why be handicapped by things he didn't want or need? Why anchor himself to one woman and inevitably tire of her?

He had to admit, though, some women were more intriguing than others.

This one, for instance.

She was tough. Or brave. Maybe that was the better word for her.

Standing up to him took courage at the best of times. Right now, looking as he did, half-naked, unkempt, hell, downright scruffy—he hadn't even shaved this morning, now that he thought about it—took *colhões*. Or *cojones*. The point was the same, in Portuguese or in Italian. Facing him down took courage. No, he didn't look like Jack the Ripper but he sure as hell didn't look like he'd stepped out of *GQ*, which was surely the kind of guy she normally dealt with.

This was, after all, the weekend haunt of the rich and famous. The I-Want-to-Be-Alone rich and famous, but that didn't change the fact that he wasn't usually the kind of guy who met you at the front door.

Given all that, he supposed you could call her foolish instead of brave. A woman who went toe-to-toe with a stranger, who walked into a house with a man she'd never seen before…

Foolish, sure.

But determined. Gutsy.

It was clear she wasn't going to give ground until she met Rio D'Aquila.

A gentleman would have made it easy. *I'm Rio D'Aquila,* a gentleman would have said, right up-front, or if he'd let things go on for a while, he'd smile at her now, apologize for any confusion and introduce himself.

A muscle flickered in Rio's jaw.

Yes, but he had not always been a gentleman. And right now, suddenly turning into one held no appeal.

The truth was, as soon as Rio D'Aquila appeared, all this would stop.

The bantering. The courage. Probably even the little blushes she tried to conceal each time she reminded herself that he wasn't wearing a shirt.

He liked it. All of it. He couldn't remember the last time he'd seen a woman blush, or the last time one had stood up to him.

It had been at least a decade on both counts, right around the time he'd made his first million.

The truth was, he was enjoying himself, playing at being someone he had once been. A man, not a name or a corporation or, even worse, a line in a gossip column.

Hell, there was nothing wrong with the game he was playing. It was just an extension of what had prompted him to buy the land and put up a house here in the first place.

He was being himself.

Rio frowned. And faced facts, because all that entire bit of justification was pure, unadulterated crap.

This was not who he was.

He didn't dig ditches. He didn't walk around half-dressed unless he was alone or unless he'd just been to bed with a woman, and what did that have to do with anything happening right now?

The point was, he was honest with people. Even with women, and that was occasionally difficult. No matter the situation, he never played games at a woman's expense.

It was just that this particular woman was a puzzle, and he had always liked puzzles.

Why was she dressed for winter when it was summer? Why was there a rip in her skirt, dirt on those come-and-get-me stilettos, a smudge on her blouse?

Now that he took a better look, there was a streak of dirt on her cheek, too.

It was an elegant cheek. Highly arched. Rose hued. And, he was certain, silken to the touch.

Her hair looked as if it would feel that way, too. It was dark. Lustrous. She'd yanked it back, secured it at the nape of her neck, but it refused to stay confined.

Tendrils were coming loose.

One in particular lay against her temple, daring him to reach for it, let it curl around his finger, see if it felt as soft as it looked.

She had great eyes. A nice nose. And she had a lovely mouth.

Pink. Generous but not, he was sure, pumped full of whatever horror it was that turned women into fish-lipped monstrosities.

One thing was certain.

Despite the classic suit, the demure blouse, the pulled back hair, that mouth was made for sin.

For sin, Rio thought, and felt his body stir.

Hell.

He swung away from her, irritated with himself for his unexpected reaction, with her for causing it. She was on his turf and she had no right to be there.

For a man who liked puzzles, the only one that needed solving was figuring out why he hadn't ended this charade before it began.

Truth time, Rio thought, and he unfolded his arms and took a long breath.

"Okay," he said, "enough."

His unwanted guest turned paper-white. *Cristo,* he thought, and cursed himself for being a fool.

"No," he said quickly, "I didn't mean…" He forced a smile. "There's nothing to be afraid of."

"I'm not afraid," she said, but, damnit, her voice was shaking.

"You don't understand." He went toward her, held out his hand. She stared at it. He did, too, saw the redness of his knuckles, the dirt on his skin and under his nails, drew his hand back and wiped it on his jeans. "I shouldn't have made things so difficult. You don't want to tell me who you are until you're positive Rio D'Aquila is here, that's fine."

"It doesn't matter," she said quickly. "I'll just—I'll just phone Mr. D'Aquila from the city—"

"Is that where you're from? New York?"

"Yes—but really, you don't have to—"

"Obviously," he said, trying to lighten things, "I'm not the butler."

He waited. After a few seconds, she gave him a hesitant smile.

"No," she said, "I didn't think you were,"

Okay. It was time. He had the feeling she was going to be furious at his subterfuge but it wouldn't matter.

He'd identify himself as the man she'd come to see, she'd tell him why she was here—something to do with town records, he'd bet, because it suddenly occurred to him that there'd been some sort of paper his lawyer had said he had to sign.

Whatever, they'd introduce themselves, he'd scribble his signature on the document she produced, and that would be the end of it.

"So," Rio said, "let's start from scratch."

He extended his hand again. She looked at it, at him, and then she put her hand in his. It was a small, feminine hand;

his all but swallowed it and yet, he could feel calluses on her fingers, which surprised him.

The coolness of her skin surprised him, too. It was a warm day. Was she still nervous about him? It was definitely time to identify himself and set her concerns at ease.

"Hello," he said, and smiled. "I'm—"

"The handyman."

He almost laughed. "Well, no. Not exact—"

"The caretaker. Sorry." She swiped the tip of her tongue over her lips, leaving them pink and delicately moist. "Nice to meet you"

"Yes." He dragged his gaze from her mouth. "And you are…?"

"Oh. Sorry. I'm the landscaper."

Maybe he hadn't heard her right. "Excuse me?"

"Well, not *the* landscaper. I'm an applicant." She looked around, then lowered her voice. "I'm late. Terribly late, but—"

"But?" he said carefully.

"But still, where's your boss? He was expecting me. You know, Isabella Orsini. From Growing Wild?"

"You?" Rio heard his voice rise. Hell, why not? He could feel his eyebrows shooting for his hairline. "You're Izzy Orsini?"

"That's me." She gave a nervous laugh. "And I hope this Rio D'Aquila isn't, you know, what I heard he was."

"What you heard he was?" he said, and wondered when in hell he'd turned into a parrot.

"Cold. Ruthless. Bad-tempered."

Rio cleared his throat. "Well, I suppose some people might say he was simply a—"

"An arrogant tyrant. But you don't have to like someone to work for them, right? I mean, here you are, Mister—Mister—"

Rio didn't even hesitate.

"My name is Matteo," he said. "Matteo Rossi. And you have it right. I'm D'Aquila's caretaker."

CHAPTER THREE

MATTEO Rossi still had Izzy's hand trapped in his.

Well, no. Not trapped. Not exactly.

Just clasped, that was all. The pressure of his fingers over hers wasn't hard or unpleasant or threatening, it was simply— it was simply—

Masculine. Totally, completely, unquestionably masculine.

Everything about him was masculine, from the drop-dead-gorgeous face to the King-of-the-Centerfolds body, but then a man who did manual labor on an estate of this size wouldn't have to work up a sweat in a gym.

He was the real thing.

That was why those muscles in his shoulders, his biceps, his chest were so—so well-defined.

Isabella's mouth went dry.

Her interest, of course, was purely clinical. After all, she did manual labor, too. Planting, weeding, all those things, even when done on Manhattan terraces rather than Southampton estates, made for sweat and muscles. Combine that with what she recalled of college physiology and she could easily con-jure up a mental image of him working, sweating…

Except, the images flashing through her head didn't have a damned thing to do with work. Not work done in a garden, anyway.

Actually, not anything a normal, healthy woman would call "work."

Or so she'd heard.

God, what was wrong with her? He was sweaty and good-looking. So what? Neither of those things had anything to do with sexual attraction…

Liar, she thought, and she pulled her hand free of his.

"For heaven's sake," she snapped, "don't you own a shirt?"

There was a moment of horrified silence. *No,* she thought, *please no, tell me I didn't say that…*

The caretaker made a choked sound. She jerked her head up, looked at him and, oh, Lord, he was trying not to laugh but his eyes met hers and a guffaw broke from his lips.

Isabella wanted to die. How could she have said such a thing?

Unfortunately, she knew the answer.

When it came to men, good-looking men, there were two Isabellas.

She met handsome men a lot. Her work took her into their homes; she accepted invitations to parties, even though she hated parties where you stood around nibbling on awful little canapés and gagging down overly sweet drinks with umbrellas stuck in them, because networking was the best way to find new clients.

Plus her brothers, gorgeous guys themselves, had recently taken to trying to find, with what they surely thought was subtlety, The Right Man for her.

"Hey," Dante or Rafe, Falco or Nick would say in the falsely cheerful giveaway tone she'd learned to recognize, "how about coming over for supper Friday evening?" Or Sunday brunch, or whatever was the latest excuse for introducing her to the latest candidate in the Orsini Brothers' "Let's Find a Guy for Izzy" plan.

To Isabella's chagrin, even Anna was getting into it, asking her to stop by and, surprise, surprise, a friend of Anna's handsome husband would just happen to stop by, too.

Hadn't any of them figured it out yet?

Put an attractive man in front of her and she either became tongue-tied or just the opposite, a woman whose mouth ran a hundred times faster than her brain.

Hi, a guy would say.

Her response? Silence, and a deer-in-the headlights stare.

Or she'd babble. He'd end up the bewildered recipient of whatever came into her head. *Did you know that shrimp you're tucking into probably came from an uninspected shrimp farm in some godforsaken place in the Far East?* Or, *How do you feel about the destruction of wetlands?*

The result, either way?

Disaster.

It had been the pattern of her life, ever since she'd first noticed that boys were not girls.

The thing was, she wasn't pretty, or clever, or the kind of woman men lusted after. Not that she wanted to be lusted after...

Okay.

A little lust would be nice.

Anna was the pretty one.

She was a great sister and Izzy adored her, but she had long ago faced facts.

Anna was the Orsini sister boys had always noticed.

She was the one with the blond hair, the one who knew, instinctively, what to say and what to wear, who knew how to charm and flirt and turn the most gorgeous guys to putty.

Izzy had long ago accepted the fact that she didn't have those attributes, and she could live with that. What she couldn't live with was turning into a jerk each and every time she found a man attractive.

Speechless or babbling. Those were her choices.

Today's winner was Izzy the Babbler.

She'd already said more to this guy than she should have about his employer. For all she knew, Mr. Heartbreaker might think Rio D'Aquila walked on water.

And now, this—this outburst about him not wearing a shirt...

She swallowed drily and risked a glance at him.

He'd stopped laughing. More or less. Actually, she was pretty sure he was choking back another guffaw.

"I'm sorry," she said miserably. "Honestly, I didn't mean—"

"No, you're right." He cleared his throat, rearranged his face until he looked as if he were the one who should do the apologizing. "I was working out back, see, and then I heard the security buzzer go off, and—"

"Really, you don't owe me an explanation. I don't know what I was thinking."

"It's the heat. It makes it hard to think straight."

He flashed a smile that sent her pulse into overdrive. Had she ever seen blue eyes so dark, lashes so long? A woman could hate a man for having lashes like those.

"And you proved it."

Isabella blinked. "Proved what?"

"That it's too hot to think straight. So here's what I suggest. Instead of standing in the foyer, why don't we head for the kitchen? On the way, I'll take a quick detour, grab a clean shirt, and then I'll get us a couple of cold drinks, and—"

"Really, that's not necessary," she said quickly. "You go on. I mean, get yourself something cold. And a shirt." She blushed. "I mean—I mean, I'll just wait here while you tell Mr. D'Aquila that I'm..." Her eyebrows rose, even as her heart sank. "What?"

"I'm afraid I can't do that."

"Can't do what?"

"I can't pass on your message." He paused. "Mr. D'Aquila isn't here."

"He isn't?"

"No," Rio said, and Isabella Orsini's face fell.

Well, so what?

He'd been cooling his heels for hours, waiting for her to turn up. Now she was upset that the man she'd come to see wasn't available.

Tough.

He wasn't in the mood to conduct an interview now. Besides, only a fool would contract with a workman—a workwoman—*Cristo,* maybe the sun really was getting to him. The point was, even if she had the necessary credentials— and it was an excellent bet that she didn't—he would never deal with a contractor who could not adhere to a schedule.

"He left about an hour ago," he said, and watched as she sank what looked like perfect white teeth into the soft fullness of her bottom lip.

Rio's gut tightened.

And that was a second excellent reason for not even considering hiring her.

The last thing he needed was to be attracted to a woman who worked for him, although what there was for him to be attracted to was beyond him to comprehend. There were things to like about her he had to admit. She spoke her mind. Those comments about his boss...

Well, no.

Not about his boss. About him. About the powerful, king-of-the-mountain Rio D'Aquila.

And then there was the shirt thing.

He couldn't think of a woman he'd ever known who'd have been embarrassed by his standing around without a shirt. And she had, indeed, been embarrassed. Stripes of crimson had risen along her sculpted cheeks.

Not that her cheeks, sculpted or otherwise, mattered.

She had a forlorn expression on her face now. Her mouth had taken a downward curve.

That made-for-sin mouth.

That silken-looking mouth.

What would she do if he bent his head and put his lips on hers? If he tasted that rosy-pink softness? If he tasted her.

Rio's anatomy responded with alarming speed. He swung away from her, feigned bending to pluck a bit of nonexistent dirt from the gleaming marble floor.

The sun had, indeed, fried his brain.

Why else react to her? She was not his type at all. He'd already admitted that once you got past the shapeless suit and pulled back hair she was pretty, he had to give her that, but a pretty face was not enough.

He liked his women sophisticated. Urbane. Sure of themselves. He liked them in silk and satin. He liked them capable of keeping up a conversation, okay, not about anything weighty but a conversation, nevertheless.

Isabella Orsini flunked all those categories. Plus, she'd wasted his afternoon and was well on the way to wasting his evening—but he wasn't going to let that happen.

He wanted a shower and a cold beer, not necessarily in that order. Then he'd head for Easthampton, fly back to the city and never mind staying overnight here or wanting a break in the endless routine of dinner—theater—clubbing. He'd phone a woman, maybe the blonde he'd met last week at that charity thing, ask her if she was busy tonight even though he knew damned well she wouldn't be, women never were when it came to interrupting their lives to accommodate him.

As for the lie he'd told Isabella Orsini about himself—it had been childish nonsense. Why had he done it? To get even with her? Whatever, it had been stupid.

Enough, Rio thought, and he turned and looked straight at her.

The woebegone look had been replaced by one of cool determination. Now what? he thought, and decided to not wait for the answer but, instead, to go straight to the truth.

"Ms. Orsini—"

"Izzy."

"Ms. Orsini," he said, with cool deliberation, "I haven't been entirely straightforward with you." An understatement, but what the hell? "What I said about Rio D'Aquila—"

"I know. You already said he isn't here."

"Right. But—"

"When will he be back?"

Aha. That explained the determined expression on her face. She was going to settle in and wait. Well, that wasn't about to happen.

"I'm going to level with you, Ms. Orsini."

"Izzy."

"Izzy. The truth is—"

"He's not coming back."

"No. Well, that isn't exactly what I—"

"He gave up waiting. And I can't blame him."

Her voice had fallen to a husky whisper. Damnit, was she going to cry? He couldn't stand it when women cried. It was always a maneuver to try and get their own way and he was impervious to that time-worn trick.

"I can't blame him at all."

Dio, better tears than this low, sad tone.

"Look, Ms. Orsini. I mean, Isabella—"

"It's Izzy. Nobody ever calls me 'Isabella.'"

Impossible. She wasn't an "Izzy." "Isabella" suited her better. Maybe she wasn't beautiful but she had a sweet voice, a pretty-enough face…

Rio acted on instinct. He reached out, cupped her chin, raised her face to his.

"Hey," he said, and suddenly he knew he'd been all wrong, thinking her pretty.

She wasn't. She wasn't even beautiful.

She was something more.

How had he missed it? Had he been put off by the game? By his own anger? By her silly outfit?

For the first time, he saw her as she was. The thick, dark lashes. The high cheekbones. That lush mouth. A nose that wasn't perfect; it had a tiny bump in the middle and, somehow, that made it perfect for her.

And, *Cristo,* her eyes.

Green. No, blue. Or brown. Or gold. The truth was, they were an amalgam of colors, and suddenly he was eight years old again, a half-starved kid pawing through a Dumpster behind a restaurant, coming across a chunk of strangely shaped glass.

He'd almost tossed it away. He'd had no need for useless things then. He still didn't, all these years later.

But a ray of sun had hit the glass and the prism—he'd later learned that that was what it was—had flamed to life. The sheer brilliance of the colors had stolen his breath.

The same thing happened now.

Rio looked into Isabella Orsini's eyes and what he saw made his heartbeat stumble.

He wanted to kiss her.

Hell, he was going to kiss her.

He was going to do something incredibly stupid and illogical and he was not a man who did things that were either stupid or illogical and, damnit, yes, he thought, dropping his hand to his side and taking a step back, he'd had too much sun.

"What you need to know," he said briskly, "is that Rio D'Aquila and I are—"

"Trust me. I understand. He got tired of waiting and left you to deliver the message. I lost the job. Well, I never had the job but I lost my chance at it, right?"

"Right," Rio said, "except—"

"I can't blame him. I'm, what, two hours late?"

"Three, but—"

"What happened was that I got a late start. A client phoned. We had lots of rain overnight and I'd just planted pansies on his terrace."

"Pansies," Rio said.

"And the rain soaked them, so I had to head into Manhattan to take a quick look. See, my place is in Brooklyn and the traffic... Anyway, I started a little bit late, and then the traffic on the L.I.E. was a nightmare, even worse than in the city, so—"

"The Long Island Expressway is always crowded," Rio said, and wondered why in hell he was letting this conversation continue. Maybe it was her eyes, the way they were fixed on his.

"I should have known. Anna warned me."

"Anna?"

"So did Joey."

"Joey," he repeated, in the tones of a man trying desperately to hang on to his sanity.

"The boy who does my deliveries." Isabella took a breath. "Then I got to Southampton—and I got lost."

"Surely my—my boss's people sent you directions."

"Well, yes. But I forgot to take them with me. The emergency call about those pansies—and then, of course, I was edgy about this interview."

"Edgy about this interview," Rio echoed. *Dio,* he really was turning into a parrot!

"I kept telling myself that I wasn't excited about it. That's even what I told Dante."

At last, a name he recognized.

"And it's what I told Anna."

So much for names he recognized.

"And then there was this rabbit in the road—"

Rabbits in the road, Rio thought. Had he stumbled into Wonderland?

"But the truth is, I really, really, really would have loved this commission." Isabella—he could not possibly think of her as "Izzy"—flung her arms wide, the gesture taking in everything that had drawn him to this place: the sea, the fields, the dunes, the privacy, the clarity of the sky that was rapidly giving up the day with the onset of dusk. "I thought it was worth going after for the money. Well, and the status of doing a job for a hotshot like Rio D'Aquila. I mean, I'm not much for status, but…"

"No," Rio said with a little smile, "I bet you're not."

"But now that I've seen the house, the setting…" A smile lit her face. "It would have been a wonderful challenge! So beautiful! So big! I'll bet the terrace is enormous, too, and I wouldn't have to think about size constraints, or whether or not rain would drain properly. It would be like—like a painter getting the chance to go from miniatures to—to murals!"

Her face glowed. So did her smile. Neither would win her the job or even an interview. Still—

"Would you like to see the terrace?" he heard himself say.

Her teeth sank into her bottom lip again.

"I shouldn't—"

Rio had started the day wearing a blue chambray shirt over the T he'd discarded. Now, he grabbed it from the table where he'd left it, slipped it on and started walking. A couple of seconds went by. Then he heard the sound of her heels tap-tapping after him.

"Maybe just a peek," she said. "I have the dimensions, of course, your employer's people sent them to me, but to see it, really see it—"

They reached the open terrace doors. Rio motioned her through. She moved past him—and tripped in those ridiculously sexy shoes. His hand shot out automatically; he caught her wrist.

Time stood still.

It was a terrible cliché, but it was precisely what happened.

He heard the catch of her breath. Saw her eyes widen as she looked up at him. The air seemed to shimmer between them.

"It's—it's the shoes," she said unsteadily, "Anna's shoes..."

Anna's shoes, he thought, but mostly he thought, *to hell with it*. He was going to kiss her, just once, and damn the consequences...

Damnit, he thought, and he let go of her, moved past her and stepped outside.

"Here we are," he said briskly.

"Oh," Isabella Orsini whispered, "oh, my."

He swung around. She stood just behind him, hands clasped at her breast.

"Look at the colors," she whispered reverently. "All those endless shades of gold and green and blue."

Rio nodded. "Yeah," he said. "It's—it's nice."

"Nice?" She gave a soft laugh. "It's perfect. I can see Russian olive all around here, and some rhododendron. And azalea, here and here and here."

Her face was as bright as the sun, her smile wide and honest.

"Mistral azalea," she said, and he nodded again as if he knew what she was talking about.

"And some weigela. For the deeper color of the blossoms."

Slowly, speaking the names of plants and trees and

flowers as easily as he'd have dropped the names of cargo ships and stocks, Isabella filled his terrace with plants and trees and flowers made so real by her voice, her words, her smile that he could almost see them.

He couldn't take his eyes from her.

All that eagerness, that joy, that animation…

She reached the area where he'd been digging, didn't hesitate, kicked off those dirt-spattered stilettos and stepped, barefoot, into the rich, dark earth.

Or maybe it was nylon-foot, he thought numbly. Not that it mattered. Whatever you called seeing a beautiful woman in an ugly outfit dig her toes into the soil, it finished him.

Rio was lost.

He took a step toward her. She was still talking, the names of plants and shrubs and God-only-knew what tumbling from that sweet-looking mouth.

"Isabella," he said.

Everything he was thinking was in the way he said her name. He knew she sensed it, too, because she fell silent and swung toward him.

Was she as lost as he?

"Mr. Rossi," she whispered, and the parting of her lips, the breath she took as he reached for her, was all the answer he needed.

"Don't call me that," he said gruffly.

"No," she said, her voice as husky as his, "you're right." They stood an inch apart, her face lifted to his. A little smile curved her lips. "Hello, Matteo."

"Isabella. You don't underst—"

She put a finger against his mouth.

"I don't want to understand," she said, and Rio gave up the battle, gathered Isabella Orsini into his arms, bent his head and kissed her.

CHAPTER FOUR

OHMYGOD, Isabella thought, *ohmygod...*

Matteo's body was hard. His mouth was firm. His arms were like steel bands, holding her to him.

The part of her brain that relied on cool logic said, *Isabella! What on earth are you doing?*

The part that was all female told that other part to shut up.

She had never been kissed like this. Never. She'd never wanted to be kissed like this...

He nipped lightly at her bottom lip. She knew he wanted her to open her mouth. To let him touch his tongue to hers. She'd never done that in her life. Well, once or twice, but never again. She hadn't liked it, the intrusion, the intimacy—

"Isabella," he whispered, "I want to taste you."

The words made her tremble, though not with fear. She felt the tip of his tongue at the seam of her lips and she parted them and let him in.

Her knees almost buckled.

His taste. Oh, his taste. Clean. Indescribable. And so amazingly sexy. How could she have ever thought having a man's tongue in your mouth was anything but glorious? Now he was framing her face with his hands, tunneling his fingers into her hair. The barrette securing it snapped open, and her wild torrent of dark curls tumbled free.

She moaned with pleasure.

How could the feel of his hands in her hair be so exciting?

"Isabella," he said thickly, and he swept one hand down her spine and pulled her tight against him.

The world began to spin.

His hand on her backside. Cupping over her bottom through the awful wool skirt.

Her body, responding to the urgency of his, her hips lifting, moving against him.

And yet, there was more.

"Kiss me back," he said in a voice rough as sandpaper.

Wasn't she doing that? What did he want her to—

"Let your lips cling to mine."

Hesitantly, perhaps a little inexpertly, she did as he'd asked and his groan told her she'd got it right.

The hard press of his sex against her belly was even greater confirmation.

He groaned again.

Both his hands cupped her bottom and he lifted her off her feet, lifted her into him. Breast against breast. Belly against belly. Hips against hips and, God, that male hardness was growing, growing, pressing into her—

A little knot of fear lodged in Isabella's throat. Things were going fast, so fast, too fast.

She tore her mouth from his.

"Matteo," she gasped. "Matteo, wait—"

But Rio was beyond waiting.

Later, he'd realize he'd been beyond thinking. Something about Isabella Orsini had turned sexual desire into sexual compulsion.

He wrapped one arm under her ass, wrapped the other around the nape of her neck, brought her mouth to his again and went on kissing her, blind to everything but the need burning white-hot within him as he strode back into the house.

"No."

At first, he didn't even hear her. But she said the word again, her voice harsh, her fists beating against his shoulders.

Sanity returned. Rio opened his eyes. Looked at the woman in his arms.

His gut clenched.

Her face was white, her eyes dark pools of terror. He'd seen all kinds of expressions on women's faces but never fear of him. *Dio,* what in hell was he doing?

"Put me down," she said in a paper-thin voice.

He drew a deep, deep breath. "Listen," he said, "Isabella—"

"Put me down!"

He nodded. Set her carefully on her feet. She took a quick step back.

"Are you crazy?" she said shakily.

Rio ran a hand through his hair. "I'm sorry."

"Sorry? You're sorry? That's it? You—you attack me and then you say you're sorry?"

A muscle knotted in his jaw.

"I did not attack you."

"No? Then, how would *you* describe what just—what just happened?"

The muscle in his jaw flickered again. He'd have described it as a complete loss of control on his part, but that was impossible.

He never lost control.

"I would describe it as a mistake," he said stiffly. "And I apologize."

Isabella blew a curl from her eyes. Calmer now, she folded her arms, glared at him and told herself she was right, that it had been all his fault.

Of course it had.

The way she'd all but thrown herself into his arms, how

she'd responded to his kisses, the wildness that had torn free within her—none of that had any relation to what he'd done…

"It's late," she said abruptly. "I have to leave."

"Yes," he said flatly. "You do."

He swung away from her, walked quickly onto the now-dark terrace, scooped up the portfolio she'd dropped, the shoes she'd kicked off and brought them inside. He could hardly wait to get rid of her; he didn't like what had happened, how he'd behaved, and he fought the urge to tell her that this had been as much her fault as his. She'd come at him with such heat, such hunger, never mind her lack of expertise…

Cristo! Her lack of expertise.

Was she a virgin? That was as impossible as his having lost control. There were no virgins over the age of puberty in today's world.

Not that it mattered.

Hell, it damned well *did* matter! He'd never bedded a virgin in his life; he had no intentions of ever bedding one. Women could be foolish enough about sex, turning it into undying expressions of love even when a man made it absolutely clear, from the start, that sex had nothing to do with anything but desire.

But sex with a virgin? The possibilities were enough to make him shudder as he held out the portfolio and shoes.

"Thank you," Isabella said coldly.

"You're welcome," he said, just as coldly.

She snatched her things from his hands, tucked the portfolio under her arm, spent a millisecond debating whether to try and stuff her size eight feet into Anna's size seven shoes and decided there wasn't a way in hell she'd perform that awful little comedy routine while Mr. Centerfold watched.

It was definitely time to go…

Oh, God! Go where? The car. The car!

"I thought you were in a hurry to leave."

She looked up. Mr. Macho was watching her as intently as a cat might watch a mouse.

"I most certainly am," she said, and she turned on her heel—her bare-but-for-her-shredded-panty hose heel... And turned back.

"Be sure and tell Mr. D'Aquila I'm very sorry he wasn't here to meet with me."

The caretaker's lips turned up in a chilly smile.

"Don't you mean, tell him you're sorry you showed up three hours late?"

"I mean exactly what I said, Mr. Rossi. Nothing more, nothing less. Is that clear?"

Silence. Then his dismissive expression wavered and, damnit, he laughed. Laughed!

"Yes, ma'am," he said, standing straight and tossing off a crisp salute.

Isabella wanted to strangle him. Instead, she chose a dignified exit, though dignity was a tough thing to maintain when you were barefoot, when a man's smug laughter followed you...

When you could still feel the heat of his kisses burning on your lips.

Rio watched her go.

An interesting woman, he had to admit. Even now, as she marched out of his life, back straight, shoulders squared, head up. Even her posture made it clear she'd been wrongfully treated.

That she wasn't wearing shoes spoiled the effect.

It made him grin.

He lost sight of her once she'd turned the corner; a few seconds later, he heard the front door slam hard enough to make it rattle.

Okay.

She was gone.

Good. Excellent. Out of his home, out of his hair, out of his life.

"Good night, Ms. Orsini," he murmured. "It's a pleasure to have seen the last of you."

What time was it, anyway? He'd left his watch somewhere before he'd started digging. Never mind. He'd search for it in the morning. Right now, he was going to have that long-awaited cold beer, take a shower, put together a meal because, by now, he was hungry as a bear. Then he'd drive to the airport.

Forget that.

He was tired. Simpler to spend the night here and fly home in the morning.

Rio yawned, stretched, headed for the kitchen. There were half a dozen bottles of beer in the fridge; he chose one at random, rummaged in a drawer, found an opener and yanked off the cap.

The first swallow went down cold, wet and welcome. He took another while he tried to find a way to describe the afternoon.

Unusual? Interesting? He smiled. A little of each, all thanks to Isabella Orsini.

He'd expected Izzy the Gardener.

What he'd got was Isabella the—the what?

She was a bundle of contradictions, charming one minute, prickly the next. Businesslike, then bumbling.

Hot as a woman could be, and then as innocent as a virgin. Unless the innocent thing had been an act. Unless she liked playing with fire, or she liked teasing a man until he went berserk, or—

What did it matter? She was gone.

And it was harmless to think about the possibility that she really was innocent.

That he'd have been the first man to touch her. To learn her secrets. To bring her pleasure again and again, because he would have done that, he'd have shown her what passion could be...

Merda.

Rio slapped the bottle on the counter and headed for the stairs. A shower would set things right, followed by the thickest steak in the freezer, and—

And, where was her car?

He paused on the second floor landing.

She'd come by car. She'd told him so, that confused tale about Manhattan traffic and highway traffic and the rabbit. Then, where was it? Why had she come down that long driveway on foot? He hadn't thought about it before but now, he wondered.

Maybe she'd parked outside the gates. He couldn't come up with a reason she would and, anyway, it wasn't his problem.

Not his problem at all.

He went up another few steps.

Yes, but where was her car?

He hesitated. Then he cursed under his breath, went down the steps, pulled open the front door and saw—

Nothing.

An empty driveway. The tall trees that lined it. The iron gate in the distance. Everything seemed eerie under the glow of the outside lights that had automatically come on at dusk.

The area past the gate was black. A moon as thin as the blade of a scythe hung in the sky but it didn't do much to illuminate the night.

Okay. He'd check. Obviously, her car had been parked on the narrow road outside the gate. It, and she, would be long gone but—

But, he'd check.

He trotted down the driveway. Reached the gate. Pushed against it, but the thing had chosen this moment to stay firmly closed. Rio cursed again. Fumbled for the number pad so he could key in the security code. The gate swung slowly open but so what? He had no idea what he was looking for, what he expected to see...

Hell.

A slender figure was marching along the road. A slender, distant figure, lit by a sliver of moonlight ghosting through the trees.

He had no doubt it was Isabella Orsini.

"Idiot," he growled, as he stepped into the middle of the road and shouted her name.

No reaction. Either she hadn't heard him, or she wasn't going to acknowledge that she had.

"Isabella!" he yelled again. "Damnit, Isabella, what the hell do you think you're doing?"

Still no answer. And she didn't stop walking. He knew she'd heard him; he'd shouted loud enough to silence the cricket symphony in the shrubs, but Isabella was not a cricket.

She was a woman determined to prove she was fearless.

Or daft.

Rio's vote was for "daft." A woman alone, on a dark country road...

Grimly, he started after her. He walked fast. Then he trotted. He'd just broken into a run when headlights appeared, coming toward him. Toward her. Their light spilled over her and, for the first time, she hesitated.

The vehicle slowed. She looked at it. The driver must have said something. Did she want a ride, maybe.

Don't say yes, Rio thought, and ran faster. Whatever you do, Iz, do not say—

She wasn't.

She was saying "no." He couldn't hear her but he could

see it. She was shaking her head, shaking it harder and now the vehicle stopped—

Rio flew down the road.

Don't panic.

The words sang in Isabella's head. *Do not panic! Do not let every Grade D horror flick you saw as a teenager take over your common sense.*

The driver who'd pulled over and asked if she needed a ride was just trying to be helpful. That he'd called her "little girl," that he looked like a sumo wrestler version of Jack the Ripper, meant nothing.

Stop that, Isabella!

The man's weight was his affair. And she didn't even know what Jack the Ripper looked like. Nobody did. She was letting her imagination run away with her...

Isabella's heart leaped into her throat.

Sumo Jack opened his door. "You ain't bein' very friendly," he said as he heaved his bulk out of the car, "an' here I am, just tryin' to be helpful."

Isabella's heart leaped in her throat. *Run,* she told herself, *run, run, run...*

"There you are, sweetheart."

That voice. Husky, lightly accented. "Matteo," Isabella sobbed, and went straight into Rio's arms.

Rio held her close against him. His heart was hammering, and not only from his crazed sprint.

"Baby," he murmured, "it's okay."

For a few seconds, nothing existed but the night and the woman burrowing against him. Then, Rio cleared his throat and looked at the guy standing next to a battered pickup. He was big and beefy. Still, under that beef there probably were slabs of muscle, but that wasn't what troubled him.

It was the way the guy stood there, motionless, his eyes hard and fixed on Isabella.

Rio's blood pounded.

I can take you, you SOB, he thought—but what if he couldn't? He wasn't a fool; he knew how to box. He was strong, his body was hard. He knew that fury at what might have happened would fuel him.

But the guy might get lucky, and win the confrontation. And if he did, what would happen to Isabella?

So Rio swallowed his rage, cleared his throat, forced a smile to his lips.

"Thanks, man," he said. Isabella stiffened against him. Rio held her even closer, hoping the unspoken warning to keep quiet would get through to her. "Offering to help my lady was really decent."

Nothing. The hulking figure didn't speak, didn't move.

Isabella shivered.

"We had an argument. She was angry as a hornet and she took off." A quick grin, this one man-to-man. "You know how it goes."

The guy shifted from one massive leg to the other. Rio waited; he was sure the man's brain was as undersized as his body was massive. Would he take the easy out—or would he come at them?

Rio almost wished he would...

No. He couldn't risk something happening to the woman trembling in his arms. Better to give the hulk the chance to hang on to whatever it was he called his honor.

Rio looked into Isabella's face.

"Sweetheart?" She looked up at him. Her eyes were wide with fear. He wanted to kiss her and tell her everything was going to be fine, soothe her until the terror left her and she sighed and melted against him...

But the thing to do now was to get moving.

"Baby," he said, "let's go home, okay?"

The big man in the road shifted his weight again.

"You need to keep an eye on your woman," he said in a low voice. "Anythin' can happen, a woman walkin' around alone out here at night."

Rio nodded. "Yeah. Thanks again. You take care, dude, okay?" He slid his arm to Isabella's waist. "Come on," he said so quietly that only she would hear him. "Start walking. Come on, Iz. That's it. Left. Right. Left. Right. Faster. The way you did when you and your ego marched out of my house."

That did it.

He felt the strength coming back into her. She'd have jerked away, but he'd expected her to react, hell, he'd counted on it, and he kept her where he wanted her, right in the curve of his arm.

"My ego had nothing to do with it," she whispered, but without as much heat as he'd have liked.

"We can argue that later. For now, just keep going."

"Is he—is he going to let us?"

"He will, if he's got half a brain. He knows I'll plaster the road with him if he tries anything."

"He outweighs you by two hundred pounds."

"Three," Rio said, "but who's counting?"

She gave a watery little laugh, which was what he'd hoped. The last thing he needed was for her to go into shock.

They walked. And walked, both of them listening for the truck, waiting for it to pass them. The gate was only a couple of hundred yards away but it seemed like miles.

Isabella's footsteps became hurried. Rio held her steady.

"Slow down. That's it. Just stay at an even pace. We're just a couple who made up after a quarrel and we're on our happy way home."

"If only he'd pass us—"

The pickup did, roaring by just as they reached the gate, its oversize tires kicking up a swirl of dust and leaves. Rio shoved her through, locked the gate after them, and Isabella flung her arms around him.

He stood absolutely still for what seemed a very long time. Then he gathered her against him, tilted her face to his and gently brushed his lips over hers.

"Easy, *cara,*" he said softly. "Everything's fine now."

"Ohmygod," she said, her voice shaking, "ohmygod..."

Her face was pale, her eyes enormous. He wanted to kiss her again, kiss her until the fear left her, until she clung to him not just for comfort but for the pleasure of being wrapped in his arms.

The thought made no sense and he knew it. He dealt with it by frowning, clasping her elbows and giving her a not-too-gentle shake.

"What in hell were you thinking? This isn't a city, or hadn't you noticed? There are no sidewalks, no people, no lights!"

"Oh, that's it! Blame me when it's your fault that—that—" The false bravado faded. "I didn't think," she whispered. "I just wanted to—to get away. To find the train station."

Rio blinked. "The train station? I thought you came by car."

"I did. It wasn't mine. It was—"

"Anna's," he said carefully.

"Yes. But—it drove into a ditch."

Despite everything, Rio had to laugh.

"The car drove itself into a ditch?"

"I told you, there was a rabbit in the road. I think it was a rabbit. It had a long, skinny nose and a long, skinny tail, and it just suddenly appeared in front of me."

"An opossum," he said, as if it mattered.

"And, of course, I didn't want to hit it."

Rio thought of the possum carcasses that littered every

country road he'd ever seen, of the trucks and cars that hit them, of the drivers who never noticed or, if they noticed, never cared.

Without thinking, he drew her close again, stroked his hand down her back.

"No," he said carefully, "of course you didn't."

"So the car sort of, it sort of lost direction, and—"

"Where was this?"

"A long way from here. I had to walk. It's why I was so late."

"Why didn't you phone? You do have a mobile phone, don't you?"

"I didn't want to ask Mr. D'Aquila for help. I didn't want to give him any reason to doubt my ability to handle things."

"Right. Which is why you figured being three hours late was better than calling and saying you needed a lift."

Her eyes narrowed. She flattened her hands against his chest and managed to put some distance between them, but only because he let her.

"Thank you for your help, Mr. Rossi."

"What happened to Matteo?"

"You can let go of me now."

"So you can do what? Go for another moonlight stroll?"

Her teeth worried her bottom lip. She had a habit of doing that. He had a habit of wanting to kiss her whenever she did.

"I'll take a bus."

He laughed, and her eyes narrowed.

"No buses? Fine. I'll phone for a taxi."

He laughed again. Her eyes got even narrower. By now, they were icy slits.

"Ask nicely," he said, "and I'll drive you to the railroad station."

The look she gave him suggested that she really wanted to ask him to do something anatomically impossible. He kept his face expressionless as he watched her struggle for control. Finally, she nodded in cool assent.

"I need a ride to the station."

"That's it? That's asking nicely?"

Any minute now, she was going to slug him. The thought made his lips twitch.

"Mr. Rossi. Would you be so kind as to drive me to the station?"

He knew what response he wanted to make. *No,* he'd say, *why should I do that when you can spend the night right here, in my bed?*

Hell, he thought, and let go of her.

"No problem," he said briskly, and headed toward the house and his truck, still parked in the driveway. She followed him and he opened the passenger door, left her to get inside on her own because touching her right now didn't seem a good idea, went around to the driver's side and slid behind the wheel.

They made the drive to town in silence. The place was buttoned up for the night. He put the windows down and heard crickets and the wind and, under it all, the distant sound of the sea.

When they reached the station, he shut off the engine and turned toward her.

"You want to tell me the location of that car-eating ditch?"

The look she shot him would have put glaciers on his stretch of beach.

"No."

Rio shrugged. "Your choice. I figured I'd arrange for a tow but if you'd rather do it—"

"Good night, Mr. Rossi. I'd say thanks for everything but except for you coming along when I was having that—that conversation with that gentleman—"

"Nothing like a nice chat with a homicidal Neanderthal

on a dark, deserted road," Rio said lightly, as he went around to her side of the truck.

"I do not require your assistance."

"No, I'm sure you don't. Still, it's late, the area is deserted, and though you may be up for another talk with a *gentleman* determined to prove himself harmless, I'm not. So give us both a break and behave while I walk you inside, okay?"

Isabella glared at the man holding her arm as if he owned her.

Matteo Rossi was insufferable!

If Rio D'Aquila was an arrogant bastard, she could only imagine what he must be like if he could tolerate having someone like this work for him.

Still, there was something reassuring about Matteo Rossi's hand at her elbow. It was late, it was dark, the place had a forlorn air to it but it wouldn't, not once she was on the station platform. Surely, there'd be other passengers waiting...

Wrong.

There was a sign on the ticket booth.

Closed.

There would be no westbound trains to Penn Station tonight.

CHAPTER FIVE

ISABELLA stared at the sign.

Impossible. A train station, closed?

She went to the door, tried to force it open. It didn't budge.

It was true, she thought numbly. Your heart really could drop to your toes.

Matteo, standing just behind her, muttered a word she couldn't decipher. Just as well. It probably would have turned the tips of her ears pink.

And no wonder.

He was as eager to see her gone as she was to go.

"It can't be closed," she said, looking over her shoulder at him. "Trains run twenty-four hours a day."

Rio's thoughts were racing. Now what? He walked to the door and tried it.

It was locked.

"Subway trains run twenty-four hours a day," he said. "But this isn't a subway, and it isn't Manhattan."

She looked at him and all but rolled her eyes. He couldn't blame her. Talk about useless comments…

And why had he done something so foolish as trying the door himself? Not foolish on the face of it, okay, but he'd had to close the slight distance between them and now he could feel her against him, smell her hair. Lemons? Something light and clean and feminine and, *Dio,* his all-male-all-the-time brain had gone to far more primitive stuff than what to do about this newest problem.

He took a step back, drew in a head-clearing breath of cool night air.

"This is turning into a comedy of errors," she said coldly. "First the car. Then your employer not even having the courtesy to wait for me. Then you. And now, this."

Rio bit back a groan. This was impossible. Who did he stand up for, himself—or himself? She'd just insulted both of them. But that was good. It brought him back to reality.

"Your car went off the road. Oh, sorry. It drove itself off the road. Never mind the rest—the traffic you should have anticipated, the directions you forgot to take with you. The point is, if you still had a car, we wouldn't be standing in the middle of town, waiting for a train that isn't going to come."

She gave him a cold glare. Then she sighed and the glare turned into a sorrowful admission that what he'd said was true.

"You're right. The only person to blame is me for agreeing to try for this job in the first place. I told Gaby it was crazy."

Gaby. A new name added to the mix. Was she referring to Gabriella Orsini, Dante's wife? Rio D'Aquila, who knew the couple, could have asked.

Matteo Rossi, who'd never heard of them, couldn't.

"And Anna. I told her the same thing. 'This job isn't for me,' I said, but did either of them listen?"

Anna, again. The mysterious Anna, so generous with her clothes and her car.

"No," Isabella said grimly, answering her own question, "they did not. They badgered me and badgered me." Her voice went from its soft, pleasing midrange to a high-pitched parody of what he figured was supposed to be Anna-Gaby. "'Think of the doors a contract like that will open, Izzy. Think of the new clients you'll get.'" Her eyebrows drew together. "Ha!"

"Well," Rio said cautiously, "they were probably right."

She snorted with derision. "Bad enough I have to deal with spoiled rich guys in the city. Why should I have to come all the way to the ends of the earth to deal with one in a place where—where creatures rule the road and trains stop running just because it's dark?"

Rio considered pointing out that creatures ruled the road everywhere, and that the dark had nothing to do with trains not running here on a Friday night.

Instead, he took the low ground.

"You have no way of knowing that Rio D'Aquila is spoiled."

"He's loaded," Isabella snapped. "And a hunk."

Rio's eyebrows rose. "Is he," he said.

"Gaby says he is. Anna's never met him but she saw him at a couple of places. Some charity party, the symphony, who knows what? The point is, she saw him. And she said yes, he's gorgeous. And that he obviously has more money than he needs, and an ego bigger than his head."

Rio folded his arms and made a mental note to add Anna to the list of people he could live without meeting.

"Interesting," he said coldly.

"Maybe she didn't say that, exactly. But why else would he build a house in the middle of nowhere when he already has God only knows how many other houses?"

"Southampton is hardly the middle of nowhere. And, ah, perhaps he found something about the area appealing."

"Do not," she said, chin lifted, eyes blazing, "do not defend your boss to me! I know what men like him are like. I work for them. Well, not on a job anywhere near the size this one is, I mean, the size this one would have been, I mean, the size it would have been if I'd gotten it—"

"I get the picture," he said drily. "So, men who have money are acquisitive fools?"

"Their egos are bigger than their heads."

"An interesting observation."

"A valid one."

"And that includes Dante Orsini, who recommended you for this position?"

Her eyes narrowed. "How do you know that?"

Idiot! "D'Aquila mentioned it."

"No, it doesn't include Dante. Of course it doesn't—but that's beside the point." Isabella shivered. The night air was surprisingly cool. "I am trapped, do you hear me? Trapped in this—this last outpost of civilization!"

It was hard not to laugh. Harder still not to kiss away the angry set of her lips, the flush in her cheeks, the glitter in her eyes.

Damnit, Rio thought, and reached for her and drew her into his arms.

"What are you doing?"

"You're shivering," he said reasonably. "I'm warming you."

"I do not need warming."

"Yes. You do. Stop fighting me and let me chase away the chill."

She stood within his embrace as rigidly as a tree. He held on to her with the determination of a Boy Scout doing a good deed—except, he had never been a Boy Scout and it was hard to think like one now. Isabella felt warm and soft. She smelled sweet and feminine. He wanted to put his lips against her hair. Lift her face to his and kiss her. He wanted to do all the things a man wanted to do to a woman who drove him crazy—

And made him feel something for her that could only be described as tenderness.

He told himself to let go of her and step back—but right at that instant, she gave a weary sigh and put her head against his chest.

Rio shut his eyes and held her closer.

"You're right," she said in a shaky whisper. "I screwed up and I'm stranded. What am I going to do now?"

He had the answer, of course.

He was Rio D'Aquila. He had a plane parked at an airport a short drive away. All they had to do was get into his truck, drive to Easthampton. An hour from now, she'd be where she wanted to be.

In the city.

So, what if he wanted her here?

There was no logic to it. He understood that. What he didn't understand was why logic didn't seem to mean a damn.

Never mind holding her to keep her warm. He was holding her because she felt so right in his arms—and what was that all about?

For what had to be the thousandth time since Isabella Orsini had walked into his life, Rio told himself that enough was enough. This foolish self-indulgence had to stop. It was time to do the logical thing. To take her to New York. It wasn't only logical, it was the right thing. All he had to do was take the first step.

The problem was, that first step was a killer.

He'd have to tell her who he really was.

The odds were good she wouldn't be happy when he revealed that this had all been a charade. Wouldn't be happy? The understatement of the year. Of the decade.

She'd be furious.

But he could get her past that. Hadn't he charmed CEOs and CFOs and COOs from here to Timbuktu into agreeing to deals they'd started out refusing?

Still, once she knew who he was, everything would change.

She'd still be Izzy the Gardener, with her ruined borrowed car and her ruined borrowed clothes and he—

He would be a liar. A rich liar. A man with too much money and an ego bigger than his head.

If only he had not lied to her. He wasn't even sure what had prompted him to do it. Boredom? Irritation? Just plain perversity? Whatever the reason, this had begun as a silly game.

But it had somehow become more.

Aside from the enormity of living a lie, he felt—he felt wonderful. Relaxed. Content. *Dio,* a few hours ago, he wasn't sure he could even have defined that word.

Most of all, he was enjoying Isabella's company. She was prickly and difficult and argumentative, but she was also gentle and honest and she made him smile.

He felt at ease with her in a way he had not felt with a woman in years.

In his teens and early twenties, when he hadn't had any money, women had been drawn to him because of how he looked. He'd known it and he hadn't much cared. What young guy would? The important thing had been to bed beautiful woman after beautiful woman; his hormones had ruled him.

Then his life changed. Hard work, good luck, some admittedly clever and dangerous risks, and he'd begun amassing a fortune. He still had the good looks—why be modest over a simple genetic fact?—but now he had money, too, and that ineffable thing called power.

People began treating him differently, especially women.

They were deferential. Eager to please. And always planning how to handle him.

At times, he could almost see them trying to figure out what response he wanted to a simple question. "Would you like to go to the opera tonight, or shall I get tickets for Eric Clapton?" Or, "Are you in the mood for seafood tonight?" Their smiles would freeze. They would hesitate. He knew they were wondering what he wanted them to say, as if there were a correct answer and it would win them a prize.

Perhaps that was the reason he didn't find many of them interesting anymore.

Isabella, on the other hand, was more than interesting.

She was fascinating. And she treated him without pretence.

He couldn't imagine another woman scowling at him, or arguing with him, or turning her back on him and walking off into a dangerous night.

He certainly couldn't imagine another woman tearing herself from his arms as she had done. Not because he was sure he was such a good lover—although he hoped he was—but because of who he was. Rio D'Aquila, who had an overblown ego and too much money.

But that was the point, after all.

He wasn't that man to Isabella. He was a caretaker. And she liked him for himself. Or didn't like him, as the spirit moved her.

And he loved it.

It was a new world for him, a place where a man was a man and a woman was a woman. It was as close to experiencing a real relationship as he'd ever had...

Rio frowned.

If a man actually wanted a relationship.

He most assuredly didn't.

He just liked being with Isabella. Liked holding her. Another minute or two, then he'd pull aside the curtain and reveal himself as the Wizard in the Emerald City. And, no, that hadn't gone so well for the real wizard but the analogy made—

"—sense."

Rio blinked. "Sorry. I was... What did you say?"

"I said, I thought of the only solution that makes sense."

"Oh?"

"I can phone Anna."

"Anna."

"My sister."

Her sister. At least he had part of the puzzle.

"Anna can come and get me. Or her husband."

She was right. That *did* make sense, and he wouldn't have to tell her the truth about himself, but what would it accomplish? Either way, she'd be out of his life tonight...

And he didn't want that.

Not just yet.

"But..." She swallowed audibly. Sank her teeth into her lip and, *Dio,* if she did that one more time, he was not going to be responsible for his actions.

"But?" he prompted.

She sighed. "But then—then everyone will know that I—that I botched this."

Rio felt a quick knot of anger form in his chest. He slid his hands up her arms, to her shoulders.

"Who is 'everyone'? Why would they judge you? Why should you care?"

"My family. And they wouldn't judge me. They'd be upset for me. See, I have four brothers. And a sister. And all of them are so successful but I'm—I'm—"

"You," Rio said fiercely, "are a beautiful, bright, talented woman."

She blushed. "That's very—it's very sweet of you but—"

"It is the truth. I've seen your sketches for the terrace."

"You have?"

Careful, Rio thought, *damnit, man, be careful!*

"Yes. D'Aquila sent them to me. I, ah, I saw the designs of all the applicants. I'll be here, supervising things on his estate, while the landscaping took shape. He thought it would be a good idea if I were familiar with the various plans."

It sounded ridiculous but she bought it. He knew she did, when she smiled.

"Well, then, I'm glad you liked what you saw."

"Very much," he said softly, and fought the urge to draw her into his arms again. "In fact—in fact, I'm going to recommend my boss set up a second interview."

Her face lit. He gave an inward groan. What in hell kind of spiderweb was he getting into? How could Rio D'Aquila interview her without giving the game away?

Never mind. He'd faced seemingly impossible situations all his life, and managed to handle them. He'd handle this, too—

But not tonight.

"Okay," he said briskly. "So, calling your sister is not a good idea."

Her smile faded. "Not really."

"Well, I have a plan."

"You do?"

"I do." He took her arm and began walking her toward his truck. "I'll put you up for the night."

"Ha!"

Isabella tried to dig her heels into the pavement but they were bare heels, really bare, because by now the feet of her panty hose were completely shredded. Rio got her to the truck without so much as breaking stride, hung on to her with one hand as he opened the passenger door.

"That," she huffed, "is one hell of a plan!"

"Calm down, Ms. Orsini. I have no interest in seducing you."

"I'm supposed to believe that after what happened before?"

He swung her toward him.

"I kissed you. You kissed me. Who, exactly, tried to seduce whom?"

Her face, lit by a streetlamp, turned red.

"I am not spending the night with you."

"Fine." Rio let go of her and folded his arms. "You can spend it here, on a bench. Or would you prefer curling up in the grass?"

She stared at him. He could almost see her brain whirring.

"In the morning," he said, "I'll arrange to have your car taken to a garage. If they can fix it, they will. If they can't, you'll rent another."

"I don't—"

"Don't what?"

She shrugged and looked down at the ground. "Nothing."

Rio rolled his eyes. "You don't have the money for either, and you don't want to ask Anna for help. Am I right?"

Another shrug, even more expressive than the first.

"I'll lend you the money."

She looked up. "You?"

"I'm a caretaker, not a drifter. I have an income. I have some savings."

"I didn't mean—"

"Yes, you did. But those of us who work with our hands are as fiscally and morally responsible as anyone else."

Dio, that sounded impossibly stiff-necked, but it was the truth. Once, he had worked with his hands. Now, he was rich. How had he become so wealthy? How had he accumulated the money to make his first investment? By working hard, living frugally and saving first every lira, then every euro, every Brazilian real that he could.

Isabella hesitated. Then she gave him a smile that lit the night.

"You're a good man, Matteo Rossi. Thank you."

She climbed into the truck. He slammed the door. Then he went around to the driver's side and got behind the wheel.

A good man?

He was a goddamned liar, was what he was.

A good man would have told her the truth. Would have taken her home, or sent her home, because he had enough money to get anyone to do anything at any hour, or so bitter reality had taught him.

Rio started the truck, backed away from the curb.

A good man wouldn't have begun this charade in the first place. At the very least, a good man would have put an end to it by now.

So much for his being a good man.

He'd told her one truth, at least. He would not seduce her. He didn't want to seduce her—

Cristo, at least be honest about that, D'Aquila. A woman who can make your belly knot, your balls ache, with nothing more than a smile? All he wanted was to seduce her.

But he had no intention of even trying.

That scene at the house earlier had been a warning.

She was innocent, or close to it. And he didn't play games with innocent women.

But would a little self-indulgence be wrong? Would it affect anything that mattered to go on letting her think he was the caretaker? Give her a room for the night, a meal, enjoy just talking with her and then send her on her way tomorrow?

No. There was no way it possibly could.

He'd help her with her dilemma, let her think her knight errant was named Matteo, and nobody would be hurt.

Not her.

Not him.

And that would be the end of it.

CHAPTER SIX

THE night was dark, the roads were empty and Isabella's brain was no longer functioning.

How else to explain why she was letting a stranger take her home with him? And what did that mean? Where was his home?

He hadn't said. And she hadn't asked.

No longer functioning, indeed.

She'd assumed he meant they were going to the D'Aquila estate. And wasn't that silly? Assuming anything was generally a mistake. Just look at today, and her assumption that Rio D'Aquila would be waiting to interview her.

Wrong on both counts.

He hadn't been waiting, and she hadn't been interviewed.

Now, she'd assumed spending the night with a man she'd just met was a good idea. But it wasn't. How could it be? He was gorgeous, he was sexy—and for all she knew, he was an ax murderer.

"Relax," he said with lazy humor in his voice. "We're going back to the house. And it's a big house. Four guest suites. You can choose the one you like."

Isabella felt color creep into her face.

"I wasn't—"

"Yes. You were." He glanced at her, his face unreadable

in the darkness. "A little late to start wondering if I have ul-
terior motives, don't you think?"

What she thought was that she didn't need him poking
around in her head, or pointing out that she'd just added one
more foolish act to a day filled with them.

"You're right," she said sweetly. "I probably should have
asked if you turn into a vampire at midnight."

He chuckled. "A hungry vampire. I don't know about you
but I can't remember the last time I ate anything today."

Neither could she, but admitting it would just mean he'd
scored another small victory in mind reading.

"You must be hungry, too."

"Not at all," she said, with the self-righteousness of a candidate for sainthood.

Unfortunately, her belly chose that moment to growl.

"Obviously not." His tone was wry but, thank God, he
didn't laugh. "So, you can just watch me eat. How's that
sound?"

Stubbornness was one thing. Stupidity was another. Even
she knew that.

"Okay," she said, "you're right. I'm starved. Is there a diner
around here? A McD's? My treat."

Her treat.

He wanted to laugh.

Or maybe not.

Women bought him gifts. Nothing new in that. An expensive watch for what one breathlessly called a one month an-
niversary. A ridiculously expensive case of wine from one
lover who'd somehow learned the date of his birthday. From
others over the years, a gold pen, sapphire studs, diamond
cufflinks.

And each time, he said, "Thank you, it's a wonderful gift,
but I can't let you spend your money on me."

The real message was that he would not let a woman forge a relationship intimate enough for him to accept a gift.

But no woman had ever offered him something like this. A hamburger and fries. He couldn't even imagine any of the women he knew admitting to liking hamburgers and fries.

For the first time in his life, Rio wanted to say yes.

Hell, no.

What he really wanted was to pull to the side of the road and kiss the lovely, messy, quirky, altogether delectable Isabella.

Rio took a deep breath.

And did neither.

Kissing her was absolutely out of the question. Hadn't he made that vow to himself just a few minutes ago?

As for going to a restaurant, even a diner or a fast-food joint...

No way.

He wasn't naive. There were a handful of other places that drew people who shunned publicity. Ski resorts, islands in the sun. He'd been to a few of them, enough to know that a town's laissez-faire attitude toward its rich and famous visitors could change after dark when the movers and shakers of the world vied for just the right table in just the right place.

For all he knew, that even applied to diners and burger places in a town frequented by high-profile names.

The very last thing he wanted was for someone to recognize him now. Living a lie, he thought as his guilty conscience gave a nasty twinge, was not easy.

"Tell you what," he said. "We'll make something when we get home."

"Home? Is that how you think of his estate?"

"Of his... Oh. D'Aquila. Well, sure. I live there."

"Will he object? To you having an overnight guest. I mean—"

"I know what you mean. Just for the record, I haven't had any overnight guests. Not the way you meant it."

"I didn't..."

"You did." His tone roughened. "What you really want to know is have I had a woman stay there with me."

Isabella flushed. "Why would I care?"

"That's an excellent question. Why would you?"

Why indeed? Isabella thought, and searched for an answer that made sense.

"Because—because I'm a little uncomfortable at the thought of staying in a house without the owner knowing it."

It wasn't the answer he'd wanted, and wasn't that ridiculous? This had nothing to do with the reason a man generally takes a woman home with him.

This was about expediency.

There was nothing else he could do with her.

You could tell her the truth.

And his conscience could just shut the hell up. Hadn't he already gone through this internal debate? Hadn't he concluded, and logically so, that there was no harm in continuing the deception for another few hours?

After that, Isabella Orsini would be a memory.

Rio shrugged.

"D'Aquila wouldn't object. Besides, he'll be away for the next few days."

"And you have—what? An apartment over the garage? A house on the grounds?"

The real caretaker lived a couple of miles away, but he could hardly tell her that.

"Over the garage," he said. When it came to telling lies, Pinocchio had nothing on him. "But it isn't finished yet. For the time being, I live in the house itself."

"Your employer doesn't mind?"

"You know," he said carefully, "it might be a mistake to judge men by the size of their bank accounts."

That won him a sigh.

"You sound like Anna."

"Your sister."

"She says I'm too judgmental when it comes to men."

Perhaps this Anna was more insightful than he'd thought.

"A woman like you should be judgmental," he said gruffly.

"A woman like me?"

A woman who's bright and beautiful, innocent and sexy, a woman any man would be taking to his bed and not to a guest room, he almost said. Thankfully, the gate to his estate loomed up just in time.

"A woman on her own," he said, and for once, *grazie a Dio,* the gate opened without difficulty and he put the moment, and the thought, behind him.

Rio headed straight for the kitchen, switched on all the lights, opened the fridge—and then realized Isabella was still standing in the breakfast room that adjoined it.

"Now what?"

She looked at him, then down at herself, then at him again.

"I'm a mess."

She was. A lovely mess, but a mess nonetheless. The torn and stained suit, the smudged blouse, the panty hose with so many runs they looked more like ribbons than nylons.

He was pretty much a mess himself.

"Is there somewhere I can wash up?"

There were five places where she could wash up, five huge bathrooms with five huge tubs and five huge shower stalls, and suddenly he saw himself with her in one of those bathrooms, saw himself slowly undressing her, baring her to his eyes, saw himself lifting her, carrying her into one of those enormous shower stalls, turning on the water so it poured down on them as gently as a summer rain, saw his hands on her breasts, his mouth on her nipples...

"Matteo? If you could just tell me where to find a bathroom..."

"No problem," he said, his voice hoarse, his erection almost painful. It was a damned good thing he was standing behind the open refrigerator door.

He gave it a minute. Then he flashed what he hoped was a smile, shut the door and led her up the stairs to the guest suite farthest from his own rooms, though how in hell he was going to explain his using the master suite was beyond him.

Everything was beyond him now.

He knew it, knew that he should never have brought her here because his vaunted self-control was gone, gone, gone—

"Okay," he said briskly, as he flung open the door to the suite, "there should be clean towels in the bathroom. New toothbrushes, soap, shampoo, all that stuff."

Isabella nodded. "Thank you."

"Hey, don't thank me. Thank the decorator. You know how these guys are. Somebody tells a guy who has a PhD in ribbons and bows to furnish a house, he goes all the way."

She laughed. Good. Keep it light. Anything to keep his mind from wandering to the one place it wanted to go.

He stepped back.

"The kitchen," he said. "Fifteen minutes."

"Yessir," Isabella said, and gave a quick salute, the same kind he'd given her hours before.

Rio narrowed his eyes. Then he pulled the door shut so hard it sounded like a thunderclap and marched resolutely down the hall.

As soon as the door shut, Isabella sagged back against it and let out a long breath.

The way he'd looked at her right before they'd started talk-

ing about toothpaste and towels... The way she'd felt, knowing he was looking at her that way...

Isabella, a stern voice that sounded a lot like Anna's said,
whatever are you doing here?

The answer was simple.

She was spending the night because her car was in a ditch
and the trains weren't running.

Could a voice in your head really say, *Pshaw?* Or as close
to *pshaw* as it could get? And, so what if the trains weren't
running? A town like this, there were sure to be private car
services.

And you didn't think of that until now because...?

Because she couldn't afford the zillion bucks a car service
would surely charge for taking her from here to the city, and
yes, she had a rich father and rich brothers and a sister who
was married to a prince. So what? She'd always insisted on
making it on her own.

Damned if she'd stop now.

Isabella turned the lock and began peeling off her clothes.
She looked at the suit jacket, then the skirt.

Ugh.

Anna, she decided, using two fingers to pick both items
from the tile floor, would surely not want this stuff back. Ditto
for the blouse. Grimacing, she dropped all three items into a
discreetly disguised wastebasket in the corner of a discreetly
disguised bathroom that had been designed to look more like
an Asiatic spa than a room meant to contain a tub, a sink, a
toilet and a shower.

Not that she'd ever seen an Asiatic spa but if she ever did,
it would probably look like this. At least, she hoped it would.
Silk wallpaper meant to look like golden meadow grass. A
soaking tub big enough to double as a houseboat. A shower
that could easily host a party or, at least, a man and a woman.

A man with dark hair and blue eyes, broad shoulders and

narrow hips. Long legs and, wait a minute, what about that square jaw, that tiny scar she'd noticed, that unabashedly sexy grin…

Isabella frowned, peeled off what remained of her panty hose, her bra and her panties—she'd never been sure whether you were supposed to wear them over or under your panty hose but it didn't much matter because she lived in jeans. As for all this stuff, bra and panties and pathetic panty hose—it went into the trash, too.

Soap, she thought. And shampoo. Matteo had said—and yes, once she'd opened a few drawers, she found it all. Soap and shampoo and conditioner, toothpaste and toothbrushes and towels. Big, fluffy towels.

She plucked a wrapped bar of soap from its shelf and sniffed it. Mmm. Vanilla. Were they all…? No. There were half a dozen different scents. Lemon. Jasmine. Lavender. Tea rose. Ginger.

Lemon, she decided. Lemon was always her favorite. And for her hair… She opened a small bottle and brought it to her nose. Lemon, again.

Perfect.

Did Matteo like the smell of lemon?

Not that it mattered, she thought quickly, as she stepped into the enormous glass shower. Why on earth would it matter? She liked it. That was all that was important. She wasn't interested in Matteo Rossi as a man. Well, he was a man, of course. An incredible man. Gorgeous. Sexy. Funny and clever, but so what?

She wasn't looking for a one-night stand.

Even if she had been—

Matteo wasn't interested in her.

He'd kissed her. So what? You didn't have to be sexually knowledgeable—and, good Lord, there had to be a better way to put it than that—to know that a kiss was just a kiss.

She had four brothers, all of them settled now into happy married lives, but she'd grown up with them, she'd overheard conversations she wasn't supposed to overhear. Meaning, Isabella thought as she rinsed conditioner from her hair, meaning a guy might well kiss a woman for no better reason than because he could.

A good-looking man saw a good-looking woman...

Not that she was good-looking, she thought, catching sight of her reflection in the mirror across from the glass shower stall.

She turned a little. To the side. To the back. To the front again.

Okay. She wasn't beautiful. She wasn't homely. What she was, she decided, was medium.

Medium height. Medium build. Medium everything, legs and hips and breasts.

Would Matteo want to kiss a medium woman? If he saw her now, would he? With her hair loose and wet, the long curls hanging down her back. With her skin glittering with droplets of water. With her nipples tightly budded by the coolness of the water.

Or by imagining him, in the stall with her.

Isabelle moved the soap slowly over her skin.

His body, hard and muscled and sleek, supporting hers as she leaned back against him. His hands, cupping her breasts; his fingers on her nipples. His mouth on the nape of her neck. His leg separating her thighs, and then his hand between them, seeking, finding, touching—

The soap fell from her fingers.

Quickly, she picked it up. Rinsed herself. Shut off the water, grabbed an oversize bath towel and wrapped herself in it as she padded into the bedroom.

Fantasizing about George Clooney was one thing. Not that

she ever did but *if* she did, well, George Clooney was George Clooney. A face, a body on the screen.

Matteo Rossi, on the other hand, was a real person. A *real, real* person, someone she knew. Someone in another room, just down the hall, maybe standing in the shower right now, naked...

Isabella bit back a moan.

What was wrong with her?

She didn't think about naked men. She didn't think about men, period. It was silly and she had better things to do with her time, like retrieving the yucky suit and equally yucky blouse from the trash because, damnit, she had nothing else to put on, and the fifteen minutes Matteo had mentioned were just about—

Knock, knock, knock.

Isabella spun toward the door. "Yes?"

"It's me."

Her heart pounded. Matteo. Who else would it be?

"I know." She winced. That was clever. "I mean, I'll be ready in—"

"I have some stuff you can wear."

She blinked. So much for his not having brought women here before.

"Isabella? Open the door."

"No, that's okay. I mean, I don't need—"

"You do," Matteo said, sounding amused. "Unless you really prefer that 'I've been dragged through the mud' look that's so popular this year."

She laughed. Carefully. Not loud enough so he'd hear it, but how could she not laugh at such a perfect description of how she'd certainly looked in what had once been a designer outfit?

She looked down at herself. The towel was tucked tightly

under her arms and went all the way down to her knees. She wore less than this to the pool.

"Okay. You want to put that stuff back on, I'll just—"

The door swung open. Wrong. Isabella had cracked it maybe an inch. Rio saw an eye, half a mouth, a tumble of dark, wet curls and a naked shoulder.

A wet naked shoulder.

His mouth went dry.

There was a long silence. Then he cleared his throat and forced his gaze to her face.

"I, ah, I brought you some things."

"What size?"

He blinked. "Excuse me?"

"I wondered what size clothes the women you haven't brought here left be—"

Isabella's voice trailed off. Oh, God! Such a dumb thing to say? What did it matter how many women he invited home? She was spending the night out of expediency, not spending it with him.

"Why, Izzy," he said softly. "You're jealous."

Heat flooded her face. "Certainly not! I simply meant—"

"I know exactly what you meant."

"No," she said quickly, "you don't. Why would I—"

"They're sweats. And socks." He smiled. "Mine."

"Oh. Well, I knew that. I mean, I figured that. I mean—"

Rio put his hand against the door. Before she had time to react, he'd pushed it open, leaned in, bent his head and captured her lips with his.

Dio, she tasted wonderful. Mint toothpaste and essence of Isabella. It was an amazing combination and when she moaned and melted toward him, he dropped the stuff he was holding and wrapped his arms around her.

She was soft. Warm. She smelled of lemon. And he wanted her, wanted her, wanted her...

It took all the willpower he possessed to slowly drop his hands to his sides and step back. Isabella was breathing hard. Well, *merda,* so was he.

"I don't," she whispered, "I really don't understand any of this. I'm not like this. I'm not. I'm really not—"

He bent to her and kissed her again. Deeper. Harder. With a hunger that he knew he'd never felt before. Then he scooped the sweats and socks from the floor and held them toward her. She looked at them. Looked at him. Then, clutching the towel to her with one hand, she took the things and pressed them against her breast.

"I'll meet you in the kitchen," Rio said gruffly.

One last kiss. One soft brush of his lips over hers. Then he stepped away, closed the door…

And wondered what she'd say if he told her he didn't understand any of it, either.

CHAPTER SEVEN

HER knees were wobbly.

Which was silly.

How could a man's kisses turn your knees to jelly?

They did, though. Isabella plopped down on the edge of the bed. Maybe it was safer to contemplate a thing that was clearly a physical impossibility sitting down.

Her lips tingled. Her heart was racing. She was breathing fast. She was a cliché-ridden mess, a bad romantic movie translated from the screen to real life.

Brilliant. Truly brilliant.

The clothes Matteo had given her lay in her lap. She looked down and choked back a laugh. Workout clothing. A sweat-shirt and pants, a pair of socks that looked big enough to fit the feet of a yeti.

And she'd accused him of bringing her stuff another woman had worn.

The laugh turned into a groan, and Isabella buried her face in her hands.

Forget silly. She'd gone straight to stupid. Why was he doing this to her? Turning not just her bones but her brain to jelly?

She drew a long, ragged breath, pushed her hair from her eyes and sat up straight.

Except—except he wasn't "doing" anything. Well, he was

kissing her, sending shivers up and down her spine each time
he did, but she was equally guilty.

She let him do it. Let him? An understatement. She was
encouraging him by kissing him back, each and every time.

The why of that was easy.

She was doing it because she loved how he kissed her. How
he held her. She loved the feel of his hard body against hers,
the heat of his hands, the tightly controlled power she could
sense when he held her.

Forget what she'd told herself about his kissing her because
he could.

He wanted more. Lots more.

And, oh, my, so did she.

Which was absolutely, totally, completely incomprehen-
sible.

She wasn't the kind who had sexy thoughts. She didn't
even have sexy dreams.

You're just inhibited, Iz, Anna had said, a long time back.
They'd been in their mid-teens then, other girls talking about
boys and sex, Isabella wondering if there was something
wrong with her because she'd go to the movies with a boy,
go to a school dance, and if her date tried to kiss her she'd
imagine what it would feel like, where his lips would go,
where hers would go, would she end up, yuck, tasting his
spit?

Her solution to the problem was invariably the same. She'd
stick out her hand and say *Thanks, tonight was fun,* and the
boy would never call again.

You think things to death, Anna had said with the loving
wisdom of a sister older by thirteen months and wiser by
what sometimes seemed a decade. *Just relax. Learn to let
go a little.*

It was good counseling. Isabella had even tried it.

She'd learned to like kissing. Not to love it but to like it.

Closed-mouth kissing, anyway. Eventually, she'd learned to tolerate a fumbled caress.

A couple of times, she'd let guys take things a little further. Open her bra. Touch her breasts. Watched, with a kind of clinical fascination, as their faces grew flushed, their breathing unsteady, while nothing even close was happening to her.

All she'd felt, each time, was embarrassed.

Finally, with all the grim determination of a woman going for a root canal, she'd decided it was time to have sex. Maybe the experience would turn out to be, well, liberating.

She'd gone to bed with a nice guy, the accountant who did her taxes. When it was over, she was out one lover...

And one accountant.

Which was when she'd decided to put sex and passion and all that nonsense out of her mind.

Until now.

Isabella drew another deep breath.

"Enough," she told the silent room.

Everything in life had a logical explanation. So did her behavior. She was hungry. Starved, was closer to accurate. That explained a lot. She might even be dehydrated.

A meal. Lots of water. After that, she'd be fine.

The thing to do was get dressed, put on Matteo's sweat suit and his socks. A classy, sexy outfit, for sure, she thought with a little smile, which was fine because sex and sexiness had nothing to with the reason she was spending the night.

Then, she'd head downstairs, help him put together some kind of supper. Sandwiches, soup, whatever. They'd eat, be casual about it, talk about banal things and then she'd come back up here, go to sleep and that would be the end of whatever was going on.

Because nothing was.

Okay. There was a little chemistry. She could admit that, she thought as she put on the clothes. And it was—it was fun, especially when you'd never had chemistry with a man before. Under the right circumstances, she just might find flirting, even sex, well, interesting.

Don't you mean, sex with the right man, Isabella?

"The right man has nothing to do with it," she said in a firm voice.

Liar, the little voice inside her whispered.

Isabella told it to shut up.

Then she opened the door and went in search of the kitchen.

Rio knew as much about kitchens as a lion would know about a canary.

This kitchen, especially. He'd told the architect to come up with a kitchen that would suit the house.

The result was this enormous room, a long stretch of stainless steel appliances that would have made a master chef smile, a variety of machines that baffled him, and the kind of lighting he figured surgeons would want in an operating room.

Merda!

He flicked switches, dimmers, took the lights down to a bearable level and thought how great it would be if he could do the same thing with his libido.

Damnit, he thought, as he opened the refrigerator, this nonsense had to stop!

He had not brought Isabella here to have sex with her.

Not that he hadn't thought of it endlessly most of the day but he'd reached a decision. There wouldn't be any sex. It was an excellent decision, and if he could just stop touching her, he would not have a problem over having reached it.

He'd brought her home with him because she had no place else to go.

Well, not exactly.

He could have flown her to New York. Or hired a limo.

But then the proverbial cat would have been out of the proverbial bag.

There was no reason to tell her anything.

After tomorrow morning, he would never see her again.

Where were those steaks his caretaker had said he'd bought? Where would you put a steak, in a fridge big enough to house a family of six and all their friends and relatives?

Right there. Inside a clear plastic drawer. And, in another drawer just below, there were lettuce and tomatoes and corn, things he'd almost forgotten the caretaker had mentioned hours ago. A lifetime ago, was more the way it felt.

Isabella had come walking up that driveway and ushered in a new dimension of time.

Which had nothing to do with turning this stuff into something resembling a late supper. And that was important because he needed a solid meal. Get something in his belly, he'd be able to think straight.

He'd made a decision and he was sticking to it.

No sex, he thought firmly, as he put the steaks on the stone counter beside the stove. It sounded like the title of a bad French farce—except there was nothing amusing about it.

Isabella was innocent. In spirit if not in fact. And he wasn't into deflowering virgins or introducing inexperienced women to the pleasures of sex, no matter how willing the women might seem.

Rio's mouth went dry.

And, *Cristo,* she was willing.

He could not think of a woman who had ever been more responsive to his caresses. He could imagine her in his bed, opening her arms to him as he slid between her thighs, as he filled her with his desire, his heat...

With the major hard-on that had just come to immediate life in his sweatpants.

Food. He needed a meal. So did she. A solid night's sleep

afterward and tomorrow, life would return to normal. She'd be back in New York and he—he'd be Rio D'Aquila again, because that was who he was. Not Matteo Rossi. He had not been Matteo Rossi for years and he'd be glad to get rid of him, for all time.

It would be a welcome relief.

The Viking stove had a built-in grill. He turned it on, then filled a pot with water and put it on to boil. He husked two ears of corn, checked the heat of the grill, slapped the steaks on it, found the water bubbling and dumped in the corn.

So much for putting a meal together, and wasn't it a lucky thing his caretaker had bought steaks because steak, scrambled eggs and grilled cheese sandwiches constituted Rio's entire kitchen repertoire.

Matteo Rossi had known how to cook. Not well, but well enough. He'd known how to make pasta sauce, chili, hamburgers, even omelets. When a man had to fend for himself and do it on the cheap…

Dio! Who gave a damn about any of that now? Why even think about it, when you had housekeepers and cooks?

He found the bottles of wine. A pair of reds, pinot noirs that carried the label of a noted South Shore vineyard. He uncorked one, set it aside to breathe; yanked open cabinets and drawers, found heavy white stoneware, equally heavy flatware, white linen napkins and salt and pepper mills. He opened another cabinet, found a pair of thin-stemmed red wineglasses…

And thought, *What the bloody hell am I doing?*

He stood still, put his hands on his hips and took a couple of deep breaths.

He was bustling around like a demented Julia Child, and for what? This was a late supper borne of necessity. It wasn't a romantic dinner for lovers.

He and Isabella were not lovers. They would not be lovers. All he had to do was get that final image of her out of his head. Her, wrapped in that towel, her hair damp and wild and sexy, water pearling on her shoulders, her eyes blurred and filled with him as he drew her to him and claimed her mouth...

"Hi."

Rio swung around.

Isabella stood just inside the kitchen. Her face was shiny. Her curls were out of control. Her sweats—his sweats—dwarfed her. The socks were the finishing touch. They reminded him of the kind of things clowns wore on their feet: long, loose and oversize.

No designer outfit. No fifteen hundred dollar blowout that would have taken away those beautiful curls. No makeup so artfully applied that he was never supposed to know it had taken an hour to do.

Just this.

Just Isabella.

His heart turned over.

He wanted to go to her, kiss that naked mouth, that shiny face, plunge his hands deep into that tumult of untamed curls...

For God's sake, D'Aquila. Weren't you paying attention to yourself? None of that is going to happen.

When he didn't answer, she colored a little and forced a laugh.

"Not exactly a *Vogue* cover, huh?"

He knew the correct, gentlemanly response. He was supposed to say she looked precisely like a *Vogue* cover but hell, he wasn't a gentleman, he was Matteo Rossi who'd grown up in an orphanage and had worked with his hands.

"No," he said a little hoarsely, "not a *Vogue* cover."

Her smile dimmed and he walked slowly toward her.

"You're far more beautiful that any cover, *cara,*" he said

softly, and what could he do then but frame her face in his hands and kiss her?

It was a light kiss, the whisper of his lips against hers, but it made him groan.

He wanted more. He wanted everything and from the way she responded, holding back for a heartbeat, then rising on her toes, sighing against his mouth, parting her lips to his, so did she.

Matteo groaned again and slid a hand under her sweat-shirt. She gasped as his fingers skated over the silken flesh of one breast, moaned as they danced across the nipple.

"Matteo," she whispered, "oh, God, Matteo…"

His body clenched like a fist. He lifted his head, looked blindly into her eyes. Then he drew his hand out from under her shirt and walked away.

When he reached one of the stone counters, he clutched the edge with both hands, waited for his heartbeat to return to something approaching normal. When it did, he faced her again.

She was standing as he'd left her, her eyes enormous, her lips slightly parted. Desire, fierce and hot, swept through him but he fought it and jerked his chin toward the plates and other things he'd set aside.

"Supper's almost ready," he said briskly. "How about setting the table?"

He saw her throat constrict as she swallowed. She swayed a little. Then she flashed a smile that he knew was as phony as his casually phrased request.

"Sure," she said, and when she turned away and went to do as he'd asked, it was all he could do not to go after her, swing her into his arms and carry her to his bed.

They ate, or pretended to eat, in a strained silence broken only by Isabella's polite, "This is very good," and his equally polite, "I'm glad you like it." Rio poured the wine but after a couple of obligatory sips, neither of them touched their glasses.

Finally, she put her knife and fork across her plate, touched her lips with her napkin and set it beside the plate.

"You know," she said, "it turns out that I'm not very—"

"No. Neither am I."

She pushed back her chair. He followed. They rose to their feet.

"I'll help you clean up," she said.

"No," he said quickly. "I'll take care of it. You go on to bed. You must be exhausted."

She nodded. "I am. Yes. I—I—"

Ah, sweet Mary, she looked so lost.

"Isabella," he said in a low voice.

She looked up at him. Her eyes were shiny with unshed tears.

"I was a fool to come here," she whispered.

"No. You weren't. I'm the fool. I shouldn't have—"

"You were kind. You took in a stray, and I— I've overstayed my welcome."

"Isabella—"

"It doesn't matter. I'll be out of your way first thing in the morning. I've thought it through and it's ridiculous for me not to phone my sister. She'll come get me and—"

"You don't need her. I'll take care of it."

She shook her head. "I'm not about to let you drive me all the way to the city."

"It's not that far."

"It's a couple of hours. At least. If there's traffic—"

"Hell, what do I care about traffic? I'll take care of you."

"I don't need anyone to take care of me."

"Yes. You do." Rio pushed aside the chair that separated them. "And I'm the one who's going to do it."

Isabella could feel fury growing inside her. He'd been tak-

ing care of her, all right, first driving her half out of her mind
with his kisses, then turning cool and distant. Did he think
she was a child?

Because she damned well wasn't.

"Look," he said, his tone so conciliatory it made her teeth
grind together, "we shouldn't be having this conversation.
It's late. You're tired. And—"

"And what?" She closed the small distance between them,
chin up, eyes molten gold, everything about her ready for a
fight. "You think I don't know what's going on? That for all
your Good Samaritan talk, you're sorry as hell you ended up
in this mess?"

"What mess?" He was bewildered. What the hell was she
so angry about? "All I did was—damnit, I don't know what
I did! What's got you so ticked off?"

"Me?" Isabella poked a finger into the center of his chest.
"I am *not* ticked off. You are. And I know the reason. You've
been stuck with me the entire day. And I haven't tumbled into
bed with you when you made those pathetic moves on me
and—"

"Pathetic moves?"

She blinked. Had she actually said that? Hadn't she just
finished telling herself he was the one who'd backed off after
each kiss? It was one or the other, she thought grimly, and
what did it matter which?

"Pathetic moves," she repeated recklessly, despite the swift
glimmer of anger in his eyes. "That's what I said."

Rio's jaw shot forward. "Damnit, woman," he said, grabbing her wrist, "do not poke your finger at me! And do not
twist the truth. If my moves were so pathetic—and, trust me,
Ms. Orsini, they weren't 'moves' at all—if they were, how
come you responded by climbing all over me?"

That made her eyes flash. Good. Why should she be the
only one hurling insults?

"You're joking. I climbed all over you?"

"Like tonight, when I brought you that clothing. There I was, being, yes, a Good Samaritan, and how did you respond?" He lowered his head until they were eye to eye. "Like a cat in heat on a back alley fence, that's how."

Her face turned crimson.

"You," she said in a voice that trembled, "are a horrible man."

"Oh, I must be," Rio snarled. "Hell, only a horrible man would tolerate the presence of a woman who showed up for an appointment six hours late."

"Two. And what's it to you? I wasn't supposed to meet with you, I was meeting with your full-of-himself boss."

"Three, and you don't know a thing about my boss."

"I know all I need to know."

"For instance?"

"He's pretentious."

Rio's eyes narrowed. "The hell he is."

"He's a cold-hearted SOB."

"And you know this, how?"

"I just do," Isabella snapped.

"Oh, that's brilliant. 'I just do,'" Rio said, mimicking her in a faux soprano that made Isabella want to scream.

The fact was, everything about him made her want to scream.

How could she have even imagined wanting to go to bed with him? He wasn't only horrible. He was arrogant and disgustingly macho and he twisted every word, every situation, to his own ends.

"You," Isabella said, her nose an inch from his, "are an arrogant example of everything I despise! You—you toady to the rich, you make excuses for them—"

"Don't hold back," Rio said coldly. "Not on my account."

"You dance to your boss's tune because he lets you play

at being him. Just look at you, living in his house, eating his food, drinking his wine… What are you laughing at? Damnit," she shrieked, "do not laugh at me, Rossi. Do not dare laugh at—"

Rio pulled her into his arms.

"Let go," she demanded, but he'd had enough.

He kissed her. And she went up in flames.

She grasped his shirt. Rose on her toes. Opened her mouth to his and sank her teeth delicately, deliciously into his bottom lip. She moaned. Whimpered. Pressed her body to his and he knew he was done pretending he didn't want her.

Rio thrust his hands deep into her hair and lifted her against him. She cried out and ground her hips against his erection.

This, he thought, this was the one real thing, the one honest thing between them.

"Matteo," she moaned, and even that was all right. He *was* Matteo Rossi; he was more him tonight than he had ever been Rio D'Aquila.

He drew back, just enough to look into her eyes, and any last remaining anger flew away.

"Isabella. *Cara mia. Bella mia.*" He ran his hand along the side of her face, her skin like silk under his callused fingertips, her eyes as filled with him as his surely were with her.

"Tell me," he said gruffly. "I need to hear the words."

Isabella sighed, and what he heard in that single expulsion of breath almost stopped his heart.

"Make love to me," she said, lifting her arms, winding them around his neck, standing on her toes so she could press herself against him. "Please," she whispered. "I want you so badly—"

Rio knew the right answer. The one logic demanded, but he was long past logic.

He said her name. Took her mouth in a deep, hungry kiss.

Then he scooped her into his arms and, still kissing her, carried her swiftly through the dark, silent house.

To his bed.

CHAPTER EIGHT

THE bedroom was an ebony sea dappled by the light of an ivory moon.

Rio's bed stood beneath a star-filled skylight.

He carried Isabella to it, still kissing her, never wanting the kiss to end, and slowly, slowly let her slide down his body until she was on her feet.

"Isabella," he whispered against her lips.

"Matteo," she sighed, and he groaned because his name—and yes, it was his name—sounded so right, coming from her mouth.

He cupped her face with his hands, lifted it to his, traced the arcs of her cheeks with his thumbs.

And kissed her.

He loved kissing her.

Loved everything about it.

The feel, the sweetness of her lips. The little moans that escaped her throat.

He'd always enjoyed sex, everything about it, from the simplicity of kissing to the hot excitement of completion, but kissing Isabella—

How could there be this much pleasure in a kiss?

She tasted of wine. Of the night. Of herself. And of desire.

For him.

Only for him.

He said her name again as he gathered her against him. She rose on tiptoe, returning kiss for kiss. He slid his hands under her sweatshirt. She cried out when he cupped her naked breasts. Her flesh was cool, the nipples pebbled.

"Oh, God," she whispered, her voice trembling, "oh, God, yes, Matteo, yes, yes."

It almost undid him.

He drew her arms up, followed the path with his hands, reached her wrists and slowly, carefully eased off her sweatshirt and dropped it to the floor. He drew her close, kissed her throat, the slope of her breast. He could feel her heart pounding beneath his lips and he ached to go further, to take her nipple into his mouth, but now her entire body was trembling; she was breathing hard and he told himself to go slowly, slowly, not to frighten her, not to do anything too quickly.

But she rose on her toes. Leaned into him. Moved against him.

"Isabella," he said roughly. "Sweetheart, when you do that—when you do that—"

He groaned, drew her to him again and kissed her, this kiss deeper, harder, and she moaned softly and gave herself up to its hot demand.

His hands dropped to her waist. She had tied the cord of the sweatpants as tightly as possible. Still, the pants were loose on her and rested lightly on her hips.

He wanted to see her.

Was it too soon?

He had to find out.

He put his thumbs under the soft cotton waistband. Isabella shook her head and burrowed against him.

"Matteo," she said, and he knew that yes, it was too soon. Instead, he wove his fingers into her hair until she raised her head and looked up at him.

She was beautiful. Real. No artifice. Just her.

Had there ever been a woman in his bed who had not done anything to enhance her looks? He didn't think so but, hell, he didn't want to think about other women now.

There was no one else.

There was only Isabella.

He kissed her. Again. And again, until he felt her relax against him. She was so warm in his arms, her naked skin like satin under his hands as he stroked her. His fingers brushed the sides of her breasts and she trembled.

"Matteo. I should have told you before this—I should have told you that I—that I haven't—" She swallowed drily and made what she knew was probably the understatement of the decade. "I haven't done this very much."

He hated the whisper of apology he heard in her voice— and hated himself for the swift, primitive response it engendered in him.

He believed firmly in sexual equality but deep in his man-as-mighty-hunter heart, he knew there was something special in being the man who would teach a woman the meaning of passion.

"I just—I just don't want you to expect—to expect—"

Rio kissed her to silence.

"All I expect is to please you," he said gruffly, and vowed to himself that he would.

Added reason to take all the time in the world to make love to her, even as—hell, especially as the urge to back her against the wall, free himself of his sweatpants and hers and thrust into her, beat hard in his blood.

He knew he could do that, despite her admission of near-innocence. He was good at sex, and at making sex last. He liked to prolong the pleasure for himself and for the woman he was with.

He liked knowing he had such complete control of himself, of his lover, of the moment.

Tonight, all that mattered was pleasuring Isabella.

He tilted her face up to his. Kissed her mouth until her lips parted and he could feast on the sweet taste of her. Kissed her throat until she moaned and her head fell back. Kissed her breast, such a delicate breast, kissed lower, lower...

She cried out as his lips closed around one nipple. The taste of her flesh was sweeter than anything he'd ever known. He tongued it and she cried out again, the sound urgent, shocked, hot with pleasure and excitement.

His hands went to the waistband of her sweatpants again. She held her breath. *Now,* he told himself, and slowly, slowly, he eased the sweatpants down her legs.

A groan broke from his throat as he gathered her against him and felt the warmth of her naked body against his.

Cristo, he wanted to see her.

But she was trembling, and he knew it was still too soon.

Sweat beaded his forehead. His pulse was going crazy. Still, he held her. Only held her. He could feel her heart racing against his, or maybe it was his heart racing against hers.

It didn't matter.

He waited, waited, waited until she sighed. Her hand crept up his chest, to his shoulders and she whispered his name.

He let go of her and pulled off his sweatshirt. Pushed down his bottoms. Stepped out of them.

Then he drew her into his arms again, closing his eyes at the hot, delicious feel of her against him.

"Isabella," he murmured, his arms tightening around her as he bent to her and took her lips in kiss after kiss, each deeper than the last. He lifted her against him, her breasts against his chest, her belly against his and she gasped when his aroused flesh pressed at the apex of her thighs.

"Matteo," she whispered, and he heard all the questions in the world in the way she said his name.

"It's all right, *cara,*" he said gruffly.

"I don't know if—I mean, I don't know if—"

He was big. He knew that. In typical male fashion, the knowledge that a woman's eyes would widen with pleasurable anticipation when she first saw him, erect and eager, when she first felt him, naked against her, had always given his ego a boost.

Those women had not been Isabella.

"Don't be afraid," he said softly. He took her hand. Brought it to him. "This is only another part of me. I won't hurt you, sweetheart. I swear it."

He caught his breath as her fingers brushed over him. Touched him. She made a soft, questioning sound. He closed his eyes. Told himself not to do anything foolish but then she closed her hand around him and he had to grit his teeth to keep from tumbling her onto the bed.

He let her explore him. He was the one trembling now, as he fought to hang on to his sanity.

At last, he groaned. It was too much.

"Isabella," he said thickly, "sweetheart—"

Her arms wound around his neck, and he took her down to the bed. When he drew back, she grabbed for the duvet bunched beneath them. He knew she wanted to cover herself, that being undressed before a man was new to her. But he had to see her and he caught her hands, kissed them, then gently brought them to her sides.

"It's all right," he whispered. "Isabella. Let me see you."

She drew an unsteady breath. He pulled back. And looked at the woman he wanted with every hard pulse of the blood beating through his veins.

His heart turned over.

She was more than beautiful.

She was exquisite.

Small, tip-tilted breasts, crowned by delicate rose nipples.

A narrow waist. A woman's hips, curved and lush. And at the juncture of her thighs, a cluster of dark curls.

He bent his head. Took one nipple and then the other into the heat of his mouth. She moaned; her fingers threaded through his hair.

"Matteo," she whispered, "oh, Matteo—"

He moved between her thighs. Kissed her eyes. Her mouth. Her throat. Her breasts. He moved lower. Lower still. Her belly. Her navel. The dark curls at the juncture of her thighs.

Her breath caught.

"Wait! You can't—"

He could. Nothing would stop him. He wanted to inhale her scent, taste the sweetness of her most intimate flesh.

Rio put his face against her. Found her, licked her and she gave a long cry of rapture that rose into the night.

"Oh, God," she sobbed, "oh, God…"

Her thighs fell open. He slipped his hands beneath her, lifted her to him, kissed her until she was weeping. He moved up her body, took her mouth in a long, deep kiss, let her taste their mingled passion on his tongue.

"Matteo," she sobbed. "Please. Please—"

He could wait no longer.

Blindly, he pulled open the drawer in the nightstand. His hands were shaking; it took an eternity to tear open the little packet, then ease the condom along his length.

He felt her eyes on him.

That she was watching him made him harder than ever— except, that wasn't possible. Any harder, he would die, he thought, and he came back to her, whispered her name, knelt between her still-parted thighs.

And paused at the entrance to her body.

Rio shuddered.

The sensation was exquisite.

And he, the man who knew how to make sex last, knew he was dangerously close to the edge.

She was wet. Hot. Tight. He moved slowly. Deliberately. It was exquisite torture. Holding back. Watching her face. Seeing her eyes blur, her lips part.

Feeling her ready to take him inside her.

Cristo, it was too much, too much, too much—

Her arms tightened around him. She lifted her hips.

"Don't," he said. "When you do that, I can't—I can't—"

She moved again, brought his mouth to hers and kissed him.

Rio closed his eyes and sank into her.

She gave a little sob.

"Did I hurt you?" he whispered.

She answered by lifting her hips again. And again. Until he was groaning, holding her against him, moving inside her, faster, harder, harder...

Isabella screamed with pleasure.

And Rio threw back his head and flew with her into the night.

Time passed.

Rio's face was buried against Isabella's throat. The delicious smell of her—woman, soap, sex—was in every breath he took.

It was the most alluring scent he'd ever known.

And, *Dio,* he was going to crush her if he didn't move. But when she felt him start to shift his weight, she tightened her arms around him.

"No," she whispered. "Stay with me, please."

"I'm not going anywhere, sweetheart. I'm just afraid I'm too heavy for you."

"You're not. I just—I just want—"

He rolled to his side without letting go of her, tucked her against him, his arms holding her fast.

"Me, too," he said gruffly, and kissed her mouth. She sighed; the soft sound, the whisper of her breath, filled him with pleasure. "You okay?"

She nodded. Her hair slid over his skin like silk.

"Are you sure? I didn't mean to go so fast—"

Isabella put her fingers lightly across his lips.

"You were wonderful."

"Yeah?" He smiled. "Not that I'm looking for compliments—" She gave a soft laugh and he brushed his mouth over hers. "You're what's wonderful, *cara*."

"You're making me blush."

Rio grinned, propped his head on his hand and looked down at her. It was true. Her face, kissed by starlight, had turned a soft shade of pink.

"I know it's silly, after—after we just had—"

"After we just made love," he said, his voice rough.

She nodded, traced the lines of his face with her fingertip.

"You have a scar on your chin."

"Uh-huh," he said, sucking her finger into the heat of his mouth.

"How did it happen?"

He shrugged. "I do some boxing. Not professionally," he added quickly, when her eyes widened. "Just to work out."

"It's very sexy."

He grinned. "So is the way you blush."

She smiled up at him. It made him want to kiss her again. Make love to her again. Bring her to the edge of the universe and hold her there before letting go.

Great.

His thoughts were turning him hard. An out-of-control lover. Just what she didn't need.

But he couldn't resist giving her one more kiss. And then another. And another...

She moved against him.

He groaned, leaned his forehead against hers.

"No. It's too soon—"

Her hand slipped between them. "Is it?" she said in tones of absolute innocence.

Cristo, she was teasing him. And he loved it.

Another little packet. Another condom. Then he gave a low growl and drew her to him, brought her leg high over his hip and slid into her.

Isabella moaned. Kissed him. Bit lightly into his lip.

This time, he set a harder rhythm. She met it, matched it, and he caught her by the waist, brought her on top of him, watched her face, her eyes as she rode him.

At the end, she collapsed against him.

They fell asleep that way, her body covering his, his arms holding her tight.

Isabella came awake with a start.

She was in a strange room. A room swathed in darkness save for a sliver of light at the far end.

Her heart leaped into her throat.

The sliver of light grew. It was from a door, and the door was opening to reveal a tall, dark figure...

"Isabella?"

The breath whooshed from her lungs.

"Matteo," she said in a shaky whisper.

Of course. She was in Rio D'Aquila's house, in Matteo Rossi's bed.

"Sweetheart. Did I startle you?"

She sat up, holding the duvet to her throat.

"What time is it?"

Matteo came to the bed, made quick work of the duvet she held and drew her into his arms. God, the feel of his skin against hers...

"It's four-something in the morning." He pressed a kiss into her hair. "Forgive me, *cara*. I didn't mean to wake you."

He smelled wonderful. Man and sex. And, of course, Matteo. She thought of how his skin would taste if she nipped his shoulder, of what he would do if she put her hands on his chest and pushed him down backward on the bed.

"Hey." He reached for a long ebony curl, let it wind around his finger and gave a gentle tug. "What are you thinking about?"

Isabella cleared her throat. "Just that—that it's fine that I'm awake. I have to get up anyway."

"Ah," he said matter-of-factly. "Sure. Let me get you my robe. The bathroom is chill—"

"No. I mean, it's time I got up."

"It is?"

She nodded.

He put a finger under her chin and tilted her face up.

"Why?"

"Well, because—because—"

She frowned.

It was a good question. She'd made love with this man. Twice. She had slept with him, literally. Draped over him— she remembered that—naked skin to naked skin. And she was going to leave his bed because it was four in the morning and instead of making love, they were having a conversation?

Why, indeed? she thought again...

And giggled.

"Isabella Orsini," Matteo said sternly. Gently, he pushed her back on the bed and came down above her. "Are you laughing?"

She shook her head. "No," she gasped, and giggled again.

"Laughter. Just what a man wants to hear after he's made love to a woman."

"I wasn't—"

"You were." His tone softened; a devilish grin lifted the corners of his lips. "I'm glad."

Isabella smiled.

"So am I. This was—"

"Indeed it was," he said solemnly, but he spoiled it with another quick grin.

She smiled. "I don't know if I can move."

"Good. I don't want you to move. Well, not for a little while, anyway."

Sighing, she wrapped her arms around him. Crazy, he knew, but that she wanted his weight on her like this made him happy.

"Matteo?"

"Mmm?"

Isabella put her hand against his jaw. His skin was bristly with early morning stubble. It felt masculine and sexy, and she thought of how wonderful it would feel against her breasts.

"Of all the things I ever thought about—about sex—"

"About making love," he said quietly.

She nodded. "I never imagined feeling so, well, so happy afterward."

Her words, her simple honesty, made his heart swell. He turned on his side, gathered her against him and pressed a kiss into her hair.

The thing was, he'd never imagined feeling like this after sex, either. Sated? Sure. Relaxed? Of course. Content? Yes, absolutely.

But happy, to use her word...

Not like this.

And *happy* was the wrong word. What he felt was bigger than that, deeper, more intense.

Much more intense, he thought, and he gave her a quick kiss and sat up.

"Okay," he said briskly. "Here's the schedule."

"Oh, God." Isabella gave a dramatic sigh. "I *hate* schedules!"

He grinned. "Now, why does that not surprise me?"

"See, I like the part where you draw up the schedule." She sat up, too, wrapped her arms around him from the back and sighed. "It's the carrying out part I'm not good at."

A moment ago, establishing emotional distance had seemed important. Now, turning around, taking Isabella in his arms and smiling at her was what mattered.

"Really," he said, widening his eyes.

"You laugh, but something always goes wrong. Like yesterday. The traffic. The directions. The car. And then, poof, so much for my schedule. It went up in smoke." She smiled. "But if it hadn't, would I have met you?"

Damned right you would have, he thought.

Hell.

He had to tell her.

Soon.

But first…

First, he thought, looking at her tousled curls, her kiss-swollen mouth, first there was that schedule.

Showering together.

Breakfasting together.

Going back to bed together.

"Isabella," he said thickly, and he brought her down beneath him and forgot everything but the woman in his arms.

Forget everything, including a condom.

Dawn was tinting the sky crimson.

Rio awoke alone in his bed. He could hear the shower running.

Isabella, he thought, smiling—

And then his smile faded as he remembered that he hadn't used a condom the last time they'd made love.

Cristo.

He had never been that careless before. He always used protection, even when a woman said she was on the Pill. Only a fool took chances. He knew the possibility that Isabella might become pregnant was small. Miniscule, really. One ejaculation? Things didn't happen that way. He knew couples who'd tried for years to conceive.

Still, he would mention it to her.

Ask if this was her so-called safe time of the month. Tell her that, of course, if anything happened, he would—he would help her with whatever had to be done.

It was a sobering thought.

Even more sobering was the fact that he hadn't remembered to use a condom.

That his naive, inexperienced Isabella had driven every logical thought from his head.

No woman had ever done that before.

His smile wavered.

He wasn't sure he liked the feeling.

The sound of the shower stopped. Rio sat up, swung his feet to the floor, went to the bathroom and quietly pushed open the door. His lover stood before the mirror. She'd knotted a bath towel around her like a sarong; she was using another to dry her hair.

Botticelli, he thought, Venus, rising from the sea—and, all at once, nothing mattered as much as coming up behind her and wrapping his arms around her waist.

She smiled at him in the mirror. "Hello," she said softly.

Rio drew her back against him. "Isabella," he whispered.

It seemed all he was capable of saying and when she sighed his name—*Matteo*—he thought, once again, how right his name, his true name, sounded on her lips.

She was Isabella. He was Matteo. Two strangers, brought together by chance.

And now, they were lovers.

Lovers.

Something swept through him. An emotion that had nothing to do with sexual pleasure and everything to do with—with—

With what? *Dio,* he had no answers for anything.

Except for this.

"I have an idea," he said.

She smiled. "I can tell."

He laughed.

"That, too. But I have another idea."

Isabella turned in his arms, placed her hands against his chest, looked up at him.

"What?"

"Don't go back to the city. Not just yet."

"But I have to. I—"

"Stay with me." He bent to her, brushed his lips over hers. "I want to show you something."

She touched her fingers to his lips.

"What is it?"

"A place. One that's all mine."

She smiled. "And where is this place?"

"You'll see."

"Ah. A secret."

"One I want to share only with you. Spend the weekend with me, *cara.* Please."

Isabella thought of all the reasons to say no.

It was Saturday, and she always worked the Union Square Outdoor Market on Saturday. Initially, she'd sold bouquets and plants; now, increasingly, she sold more elaborate flower arrangements. It was excellent and inexpensive advertising for her business.

There was more, too.

She did her weekly food shopping Saturdays: staples at

Costco, fresh stuff at—naturally—the Union Square market and at Whole Foods. Plus, she was supposed to meet Anna for lunch and—oh, hell—return her car. Okay. That was another story altogether.

"Isabella," Matteo said, "stay with me."

The towel fell away as she went up on her toes and gave him her answer with a kiss.

CHAPTER NINE

A LITTLE after dawn, Isabella announced it was time for breakfast, and that she would prepare it.

"Not to boast or anything," she said, fluttering her lashes, "but I make the world's best scrambled eggs. And bacon. And toast. And coffee."

When Rio said he'd help, she pointed to a kitchen chair and said, "Sit."

He laughed.

He couldn't remember the last time someone had told him what to do, even in a teasing way. He could just picture the looks on the faces of his staff if anyone had.

But this wasn't anyone, it was Isabella.

And he certainly couldn't recall a woman making him breakfast. Not that women didn't offer. He simply never took them up on it. There was something far too intimate in letting a woman cook your breakfast, even if she'd spent the night in your bed.

Sex was one thing.

Breakfast was another.

It was the kind of logic only another man could understand.

In fact, he'd once had that conversation with Dante Orsini, when Dante was still a bachelor.

They'd bumped into each other at a Starbucks a little past

eight one morning, Dante paying for a *caffé Americano* just as Rio ordered a *caffé Macchiato*.

For some reason, they'd exchanged slightly embarrassed looks.

Dante had spoken first.

"I, ah, I didn't have time for coffee at home this morning," he'd said.

"Me, neither," Rio had said, his tone as uncomfortable as Dante's. Then he'd laughed a little shamefacedly and admitted that the problem was a woman who'd wanted to make coffee for him, and Dante had grinned and admitted to the same thing.

"Too much togetherness," Rio had said. "Last thing I want to face in the morning is a woman hell-bent on showing me her domestic side."

Dante had grinned and agreed.

Talk about your own words coming back to haunt you, Rio thought. What would Dante say right about now, if he knew his relative was in this kitchen, doing exactly that?

It was not a good thing to dwell on.

"Matteo." Rio blinked. Isabella, arms folded, gave a dramatic sigh. "I don't see you sitting down and leaving this to me."

He grinned.

"Yes, ma'am," he said, and then he grabbed her, lifted her off her feet and kissed her.

Then he sat down and hoped he was remembering correctly, and that there actually were bacon and eggs in the refrigerator.

There were. Free-range eggs, Isabella said with approval, and explained why hens should be kept cage-free. There was bacon, too, from—he lost track of the "from" part, but Isabella pronounced it perfect.

She was what was perfect, Rio thought.

And made a mental note to thank his caretaker for laying in the right foods.

He'd have to thank the guy for a lot of things, starting with leaving before Isabella arrived yesterday.

Was it only yesterday?

It seemed impossible that he'd only known her so short a time. He felt as if he'd known her for a lifetime. He was so at ease with her, so relaxed.

He couldn't remember feeling this way with another woman.

With anyone.

No pressures. No demands. No trying to read the true meaning behind her words or actions.

She was with him because she wanted to be with him, not because of who he was or what he might be able to do for her. He couldn't recall that ever happening. Everybody wanted something from him. It was part of his life and though he hated it, he'd learned to endure it.

Nothing about yesterday, last night or this morning had anything to do with endurance... Except in bed, he thought, biting back a smile. Not that he'd ever had any complaints but, *Cristo,* there wasn't an eighteen-year-old out there who could possibly have anything on him today.

And it was Isabella's doing.

The cold truth was that a woman who said "no" to a man's sexual advances often became a prize to pursue. The even colder truth was that once a man captured that prize, his interest lessened.

Nothing even close to that was happening to him.

The more he made love to Isabella, the more he wanted her. And it wasn't because she was so innocent that every touch, every caress brought her such unabashed delight and surprise.

It was because making love to her, with her, had a power

that went beyond the physical. He couldn't explain it to himself except to suspect it had to do with, well, with friendship. He liked being with her, outside of bed as well as in it.

His life in what he increasingly thought of as the real world was a full, successful one. He liked who he was, his achievements, the complexities of business…

But now—now, he had the sense that something had been missing from it. A day didn't have to begin and end with appointments and conferences, it could begin and end with a woman.

With this woman.

Rio frowned.

Not that he could imagine his life centering on her. On any woman, but—

"—or runny?"

Rio blinked. Isabella was looking at him, her winged eyebrows arched, waiting for an answer to a question he hadn't heard.

"Sorry, *cara*. What did you ask me?"

"I asked if you like your eggs well-cooked or runny?"

"Runny," he said with dignity, "is not a word meant to pique the appetite."

She grinned. She had an extraordinary grin, one that involved her nose wrinkling with delight.

"Okay, I'll rephrase that. Soft or hard?"

It was his turn to grin.

"I can think of a lot of answers to that question but none that have to do with scrambling eggs."

"Keep your mind on eggs," she said with mock severity, "unless you want us both to die of hunger."

She was right. They'd eaten hardly anything last night. Rio gave a sigh suited to a long-suffering male in torment.

"Soft," he said.

"Good. Because—"

"But definitely not runny. And while you're asking, I like my bacon crisp, my toast light, my coffee black—"

She poked out her tongue. He grinned again.

"Is that a no? Or is it an invitation?"

She blushed. He loved it when she did but for all those charming blushes, he could see her becoming more and more relaxed with him.

She'd begun touching him more. Exploring him, during sex. She was more comfortable with him in other ways, too. What she'd just done, for instance, giving him little teasing answers to his questions.

He had the feeling she'd learned to keep herself quietly in the background most of her life.

But not with him.

She'd been feisty from the second she'd come limping up his driveway.

Now, she was giving him orders.

And she was sexy as hell.

He wanted to know more about her. He wanted to know *all* about her. He usually made a point of avoiding learning more than necessary about his lovers. Where they came from, what they wanted out of life... He knew it might seem—that word again—cold not to show an interest.

It wasn't. It was just that those things were too personal.

A man and woman didn't have to open themselves to each other's scrutiny just because they slept together.

Now, watching Isabella beating eggs hard enough so every part of her was jiggling—and, *Dio,* those jiggled parts were distracting—he realized he didn't feel that way this time.

He wanted to know everything about Isabella. Everything, from her favorite books to her favorite foods. What she'd been like as a little girl, although he knew she had to have been bright and sweet and adorable. How she'd come to love working with her hands in the soil.

Most of all, he wondered why sex was so new to her.

Male chauvinist bastard that he was, he loved sensing that he was the first man to make her cry out when he brought her to the brink of orgasm and held her there, suspended, until neither she nor he could wait another heartbeat for the incredible pleasure of release.

They'd come close to not even making it out of the bedroom a little while ago.

Each time she'd tried to get dressed, he'd grabbed the top or bottom of the sweat suit and demanded ransom in the form of a kiss. He'd finally relented, or so he'd allowed her to think, letting her put on the bottoms before he danced away with the top.

Isabella had narrowed her eyes and slapped her hands on her hips. It had made for a delectable sight, the pants riding low, her lovely breasts naked, the pink nipples delicately peaked.

"I cannot get dressed if you keep undressing me," she'd said with an indignation that didn't match the laughter in her eyes. "And you did say you wanted an early start to take me to this secret place you absolutely refuse to talk about!"

He'd grabbed her, bent her back over his arm for a dramatic kiss, told her fine, she could banish him now.

"But just think of what you'll be missing," he'd said, curving his hand around one sweet breast and putting his mouth to the tip.

She'd moaned—*Dio,* he loved that moan of hers—but then she'd turned the table on him, putting her lips to his ear and whispering, "You think of what *you'll* be missing, too," and the sexy taunt had made him so hard he'd kissed her mouth— and gotten the hell out of there before he tumbled her back on the bed again.

He damned well wanted to. But there wasn't time.

Isabella didn't know it yet, but they had several hours of flying time ahead of them.

So he'd gone downstairs, into the freshness of the morning where he'd listened to the heartbeat of the ocean while he breathed deep and got his hormones under control.

Then he'd phoned the Plaza and left a message for a visiting Greek ship owner, canceling an appointment for drinks that evening. He gave it a couple of minutes and then he made another call, this time to his office where he left voice mail for his PA to pick up on Monday.

"I won't be in today, Jeanne. Reschedule my appointments for the middle of the week."

Jeanne would be shocked.

Well, so was he.

He never canceled appointments, much less cleared his entire calendar, but then, he'd never been—he'd never been eager to spend time alone with a woman before.

If things went as he intended, he and Isabella would still be in Mustique come Monday and Tuesday and, for all he knew, Wednesday.

Mustique.

A beautiful little island in the Caribbean. That was his surprise; that was where he was taking her. It was a long flight but worth it.

He was certain she would love the villa he owned there.

Rio sat back in his chair, feet crossed at the ankles, arms folded, watching Isabella bustle around the kitchen in his sweat suit.

She looked spectacular in it but he suspected he'd have to do a lot of fast-talking to convince her to go on wearing it while he flew them to the island.

There wasn't much choice.

It was early. Just after 6:00 a.m. The village boutiques

wouldn't be open yet. They *would* open, he was certain, for Rio D'Aquila, but that wasn't who he was.

He was Matteo Rossi.

And until the moment was right, that's who he would remain.

As for the villa—he'd bought it with part of his first big chunk of money. Five million dollars, more money than he'd imagined existed in the entire world.

His lawyer had invited him to celebrate by flying down to what he'd called his hideaway in the Caribbean for the weekend. That "hideaway" had turned out to be Mustique.

Gentle green hills. A pure blue sea. White sand beaches. And best of all, the attorney said, privacy.

Mustique, privately owned, was a getaway destination for lots of rich, famous people. There was no guarantee a reporter or photographer wouldn't leap out of a shrub, but if you were careful, the odds were good no one would point a finger and say, "Ohmygod, look who that is!"

Rio, who hadn't been famous back then, couldn't imagine needing a place like that but the beauty, the quiet of the island had enthralled him. His lawyer had turned him on to a small villa with a private stretch of beach that was going at a bargain price, thanks to some unfortunate soul's bankruptcy. Rio had taken a deep breath and bought it.

A couple of years later, he'd legally changed his name from Matteo Rossi to Rio D'Aquila. Everything he now owned— his Manhattan condo, the place in Southampton, his homes abroad, his Brazilian estate—were Rio's.

For some reason, he'd left the deed to the villa untouched. Matteo Rossi, not Rio D'Aquila, owned it.

One less lie to deal with today, he thought, and despite Isabella's command that he sit, he rose, went to the stove, put his arms around her, nuzzled aside her dark curls and kissed the nape of her neck.

"Careful or the bacon will burn," she said, but she turned in his embrace and kissed him.

It was a long, deep kiss. It made him want her. Again. He hardened against her and she gave one of those sexy little moans he'd come to love, but then she put her hands against his chest and said, with a breathless little laugh, that he was better than any of the diets she'd ever tried when it came to keeping down the daily calorie count.

"Why would you need a diet?" he said with absolute truthfulness. One of the things he lov—he liked about her was that she didn't look like a toothpick.

"Flattery," she said, "will get you a burned breakfast."

He laughed. She grinned, her nose doing that cute wrinkly thing, gave him another quick kiss, and he went back to the table, swung a chair around so he could sit on it and watch her some more, his arms folded along the back, his chin propped on his folded arms.

She was going to love the villa.

He hadn't been there in a long time. He'd been too busy, making deals and making money. A housekeeper and groundskeeper came by every couple of weeks to keep things organized.

And he'd never taken a woman there.

That was another good thing. A very good thing. Mustique would be about fresh starts. And honesty.

It would also be about being in a place where he could take Isabella out to some small, intimate café for dinner. Hold her in his arms as they moved to slow music on a tiny dance floor. Behave like real people. And any time, in the cool of the house or the heat of the sun, they could go into each other's arms and make love.

And then…

A muscle flickered in Rio's jaw.

Then, when the time was right, he'd admit everything.

That he had not been—not been completely forthright with her but then, this had begun as a clever game.

How could he possibly have known it would turn into something else?

Isabella, his Isabella, would understand. He was certain of it. She wasn't a prima donna. Okay, she might be a little miffed at first but once she got over the shock, she'd laugh along with him at how he'd dug the hole he'd made for himself deeper and deeper.

She would, wouldn't she?

Wouldn't she?

"What a long face!"

Rio jumped. Isabella was standing beside him, smiling.

"A long face, and *before* you've tasted my cooking!"

She had two plates in her hands. Rio shot to his feet and took them from her. He smiled, leaned in and kissed the tip of her nose.

"Everything looks perfect," he said.

Perfect eggs, perfect bacon, perfect toast...

Perfect woman, he thought, and his heart did something it had never done before.

It soared.

They were almost at the airport when he told her what his "surprise" was.

Isabella looked at him as if he'd lost his mind.

"We're flying to where?"

"Mustique. It's an island—"

"—in the Caribbean. I get that. But—but I can't just—just do something so—so outrageous on the spur of the moment!"

"That's what doing things on the spur of the moment is all about," Rio said, steering around a pickup truck loaded with crates of lettuce. "If it's not outrageous, what's the point?"

She stared at him. There was truth in that, if you were into doing outrageous things, but—

"But?" he said, and flashed her a smile. "I can hear the *but* from here, sweetheart."

"But," she said, "I can't."

"Because?"

"Well, because—because I have commitments."

"What commitments?"

What, indeed? Or maybe the question was, what commitment could possibly supercede the sheer joy of flying to an island in the sun with her lover? Her gorgeous, sexy, amazing lover.

"Well—well, I'm supposed to have lunch with Anna."

Rio reached into the pocket of his blue chambray shirt, took out his cell phone and handed it to her.

"Call her. Tell her you can't make it."

"I'm supposed to return her—" Isabella sucked in her breath. "Oh, boy. I'm supposed to return her car."

"Ah. The car. Right. I almost forgot that. Where'd you have the accident? Can you give me some kind of location?"

"No, not really. I just… Wait. There was a field of corn on my right."

Based on what he knew of the area, that narrowed things down to something like a zillion square miles.

"How about some visual clue? A house. A store. A sign."

"A sign," she said eagerly. "I passed it maybe five minutes before the car drove off the road."

"Uh-huh," Rio said, trying not to laugh. "Can you remember what it said?"

She frowned. "A man's name. James. Jack. Jeffrey." She snapped her fingers. "Jonas," she said happily. "Jonas's Organic Vegetables."

"Excellent. Call Anna, then give me the phone. I'll call—"

He'd almost said he'd call his caretaker. "I'll call a service station and arrange to have the car towed."

"But Anna—"

Rio checked his mirrors and pulled his truck onto the shoulder of the road. He undid his seat belt, reached over, cupped Isabella's face with his hands and gave her a long, deep kiss.

"I want us to be alone," he said gruffly. "In a place that's entirely mine." He stroked a curl from her temple. "If that's what you want, call your sister. If it isn't—" He took a deep breath. "If it isn't, I'll drive you back to the city, right now."

Isabella could feel her pulse racing.

This was crazy.

All of it.

And she didn't do crazy things.

She was not the driven-to-succeed type like Anna. She was not a walk-the-tightrope-over-the-chasm daredevil like her brothers. She was—she was Izzy, who liked to plant things and watch them grow. She was steady and nurturing.

Except, she wasn't only that Izzy anymore.

She was also Isabella, a woman sexually and emotionally awakened. A woman who had found a man who made her heartbeat rise into the stratosphere. Life had handed her a gift. It was something that probably would never come her way again.

"Isabella?" Matteo, her wonderful lover, looked deep into her eyes. "Am I taking you to the city, or to Mustique?"

Isabella took a steadying breath and punched Anna's number into the cell phone.

One ring. Two. Four and then, at last, Anna's voice, husky with sleep.

"Hello?"

"Anna. It's me. Izzy."

"Izzy? What time is it?" Anna's voice sharpened. Isabella

could picture her getting a look at the clock, then sitting upright in bed. "Are you okay?"

"I'm fine. I just—I just called to tell you I can't meet you
for lunch."

"Why not?" A pause, and then Anna's voice hardened.
"Isabella. Something's wrong. I can tell."

"Nothing's wrong. Why should anything be wrong? I told
you, I can't—"

There was mumbling in the background. Isabella rolled her
eyes. Wonderful. Anna's husband, Draco, was awake now,
too.

"No," Anna said, "it's just Izzy."

It's just Izzy. Isabella reached across the truck's console
and felt Matteo's warm, strong hand clasp hers.

"Also," she said, "I wrecked your car."

"Ohmygod! Izzy! You're not all right! You're in the hospital. Where? I can be there in—"

"Anna," Isabella said, "will you listen to me? The car's a
mess. I'm fine."

"Not fine," Matteo said softly, lifting her hand to his lips.
"You're perfect."

"Izzy? Who is that? You're with someone. A man? Izzy?
Are you with a—"

"I am," Isabella said, her breath catching as Matteo sucked
her finger into the heat of his mouth. "I am with a man. I've
been with him since yesterday. And I'm going to spend the
weekend—"

"The week," Matteo murmured. To hell with returning to
the city by Wednesday.

"And I'm going to spend the week with him."

Silence. Then she could hear Anna drag in a deep breath.

"Iz. Remember when I phoned you from Rome that time?
And I asked you if you remember Psych 101, that stuff about
fantasizing sex with a stranger?"

Isabella looked at her lover. She held up a finger, opened the door and stepped onto the grass.

"I do, indeed," she said calmly.

"Remember the rest of what you said?" Anna's voice rose. "About fantasizing sex with a stranger? A dark and dangerous stranger? You warned me against it. *You warned me!*"

"And you really listened," Isabella said with saccharine sweetness.

"Isabella. Damnit, when did you meet this man? Where? What do you know about him? For God's sake, Iz—"

"When did you meet Draco? What did you know about him? As I recall, you fell into bed with him, what, a couple of hours after you set eyes on each other."

"I am not going to discuss that with you," Anna said coldly. "Besides, that was different."

Isabella laughed. "Really?"

"Of course! I knew what I was doing. I had some experience dealing with men." Anna's tone softened. "This could be an awful mistake, Iz. Do you realize that?"

Isabella hesitated. She looked into the truck, at Matteo. His eyebrows rose. Did she need him with her? he was asking.

Yes, she thought, *oh, yes.*

"Izzy? Did you hear what I said? This could be a terrible, terrible mistake!"

Isabella shot her lover a reassuring smile. Then she turned away from him again.

"It could be," she said quietly. "I know that. But I'm happy, Anna. I've never been so happy before."

"Oh, Izzy! Honey, I want you to be happy, but—"

"Isabella?"

Matteo had gotten out of the truck, He came to Isabella and held out his hand. Isabella's heart lifted. She smiled and put her hand in his.

"Anna. I have to go. We're flying to—to—" She looked at Matteo, who leaned down and kissed her.

"Mustique," he said softly, and kissed her again.

"Mustique," Isabella said.

"Mustique?" Anna shrieked. "That's halfway around the world!"

"It's in the Caribbean."

"Jeez, Izzy, I know that! I only meant—" A long breath; Draco's low voice saying something. "Yes. Right. Iz? At least tell me who this man is. What's his name? How did you meet him? What does he do?"

"His name is Matteo Rossi. I met him at Rio D'Aquila's estate in Southampton. Matteo is the caretaker."

"And a pilot," Matteo said, with a smile.

"And a pilot," Isabella added, her eyes widening.

"The caretaker?" Anna said. "Ohmygod, Iz, this is a bad remake of *Lady Chatterley's Lover!*"

Isabella laughed. "Wrong," she said. "It's an excellent remake."

Then she closed the phone, gave it back to Matteo and when he kissed her this time, she knew she hadn't told Anna the most important thing of all.

She was more than happy.

She was in love.

CHAPTER TEN

ISABELLA had flown before.

Her brothers owned a sleek, private jet. She'd been up in it, of course. And she'd flown in commercial jets. Not often, but a few times.

This was different.

She was in the copilot's seat of a handsome plane Matteo said was a prop-jet.

And the man beside her, the pilot, was her lover.

She hadn't had time to think about that for very long. They'd parked at the airport, gone into a small building, Matteo had talked with a pleasant man behind a desk, and then he'd led her to a plane tethered near the runway.

"Does the plane belong to Rio D'Aquila?" she'd asked.

"It's mine," Matteo had answered, and then he'd quickly corrected himself. "I mean, I feel as if it's mine."

"Because you're the one who flies it?"

"Yes," he said, running a hand lightly over the fuselage. "But D'Aquila pilots it, too."

"Not as well as you, I bet."

Matteo had turned to her and ruffled her hair.

"Actually, he's pretty good."

"He doesn't mind that we're using it? Well, I mean, he doesn't know about me, but—"

"He doesn't mind," Matteo had said a little brusquely. "I wouldn't do this if I thought he would."

Isabella had put her hand on his arm.

"No," she'd said softly, "of course you wouldn't." She'd paused. "You really like him."

"I like some things about him. Other things... Yeah. There are things about him that definitely need changing. Basically, he's just a man, you know? He isn't all good or all bad."

He'd kissed her, a quick kiss, and then he'd become all purpose and efficiency as he made his way around the plane for what he'd called an inspection.

"Okay," he'd finally said.

He'd held out his hand, the same as he had at the truck, and Isabella had taken it and stepped into the sleek aircraft. He'd motioned her into a seat in the cockpit, told her to buckle herself in. Then he'd checked to make sure her seat belt was tight; he'd buckled himself in, too, put on a set of headphones, reached for what looked like a sea of dials and knobs and controls that had to be scrutinized to complete what he explained was a preflight checklist.

Isabella watched him. What an amazing man he was, capable of doing such varied things.

"I've never known anybody who knew how to fly," she said. "I mean, it's such an unusual thing to do—"

"I loved planes from the time I was just a kid, so when I had the chance to learn, I jumped at it." He glanced at her, warmed by the interest he saw in her expression. "I was a roughneck—a guy who's part of the drilling crew—on an oil field in Brazil. The foreman had a small plane." That all-business mask slipped just enough for him to turn to her and flash a boyish grin. "I probably made an ass of myself, hanging around, asking questions, and finally he figured the only way to get rid of me was to take me up and teach me."

Isabella smiled. "You make going after what you want sound easy."

"Nothing really important is ever easy to come by." Rio's smile tilted. "But some things are worth the cost." He leaned over and kissed her. Then he shot her another of those fantastic grins. "Sit back, sweetheart, and enjoy the view."

She knew he meant the view of the earth, slipping beneath them. But what her eyes feasted on was her lover.

Her lover was relaxed, obviously very much in command, pointing out things to her, his voice taking on quiet authority when he spoke with the various air traffic controllers along their flight path.

If Anna saw him now, Isabella suddenly thought, she wouldn't have called him a caretaker with such derision.

Okay. Not derision. Anna wasn't a snob. Had Isabella said the man she was going away with was a lawyer or an accountant or a doctor, Anna would still have warned her against it, but would her voice have climbed the scales?

"Your sister wasn't happy."

Isabella stared at Matteo. "Don't tell me you read minds, too." She sighed. "No. She wasn't."

"I understand that." He looked at her, took her hand and brought it to his lips. "She worries about you."

"Uh-huh. Anna's just a little more than a year older than I am but there are times you'd think she was my mother." She looked at him and grinned. "I already have a mother. Honestly, why would I want two?"

"So you have a sister and four brothers. A big family."

"Did I tell you all that?" She shook her head. "I talk too much."

"You don't," Rio said quickly, silently cursing himself for that slip of the tongue, "I'm just envious, is all."

"No brothers or sisters?"

"No family," he said. "I grew up in an orphanage." Hell,

what was he doing? He was telling her things he'd never told anyone else. Working as a roughneck, learning to fly, now this.

"Oh." Her voice was soft. "I'm sorry."

"Don't be," he said briskly. "Life is what it is, isn't that what people say?"

"Yes. But to have nobody—"

I have you.

The words were on the tip of his tongue. That they were, terrified him. He didn't have her. He didn't have anyone, didn't need anyone, didn't want anyone...

A voice crackled in his headset. They were coming up on an airport in the Carolinas, where he'd planned to touch down, refuel, and have a quick lunch.

Grazie Cristo for interruptions, Rio thought, and busied himself with the controls.

He tried to keep the conversation light once they were airborne again.

What had drawn Isabella to gardening?

A simple question, but she gave him an answer that made him see her as a little girl, growing up in a big house with a father she'd started out worshipping and ended up despising.

"An old country despot?" Rio said.

She shook her head.

"A crook," she said, so softly he had to strain his ears to hear her. "A *don*. A godfather. You know what that is?"

He knew, all right. How could you grow up in Italy without knowing? It occurred to him now that he'd seen the name *Cesare Orsini* in the papers, heard it on the news, never in a good way.

He'd just never associated that Orsini with his friend Dante.

Dio, how hard it must have been for Isabella, growing up

with that kind of ugly notoriety. It would have been difficult enough for the Orsini brothers, but for a daughter…

"My brothers broke with our father when they were still in their teens. It was harder for Anna and me. Girls, especially good Italian girls, aren't supposed to tell their father to go to hell."

"Cara." Rio reached for her hand. "I'm so sorry you had to go through something like that."

"No. It was all right. It made us strong. You know, pretending, for our mother's sake, that we were blind to the truth…" Her tone lifted; she gave a little laugh. "And we got even. Anna became a lawyer. A damned good one. I can still remember our father saying now he'd have a consigliere of his very own and Anna looking him in the eye and saying she'd sooner represent the Borgias than him."

Rio grinned. "I like your sister already." He looked at her. "And you? What was your act of rebellion, *bella?* Wait. Don't tell me. You wanted to nurture things, which is the very opposite of what your father does in his world. And, maybe, to get your hands dirty literally, not figuratively."

"Wow." Isabella smiled. "Now you're going to tell me you're a shrink and a philosopher, along with everything else."

"I am a lot of things," Rio said, after a few seconds. "Some good. Some bad. The more you get to know me, the more you'll see that." Another pause, and then he cleared his throat. "What I hope is—is that you'll believe that the good outweighs the bad. That you will—that you will care for me—"

"I will always care for you," Isabella whispered.

And, just as suddenly as that, Rio saw the truth.

He had fallen in love with her.

The realization stunned him.

He was not a man who had ever looked for love. He was not a man who believed in love. How could this have happened? Because, like it or not, it *had* happened. He didn't doubt his feelings, not for a minute. He was in love—deeply in love—with a woman who thought he was a man he was not.

Tell her. Tell her. Tell her...

"Your turn."

Rio swung his head toward her. "My turn?"

"To tell me more about yourself."

But it wasn't. Not when they were thousands of feet above the earth. When he told her the extent of the lie he was living, the lie he'd involved her in, he wanted to be able to take her in his arms, kiss her, make her see that it wasn't important if he called himself Rio or Matteo because they were the same man.

"I want to know more about that little boy in the orphanage," she said softly. "And how he grew up to be you."

Rio nodded. He could surely tell her that. If anything, she could look back on this conversation when the time came and see that he had never lied to her about the things that mattered.

Yes, he thought. He would tell her about that little boy, and the man he'd become.

It was a story he'd never before revealed to anyone.

He told her about living on the streets of Naples after he ran away from the orphanage. He told her the truth of it, not some sanitized version. The petty thefts. The pockets he'd picked. The cars he'd broken into so he could steal things left in them.

He told her without excuses, without emotion, and though her hand tightened on his, she never interrupted, never offered stupid platitudes, and he loved her all the more for it—but the more he talked, the more he wondered if he were making a mistake.

How would she look at him, once she knew all the sordid details of his early years? But it was too late to stop. She had the right to know everything about Matteo Rossi, and why and how he had become Rio D'Aquila.

He took a deep breath.

"I had a run-in with the *polizia* right around the time I turned seventeen. I got off easy but I knew everything would change once I turned eighteen. So I stowed away on a freighter and ended up in Brazil. I was broke and scared. There must have been a hundred times I thought about getting back on another freighter and heading home."

"But you didn't."

"No. The truth was, I didn't have a home to go back to. That was why I'd stowed away on that ship. To make a fresh start. New me, new life, new world." He laughed, his belly knotted with tension. "So, what do you think, *cara?* A sordid tale? A bad movie?"

"I think," Isabella said gently, "you must have been a brave, terrified, amazing boy." She reached for his hand. "You did what you had to do, and you made that new life for yourself."

A sweet sense of relief swept through him.

"I am happy you see that," he said softly.

"What happened after you stowed away? When you got to Brazil?"

"I made a plan."

"A plan?"

"I'd educate myself. Learn things that would help me find that new life. I began by studying Portuguese and English. I took some night classes. Math. Science. History. Business. I wasn't particular." He laughed. "I'd never tried putting anything in my head before so there was lots of room up there to fill. And I worked at every possible kind of job. Loading cargo. Construction. The oil fields. You name it, I did it. I took some risks, made a little bit of money, took some additional risk and made more. And I discovered I had a talent for—for organizing things."

"Like managing property."

His gut twisted.

"Something like that, yes."

"When did you meet Rio D'Aquila?"

When, indeed. Rio took a deep breath. He had to be careful now, very careful until tonight, when he could tell her everything.

"Remember the dot-com thing? The incredible rise in the stock market? Well, I'd played it. Invested in some of the companies. And—"

"And lost your money." Isabella sighed. "I remember."

The fact was, he hadn't lost anything. His investments had been wise ones; he'd made his first millions on that Wall Street stampede but if he told her that—

"Is that when you met D'Aquila?"

"Yes," he said, and damned if it wasn't true. He'd looked in the mirror, said goodbye to Matteo Rossi and hello to Rio D'Aquila, and he'd never looked back.

Until now.

"So, he offered you a job? Managing property for him?"

"It's probably more accurate to say I handle a variety of things for him."

"You like him."

"I, ah, I think we get along well enough."

"We. You say that so easily. Is he really a nice man?"

A good question. Rio felt a muscle knot in his jaw.

"I think he wants to be," he said, after a minute, "but there are lots of pressures on him."

"I guess he's not so awful. Here we are, using his plane."

Was a lie still a lie when it actually was the truth?

"Right," Rio said, "here we are, using his plane."

"But the villa we're going to... You said it's yours."

"Absolutely mine," he said without hesitation. "I bought it a long time ago with—with some winnings. It was the first home I'd ever owned." He reached for her hand and squeezed it. "It means a lot to me," he said gruffly. "But it will mean even more if you like it."

"I'll love it," Isabella said.

"Will you?" he said, his voice filled with relief.

How could she not? she thought, when she loved its owner with all her heart.

They reached Mustique in late afternoon.

Isabella's first glimpse of the island made her catch her breath.

Pale blue sky. Fluffy cotton clouds. A vivid blue sea, endless white beaches, lush emerald jungle. The colors of paradise, she thought happily.

An old Jeep was waiting for them at the small airport, keys dangling from the ignition. They got in and drove along a narrow road that climbed into the low hills. Just when it seemed as if the surrounding jungle was going to swallow them up, the trees opened onto a clearing and a graceful white building.

Matteo pulled the Jeep to a stop before it.

"Well," he said, as if his heart wasn't in his throat, "this is it."

"Oh," Isabella said, "oh, Matteo…"

He felt the tension within him ease, if only a little.

"You like it?"

"Like it?" She flung herself into his arms, gearshift be damned. "It's wonderful! Like a painting. Something by, what's his name—"

"Gauguin?"

She laughed with delight. "Exactly."

"Si. Sim." He grinned. "Yes. I thought the same thing the first time I saw it. Want to get out and take—"

But Isabella was already out of the Jeep, her face alive with pleasure. Rio followed, and took her hand.

"Thank you," she said, her eyes shining, "for sharing this beautiful place with me."

She turned to him, lay a hand on his chest, rose on her toes and kissed him.

Rio felt his throat constrict.

Showing her the pool, the beach, the sea, could wait.

It was far more important to scoop her into his arms, carry her into the villa and make love to her with a tenderness that made her weep.

They fell asleep in each other's arms but when Isabella woke, she was alone.

Shadows had crept across the bedroom; she could see the pink and violet of twilight through the open glass that led to the patio.

She could see her lover, as well.

Matteo stood at the teak railing, his back to her as he looked out over the sea.

The breeze ruffled his hair. He had thick, dark, short hair; she loved the feel of it under her hands.

She loved the feel of every part of him.

Her heart skipped a beat.

He was so strong, so masculine. He was a feast for her eyes and without him watching her, she could take all the time she wanted to enjoy the view.

Matteo wore faded jeans and a white T-shirt. The simple clothes emphasized his broad shoulders, long body, narrow hips and long, muscled legs.

He was—God, he was gorgeous.

And he was hers.

Not for forever. She knew that. They had not talked about

forever; how could they, when they'd only just met? Still, the truth was that she was already his, forever, in her heart.

She thought of Anna, always cynical about men, and how she teased Isabella about her love life. Her lack of a love life, to be accurate. Anna's teasing was a cover-up for sisterly concern.

You're waiting for Prince Charming, Iz, she'd say, *but there's a problem. He only exists in a fairy tale.*

Not true.

Pessimist or not, Anna had found her very own Prince Charming. Now, Isabella had found hers. Unfortunately, there was one huge difference. Anna and her prince had fallen in love. Isabella's story had not gone that way.

She'd fallen in love. Her prince had not.

Isabella sat up in the bed, sighed and thrust her hands into her hair, dragging the heavy mass back from her face.

Her prince was her lover but that wasn't the same as loving her. Okay. So be it. She was a grown-up, not a dreamy-eyed girl, and this wasn't a story, it was reality, and when it ended, she'd survive.

She'd survive. She'd have to survive, no matter how it hurt to think of a future without Matteo, and she must never let him know—

"Hey, sleepyhead. You're awake."

Quickly, she ran her hands over her eyes, turned toward him and forced a smile.

"Hi."

He sat down beside her, opened his arms and gathered her into his embrace.

"Mmm." He pressed his lips to her hair. "I love the way you smell when you wake up. All soft and female."

Her lips curved in a smile. "I like the way you smell, too. Sea and sky and Matteo." She leaned back in his arms and looked at him. "If only somebody could bottle that and turn it into cologne…"

He laughed. Then, his eyes searched hers.

"You really like it here, sweetheart?"

"How could I not? This beautiful island. This wonderful house." She smiled again. "And you. It's all perfect."

Rio linked his hands at the base of her spine.

"We can make it more perfect," he said softly.

"I don't see how."

"Dinner in a quiet little restaurant by the sea would be a start."

"Uh-huh. A quiet little restaurant, and me in those sweats." She laughed and wrinkled her nose. "I think there might be Health Department rules to keep me out."

He grinned and planted a kiss on the end of her nose.

"I took care of that."

"You did, huh?"

"I did."

"You bribed the department of health?" she said, laughing.

"I bought you some stuff to wear."

"What?"

"I said, I bought you—"

"Matteo. You can't do that."

He smiled. "Too late. I already did."

"But—"

"A dress. One of those floaty things with skinny straps. Brown. Well, maybe it's amber. Or dark gold."

"Matteo, listen to me. You cannot—"

"Shorts. A couple of T-shirts. Sandals. I guessed at the sizes."

"Would you listen?"

"So I went with size sixteen for the clothes and size ten for the sandals."

"Matt—" Isabella slapped her hands against his chest. "Size what for the clothes? And for the sandals? Do you really think—" Her eyes narrowed. "You're making that up."

"The part about the sizes?" He smiled. "Absolutely."

"But you really spent money on clothes for me? I can't let you do that. Really, I—"

"Really, you can. Things are inexpensive here." It was a lie of monumental proportions but what did one more matter? "I guessed at the sizes. And the colors." He nuzzled a curl from her cheek. "I ordered everything by phone, sweetheart, and they delivered it while you were sleeping. So if things don't fit, or if you don't like them—"

"If I don't like them? Are you crazy? I'm going to love them! How could you even think—"

Rio kissed her. Kissed her gently, then more deeply. She made a soft, sexy little sound; he groaned as she melted against him.

"Isabella," he whispered, and she fell back on the bed, her arms taking him down with her, and he made love to her as Matteo Rossi for the very last time because tonight, after he'd showed her off to the world…

Tonight, he was going to take the biggest risk of his life.

He was going to tell Isabella he'd been deceiving her.

And that he loved her, with all his heart.

A couple of thousand miles away, Anna Orsini Valenti was pacing the office at the rear of the bar her brothers owned in SoHo.

That she was able to pace it was proof of how carefully everyone else was maintaining their distance.

Eight of them—Anna, her husband, three of her brothers and their wives—were packed into the relatively small room.

The bar—*The Bar,* to use its semiofficial name—was still a real bar. Rafe, Dante, Falco and Nick had bought it for the express purpose of keeping it that way as the area all around it turned upscale and expensive.

They had done little to change it, and the little they had done had not included expanding the office. It was small. Very small. On a good day, all four brothers, big men every one, constituted a crowd.

"For the tenth time, Anna," Rafe said, "what's this all about?"

Anna glared at him.

"For the tenth time," she snapped, "I'll tell you once we're all here."

"Well, then," Falco said impatiently, "where in hell is Dante?"

"He's on his way, with Gabriella."

"And Izzy?"

"Izzy's not coming."

"Maybe Dante and Gaby aren't, either," Nick said logically. "Maybe they're away. Maybe they're out for the evening. Damnit, Anna—"

The office door edged open. Dante Orsini and his wife squeezed into the small room. One glance at Dante's grim face and Gaby's swollen eyes and the Orsini-Valenti clan fell silent.

"Okay," Rafe said grimly. "Let's hear it."

Anna took a deep breath. "Izzy phoned me this morning."

Nick: "So?"

"She phoned to tell me she was going away for the weekend."

Rafe: "And?"

"She was in Southampton."

Falco: "Southampton, Long Island? What was she doing all the way out there?"

Anna looked at Dante, who cleared his throat.

"She went to interview for a job. A landscaping job. We— I got her the interview."

"It was me," Gabriella Orsini said quickly, touching her husband's arm. "I thought it was a wonderful opportunity. It was such an important commission..."

"I'm the one, darling," Dante said softly. "It's entirely my fault, not yours."

"Goddamnit," Falco snarled. Elle, his beautiful wife, grabbed his hand and clutched it. "Will somebody get to the point?"

"I convinced Rio D'Aquila to add her to his short list of landscaping applicants."

"Rio D'Aquila?" Nick raised an eyebrow. "Smart guy. Lots of money. He's into shipping, freight, oil, computers—"

"He's into women, too," Rafe murmured. Chiara Orsini dug a sharp elbow into her husband's side. "Hey," he said, "I'm only saying what I've heard."

"You're right," Dante said tersely. "Lots of money. Lots of women. Not much heart."

"Well, so what?" Nick said. "The guy doesn't have to pass a morals test before Iz can go to work for him."

Anna narrowed her eyes.

"Izzy drove out there yesterday. She took my car. She had some kind of accident."

A communal gasp almost sucked the air from the room.

"No," Anna said quickly, "she's fine. She's okay. But—"

"But?"

"She met someone. A man. And she called to tell me she was going away with him for the week."

Silence descended on the tiny room again.

Falco: "Wow."

Nick: "Our Izzy?"

Rafe: "Going away, with a guy?"

The brothers looked at each other.

"Well," Rafe said, "okay. I mean, she's a big girl. I mean, hell, we're happy for her. I mean—"

"His name," Anna said, "is Matteo Rossi."

Frowns all around. Nobody knew a Matteo Rossi.

"Who?" Nick's wife, Alessia, said.

"Exactly. So, I asked her, who was this Matteo Rossi? And she said that Rossi worked for Rio D'Aquila. That he was the caretaker at D'Aquila's Southampton estate."

"A caretaker?" a male voice asked.

Throats were cleared.

"Okay," Falco said, "well, hell, we're not snobs—"

"Except," Dante said, "except, D'Aquila's caretaker is a guy named Bill Foster."

This time, the silence in the room was a palpable force.

"What the hell is going on?" Nick said softly. "Has Izzy been kidnapped?"

"Worse."

"Sweet Mary, what could be—"

"Matteo Rossi and Rio D'Aquila are the same man."

Rafe shook his head. "I don't understand."

"They're the same man, damnit! Anna called me, told me Iz had called and said that she was leaving the country with some stranger."

"Leaving the—"

"She didn't like how it sounded. Neither did I. So I tried to get hold of D'Aquila to see what he could tell me about Rossi."

"And?"

"And, I couldn't reach him. And something didn't smell right. And," Dante said, his voice becoming flat, "I decided to do some checking. I used that guy, the private investigator who's done some work for Orsini Brothers Investments in the past."

"And?" Falco said, through his teeth.

"D'Aquila's real name is Matteo Rossi. He's the man Izzy's gone away with. He lied to her, told her he's a caretaker, told her God only knows what other lies, and now she's in the middle of nowhere with him."

Silence wrapped around the office again. This time, it was ugly.

Isabella, sweetly innocent Isabella, the girl who worried over each flower she grew, who picked up half-dead plants left for the trash collector on the curb so she could nurse them back to life—she, the baby they all adored, had been seduced by a man reputed to be a heartless bastard, a man who had lied to her, who was pretending to be someone he wasn't—

"Why?" Draco said.

They were all bewildered. Was it a cruel joke? A vicious prank? They talked. And postulated. And came up with only one obvious point of agreement.

Their Izzy needed them.

"They're not in the middle of nowhere," Anna said in a low voice. "They're on Mustique."

An hour later, the Orsinis' private jet was in the air.

CHAPTER ELEVEN

A LITTLE before eight, Isabella shooed her lover from the bedroom.

They had showered. Together, of course, which took a little longer—a lot longer—than if each had showered alone.

Matteo was shaved and dressed. Chino trousers. Dark brown moccasins with no socks. A black T-shirt that clung to his wide shoulders and hard body in a way that made her want to drag him down into the rumpled sheets, but he'd made dinner reservations at what he said was "just a restaurant" and said it in a way that made her suspect it was much more than that.

She knew he was spending far too much money and she'd tried to come up with a way to split costs. But she came from a family of strong, proud and, yes, occasionally arrogant brothers. Matteo had those same qualities and she'd decided it was best to let him spoil her, at least for a little while.

Besides, the selfish truth was that it felt lovely to be spoiled by a man like him.

So she let him bend her back over his arm for a dramatic kiss that made her laugh, and then she banished him to the patio.

"Give me fifteen minutes."

Her gorgeous, sexy, amazing lover rolled his eyes. "A likely story."

She grinned, he grinned back, stole one last quick kiss and went out the glass doors to the patio.

Isabella shut the doors. She wanted to look perfect for him, and to make her entrance a surprise.

How many other women had made him wait while they dressed? A legion, she thought as she dropped the bath towel she'd wrapped around her on the bed.

Matteo probably had to beat the women off with a stick— or with a kind word, because she couldn't imagine him not being less than honorable in his dealings with anyone.

She had only to think of how honorable, how honest he'd been with her, telling her things about himself most men would try to keep buried. On top of that, he was gorgeous. Generous. Kind. Sexy as a man could be.

He was a modern Prince Charming—and he was hers. For tonight, for the next few days...

Don't think too far ahead, Isabella.

No. She wouldn't. But there was always a chance. What good were fairy tales, if one didn't occasionally come true?

The clothes he'd bought her were laid out on a love seat in the corner of the bedroom.

They were beautiful. And he'd thought of everything. Well, almost. No comb and brush, but she had used his. No makeup but she rarely wore makeup anyway. Besides, lovemaking had left her eyes and skin glowing, and her lover's kisses had left her lips rosy pink and delicately swollen.

The rest? Well, yes, he'd remembered to get panties.

But no bra.

Her heart did a little stutter step.

She'd just have to wear this bit of silk, this dress that reminded her of gossamer-winged lavender and blue butterflies, without one.

Her breasts would be bare behind the thin fabric. When

Matteo spoke to her in a low, husky voice, when he took her in his arms, he'd be able to see the effect he had on her.

Isabella let out a shaky breath.

Amazing. She was turning herself on just by thinking about him, and who'd ever imagined that?

The dress fit as if it had been made for her. So did the sandals of soft gold leather with delightfully wicked heels. She fluffed her hair, sent up a silent thank-you to whichever of the Fates it was who'd decreed that her long, dark curls would not, for once in her life, turn to frizz.

There could not be a woman on the entire planet even half as happy as she was tonight.

Fifteen minutes, Isabella had said.

Rio knew what a woman's fifteen minutes meant, that the actual time could run to an hour or more. But a quarter hour later, he heard the doors slide open. He turned around—

And there she was.

My God, he thought, in English and Portuguese and Italian and half a dozen other languages he'd picked up doing business around the world, *My God, how beautiful she is!*

Her hair, black and lustrous, fell in sexy curls over her shoulders. Her eyes were wide, glittering as if they were filled with starlight. And the dress…

Dio, the dress.

Over the years, he had spent thousands on couturier designs for his mistresses. This dress had cost him an almost pitiful fraction of that, but he was certain that *Vogue* or any fashion magazine would have fought for the privilege of taking a photo of it now.

Except, he thought, as he drank in the sight, except it wasn't the dress that was special. It was his gorgeous, sweet, sexy Isabella.

Her smile turned questioning.

"What do you think?" she said. "Do I look—"

Rio swept her into his arms, angled his mouth over hers and kissed her. She made one of those little sounds that drove him half-crazy; her arms went around his neck and she returned his kiss with such passion, such honesty that he could have sworn he felt the earth tilt.

He kissed her again but it wasn't enough. Not even taking her to bed again would have been enough because—

Because he loved her.

He had known it on the plane. Now, the realization swam in his blood.

He loved her.

Deeply. With everything he was, everything he had ever been or would ever be. He loved her, and it was time he told her the truth.

"Sweetheart," he said softly, "Isabella *mia*..."

"I want to look beautiful for you tonight," she whispered.

"You are more than beautiful, sweetheart."

"You think?"

He smiled. "I know."

And he knew, too, that all the things he had to tell her could wait. She deserved this night, a perfect night. Lovers going out for dinner, sharing a bottle of wine, holding each other close on a tiny dance floor.

Then he'd bring her home, and embark on a voyage that would make that long-ago trip in the forecastle of a rusting freighter seem simple.

He would bare his soul and his heart to the woman he adored, and pray she'd forgive him for his lies.

Isabella was almost dizzy with joy.

An ivory moon had risen majestically from a turquoise sea after the sun had made a spectacular exit over the horizon. The air was warm and scented with flowers.

Matteo drove them to a tiny restaurant that seemed to hang over a sea that rolled in on a whisper of sound that spoke of ancient mysteries.

The night and the setting were wonderful but *wonderful* was not sufficient to describe the man who was her lover.

He was all a woman could dream of or want.

Not just the way he looked, though she had to admit to a moment of foolish pride when they'd been shown to their table in this casual but elegant little place and all the women in it had given him looks of longing.

I agree, Isabella thought, *he's spectacular—and he's all mine.*

Maybe it made more sense to say, she was all his.

And oh, if only he wanted to be hers...

Thinking like that was dangerous. She knew that it was. They were in a sexual relationship and she wasn't naive, she understood that, too. But—

But maybe, just maybe, Matteo felt more for her than desire. He had to, otherwise how could he make her feel as if she were the center of his universe?

When the captain took them to their table and started to pull out her chair, Matteo politely demurred, moved forward and pulled it out himself.

His hands brushed over her shoulders; he moved her chair in and, as he did, he stroked his thumb lightly over the hollow in her throat.

Her breath caught.

His touch sent a rush of desire through her body. He knew it; she felt her nipples peak and his gaze dropped to her breasts and when he looked up at her again, his eyes burned with flame.

"I'm going to have a lot of trouble keeping my hands off you tonight," he said in a rough whisper.

Just that—his words, his glance—and Isabella felt herself go hot and wet.

"Good," she whispered back, and the flames in his eyes narrowed to pinpoints of light.

He ordered for them both.

"Is that all right, *cara?*"

She, the woman who bristled when one of her own brothers was foolish enough to think he could decide if she wanted a burger or a hot dog at a Fourth of July barbecue, she smiled and said that would be fine.

His choices were eclectic and wonderful. A drink that tasted deliciously of coconut and rum arrived in a tall glass garnished with gorgeous flowers. A cold fruit soup dotted with freshly ground black pepper, a combination that seemed incongruous until she tasted it, was next. And then white wine that was cool and crisp, crab cakes hot with spices, pan-blackened grouper, bananas sautéed in butter and cinnamon and nutmeg and who knew what else.

The meal was decadently delicious.

The service was wonderful.

But being with Matteo...

No words could do that justice.

They ate. They talked. They laughed. And, in between, Matteo led her onto a miniscule dance floor where he wrapped his arms around her, gathered her close against him, and they swayed in rhythm to soft music.

Isabella sighed as he drew her to him, as she felt his hard body against the softness of hers, his muscled thighs against the length of hers.

She put her arms around his neck. He put one hand in her hair, the other at the base of her spine.

She buried her face against him, inhaling him, feeling him harden against her, feeling the power of knowing she could make him want her just by being in his arms.

It happened over and over. Dancing, or pretending to dance. The teasing of him against her, her against him, until they were both half out of their minds.

Isabella moaned.

"Matteo," she whispered, "take me to bed."

Rio had done a lot of tough things in his life but nothing compared to getting off that dance floor without lifting her in his arms, taking her down to the beach and making love to her right there.

Somehow, he managed to hang on to what little sanity he had left. He clasped her hand, never broke stride as he dug a handful of bills from his pocket and dropped them on the table.

He drove home fast, his hand under her skirt, her hand on him, taking the narrow, curving roads at speeds his brain warned were dangerous, even when he wasn't almost blind with desire, but all that mattered was getting home.

When they reached the villa, he drew her from the car before she had time to get her door open.

"Isabella," he said, just that, because her name was infused with everything a man could need or want.

She went into his arms.

He held her to him, kissed her mouth and throat. And fought to hang on to his control.

"Isabella." He drew back, framed her face with his hands. "Sweetheart, we have to talk."

"Not now," she said in a broken whisper, and when she went up on her toes, dug her hands into his hair and kissed him, her mouth open and hot and greedy against his, Rio forget everything except his need for her.

There would be plenty of time, later.

He carried her through the dark house to the bedroom where they tore at each other's clothes.

When they were naked, she moved against him.

"Now," she said, and the urgency in her voice all but finished him.

They fell to the bed in each other's arms and made love, again and again and again, while the moon sailed across the heavens and the earth spun through the mantle of the night...

And, fell asleep, at last, wrapped in each other's arms.

Isabella came awake abruptly from a deep, dreamless sleep. The moon had set. The night had turned black and impenetrable.

Something had awakened her—

A sound. A noise. Something growling just beneath the hiss of the waves rolling in from the sea.

She recognized it now. What she heard was a car, coming up the narrow road to the villa—and where was Matteo? She was alone in the big bed.

Fear turned her skin icy.

She sat up quickly, grabbed the first thing at hand—a cotton throw from the foot of the bed—and wrapped it around herself.

"Matteo?" she whispered as she padded out of the bedroom. "Matteo? Where—"

A hand closed around her wrist.

"Easy, sweetheart. I'm right here."

Her heart felt as if it were going to burst from her chest. Her lover had all but materialized from the shadows in the hallway; her eyes had adjusted to the dark and she saw that he'd pulled on a pair of jeans and nothing else.

Shivering, Isabella moved closer to him.

"It's a car, isn't it? Who—"

"I don't know," Rio said, and, damnit, he didn't.

Who would come to the villa in the middle of the night? Crime was practically nonexistent on the island but things happened, no matter how safe and tucked away a place seemed.

"Matteo. I'm frightened."

He was, too. Not for himself. For her. A dozen ugly headlines, splashed across newspapers everywhere, shot through his mind.

"Don't be," he said. "It's probably nothing. Kids out, having fun. Or somebody tipsy who made the wrong turn." He put his hand against her cheek. "Isabella. I want you to go into the bedroom and lock the—"

"No! I'm not leaving you."

The sound of the engine died and the night filled with silence. A car door slammed, and then another.

"Isabella," Rio said urgently, "get inside that room and lock yourself in."

"I am not leaving you, Matteo. Whatever happens, I want to be with you."

Rio's heart swelled with love.

"Ah, Izzy," he said softly, "Izzy, sweetheart—"

A fist hammered against the door. "Open up!"

A heavy wooden statue stood on a table near the door. It wasn't a hell of a good weapon, but it was all there was. Rio grabbed it.

"Isabella," he hissed, "go into the bedroom and—"

Bam! "You open this effing door or—" *Bam!* "—you effing son of a bitch, or so help me God—" *Bam!* "—I'll break it down!"

Isabella stiffened. No. It couldn't be—

"D'Aquila, you no good, sleazy, bastard! I've come for my sister. If I have to take this place apart to get to her, I will!"

Isabella stared at her lover.

"That's—that's my brother," she said. "But what's he doing here?"

"D'Aquila!"

The door shuddered under Dante Orsini's fist.

"He thinks—" She shook her head. "He thinks you're Rio D'Aquila."

"Isabella," Rio said in a low voice, "Isabella, you must listen to me."

"My God, what a mess!" Isabella gave an unsteady laugh. "My brother, come to rescue his little sister from the clutches of big, bad Rio D'Aquila... I'm so sorry, Matteo!" She moved past him, reached for the lock on the door. "I'm horrified. Humiliated. I don't know how this could have happ—"

"Isabella!" Rio caught her by the shoulder. She could feel each finger digging into her flesh. "Don't open that door."

"What do you mean, don't open it? I know this is awful but he's got things all wrong. I most certainly don't need rescuing. He had no right to come here. And you most certainly are not—"

"But I am," Rio said. "I am Rio D'Aquila."

Isabella stared at him. He saw the color drain from her face. Her lips formed a word—*No*—but it was soundless.

Rio cursed violently. He dropped the wooden statue and reached for her but she stumbled back. *Cristo,* he was running out of time! The pounding at the door had stopped, but he wasn't foolish enough to think Dante Orsini had gone away.

He knew he had only minutes to explain everything. How what had started as a farce had become all that mattered, all that ever would matter for the rest of his life.

"It's true," he said in a low voice. "I am Rio."

Isabella shook her head. Her eyes were wide with disbelief.

"No. You're not. You're not! You're his caretaker. His property manager. His pilot. You're Matteo Rossi."

"*Si. Sim.* I am him, as well. Matteo Rossi is my real name. Hell, not my real name. It's the name I was given. I took the name Rio D'Aquila years ago." Desperate, he ran his hands through his hair. "Isabella *mia*. Sweetheart, it's all so damned complicated—"

Tears ran down her face.

"Why?" she whispered. Her voice broke. "Why did you lie to me? Why did you let me think—"

Glass shattered in the bedroom. Rio knew it meant that Dante Orsini had broken open the patio doors, that he had only seconds left.

"Why?" she said. Her voice rose to a sobbing cry. "Why?"

"I don't know. It was on the spur of the moment. It was nothing—"

"Nothing?"

"Yes. No. It was—it was a harmless prank."

"A prank," she said, through bloodless lips.

"We were strangers. We were never going to see each other again. And then—and then—"

Dante stormed toward Rio, eyes blazing.

"You SOB," he snarled, and hit Rio with a fist that felt as if it were made of iron.

Rio staggered back but his eyes never left Isabella's.

"I wanted to tell you. I tried to tell you. Even tonight—"

"A prank," she whispered, while her heart shattered. "Pretending to be someone you weren't. Telling me we were in his house when it was yours. Telling me stories about how you'd come to be working for him—"

"Isabella, please, I beg you—"

"And—and you—you made love to me…"

A sob broke from her throat. Rio groaned and reached for her; Dante put a hand in the center of his chest and pushed him back.

"Iz," Dante said harshly, "Anna's outside. Get out of this house, go to her and wait in the car."

"No," Rio shouted. "Don't listen to him. Stay where you are. Let me talk to you. Let me explain—"

"You already did," Isabella whispered. "You said it was nothing. You said it was a prank."

"I wanted to tell you. A dozen times. A hundred. But—"

"When?" Isabella said brokenly. "Before you seduced me? Or after?"

Dante hit him again. It was a good, solid shot. Rio, who was a boxer, could have put Dante down with one blow. Instead, he snarled with pain, anger and rage.

At himself.

"I made a terrible mistake, *cara*. What I did was wrong. And not admitting to it sooner was cowardly but—"

Isabella had stopped listening. He could see it happen, that she was gathering herself together, leaving him behind. She had never looked more beautiful than now, standing straight and proud, her chin lifted, wearing the cotton throw as if it were a queen's cloak.

"Orsini," Rio said desperately, "give us five minutes alone."

"Not in this lifetime," Dante growled. "Iz? We're leaving, baby. You just take my arm and—"

"Amazing," Isabella said. "Here I thought I was the one playing games."

Rio blinked. "What?"

"A caretaker. A man who lives in another man's home, eats another man's food, takes another man's orders."

"No. I'm telling you, I am—"

"Oh, I believe you. You're Rio D'Aquila."

Isabella's voice had turned chill and smooth. She smiled, and told herself that all she had to do was get through the next couple of minutes and then this would all be nothing more than a bad dream.

"And I—I enjoyed our little idyll but the thing is, if I'd know who you really were, I'd probably never have bothered with you in the first place."

She saw the man she knew as Matteo narrow his eyes. Good. Better than good. But it wasn't enough. She wanted to put the knife in deep and then give it a twist.

"I mean, men with lots of money, you know, power brokers like Rio D'Aquila, are a dime a dozen in my world." She forced a smile; she hoped it held amusement and not anguish. "But guys with dirt under their nails, studs like Matteo Rossi—"

"Izzy," her brother said softly, "honey, it's okay. Just go outside to Anna."

"Dante can tell you," she said, putting her hand on her brother's rigid-with-fury arm, praying he wouldn't spoil the lie. "I'm not exactly the little innocent you decided I was."

"Iz." Her brother's voice was rough. "Iz, honey—"

"I wanted something different. Well, Matteo Rossi was different. And—and it was fun," Isabella said, and prayed her voice would not break into the same tiny shards as her heart. "But you used me. You lied to me. And I'll despise you for it, for the rest of my life."

Rio's face had gone blank. Isabella looked at her brother.

"Dante," she said, "leave him alone. He's not worth the effort."

Somehow, she made it to the door. She heard Dante say something sharp and ugly. Then they were outside, where the air was cool and clean and she could let the darkness enfold her.

"Izzy," someone said, "oh, Izzy, baby..."

"Anna," Isabella whispered.

Anna's arms opened wide. She flew into them and then, only then, was it safe to give way to racking sobs.

CHAPTER TWELVE

ISABELLA knelt in the middle of her sister's penthouse garden, carefully pulling weeds and deadheading spent flower blossoms.

She was dripping with sweat, her back ached, the lightheadedness and vague nausea that had plagued her for the past couple of weeks seemed ever-present, but she'd be damned if she'd give in to a summer virus when she had so much work to do.

Summer could be tough in New York.

Pavement. Concrete. Skyscrapers that created man-made canyons trapped the heat and reflected it back with the ferocity of a gigantic convection oven.

The result was predictable.

Horns blared, tempers rose, pedestrians wilted.

So did plants. Isabella always warned her clients about that.

"Plants are living things," she'd say. "They need food some of the time and unless they're succulents, they need water all of the time, especially in summer."

She gave them handsome calendars filled with instructions on caring for their gardens if they didn't hire her to do it for them and when summer arrived, she emailed cheerful reminders to water, water, water.

Some people, she thought grumpily, didn't get the message.

An end-of-season heat wave had the city in its cruel clutches. Isabella's phone rang and rang with desperate pleas for help.

My hydrangeas are dying!

You know that green and yellow shrub with the funny leaves? Well, the leaves are all brown and now they're falling off!

And there was always her favorite complaint: *Really, Ms. Orsini, we are very upset! You said these flowers would last forever!*

Nothing lasts forever, Isabella had finally told a caller after one angry voice mail too many.

Because, of course, nothing did.

"Hell," she muttered, and sat back on her heels.

She was not going there.

Ridiculous, that after four weeks she could still say something, see something, hear something and just like that, the entire horrible interlude with Rio D'Aquila would pop into her mind.

The Horrible Interlude.

Isabella snorted, ran the back of her hand over her dripping forehead, then gave another dig to a particularly hardy weed.

It sounded like a bad movie title but what else would you call what had happened? *Interludis Horribilis?*

She laughed.

Not bad, she thought, not at all bad—and then her throat tightened and what had started as laughter turned into a lump and she heard herself make a pathetic little sound, really pathetic, painfully pathetic—

"Izzy, for God's sake, what are you doing out here?"

Isabella shaded her eyes with a grimy hand and looked up. Anna stood over her, looking cool and elegant in a silk suit and high heeled pumps.

"Anna," she said brightly. "You're home."

"It's after six. Even lawyers know when to knock off for the day. What are you doing?"

"Playing in the dirt. Or trying to save your pansies. Which does it look like?"

"What it looks like," Anna said, "is that you're trying to get sunstroke. For goodness sake, come inside. Those pansies are fine. You said so yourself last week."

"Exactly. Haven't you touched them at all since then? Thinned them out? Weeded them? Watered them?"

"Draco did."

"Nobody did. Honestly, Anna—"

"Honestly, Izzy, enough is enough. Get up and come inside."

"Ask me nicely and I might."

"What?"

"I'm not a child, Anna. I know you mean well, but—" Isabella sighed. "Never mind. Just give me another couple of minutes."

"You're very prickly lately, Iz."

"I'm not prickly at all," Isabella snapped. Anna rolled her eyes and Isabella let out a long breath. "Look, I don't want your flowers to die, okay?"

"So you had to pick the hottest day of the year to give them a manicure?"

"It's not a manicure. And this was the first chance I had to come by. I've been so busy with other idiots that—"

"Other idiots?" Anna folded her arms. "That's really nice."

"Hell," Isabella said wearily. "Okay. Point made. It's time to call it a day."

"Good. Come sit inside and we'll have some iced— Izzy?" Anna grabbed Isabella's arm as her sister swayed like a sapling in a breeze. "My God, you're white as a sheet."

"I'm—I'm okay. I got up too fast. The sun. And being on my knees all this time—"

Anna put her arm around Isabella and led her into the cool comfort of the penthouse living room.

"Sit down on that chair. I'll get some water."

"I'm filthy," Isabella said shakily.

"Sit down," Anna said in her best courtroom voice.

Isabella sat.

The room was spinning and her stomach was somewhere just slightly south of her throat. She bent forward, shut her eyes and took long, deep breaths.

Okay. She'd have to deal with this summer virus.

Because it *was* a summer virus. It had to be.

"Here you go."

Anna pressed a tall glass of iced water into Isabella's hands. She drank it slowly. Over the past few days she'd learned, the hard way, that when she felt like this, even a drink of water might trigger a gag reaction.

"Better?"

Isabella nodded. "Yes, thank you. Much better."

"It's a good thing I came along when I did. You'd still be out there, working in the Sahara and saving our pansies." Anna peered at her younger sister. "You look like hell."

"Thank you."

"Okay, here's what we're going to do," Anna said briskly, taking the glass from Isabella. "You take a nice cool shower, I'll give you something to wear and then we'll have a glass of Pinot Grigio while we wait for Draco to come home. We're having broiled halibut for supper and—Izzy?"

Isabella ran for the powder room and made it just in time to slam the door and bend over the toilet before her stomach emptied itself of the crackers and chicken soup she'd managed to get down for lunch.

She flushed the bowl. Washed out her mouth, washed her

hands and face. Her reflection was not reassuring. Her cheeks were colorless, her hair was wild—and the worst was yet to come.

She had to face Anna.

A long, deep breath. Then she opened the bathroom door. Her sister was standing right outside, arms folded, expression grim, looking exactly the way Isabella felt—

As if the world as they both knew it was about to end.

"You're pregnant," Anna said flatly.

Isabella tried for a laugh. "You certainly have a way with words."

"You," Anna repeated, "are pregnant."

"I just said—"

"I heard what you said, and it wasn't 'no, I'm not.' Answer me, Izzy. Did that lying SOB get you pregnant?"

Isabella narrowed her eyes. "He didn't 'get' me anything! I'm a grown woman. I'm responsible for myself."

"Damnit, answer the question! Are you pregnant?"

"This is not a courtroom, and I am not on the witness stand!"

"Meaning?"

"Meaning…" Isabella's shoulders slumped. "Meaning, I don't know."

"What do you mean, you don't know?"

"Read my lips. I mean, I—don't—know."

"How can you not know? Have you missed your period? Have you seen a doctor? Bought an EPT? It is not possible to answer a question like, 'Are you pregnant?' by saying, 'I don't know.'"

"It is, if you're a coward."

"Oh, Iz…"

"See? This is why I didn't want to tell you. That 'oh, Iz,' as if you were thirteen and I were twelve and I'd just spilled your favorite nail polish all over your favorite sweater."

"Izzy, honey—"

"And that. That look. That tone. 'Izzy, honey,' meaning 'Izzy, you pathetic little incompetent, you sad underachiever, what have you done now?'"

Anna threw up her hands in defense. "I never—"

"Maybe not, but that's how it always sounds."

"How *what* always sounds? Izzy—"

"And that's another thing. My name is Isabella."

The sisters stared at each other.

"We need to talk," Anna finally said.

Isabella nodded and Anna led the way to the kitchen. Isabella sat at the glass-topped table. Anna poured another glass of iced water and gave it to her, started to pour water for herself, muttered "to hell with it" and instead took an opened bottle of Pinot Grigio from the fridge and poured herself half a tumbler of it.

Then she plopped into a chair opposite Isabella's.

"I have never," she said softly, "not once in our entire lives, thought you were anything less than smart, capable and altogether competent. Okay? I mean, let's get that out of the way first."

Isabella used her damp glass to make a ring of intersecting circles on the tabletop.

"You're my sister," Anna continued. "My baby sister, and—"

"I'm your sister," Isabella said, looking up. "And you're mine. And I love you like crazy, but—"

"But," Anna said, "you're all grown up. And I need to remember that."

"You do." Isabella gave a little laugh. "Except when my stuff isn't as grown up as I am, and I need to borrow your clothes or your car…"

Her smile faded. Anna reached for her hand.

"Which takes us," she said gently, "back to the beginning."

Isabella nodded. "The old square one."

"You want to tell me about it?"

Isabella hesitated. Then she swallowed hard.

"More than anything," she said, and the entire sad story tumbled out. It took a while, because she had not told anyone anything after Dante and Anna had brought her back to the States.

But she knew the time had come.

She told Anna how she'd gotten stuck in traffic en route to Southampton. How she'd gotten lost. The accident that had left her on foot. How she'd stumbled through the gate at Rio D'Aquila's estate hours late.

"And D'Aquila was waiting for you," Anna said grimly.

"I didn't know who he was," Isabella said. "He was just a guy." *A big, shirtless, gorgeous sexy-looking guy...*

"Go on."

Isabella cleared her throat.

"We talked. And talked. He was—"

"Rude. Insolent."

"Actually, he was charming. He was fun. And then—"

"And then, he seduced you."

He kissed me, Isabella thought, *God, he kissed me and I melted...*

"No. He didn't. I—I left. And he came after me. It was dark by then and he said—he said he'd take me to the train station."

"But he didn't, the no-good, testosterone-crazed SOB."

"He did. Trouble was, the trains weren't running."

Anna snorted. "How could you have bought such a lie?"

"It was true. The station was closed. So, he said I could spend the night—"

"And then he seduced you."

"He showed me to a guest room and he gave me something

to wear. I was a mess, your suit all torn and dirty—and I'm sorry about that. I'll pay you back—"

"Forget the suit," Anna snapped. "I'll just bet he gave you something to wear, something left over from some other damsel in distress who'd spent the night in his—"

"He gave me one of his sweat suits. And then we went to the kitchen—"

"Naturally. Men like him always want a woman manacled to the stove with a skillet in her free hand."

"Anna," Isabella said carefully, "you think you're being just a little judgmental here? Actually, *he* did the cooking. But we never got around to eating much because—"

"Because he sed—"

"My God," Isabella said, yanking her hand free of her sister's, "will you let me talk? Because we quarreled. But you're right. We did get around to seduction..." Isabella's voice trembled. "And I'm not really sure who seduced who."

Anna stared at her sister. "Please," she said, "please, *please* do not tell me you think you still feel something for this man!"

"Of course not."

"Because he has the morals of the manure you use for fertilizer."

"I don't feel anything for him, but he's not—not..."

"Izzy. I mean, Isabella, how can you say that? He seduced you, and don't waste your breath saying you were equally responsible. You don't know a thing about sex, Iz. And he—"

"He knew everything," Isabella whispered. "And it was—it was wonderful."

Anna Orsini Valenti looked at her sister. *Ohmygod,* she thought, and grabbed her hand again.

"Isabella," Anna said firmly. "You're forgetting all the rest. He spirited you out of the States."

Isabella laughed.

"Okay, so that sounds dumb. What I mean is, he took you

away from everything familiar, everything that could have kept you safe—"

"He kept me safe. I'd never felt that safe in my life. When I was with him, when he held me in his arms… Can you possibly understand what I mean?"

Anna could. She had only to think of how it felt each time her husband touched her, and she understood.

In fact, she was starting to think she understood everything.

Her sister—her baby sister, though she wouldn't make the mistake of calling her that ever again, had fallen head over heels for a rat.

"Yes," she said gently, "I do understand. But you're leaving something out, honey. He lied to you. And it was one hell of a lie, pretending he was someone he wasn't."

Isabella shook her head. "He didn't."

"He did! He's Rio D'Aquila but he told you he was Matteo Rossi."

"He's both. Matteo Rossi was the name the orphanage gave him." Isabella's eyes glittered with sorrow. "Can you imagine being raised in an orphanage?"

Anna could come close. Her own husband had been raised in a boarding school that seemed, each time she thought about it, straight out of a Dickens novel.

"He never lied, Anna. Not about what mattered, not after we'd become lovers. He told me the villa was his, and it was. He told me about his life as Matteo Rossi, and what he told me was the truth. And—and he would have told me the rest, if we'd had time."

"You had plenty of time. Three days—"

"Two days. And two nights. And that last night, he kept saying we had to talk, that it was important, but I wouldn't listen. I just wanted to—to be in his arms, to be with him because I—because I loved him, God, I loved him—"

Isabella began to weep. Anna came around the table, knelt beside her and took her in her arms.

"Oh, honey," she said softly.

"I still love him," Isabella said. "I always will. And sometimes—sometimes I think he was starting to fall in love with me. Oh, God, Anna, if I'd let him talk to me. If I'd said 'yes' when he asked Dante to give us time alone." Her voice broke. "If I hadn't lied to him because I'll never forget how he looked when I said those terrible things…"

"What terrible things?"

"I was so hurt. I was in agony." Isabella drew a shuddering breath. "So I lied. I said I'd never have bothered with him if I knew who he was. I made it clear that I'd been slumming by—by sleeping with a man I thought was—was socially beneath me."

"Oh, Iz!"

"And I said—I said I'd let him think I was—I was sexually naive but that I wasn't."

"Oh, Iz!"

"I hurt him. I could see it. His feelings, his pride, the whole male thing. You know that whole male thing?"

Anna thought of her husband, the man she'd thought of as the Ice Prince. She thought of her brothers, the strength of their characters—and the fragility of their male egos.

"Oh, Iz!"

Isabella drew back and looked at Anna.

"I told you not to call me that," she said on a sad little laugh, and Anna burst into tears and wept with her.

That was how Draco found them a little while later.

"What happened?" he asked in bewilderment, and his beautiful wife said he would never understand, and then she relented and said okay, they'd tell him. And they did—well, not everything, not about the possibility of Isabella being pregnant.

But they told him all the rest, that Isabella hated Rio D'Aquila except she didn't hate him, and they were right. He didn't understand.

All he understood was that men were helpless at moments like this, which was when he went to the phone and called his brother-in-law, Dante Orsini.

CHAPTER THIRTEEN

THE four Orsini brothers were sitting in their favorite booth at The Bar, their place in SoHo. Their brother-in-law, Prince Draco Valenti, was with them.

The booths at The Bar were big, easily accommodating six adults, but the men of the Orsini clan were all tall, broad-shouldered and long-legged. The result was that they were crammed into what should have been a sufficient space but wasn't.

It would have been nice to think that was why they were all glowering at each other, but they knew better.

They had a problem to deal with, and not one of them wanted to touch it.

So they ordered hamburgers and beer, but the burgers remained untouched.

The beer, on the other hand, was getting a good workout.

And the silence was almost deafening.

Raffaele and Falco seated at the ends of the booth, finally got to their feet, took away the hamburgers, the empty beer mugs and bottles, and came back with fresh liquid supplies.

Dante took that as a signal.

"Okay," he said, as his brothers slid back into the booth. "Let's get this over with."

Nicolo nodded. "Damned right. Not that it's gonna take

very long. What I think is that Izzy's kind of dealing with post traumatic shock. She just needs time, is all."

"I agree," Rafe said. "Hell, when you think of what she went through—"

"Think all you like," Dante said. "The bottom line is that Anna suspects we may have overreacted."

There were snorts of disbelief all around the big, scarred wooden table.

"We sure as hell underreacted," Falco said coldly. "We should have all flown to Mustique with you and beaten the crap out of D'Aquila." His dark eyes narrowed. "It's still not too late for that."

There were murmurs of agreement, but Nick held up his hand.

"We agreed to leave him alone, remember? For Izzy's sake. She said she just wanted to forget he existed."

"Well, what's changed?"

Dante shrugged.

"Anna and Izzy had a talk. Draco came in on the tail end of it."

Draco nodded.

"And? What did Izzy tell you?"

Draco laughed, though it was not a happy sound.

"You ever try and get a woman who doesn't want to tell you something to tell it to you?"

Sighs all around the table.

"Okay," Rafe said. "Then, how did Iz seem to you? Like she was still carrying the torch for this guy?"

Draco looked at his brothers-in-law. He had been accepted as one of them and he knew it was an honor. They were smart, tough, successful men who adored their wives as much as he adored his.

Until last night, he'd felt as they did, that the man who'd broken Isabella's heart should have been drawn and quartered.

But what he'd seen in his sister-in-law's face the prior evening had been raw emotion, and what his wife had told him afterward had given him pause.

There'd been a time he, too, had believed the woman he loved despised him, a time he'd come to this very place with his heart on display, knowing that he had to make the Orsini brothers understand that he loved his Anna, that nothing would keep him from loving her, no matter what they did to him.

"Draco? What do you think?"

Draco cleared his throat.

"I think Isabella is deeply in love with Rio D'Aquila or Matteo Rossi or whatever you want to call him," he said quietly.

"I know what to call him," Falco said. "He's nothing but a scheming, lying—"

"What you mean is," Rafe said, "is that she's infatuated with him. Okay. I guess that's understandable. She's just a baby and—"

"She's a grown woman," Draco said. "She made that point to Anna." He grinned. "With enough fervor that Anna was still apologizing for treating her as if she wasn't when they shooed me out of the room."

"Anna, apologizing?" Dante grinned, too. "I'd have paid to see that."

"Yeah," Falco said, "well, even if Iz thinks she loves the bastard, he's still a bastard."

"You really have a way with words," Nick said drily.

"Come on, dude, you know what I mean. Besides, D'Aquila or Rossi or whoever he is, doesn't give a damn for our Izzy."

"And you know this because…?" Rafe said.

"Well," Falco said, "where is he? A man who cares about a woman doesn't just let her go."

Falco's brothers looked at him.

"Okay," he said, the color rising in his face, "but it was different with Elle and me."

"Uh-huh."

"It was. Besides, we're talking about a whole other situation. The fact is, the bastard hasn't made any attempt to contact Iz, and—"

"You're right, he hasn't," a husky, slightly accented male voice said. "He's been much too busy nursing his wounded pride."

Startled, Rafe, Dante, Nick, Falco and Draco turned toward the man who'd appeared beside their booth. He was tall, same as them. Powerfully built, same as them. Dark-haired, same as them. He wore a custom-tailored suit, same as them.

And, in a heartbeat, they knew who he was.

Falco shot to his feet.

"D'Aquila," he snarled.

Rio nodded. "Yes."

The others rose, jostling each other as they got to their feet in the crowded booth.

"What the hell are you doing here?" Dante said coldly.

"I'm here to talk to you. All of you."

Cristo, Rio could almost smell the adrenaline in the air. Every muscle in his body was on alert.

"Back there," Nick growled, jerking his head toward the rear of The Bar.

The men surrounded Rio and led him to a door. *Dead man walking,* he thought, and knew that could end up pretty close to the truth.

If Isabella's brothers, plus the one additional guy he vaguely recognized as some sort of financial guru with a title, wanted to beat the crap out of him and leave him in the alley he figured was beyond that door, so be it.

He deserved it.

But the door opened into a small, very plain office. A hand

shoved him forward, the door slammed behind him, and then the five men faced him, faces like stone, arms folded, legs planted slightly apart.

Rio stood with his hands at his sides.

"So, this is the SOB, Rio D'Aquila," one of the men growled.

"Maybe he prefers his alias," another man snarled.

"Not that it matters," a third added.

"It damned well doesn't," a fourth said, "because he's going to be hurting really bad, whatever he calls himself."

Rio nodded. "Fists first, facts later? That's fine, if that's what you want, but at least leave me conscious long enough so I can tell you why I'm here."

Nobody laughed but then, Rio hadn't meant it as a joke.

It had taken him three weeks to get past his rage at being used by Isabella, another week before he'd let himself feel the pain of what had happened—

And then, finally, a couple of days ago, he'd come to his senses.

He didn't believe a word she'd said about sleeping with him because he was socially beneath her. That absolutely was not his Isabella.

As for her having pretended to be inexperienced—he didn't believe that, either. And even if she had been sexually experienced, it wouldn't have mattered.

He loved her. He adored her.

And she loved him.

What else could possibly matter?

Her love for him had been in her smile, her touch, her voice, her kisses. She loved him, he loved her, and they were apart because he'd been a stupid, arrogant ass.

He'd told himself she had to give him a second chance.

Really? a sly voice within him had whispered. *Just think of how you hurt her. She doesn't "have" to give you anything.*

By last night, he'd been close to crazy. He needed a plan. A logical plan. Logic was what had built him a fortune. Surely, it could win back a woman's heart.

And suddenly, late this afternoon, it had come to him. A plan. Logical, imaginative, one that would surely work.

He'd headed straight for Tiffany's.

A gift a day. A heart a day. Diamonds, rubies, sapphires. Yellow gold. White gold. Platinum. All with notes saying he loved her. What woman would resist?

His Isabella. That was who.

The realization hit him as he looked at an exquisite array of jeweled hearts. Pendants. Earrings. Bracelets. Beautiful, all of them—but nothing like this would win Isabella.

Flowers, perhaps. Something simple and beautiful, flowers every day for a week, for a month…

Flowers? For a woman whose life was filled with them?

Rio had thanked the sales clerk. He said he'd look around a little more and he strolled slowly through the store, hoping some brilliant idea would come to him.

A couple was standing near a display case. Rio barely noticed them—but he overheard them.

"Someday," the man said softly, "someday, babe, I'll buy you everything in this case. I love you, you know. You—and our baby, growing inside you."

Our baby, growing inside you…

Rio damned near stopped breathing. He swung toward the couple. The man had his arm around his wife.

His very, very pregnant wife.

Dio! How could he have forgotten that night he'd made love to Isabella without a condom? For all he knew, she might be carrying his child.

Suddenly, there was no time to waste on plans. He knew exactly what he had to do.

A quick call to his lawyer to set things in motion. Within a couple of hours he had what he needed: the location of the bar he'd heard Dante and the rest of the Orsini brothers owned—and the fact that the brothers met there almost every Friday night.

This was a Friday night.

And now, he was here, facing her brothers and a man he figured had to be the formidable Anna's husband.

They looked as if they wanted to kill him.

He didn't blame them—but they couldn't kill him before he told them the truth. Part of the truth, anyway. He had no intention of telling them Isabella might be pregnant. That was too private, too special.

It was between the two of them.

"Well?" the one called Falco said. "You have something to say, say it. Then we'll beat the crap out of you."

Rio took a deep breath. "I'm in love with Isabella."

Four of them laughed. Not Dante, the man who had once been his friend. Dante simply narrowed his eyes.

"We're supposed to believe a lie told by a liar?"

Rio flushed.

"I lied about who I was. It was stupid but—"

The man called Nick said something vicious and moved forward. Dante put out a hand.

"Let him finish."

"But I thought it was harmless. I never intended to—to become involved with your sister."

"Involved," the one called Rafe said coldly.

All of the men had moved closer, as if to wall him in.

"That was what it was, at first," Rio said flatly. "Then it changed. And I wanted to tell her the truth."

"Why didn't you?" Anna's husband said.

A muscle knotted in Rio's jaw.

"I would have," he said. "But I was afraid I'd lose her."

"You mean," Falco said, "you'd lose your innocent little toy."

"I mean," Rio said quietly, "I was afraid I'd lose the woman I'd fallen in love with."

"That's an interesting story," Falco said coldly. "Let's see if we have it straight. You wanted to take our sister to bed, so you told her a lie. Then you fell in love with her, so you went on with the lie."

Rio looked at Dante. "I was going to tell her that night you showed up. I asked you to give us a few minutes alone, remember?"

"And he didn't," Nick said. "Tough."

"He didn't, no. And then Isabella said some things—"

"Oh," Dante said with icy sarcasm, "and she hurt your feelings."

Rio flushed. "I'm not proud of it, of being so—so god-damned pathetic that I let myself believe what my heart should have known wasn't true."

"Pathetic is right," Falco said. "If a man loves a woman he'd never believe lies about her."

"Not necessarily true," said Nick uncomfortably. He knew, all too well, how easy it was to be a dumb SOB who'd listen to his head instead of his heart.

Silence. Then Rafe said, "So, what now? Why are you here?"

"Yeah," Dante said. "If any of this is true, why are you here instead of at Izzy's?"

"I'm here," Rio said, "because I was born in Italy and I've lived my life in Brazil. Both cultures are my own—and there are still those Italians and Brazilians who think it proper to go to the family of the woman you love and tell them you are going to marry her."

For some reason, the Orsini brothers all looked at Draco

Valenti, who nodded in a way that made it clear confronting the family of the woman you loved made a lot of sense to him.

"You sound very sure of yourself, D'Aquila."

"I am sure of the fact that I love Isabella and she loves me."

In any other circle, such male arrogance might have raised some eyebrows. In this bunch, it brought nods of the head.

"We love each other," Rio said. His voice took on an edge. "And all of you better get used to it."

Dante raised his eyebrows. So did the others.

"Well, well, well," he said softly. Then he stuck out his hand. "Go for it," he said.

Rio shook Dante's hand, then the hands of the others.

"I'm happy to have met you all," he said formally.

"Yeah," Falco said. "But if our Izzy kicks you out, you'll meet us again—and next time, you won't be so happy about it."

The six men grinned at each other, and then Rio hurried from the room.

Isabella sat on the sofa in her tiny living room, shoes kicked aside, bare feet up on the coffee table.

She was exhausted, but not from gardening.

She'd had to stop digging and kneeling and sweating in the sun. You couldn't do those things and then toss your cookies all over a client's toes, not if you wanted to keep those clients.

Besides, she'd had something more important to do today.

She'd bought half a dozen early morning pregnancy test kits on her way home from Anna's last night and finally found the courage to use them this morning.

The EPTs had made things worse.

Two said she wasn't pregnant, three said she was, and she'd been so nervous she'd dropped one in the toilet before she could pee on it. So she'd phoned her GYN's office and said she had to have an appointment, no, not in two weeks, not next week.

"Today," she'd said in the firm voice of the new Isabella. And then the old Izzy had added a very polite "please."

And she was still in the dark.

Her gynecologist said she might be pregnant. On the other hand, she might not be. The doctor was rushed, the lab was busy, and the upshot was that the earliest she'd have a definite answer was tomorrow or, more probably, Monday, because tomorrow was Saturday and, *really, Ms. Orsini, the lab only works half days on Saturday and then it's only for emergencies...*

Isabella groaned and put her head back against the couch.

A few days ago, she'd refused to consider pregnancy as a possibility. Denial had her convinced she had a summer virus. Even when she'd let herself think about pregnancy, she'd done nothing to find out the truth.

Now, she wasn't sure she could endure the next twenty-four or forty-eight or how many endless hours it would be until she knew.

She wanted to know, right now. She *had* to know; she had plans to make, whether to remain pregnant, assuming she really was, or to terminate it, or have the baby and give it up for adoption...

Except, she knew the answer.

She'd have her baby. Keep it. Nurture it. Love it, this life she and her lover had made together. Her lying lover...

Had he intended to tell her the truth? That was what he'd said, but—but, it didn't matter.

Matteo was history, and it was funny but now she thought of him as Rio, because that was who he really was. A strong, proud man who'd created an existence out of nothing.

It didn't matter what name she gave him.

They'd both lived a lie and now—now they were lost to each other, forever.

A sob burst from her throat.

"I love him," she whispered, "I'll always love him—"

Isabella's cell phone rang. She wiped her eyes with her hand and checked the screen. Anna. She'd call her back. She wasn't up to speaking with anybody right now, not while she was being such a fool, crying over a man who could have come after her if he'd really loved her, who shouldn't have believed her terrible lies except yes, he should have, that was why she'd told him those lies, so he *would* believe them—

Brring, brring, brring.

The doorbell. Of course. Anna had phoned while she was climbing the five flights to Isabella's flat. Now what? Answer the door? Not answer it? Leave Anna, and all her good intentions, in the hall?

Brring, brring, brring.

Isabella sighed, rose to her feet, went to the door. Such impatience was so typically Anna.

"Okay," she said wearily as she undid the lock, the chain, the dead bolt. "Can't you take a hint? Somebody doesn't answer the bell, somebody doesn't want visit—"

The words caught in her throat as the door swung open. It wasn't Anna standing in the hall. It was Matteo. It was Rio. It was the love of her life. Tall. Handsome.

And angry.

Angry? Isabella frowned. What did he have to be angry about?

She would have asked him but he caught her by the shoulders, gave her a little shake and said, "Damnit, Isabella—"

And then his mouth captured hers.

It wasn't what he'd planned.

He'd rehearsed his lines in the taxi, gone over and over what he was going to say. That he'd lied about his name but

not about who he was and never about his feelings for her.
That he loved her and she loved him and, damnit, she'd lied,
too—

Reality had driven all that logical planning from his mind.

His Isabella lived in a neighborhood that could, at best,
be described as diverse. Her building was decrepit. She had
five flights of steps to climb.

He was ticked off by the time he reached her door. And
when he heard her undoing all those locks, when he saw her
looking pale and exhausted and thin, when all of those things
happened, he grew so angry at himself for not having told
her what a liar he was, for not having confessed his love, for
not having carried her off and made her his bride weeks ago
that the only thing he could do was kiss her.

That, at least, was logical.

So was the fact that after a few seconds of struggle, she
wrapped her arms tightly around his neck, lifted herself
against him and kissed him back.

It took all the determination he possessed to take his lips
from hers.

"You are the love of my life," he said.

And he waited.

For the first time in more than a decade, Rio D'Aquila
waited.

It seemed to take forever. Then, at last, Isabella smiled.

"And you are mine," she said.

Rio's heart, frozen solid as ice the past endless weeks, the
past endless years, thawed at the sound of those sweet words.

"Isabella," he whispered against her mouth, and he followed
her name with a string of words in Italian, in Portuguese, none
of which she understood, but she didn't have to.

He loved her. Her lover loved her.

"Isabella, *mia bella* Isabella, forgive me. I loved you from
the minute I saw you."

"I don't believe you," she said, her lips curving in a smile. "You'll have to keep kissing me until I do."

"I love you," he said huskily. "That's why I was so afraid to tell you the truth. I thought you would hate me—"

"I did," Isabella said, between kisses. "That's why I told you my own lies. Here's the truth. I love you. I'll always love you."

Rio grinned. "Say it again."

"I love you. I love you. I love—"

More kisses. Then Rio framed her face with his hands.

"Marry me, Isabella."

Her eyes glittered with happy tears. She smiled—and then her smile dimmed.

"Ask me on Monday."

"What?"

"By Monday—" She hesitated. Should she tell him the truth? Yes. Absolutely. She would never lie to him again. "By Monday, I'll know if—if I'm pregnant. You might feel differently if—"

"Trust me, sweetheart," Rio said, with a smile so sexy it made her breath catch. "If you're not pregnant now, I'll make you pregnant as soon as I can."

Isabella laughed. "You will, huh?"

"I want a tiny Isabella in our lives."

"It could be a tiny Rio. Or a Matteo… Which reminds me, what do I call you?"

Rio smiled.

"Call me your beloved," he said huskily, "as I will call you mine."

EPILOGUE

EVERYONE agreed that Isabella was the most beautiful bride in the world, just as her sister and her sisters-in-law had been before her.

She wore a floor-length gown of ivory lace, her mother's lace veil and an antique diamond tiara Anna had found in a tiny Greenwich Village shop.

"It just had your name on it," Anna explained when she pinned it carefully into Isabella's dark curls.

The sisters smiled, hugged each other…and wept.

There was, Rio noticed, a lot of weeping going on.

"It's what happens when you have six sisters at one wedding," Rafe said drily, but they all knew how lucky they were that Anna and Isabella, Gabriella and Elle, Alessia and Chiara felt as if they were sisters by blood, not only by marriage.

All of them were Isabella's bridesmaids, though Anna, of course, was her matron of honor.

Raffaele, Falco, Nicolo, Dante and Draco, handsome in their Armani formal wear, stood witness for Rio, equally handsome in his.

They all called him Rio; it was what Isabella called him because it was his legal name and it seemed to suit him better than the name the orphanage had bestowed upon him.

This time, the wedding planner—they'd used the same one

for all the Orsini nuptials—knew there was no point telling them you couldn't have that many best men at the altar.

In fact, she said, with a little sigh, she'd decided that this was how things *should* be done, if only a groom and his friends looked like these.

After the ceremony at the little Greenwich Village church, limousines took them to the Orsini mansion. The enormous conservatory behind it had been decorated with baskets and baskets of flowers from Isabella's shop.

There was music and incredible food—Anna, experienced at this by now, had dealt with the catering. And there were endless bottles of vintage champagne, though, as in the past, the brothers—or maybe, this time, it had been Draco—somebody, at any rate, managed to sneak in a few bottles of chilled beer.

Isabella drank only chilled Pellegrino.

She was pregnant, and she glowed as only a happily pregnant woman can glow.

The day was winding down. All the guests had left. Only the band and the family remained when Cesare Orsini stepped up to the microphone, tapped on his champagne flute, cleared his throat and announced he had something to say.

Everyone was surprised.

Their father—the don—had not made any kind of speech at any of the other weddings. He had, if anything, kept to the background, for which his sons and daughters had been grateful.

None of them had any illusions about what he was.

None except Sofia, Cesare's wife and their mother. It was for her that Rafe, Dante, Falco and Nick, Anna and Isabella maintained an illusion of peace with their father.

So when he commandeered the microphone, the Orsini offspring frowned at each other.

The brothers and brothers-in-law instinctively offered their wives protection from whatever their father might say.

Rafe put his arm around Chiara; Dante did the same with Gaby. Falco took a stance behind Elle and wrapped his arms around her waist. Nick reached for Alessia's hand. Anna settled in the curve of Draco's arm, Isabella in the curve of Rio's.

The Orsini grandchildren—there were six of them by now—had long ago been put down for naps by their nannies.

Silence descended over the conservatory.

"This," Cesare said into the mike, "is a very happy day." He smiled and raised his champagne flute to Isabella and Rio. "Isabella, my daughter, your mama and I wish you and your new husband joy."

Isabella nodded. "Thank you," she said stiffly.

Cesare grinned slyly. "Can you imagine what might have happened if I had not told you that accepting a job as a landscaper was not the right thing for you to do, hmm?"

Isabella stared at her father. "What?"

"Ah, *i miei amati figli,* my beloved sons and daughters, you have no idea how much you mean to me."

"He's right," Falco said, sotto voce, "we sure as hell don't."

"Shh," Elle said softly, but she turned her face up to his and smiled.

"And you have no idea how much I respect you," Cesare said. His voice wobbled and he cleared his throat. "None of you chose to follow in my footsteps, for which I am very, very grateful."

A murmur swept through the room.

"When I was a young man, I dreamed of having children who would make your mama and me proud. And you have done exactly that. We are proud of you all."

The murmur grew in intensity. Cesare cleared his throat again.

"You have chosen your professions and your mates wisely.

You are happy, and that is what we wanted most in this sometimes ugly world." He turned to his wife and held out his hand. Sofia took it and stood beside him. He bent his head, whispered to her, and she smiled. "Your mama has something she wishes to say."

Cesare took her hand and lifted it to his lips, which sent another murmur through the room. Sofia looked at her children and their spouses. Her eyes glittered with unshed tears. She looked, Isabella would say later, like a bride herself.

"Your papa has told you how much we love you," Sofia said softly. "How much we respect you for your choices." She paused and looked up at her husband. "My wish for you all is that you will love each other as much as your father and I."

This time, the murmur that went through the room was filled with amazement. Quiet, docile Mama, professing love for her crime boss husband?

Sofia put her hand on Cesare's arm.

"I know it is difficult for you to understand. I know what your father is, what he has had to become. I know it in ways you cannot possibly comprehend and while I deplore the life he had to choose, I love him with all my heart." She looked at each of her sons and daughters in turn. "And because we love each other, we hoped that you would all find love, too." She paused. "But we began to worry—*I*—began to worry that you would not."

Isabella stepped forward. "What are you talking about, Mama?"

"Cesare," Sofia said, "you tell them, *si?*"

Cesare Orsini put his arm around his wife's waist.

"Your mama was concerned. Our sons, she said, were too content with bachelorhood. Our daughters were even worse. One was sometimes arrogant and opinionated."

Anna blushed. They couldn't possibly mean her.

"The other was filled with quiet strength and courage, but unable to see her true self."

Now, it was Isabella who blushed. Her new husband smiled and drew her to him.

"So," Cesare said, "we looked around. We saw things. Heard things. We put our heads together. What kinds of situations would catch the interest of our sons? Our daughters? And then, we sent you on errands we hoped might change your lives."

The Orsinis looked at each other. No. It was too much to absorb. Their parents, their quiet mother and tough father, playing cupid?

"Could it be true?" Isabella whispered to Rio.

Rio gathered his wife into his arms.

"I found you, didn't I, *bella mia?* So, I would say, yes, when it comes to love, anything can be true."

"Le nostre benedizioni su di voi e ai vostri figli," Cesare said. "Our blessings on you and your children. And now, *per favore,* your mama and I would like to share the dance floor with you before this beautiful day ends."

The band began to play. The tune was soft and haunting.

Rio led his wife onto the dance floor. Draco did the same with Anna. Rafe, Dante, Falco and Nick followed with their wives until the entire Orsini clan, Cesare and Sofia included, was waltzing to the beautiful music.

It was Anna who caught on first.

"Ohmygod," she said to Draco, "it's the theme from *The Godfather!*"

Everyone heard her. They all began to laugh.

"Now," Isabella whispered to her bridegroom, and Rio grinned, swept his wife into his arms and carried her off into the night while his new family cheered.

* * * * *

SECRETS, LIES & LULLABIES

HEIDI BETTS

To Rob and Michelle (Timko) Massung,
for all of their amazing computer help recently.
You saved my butt more than you will ever
know, and I just can't thank you enough.

One

Alexander Bajoran swiped his key card and pushed open the heavy oak door to his suite. He'd been halfway down the winding mile-long drive leading away from the luxurious yet rustic resort—aptly named Mountain View Lodge—when he realized he'd forgotten a stack of much-needed paperwork. Now he was late for his meeting, and it was going to be nearly impossible to make it into downtown Portland on time.

He let the door swing closed behind him as he marched toward the large cherrywood desk on the far side of the sitting area. Six steps in, he stopped short at the sound of someone else moving around in the suite. Turning toward the bedroom, he paused in the doorway, taking note of the woman stripping his bed and shaking her rear end to a song only she could hear.

She was wearing a maid's uniform, but sadly not one of the sexy French variety. Just a simple gray dress that did nothing to compliment her figure or coloring.

Her blond hair was pulled up and twisted at the back of her head, held in place by a large plastic clip, but he could still see bits of color peeking out here or there. A thin streak of black, then auburn, then blue running down one side and blending into the rest.

Yes, blue. The woman had blue hair. At least a few bits of it.

She was humming beneath her breath, the occasional odd lyric tripping off her tongue as she whipped back the top sheet, then a corner of the fitted one. The quilted coverlet was already in a heap on the floor.

As she danced around, oblivious to his presence, he noticed the glitter of earrings lining the entire length of one ear. Studs, hoops, dangles; there must have been seven or eight in her right ear alone. The left had only four that he could see—three near the lobe and one higher up near her temple.

Despite all the silver and gold and jeweled settings, he knew they had to be fake. No way could a chambermaid afford the real thing. Which was a shame, because she'd look good in diamonds. And he should know—diamonds were his business.

Soiled sheets balled up in her arms, she turned suddenly, jumping back and giving a high-pitched shriek when she saw him standing there.

He held his hands up in the universal I-mean-you-no-harm gesture. "I didn't mean to startle you," he offered by way of apology.

Reaching up, she yanked the buds from her ears and tucked them into the pocket of the white apron that must have held her MP3 player. He could hear the heavy beat of her music as she fumbled to turn down the volume.

Now that he could look at her straight on, he noticed she wasn't wearing makeup...or not much, at any rate. Strange, considering her hair and jewelry choices. She even had a small gold hoop with a tiny fleck of cubic zirconia hanging from the outer edge of her right eyebrow.

Eyes still wide from the scare he'd given her, she licked her lips. "I'm sorry, I didn't know anybody would be here. I didn't see the sign on the knob."

He shook his head. "There wasn't one. I expected to be gone for the day, but forgot something I need for a meeting."

He didn't know why he was telling her this. He didn't normally spend a lot of time explaining himself to anyone. But the longer he stood here talking, the longer he got to look at her. And he did enjoy looking at her.

That, too, was unusual for him. The women he dated tended to be socialites from wealthy families. Polished and sophisticated, the type who spent their days at the garden club doing nothing more strenuous than planning their next thousand-dollar-a-plate fundraiser for the charity du jour.

Never before had he found himself even remotely attracted to someone with multicolored hair and excessive piercings. But the young woman standing in front of him was fascinating in an exotic-animal, priceless-piece-of-artwork way.

She seemed to be slightly disconcerted by his presence, as well, staring at him as if she expected him to bite.

"Is there anything you need, as long as I'm here?" she asked, nervously licking her lips over and over again. "Extra towels or glasses, that sort of thing?"

He shook his head. "I'm fine, thank you."

Then, because he couldn't think of anything else to say or any other reason to stand there, staring at the help as though she was on display, he moved away, heading back across the sitting room and grabbing up the file he'd forgotten. It was her turn to stand in the bedroom doorway while he slapped the manila folder against his free hand a couple of times.

"Well," he murmured, for no particular reason, "I'll leave you to it, then."

She inclined her head in acknowledgment, still watching him warily.

Walking to the suite's main door, he pulled it open and set one foot across the threshold into the hall. But before walking off, he couldn't resist turning back and taking one last glance at the intriguing young woman who had already returned to her job of changing his sheets.

"It was Alexander Bajoran," Jessica said in a harsh whisper, leaning so far across the small round deli table that her nose very nearly touched her cousin's.

"You're kidding," Erin returned in an equally hushed voice, her eyes going wide in amazement.

Jessica shook her head, crossed her arms over her chest and flopped back in her chair, causing her cousin to move forward in hers. Their sandwiches sat untouched in front of them, their ice-filled fountain drinks slowly producing rivulets of condensation down the sides of the paper cups.

"Did he recognize you?" Erin asked.

"I don't know. He didn't say anything, but he *was* looking at me a little funny."

"Funny, how?"

Jessica flashed her a tiny grin. "The usual."

"Well, you do tend to stand out."

Jessica stuck her tongue out at her cousin's teasing. "We can't all be prim and proper Jackie O wannabes."

"Nobody's asking you to be Jackie O. The family just wishes you weren't quite so intent on being the next Courtney Love."

Following through on the natural instincts that had probably earned her that reputation in the first place, Jessica flipped her cousin a good-natured hand gesture. Not the least offended by the response, Erin merely rolled her eyes.

"Actually, your unique personal style may work in our

favor. You don't look at all the way you did five years ago. Chances are, Bajoran won't have a clue who you are."

"I hope not. I'll try to switch floors with Hilda, though. That should keep me from accidentally bumping into him again."

"No, don't do that!" Erin said quickly. "The fact that he doesn't recognize you is a good thing. You can move around his suite freely without arousing suspicion."

"Arousing suspicion?" Jessica repeated. "Who am I— James Bond?"

"If I could do it, I would, believe me," Erin told her with no small amount of bitterness leeching into her voice. "But you're the one he already thinks is a chambermaid."

Jessica narrowed her eyes. "Why does that matter?"

"Because it means you can move around the lodge without being noticed. You know what men like Bajoran are like. Rich and self-absorbed…to him, you'll be all but invisible."

Jessica understood her cousin's anger, really she did. Fifty years ago, Alexander Bajoran's grandfather and great-uncle had launched Bajoran Designs. Soon after, they'd begun a partnership with Jessica's and Erin's grandfathers, who owned Taylor Fine Jewels. Both companies had been based in Seattle, Washington, and together they'd been responsible for creating some of the most beautiful and valuable jewelry in the world. Million-dollar necklaces, bracelets and earrings worn by celebrities and royalty across the globe.

The Taylor-Bajoran partnership had lasted for decades, making both families extremely wealthy. And then one day about five years ago, Alexander had taken over Bajoran Designs from his father, and his first order of business had been to steal *her* family's company right out from under them.

Without warning he'd bought up a majority of shares of Taylor Fine Jewels and forced Jessica's and Erin's fathers off the Board of Directors so he could absorb the company into his own and essentially corner the market on priceless jewels and their settings.

Thanks to Alexander's treacherous move, the Taylor family had gone bankrupt and been driven out of Seattle almost overnight. They were far from destitute, but all the same, the Taylors were *not* used to living frugally. Jessica didn't think her mother was used to her new, more middle-class lifestyle even now, and Erin's mother had taken the reversal of fortune hardest of all.

Jessica was doing okay, though. Did she *enjoy* being a maid at a resort where she used to be a guest? Where she used to stay in a three-thousand-dollar-a-night suite and that her family could easily have purchased with a flick of the wrist?

Not always. But being a maid, working at a normal job like a normal person, gave her a freedom she'd never felt as a rich, well-known socialite. No way could she have gotten away with streaks in her hair and pierced everything when she'd been one of *those* Taylors. When she'd been attending luncheons at the country club with her mother and been the subject of regular snapshots by local and national paparazzi.

Money was good, but she thought anonymity might be a little bit better. For her, at least. For Erin, she knew the opposite was true.

"Why do I need to be invisible?" she asked finally. "It's lucky enough he didn't recognize me the first time. I should switch floors and maybe even shifts with one of the other girls before he does."

"No!" Erin exploded again. "Don't you see? This is our chance! Our chance to get back at that bastard for what he did to us."

"What are you talking about?" Thoroughly confused, Jessica shook her head. "How could we possibly get back at him for that? He's a millionaire. Billionaire. The CEO of a zillion-dollar company. We're nobodies. No money, no power, no leverage."

"That's right, we're nobodies. And he's the CEO of a zillion-dollar company that *used* to be ours. Maybe it could be again."

Before Jessica had the chance to respond, Erin rushed on. "He's here on business, right? That means he has to have business information with him. Paperwork, contracts, documents we could use to possibly get Taylor Fine Jewels back."

"Taylor Fine Jewels doesn't exist anymore. It's been absorbed into Bajoran Designs."

"So?" Erin replied with a shrug of one delicate shoulder. "It can always be un-absorbed."

Jessica didn't know how that would work. She wasn't sure it was even possible. But whether it was or it wasn't, what Erin was suggesting was insanity.

"I can't go poking around in his things. It's wrong. And dangerous. And corporate espionage. And *definitely* against Mountain View policy. I could lose my job!"

Her cousin made a sound low in her throat. "It's only corporate espionage if you're employed by a rival company. Which you're not, because Alexander Bajoran *stole* our company and put us all out on the street. And who cares if you lose that stupid job? Surely you can scrub toilets for the wealthy elite at some other high-priced hotel."

Jessica leaned back, stunned by the venom in her cousin's voice, as well as her obvious disdain for Jessica's occupation. Yes, she scrubbed toilets and stripped beds and vacuumed carpets instead of folding scarves and dressing mannequins at an upscale boutique like Erin, but she kind of liked it. She got to spend most of her time alone, got along well with the rest of the housekeeping staff and didn't have to claim her sometimes quite generous tips on her taxes.

And it kept her busy enough that she didn't have time to

dwell on the past or nurse a redwood-size grudge against an old enemy the way her cousin obviously did.

"Come on, Jess. Please," Erin begged. "You have to do this. For the family. We may never get another opportunity to find out what Bajoran is up to, or if there's some way—*any way*—to rebuild the business and our lives."

She wanted to refuse. *Should* refuse. But the pain in Erin's voice and in her eyes gave Jessica pause.

She could maybe poke around a little.

"What would I have to do?" she asked carefully. "What would I be looking for?"

"Just…see if you can find some paperwork. On the desk, in his briefcase if he leaves it. Interoffice memos, maybe, or documents outlining his next top secret, underhanded take-over."

Against her better judgment, Jessica gave a reluctant nod. "All right, I'll do it. But I'm not going to get caught. I'll *glance around.* Keep my eyes open. But I'm not going to rummage through his belongings like a common thief."

Erin's nod was much more exuberant. "Fine, I understand. Just look around. Maybe linger over fluffing the pillows if he's on the phone…listen in on his conversation."

She wasn't certain she could do that, either, but simply acting like she would seemed to make her cousin happy enough.

"Don't get your hopes up, Erin. This has 'Lucy and Ethel' written all over it, and you know how their crazy schemes always turned out. I'm not going to jail for you, either. A Taylor with a criminal record would get even more press than one having to work a menial, nine-to-five job cleaning other people's bathrooms."

Two

This was insane.

She was a former socialite turned chambermaid, not some stealthy spy trained to ferret out classified information. She didn't even know what she was looking for, let alone how to find it.

Her cart was in the hall, but she'd dragged nearly everything she needed to clean and restock the room in with her. Sheets, towels, toilet paper, the vacuum cleaner... If there were enough supplies spread out, she figured she would look busier and have more of an excuse for moving all over the suite in case anyone—specifically Alexander Bajoran—came in and caught her poking around.

The problem was, his suite was pretty much immaculate. She'd been cleaning it herself on a daily basis, even before he'd checked in, and the Mountain View's housekeeping standards were quite high. Add to that the fact that Alexander

Bajoran was apparently quite tidy himself, and there was almost *nothing* personal left out for her to snoop through.

Regardless of what she'd let her cousin believe, she was not going to ransack this room. She would glance through the desk, under the bed, in the nightstands, maybe inside the closet, but she was not going to root through his underwear drawer. Not when she didn't even know what she was supposed to be looking for.

Business-related what? Compromising...what?

Jessica couldn't blame her cousin for wanting to find *something* incriminating. Anything that might turn the tables on the man who had destroyed the Taylors' livelihood and a few members of the family personally.

But how realistic was that, really? It had been five years since Bajoran's hostile takeover. He had moved on and was certainly juggling a dozen other deals and business ventures by now. And even if *those* weren't entirely on the level, she doubted he was walking around with a paper trail detailing his treachery.

The sheets were already pulled off the bed and in a heap on the floor, so it looked as though she was busy working. And since she was close, she quickly, quietly slid open one of the nightstand drawers.

Her hands were shaking, her fingertips ice-cold with nerves, and she was shivering in her plain white tennis shoes. Sure, she was alone, but the hallway door was propped open—as was lodge policy—and at any moment someone could walk in to catch her snooping.

She didn't know which would be worse—being caught by Alexander Bajoran or by her supervisor. One could kick up enough of a stink to get her fired...the other could fire her on the spot.

But she didn't need to worry too much right that second, because the drawer was empty. It didn't hold so much as a

Bible or telephone directory. Mountain View wasn't *that* kind of resort. If you needed a Bible or phone book or anything else—even items of a personal nature—you simply called the front desk and they delivered it immediately and with the utmost discretion.

Closing the drawer on a whisper, she kicked the soiled sheets out of her way and shook out the clean fitted sheet over the bare mattress as she rounded the foot of the bed. She covered one corner and then another before releasing the sheet to open the drawer of the opposite nightstand.

This one wasn't empty, and her heart stuttered in her chest at the knowledge that she was actually going to have to follow through on this. She was going to have to search through her family's archenemy's belongings.

The bottom drawer of the bedside bureau held a decanter of amber liquid—scotch, she presumed, though she'd never really been in charge of restocking the rooms' bars—and a set of highball glasses. The top drawer held a thick, leather-bound folder and dark blue Montblanc pen.

She swallowed hard. Once she moved that pen and opened the folder, that was it…she was invading Alexander's privacy and violating the employee agreement she'd signed when she'd first started working at the lodge.

Taking a deep breath, she closed her eyes for just a split second, then reached for the pen. As quickly as she could she flipped open the folder and tried to get her racing mind to make sense of the papers inside.

Her eyes skimmed the print of the first two pages, but nothing jumped out at her as being important or damaging. And the rest was just pictures of jewelry. Snapshots of finished pieces and sketches of what she assumed were proposed designs.

Beautiful, beautiful jewelry. The kind her family used to create. The kind she used to dream of being responsible for.

She'd grown up pampered and protected, and was pretty sure her parents had never expected her to do anything more than marry well and become the perfect trophy wife. But what she'd truly aspired to all those years she'd spent primping and attending finishing school was to actually work for Taylor Fine Jewels. Or possibly more specifically their partner company, Bajoran Designs.

Like any young woman, she loved jewelry. But where most of her peers had only wanted to wear the sparkly stuff, she'd wanted to *make* it. She loved sifting through cut and uncut gems to find the perfect stone for a setting she'd drawn herself.

All through high school her notebooks and the margins of her papers had been filled with intricate doodles that were in reality her ideas for jewelry designs. Her father had even used a few for pieces that had gone on to sell for six and seven figures. And for her sixteenth birthday, he'd surprised her with a pearl-and-diamond ring in a setting that had always been one of her very favorites.

It was still one of her favorites, though she didn't get many opportunities to wear it these days. Instead, it was tucked safely at the bottom of her jewelry box, hidden amongst the much less valuable baubles that suited her current level of income.

But, heavens above, these designs were beautiful. Not perfect. She could see where the size of one outshone the sapphire at its center. Or how the filigree of another was too dainty for the diamonds it surrounded.

She could fix the sketches with a sharp pencil and a few flicks of her wrist, and her palms itched to do just that.

When she caught herself running her fingers longingly across the glossy surface of one of the photographs, she sucked in a startled breath. How long had she been standing there with a target on her back? All she needed was for Alexander or another maid to walk in and catch her staring at his portfolio as if she was planning a heist.

Slamming the folder shut, she returned it to the bedside drawer and placed the pen back on top in exactly the same position it had been to begin with. She hoped.

With the nightstand put to rights, she finished stretching the fitted sheet over the other two corners of the mattress, then added the top sheet. She needed to get the room cleaned, and the best way to snoop was to search the areas nearest where she was working, anyway.

So she got the bedroom fixed up and cleaned but didn't resupply the bathroom before moving back into the main sitting room. She ran the vacuum over every inch of the rug, just like she was supposed to, but took her time and even poked the nose of the sweeper into the closet near the hallway door. The only thing she found there, however, was the hotel safe, which she knew she didn't stand a chance of getting into.

The only place left that might hold something of interest to her cousin was the large desk along the far wall. She'd avoided it until now because she suspected she didn't really want to find anything. She didn't want to be put in that spot between a rock and a hard place; didn't want to hand something over to Erin that might put her cousin in an even more precarious situation; didn't want to stir up trouble and poke at a sore spot within her family that *she'd* thought was beginning to heal over. She'd thought they were all moving on.

Apparently, she'd been wrong.

Leaving the vacuum nearby, she did a quick sweep of the top of the desk. There were a few sheets of hotel stationery with random notes written on them, but the rest seemed to be the typical items supplied by the lodge. Hotel directory, room-service menu, et cetera.

Inside the desk, though, she found a heck of a lot more.

Namely a small stack of manila folders and a laptop computer.

Jessica licked her lips, breathing in shallow bursts that matched the too-fast beat of her heart against her rib cage.

She was not opening that laptop, she just wasn't. For one thing, that would be *too much* breaking and entering, and sticking her nose where it didn't belong, for her peace of mind. For another, it would take too long. By the time it booted up and she figured out how to explore the different files and documents, her supervisor would surely be kicking in the door demanding to know why she was still in this suite when she should have been done with the entire floor.

She was sticking to her guns on this one. Erin might not like that decision, but she would just have to deal with it.

So she stuck with the folders lying beside the laptop, opening them one at a time and scanning them as quickly as possible.

Nothing jumped out at her as being out of the ordinary—not that she really had a clue what she was looking at or for. It was all just business jargon, and she certainly hadn't gone to business school.

But there was no mention of Taylor Fine Jewels in any of the papers...not that she'd expected there to be. And there was no indication of anything else that put her instincts on red alert.

She was just letting out a huff of air that was part frustration, part relief when she heard a creak and knew someone was entering the suite behind her. Her eyes flashed wide and she all but slammed the desk drawer shut—but slowly and quietly to keep from looking as guilty as she felt.

Putting her hand on the rag that she'd left on top of the desk, she started to wipe it down, just as she was supposed to. *Act natural. Act natural. Try not to hyperventilate. Act natural.*

Even though she knew darn well someone was behind her...likely standing there staring at her butt in the unappealing, lifeless gray smock that was her work uniform...she didn't react. She was alone, simply doing her job, as usual. The trick would be to feign surprise when she turned around and "discovered" that she *wasn't* alone.

Schooling her breathing...*act natural, act natural*...she hoped her cheeks weren't pink with the guilt of a kid caught with her hand in the cookie jar. Luck was on her side, though, because as she finished wiping down the desktop and twisted toward where she'd left the upright vacuum cleaner, whoever was standing behind her, silently monitoring her every move, cleared his throat.

And it was a he. She could tell by the timbre of that low rumble as it reached her ears and skated straight down her spine.

The air caught in her lungs for a moment, and she chastised herself for having such a gut-level, feminine response to something so simple. This man was a complete stranger. Her family's sworn enemy. And since he was a guest of Mountain View, and she worked for the lodge, he might as well be her employer.

Those were only the first of many reasons why her breathing should not be shallow, her blood should not be heating, and the clearing of his throat should not cause her to shiver inside her skin.

Doing her best to snap herself out of it, she straightened and twisted around, her hand still on the handle of the vacuum cleaner.

"Oh!" she exclaimed, letting her eyes go wide in mock startlement, praying the man standing in front of her wouldn't see right through it. "Hello again."

"Hello there," Alexander Bajoran returned, his mouth curving up in a small smile.

Jessica's pulse kicked up a notch.

It was nerves, she told herself. Just nerves.

But the truth was, the man was devilishly handsome. Enemy or no enemy, a blind woman would be able to see that.

His ink-black hair was perfectly styled, yet long enough in places to look relaxed and carefree. Eyes the color of blue ice glittered against skin that was surprisingly tan for a resident of the Pacific Northwest. But she knew for a fact it wasn't the result of time spent in tanning beds or spray-on booths; the entire Bajoran family leaned toward dark skin, dark hair... and ruthless personalities.

She had to remember that. The ruthless part, anyway.

Never mind how amazing he looked in his black dress slacks and dark blue blazer. Like he belonged on the cover of *GQ.* Or *Forbes,* thanks to his ill-gotten millions.

Never mind that if she saw him on the street, she would probably give herself whiplash spinning around to get a second look.

"We seem to have conflicting schedules this week," he said in a light, amused tone. His voice immediately touched deep, dark places inside of her that she *really* didn't want to think about.

He gave her a look, one she'd seen thousands of times in her adult life and had no trouble recognizing. Then his voice dropped a fraction, becoming sensual and suggestive.

"Or maybe they're matching up just right."

The heat of his voice was like sunshine on budding little seedlings, making *something* low in her belly shiver, quiver and begin to unfurl.

Oh, no. No, no, no. No more charming-but-dangerous men for her—and Alexander Bajoran was the most dangerous of all.

She'd been hit on and leered at by any number of male guests in her time at Mountain View. Traveling businessmen, vacationing husbands with a wandering eye, rich but useless playboys with a sense of entitlement…. But whether they'd pinched her on the rear, slipped her hundred-dollar tips or attempted simple flattery, she had never once been attracted to a single one of them.

Yet here she was, face-to-face with the man who had stolen her family's company and whom she was supposed to be spying on, and caterpillars were crawling around under every inch of her skin.

He took a step toward her, and her hands fisted, one around the handle of the vacuum, the other near her right hip. But all he did was set his briefcase—which was really more of a soft leather messenger bag—on the nearby coffee table before sinking into the overstuffed cushions of the sofa behind it.

Releasing a pent-up breath and sending some of those annoying creepy-crawlies away with it, Jessica reached down to unplug the sweeper and started to coil up the cord. The sooner she got out of there now that he was back, the better.

"I can leave you alone, if you need to work," she said, because the growing silence in the room was killing her.

But even though he had the brown leather satchel open on the glass-topped table and had pulled out several stacks of paperwork, he shook his head.

"Go ahead and finish what you were doing," he told her. "I've just got a couple of things to look over, but you won't distract me. In fact, the background noise might do me some good."

Well, shoot. How was she supposed to make a smooth but timely exit now?

She guessed she wasn't.

Dragging the vacuum across the sitting room, she set it in the hallway just outside the door of the suite. Then she gathered up an armful of fresh towels and washcloths for the bathroom.

It wasn't hard to go about her business this far away from Alexander. It was almost as though the air was normal in this tiled, insulated room instead of thick with nerves and guilt and unspoken sexual awareness. From her standpoint, at any rate. From his the air probably seemed absolutely normal. After all, he wasn't the one snooping, breaking the law, fighting a completely unwanted sexual attraction to someone he was supposed to hate.

She spent an inordinate amount of time making sure the towels hung just right on the towel rods and were perfectly even in their little cubbies under the vanity. Even longer putting out new bottles of shampoo, conditioner, mouthwash and shaving cream.

There were decorative mints and chocolates to go on the pillows in the bedroom, but she didn't want to go back in there. From the bathroom she could wave a hasty goodbye and get the heck out of Dodge. But if she returned to the bedroom, she would have to pass by Alexander. See him, smile at him, risk having him speak to her again.

That was one corner she was willing to cut today. Even if he complained to her superiors and she got in trouble later, missing mints were easier to apologize for than snooping or blushing herself into heat stroke in front of a valued guest.

Stepping out of the marble-and-gilt bathroom, she rounded the corner and was just congratulating herself on a narrow escape when she lifted her head and almost ran smack into Alexander, who was leaning against the outside wall waiting for her.

She made a tiny *eep* sound, slapping a hand over her heart as she bounced back on her heels.

"Sorry," he apologized, reaching out to steady her. "Didn't

mean to scare you, I just wanted to catch you before you took off."

If ever there was a word she didn't want to hear pass this man's lips, it was *catch*. Was she caught? Had he noticed something out of place? Figured out that she'd rifled through his things?

She held her breath, waiting for the accusations he had every right to fling at her.

Instead, as soon as he was sure she wasn't going to topple over, he let go of her elbow and went back to leaning negligently against the wall. It was a casual pose, but all Jessica could think was that he was standing between her and the door, blocking her only exit from the suite.

"I know this is probably out of line," he murmured, "but I was hoping you'd have dinner with me tonight."

His words caused her heart to stutter and then stall out completely for several long seconds.

"I'm here on business, so after I finish with meetings and such during the day, my evening hours are a bit...empty."

He shrugged a shoulder, and because he'd taken off the blazer, she could see the play of muscle caused by the movement beneath his crisp white dress shirt. Something so minor shouldn't make her hormones sit up and take notice, but they did. Boy, howdy, did they ever.

Licking her lips, she cleared her throat and hoped her voice didn't squeak when she tried to speak. It was bad enough that her face was aflame with nerves; she could feel the heat all but setting her eyelashes on fire. She already looked like a clown, in many people's estimation—she didn't need to open her mouth and sound like one, too.

"Thank you, but fraternizing with guests is against resort policy."

Ooh, that sounded good. Very confident and professional—and squeak-free.

Alexander lifted a brow. "Somehow I find it hard to believe a woman with blue hair is afraid of breaking a few rules."

She reached up to toy with the strip of chemically altered hair he was referring to. "It's not *all* blue," she muttered.

That bought her a too-handsome grin and flash of very white, perfectly straight teeth. "Just enough to let the world know you're a rebel, right?"

Wow, he had her pegged, didn't he? And he wasn't taking no, thank you, for an answer.

Dropping the hank of hair, Jessica pushed her shoulders back. She was a rebel, as well as a confident, self-reliant woman. But she wasn't stupid.

"I could lose my job," she said simply.

He cocked his head. She wasn't the only self-assured person in the room.

"But you won't," he told her matter-of-factly. Then, after a brief pause, he added, "Would it make you feel better if I said I won't let that happen?"

With anybody else she would have scoffed. But knowing who Alexander Bajoran was and the power he held—even here in Portland—she had no doubt he meant what he said and had enough influence to make it stick.

"You'll be on your own time, not the resort's," he pointed out. "And I'll let you decide whether we order from room service or go out somewhere else."

She should say no. Any sensible person would. The entire situation screamed danger with a capital *D*.

But she had to admit, she was curious. She'd had male guests proposition her before, give her that salacious, skin-crawling look reserved for when they were on out-of-town business trips without their wives and thought they could get away with something.

Alexander was the first, though, to ask her to dinner without the creepy looks or attempts at groping. Which made her wonder why he was interested.

Did he suspect her of snooping around where she didn't belong, or was he just hitting on a pretty, no-strings-attached maid? Did he recognize her as a Taylor and think she was up to something, or just hope to get lucky?

Of course she *was* up to something, but now she wanted to know if *he* was up to something, too.

So even though she knew she should be running a hundred miles an hour in the opposite direction, she opened her mouth and made the biggest mistake of her life.

"All right."

Three

Jessica didn't get many opportunities to dress up these days. But she was having dinner this evening with a very wealthy, very handsome man, and even though she knew it was a terrible idea, she wanted to make the most of it. Not so much the man and the dinner but simply the act of going out and feeling special for a little while. Putting on something pretty rather than functional. Taking extra time with her makeup and hair. Wearing heels instead of ratty old tennies.

She even went so far as to dab on a couple drops of what was left of her favorite three-hundred-dollar-an-ounce designer perfume, Fanta C. Alexander Bajoran might not be worth a spritz or two, but she certainly was.

She was wearing a plain black skirt and flowy white blouse with a long, multi-strand necklace and large gold hoop earrings in her primary holes. The others held her usual array of studs and smaller hoops.

As she strode down the carpeted hallway, she fiddled with

every part of her outfit. Was her skirt too short? Did her blouse show too much cleavage? Would the necklace draw Alexander's eye to her breasts? Or worse yet, would the earrings pull too much of his attention to her face?

Flirting—even flirting with danger this way—was one thing. Truly risking being recognized by her family's greatest enemy, though… No, she didn't want that.

Which was why she'd chosen to meet him here, in his room at the resort, rather than going out to a public restaurant where they might be seen by someone they—especially she—knew.

Getting caught in a guest's room after work hours would be bad, but being spotted out on a date with Alexander by one of her relatives or somebody who might tell one of her relatives would be exponentially worse. She would rather be fired than deal with the familial fallout.

Reaching the door of his suite, Jessica stopped and took a deep breath. She straightened her clothes and jewelry for the thousandth time and checked her small clutch purse to be sure she had her cell phone, a lipstick, a few bucks just in case. She didn't know if she would end up needing any of those things, but wanted to have them, all the same.

When there was nothing left to double-check, no other reason to put off the inevitable, she took another deep, stabilizing breath, held it and let it out slowly as she tapped on the door.

The nerves she'd tamped down started to wiggle back toward the surface as she waited for him to answer. Then suddenly the door swung open, and there he was.

Six foot something of dark, imposing good-looks. Slacks still smooth and pressed, despite being worn all day. Pale, pale lavender dress shirt unbuttoned at his throat and sleeves rolled up to his elbows, but no less distinguished than when he'd been wearing a tie and suit jacket.

He smiled in welcome and a lump formed in her throat, making it hard to swallow. Suddenly she was almost pathologically afraid to be alone with him. It was two mature adults sharing a simple meal, but almost as though she was watching a horror movie, she could see around all the corners to where scary things and maniacal killers waited.

A thousand frightening scenarios and terrible outcomes flitted through her brain in the nanosecond it took him to say hello—or rather, a deep, masculine, "Hi, there"—and step back to let her into the suite.

She could have run. She could have begged off, hurriedly telling him she'd changed her mind, or that something important had come up and she couldn't stay.

She probably should have.

Instead, a tiny voice in her head whispered, *What's the worst that can happen?* and showed her images of a lovely, delicious meal at an establishment where she worked but never got the chance to indulge, with an attractive man the likes of which she probably wouldn't meet again for a very long time. Not given her current circumstances.

So she didn't run. She told herself she was here, he was a gentleman, and everything would be fine.

"Thank you," she murmured, surprised when her voice not only didn't crack, but came out in a low, almost smoky tone that sounded a lot sexier than she'd intended.

She stepped into the suite, and he closed the door behind her with a soft click. More familiar with these rooms than she cared to admit, she moved down the short hallway and into the sitting room where there was already a table set up with white linens and covered silver serving trays.

"I hope you don't mind, but I took the liberty of ordering," Alexander said, coming up behind her. "I thought it would save some time."

True enough. Mountain View employed one of the best

chefs in the country and served some of the best food on the West Coast, but room service was room service. It sometimes took longer than guests might have liked for their meals to arrive, especially if the kitchen was busy trying to get food out to the dining room.

Cupping her elbow, he steered her around the table and pulled out her chair. She tried not to let the heat of his hand do funny things to her pulse. Of course, her pulse had a mind of its own.

He helped her get seated, then began uncovering plates of food. The smells hit her first, and they were divine. Even before she could identify them all, she saw that he'd ordered a sampling of some of the very best culinary creations the resort had to offer.

From the appetizer section of the menu he'd asked for watermelon gazpacho with tomato; cucumber and borage; seafood tomato bisque; eggplant ravioli; and oysters in red wine mignonette.

As entrées, he'd gone with pheasant with green cabbage, port wine-infused pear and black truffle shavings, and something she could rarely resist—crab cakes. Mountain View's particular recipe consisted of large chunks of Dungeness crab, tiny bits of lobster, corn and faro lightly seared to a golden brown.

He had no way of knowing they were one of her all-time favorites, though. Most likely he'd ordered them because they were nearly world renowned and one of the most popular items on the resort's menu.

But her stomach rumbled and her mouth began to water at the very sight. She might work here, might have skated past the kitchen or dining room a time or two, but since she couldn't exactly afford fifty-dollar-a-plate dinners any longer, she'd never been lucky enough to actually taste them.

"I hope there's something here you'll like."

Like? She wanted to take her clothes off and roll around on the table of food, then lick her body clean.

Because she wasn't certain she could speak past the drool pooling on her tongue, she merely nodded and made an approving *mmm-hmm* sound.

"I ordered dessert, as well, but let's wait until we finish this before we dig into that."

Oh. She'd heard wonderful things about Mountain View's desserts, too.

"So..." he murmured, "where would you like to start? Or should I just hand over the crab cakes before someone gets hurt?"

The mention of crab cakes and the slight amusement in his tone brought her head up, and she realized she'd been concentrating rather intensely on that particular platter.

"Sorry, they just...smell really good."

He grinned at her candid response. Reaching to the side and lifting the plate, he set it back down directly in front of her.

"They're all yours," he told her. "As long as you don't mind if I keep the pheasant to myself."

Well, she would have liked at least a *tiny* bite—she'd never had the pleasure of trying that particular dish, either—but if the crab cakes were as delicious as they looked, smelled and she'd heard they were, she supposed it was a sacrifice worth making.

Her silence seemed to be answer enough. He moved the pheasant to his place setting, then reached for the bottle of wine in the center of the table and pulled the cork. While she shook out her napkin and laid it across her lap, he poured two glasses of the rich, dark liquid and handed one to her.

She took it with a murmured thank-you and brought it to her nose for a sniff. Mmm. It had been a while since she'd enjoyed a glass of really good, expensive wine. This one was full-bodied, with the scents of fruit, spice and just a hint of chocolate.

She was tempted to take a sip right away, but didn't want to ruin her first taste of the crab cakes and had also promised herself she would be careful tonight. A little bit of wine with dinner wouldn't hurt, but she didn't want to risk drinking too much and forgetting who she was…who he was… and exactly how much was on the line if she accidentally let any part of the truth slip past her lips.

So she set the glass aside and picked up her fork instead.

"At the risk of scaring you off now that you're already here," Alexander said, shaking out his own napkin and placing it across his lap, "it occurred to me that I invited you to dinner tonight without even knowing your name. Or introducing myself, for that matter."

Jessica paused with her first bite of crab cake halfway to her mouth. Uh-oh. She hadn't been concerned with introducing herself to Alexander because she already knew who he was. And keeping her own identity under wraps was critical, so she hadn't exactly been eager to share that information, either.

Now, however, she was cornered, and she'd better come up with a response soon or he would start to get suspicious.

To buy herself a little bit of time, she continued the trajectory of her fork and went ahead with that first bite of food she'd so been looking forward to. Her anticipation was dampened slightly by the tension thrumming through her body and causing her mind to race, but that didn't keep her taste buds from leaping with joy at the exquisite spices and textures filling her mouth.

Oh, this was so worth the stress and subterfuge of pretending to be someone she wasn't. With luck she would only have to lie to him for one night, and not only would he be none the wiser, but she'd have the experience of a lovely meal with a handsome, wealthy playboy-type tucked away in her memory banks.

The part about deceiving him and searching his suite like a wannabe spy would maybe have to be deleted, if she hoped to live with herself for the next fifty years, though.

Making a satisfied sound deep in her throat, she swallowed and finally turned her attention to Alexander—since she couldn't justify ignoring him any longer.

"My name is Jessica. Madison," she told him, using her middle name instead of her last. If he questioned anyone at the resort, they would either deny knowing her or correct her little fib without realizing they were revealing anything significant. He obviously hadn't asked around about her or he would already know her name, and she doubted he would bother after this, as long as she didn't give him cause to become curious.

He offered her a small grin and held his hand out across the table. She had to put her fork down to take it.

"Hello, Jessica. I'm Alexander Bajoran. You can call me Alex."

A shiver of heat went through her at both the familiarity of his invitation and the touch of his smooth, warm hand.

Darn it! Why did she have to like him so much? And she really did. He was charming and good-looking and self-assured. Knowing he had a nice, hefty bank account certainly didn't hurt, but it was his easy friendliness that made her regret her bargain with Erin and the fact that she was a Taylor.

If she didn't have that baggage, she suspected she would be extremely flattered by his apparent interest in her and excited about tonight's "date." But she would be self-conscious about the fact that she was a lowly chambermaid, while he was clearly blessed financially, even though there was a time when her fiscal worth possibly rivaled his own.

She would have been fidgeting in her seat, careful to say

and do all the right things in hopes of having him ask her out again.

And she probably also would have been imagining going to bed with him. Maybe not tonight, on their first date, or even on their second or third. But eventually—and sooner rather than later considering her deep and sudden hormonal reaction to him.

Shifting in her chair, she returned her attention to her plate, playing with her food in an attempt to get her rioting emotions under control. Not for the first time, she realized how truly foolish it was for her to have agreed to spend any more time alone with him than absolutely necessary.

Alexander—Alex—didn't seem to be suffering from any such second guesses, however.

"So…" he muttered casually, digging into his own perfectly roasted pheasant. "Tell me something about yourself. Were you born here in Portland? Did you grow up here? What about your family?"

All loaded questions, littered with pitfalls that could land her in very hot water. Without getting too detailed or giving away anything personal, she told him what she could, stretching the truth in some places and avoiding it altogether in others.

Before long, their plates were clean, their glasses of wine had been emptied and refilled at least once and they were chatting comfortably. More comfortably than Jessica ever would have expected. Almost like new friends. Or new ones, hoping to become even more….

Four

Reaching across the table, Alex topped off Jessica's glass before emptying the rest of the bottle into his own. He leaned back in his chair, watching her, letting the bouquet of the expensive wine fill his nostrils while his eyes took in every detail of the woman sitting before him.

He couldn't remember a time when he'd enjoyed a dinner more. So many of his meals were spent with business acquaintances, hammering out a new deal, discussing the aspects of a new publicity campaign or simply blowing smoke up someone's proverbial skirt in an effort to preserve continued goodwill. Even dinner with his family tended toward business talk over anything personal.

Jessica, however, was a breath of much-needed fresh air. Without a doubt she was a beautiful woman. It was hard to miss her streak of blue hair or the multiple piercings running along her ear lobes and right eyebrow, but rather than detracting from her attractiveness, they added a unique flare to her classic good looks.

She was also much smarter and more well-spoken than he would have expected from a hotel maid. Truth be told, he hadn't known what to expect from the evening after his completely impromptu invitation. But Jessica was turning out to be quite entertaining. Not only were her anecdotes amusing, but her warm, whiskey-soft voice was one he wouldn't mind hearing more of. For how long, he wasn't sure. The rest of the night might be nice. Possibly even in the morning over breakfast.

Jessica chuckled at whatever she'd just said—something he'd missed because he was preoccupied by the glossy pink of her bow-shaped mouth, the smooth half-moons of her neat but unmanicured nails and the soft bounce of her honey-blond curls. She tucked one of the shoulder-length strands behind her ear and licked those delectable lips, and Alex nearly shot straight up out of his chair. And while he managed—barely—to remain seated, other portions of his anatomy were beginning to inch their way north.

Knowing his behavior probably came across as bordering on strange, he shot to his feet, nearly tipping the heavy armchair over in the process. In the next instant he'd grabbed her hand and yanked her up, as well.

She made a small sound of surprised protest, but didn't resist. She did, however, dig in her heels and catch herself on the edge of the table just before she would have smacked straight into his chest.

Too bad; he would have liked to feel her pressed against him for a moment or two. Her warmth, her curves, the swell of her breasts.

When he'd walked into his suite to find her making his bed that first time, he'd caught a whiff of lemon and thought it came from whatever cleaning solutions she'd been using.

Now he realized the tangy scent had nothing to do with dusting or scrubbing. Instead, it came directly from her. From her shampoo or perfume, or maybe both. It was a peculiar blend of citrus and flowers that he'd never smelled before, but that seemed to suit her perfectly.

He took a deep breath to bring even more of the intoxicating fragrance into his lungs, then reached around her to pick up both glasses of wine.

"Come on," he invited, tipping his head toward the French doors and the balcony beyond.

He left her to follow—or not—but was pleased when she did. Even more pleased that it seemed to take her no time at all to decide. No sooner had he turned and started walking than she was on his heels.

Though Jessica had arrived while it was still light out, the sun had long ago slipped beyond the horizon, leaving the sky dark and star dappled. A slight breeze chilled the evening air, but nothing that required jackets or would hinder them from enjoying being outside for a while.

Moving to the stone balustrade, he set down the two glasses, then turned, leaning back on his rear and crossing his arms over his chest. As large as the Mountain View resort was, and as many guests as he was sure were in residence, the wide balcony that ran the entire length of his suite was completely private.

Tall, waffle-patterned trellises protected either side from the balconies beyond. He didn't know what the lodge did about them in the dead of winter, but at this time of year, they were covered with climbing flowering vines, creating a natural barrier to sound and sight.

When Jessica came close enough that he could have reached out and touched her, he uncrossed his arms and reached behind him instead. "Your wine," he offered in a low voice.

She took it, raising it to her mouth to sip. For long minutes neither of them said anything. Then she moved to the low chaise longue a few feet away and carefully lowered herself to its cushioned seat.

Her skirt rode up, flashing an extra couple of inches of smooth thigh. More than he'd been able to see while she'd cleaned his rooms in that frumpy gray uniform. A shame, too, since she had *amazing* legs. Long and sleek and deliciously toned.

He had the sudden urge to sit down next to her and run his hand along that silken length. Even through her stockings he wanted to feel the curve of her knee, the sensitive dip beneath, the line of her outer thigh and the perilous trail inside.

Alex sucked in a breath, his mouth gone suddenly dry.

When was the last time he'd been this attracted to a woman? Any woman?

He'd had affairs, certainly. A few relationships, even. At one time, he'd dated a woman long enough to consider marrying her. He hadn't loved her, not really, but it had seemed as if it might be the right thing to do. The most sensible next step, at any rate.

He was no stranger to lust, either. He'd been with women who'd caused it to flare hot and fast. But to the best of his recollection, he'd never been with a woman who stimulated his libido *and* his brain both at the same time.

Oh, it wasn't as though he and Jessica were waxing poetic about astrophysics or the effect of global warming on penguins in Antarctica. But that was just the point: he'd *had* those discussions—or similar ones, at least—with certain women without a single erotic nerve ending tingling to life. Just as he'd found himself burning with passion and rolling around on the sheets with others without a single intelligent thought passing between them.

And then there was Jessica Madison. Nearly anonymous

housekeeper at a resort he'd only decided to patronize a week and a half ago. If he'd booked a suite at the downtown Hilton instead, as had been his first inclination, he never would have bumped into her.

Damned if he wasn't glad they'd been booked up and someone had recommended Mountain View as a second choice. This dinner alone was worth every penny of the added expense and every extra mile it took to get into downtown Portland for his scheduled meetings.

Jessica wasn't just lovely to look at, but entertaining, too. Not only conversationally but in her silent self-assurance.

The hair and jewelry choices were the physical aspects of that, he supposed; a way to tell the world without words that she knew who she was and didn't care what anyone thought of her or how she lived her life. But whether she realized it or not, her body language conveyed the same message.

Once she'd spotted those crab cakes and decided she wanted them, it had been difficult to draw her attention away from the plate. And when he'd told her she could have them all to herself, she'd set about eating them as passionately as an artist struck by sudden creative inspiration.

No worries about how she'd looked or what he might think. Which wasn't to say she'd been a ravenous wolf about it. Her table manners had been flawless. But she'd enjoyed her meal the way he enjoyed a quick bout of neat, no-strings lovemaking.

And there it was. Sex. No matter where his mind started to wander when he got to thinking about this woman, it always seemed to circle right back around to *S-E-X*.

It didn't help that she was stretching now, lifting her legs onto the long seat of the chaise and leaning back until she was nearly sprawled out like a virgin sacrifice.

Blood pooled in his groin, heating, thrumming, creating a beat in his veins that matched the one in his brain. *Pa-dump.*

Pa-dump. Pa-dump. His heart, his pulse and his head kept the same rhythm, one that he could have sworn was saying, *Do it, do it, do it.*

He was very afraid "it" could be defined as something ill-advised. Like kissing her. Touching her. Taking her to bed.

Indulging in another sip of wine, Jessica let out a breathy sigh and crossed her legs—those damn tempting legs—at the ankle. She rested her arms on the armrests and her head back against the chaise.

"I'm sorry," she said. "I've been doing all the talking and not letting you get a word in edgewise."

Something he'd noticed, but certainly hadn't minded. He'd much rather listen to her speak than himself. On his best day he was a man of few words, and his only response now was to arch his brow and lift his own wine to his mouth for a drink.

"So…" she prompted. "Tell me about yourself. What do you do? Why are you in town? How long will you be staying at our fine establishment?"

"How long will you be making my bed and restocking my wet bar, you mean?" he retorted with a grin.

She chuckled, the sound filling the night air and doing nothing to quiet the pounding in his blood, his head, his gut.

"I don't stock the bars," she told him, returning his grin. "They don't trust us near the pricey liquor—because they're afraid we'll either steal it…or drink on the job."

He laughed at that. "I might be tempted to drink, too, if I had to clean up after strangers all day. Especially the kind who stay here. I imagine a lot of us come across as quite demanding and entitled."

She shrugged a shoulder. "It's not so bad. For one thing, I don't usually have to interact with you demanding, entitled types. Most of the time the rooms are empty when I clean, and I get to work alone. The pay could be better—and for rich people, you guys sure can cheap out when it comes to tipping—but I like my coworkers, and the view is stunning when I get the chance to stop and actually enjoy it."

He inclined his head. "Duly noted. In the future, I'll be sure to leave a generous tip anytime I stay out of town."

"Every morning before you leave your room," she clarified, "not just the day you check out. Shifts change, and the same maids don't always clean the same rooms every day."

As hard as he tried, he couldn't completely hold back the hint of a smile. She was a pretty good advocate for her fellow service workers.

"I'll remember that. Have my tips so far been acceptable?" he asked, half teasing, half genuinely curious of her opinion.

She slanted her head, thinking about it for a minute. Then she shrugged a shoulder. "You've been doing well enough. And tonight's dinner definitely makes up for any corners you may have cut."

"Glad to hear it," he drawled.

"You never answered my question," she said after a moment of silence passed. The only sounds in the growing darkness were the muted voices of guests far off in the distance, perhaps strolling along one of the lodge's moonlit paths, and the occasional chirp of crickets.

"Which one?"

"Any of them. All of them." She uncrossed her ankles only to cross them again the other way. "Just tell me something interesting so I won't feel like I monopolized the conversation tonight."

"All right," he replied. Pushing away from the stone barrier, he strode toward her, dragging the second chaise closer to hers one-handed and sitting down on the very end to face her.

"My family is in jewelry. Gems and design. Maybe you've heard of us—Bajoran Designs?"

Her eyes widened. "*You're* Bajoran Designs?"

"I'm one of the Bajorans of Bajoran Designs," he clarified. "As much as I might feel or wish otherwise at times, it isn't a one-man operation."

"Wow. Your jewelry is amazing."

"You're familiar with it?"

"Isn't everybody?" she retorted. "Your ads are in all the magazines, and on TV and billboards everywhere. Didn't you design a bracelet for the Queen of England or something?"

"Again, *I* didn't, but our company did."

"Wow," she repeated. And then her head tilted to one side and she raised a brow. Her lips curved. "I don't suppose you have any free samples you'd like to share."

The sparkle in her eyes told him she was teasing, but he wished suddenly that he had more than just a few proposed design sketches with him. He wished he had a briefcase full of priceless jewels surrounded by exquisite settings to regale her with.

He would love to see her draped in emeralds and platinum or diamonds and gold. Earrings, necklace, bracelet, perhaps even a small tiara to tuck into those mostly blond curls.

He could think of any number of his companies' designs that would look stunning with what she was wearing. But he imagined that they'd look even better on her while she was utterly naked.

Naked in his bed, her skin alabaster against dark sheets, her hair falling loosely about her shoulders. And at her lobes, her throat, her waist…maybe her ankle, too…*his* jewels, *his* designs, in essence his *marks* lying cool on her warm, flushed flesh.

The picture that filled his head was vibrant and erotic and so real, he nearly reached out to touch her, fully expecting to encounter nothing but the blessed nudity of a gorgeous and waiting female.

Arousal smacked into him with the force of a freight train

late to its final destination. His fist closed on the wine in his hand, so tight he was surprised the glass didn't shatter. Every muscle in his body turned to iron, and that most important one—the one that desired her most of all—came to attention in a way that made its wishes clearly known.

Sweat broke out across Alex's brow and his lungs hitched with the effort to breathe. Jessica was still staring at him, the amusement at her teasing about the jewelry slowly seeping from her eyes as she realized he wasn't laughing.

She probably thought she'd insulted him. Or come across as a gold digger. The difference in their stations—her minimum wage chambermaid to his multimillionaire business tycoon—was patently obvious, and something he supposed she hadn't forgotten for a minute. Add to that the fact that he felt ready to explode, and he probably looked like Dr. Jekyll well on his way to becoming Mr. Hyde.

Forcing himself to loosen his grip on the wineglass, he concentrated on his breathing. *Relax,* he told himself. *Breathe in, breathe out. Don't scare her off before you have a chance to seduce her.*

And he was going to seduce her. He'd been attracted to her from the moment they'd first met, which, of course, meant he'd thought about sleeping with her about a thousand times since. But thinking about it and making a conscious decision to go through with it were two different things.

He hadn't realized until just this minute that he *was* going to make a move on her. He *was* going to kiss her and do his best to convince her to go to bed with him.

Pushing to his feet, he leaned across to set his wine on the wrought-iron table that had been between the two chaises. He locked his jaw and cursed himself when she jerked at his sudden movements. His only hope was that he hadn't frightened her so much that he couldn't smooth things over. Seducing a woman on the first date could be hard enough without adding "acted like a jackass" to the mix.

"Sorry," he said in a low voice, hoping the single word would be suitable as a blanket apology. And then in answer to her earlier question, "I don't have any samples. I'd need a 24/7 armed guard to carry that kind of merchandise around with me."

At his friendly tone, she seemed to relax. And when she did, he did.

"If you like, though, I can arrange a tour of our company. You can see how the pieces are put together, watch some gems being cut, maybe even catch a peek at a few designs that haven't been released yet. You'd have to come to Seattle, though. Think you can get the time off?"

If he'd expected her to be impressed, he was sorely disappointed. Her expression barely changed as her tongue darted out to lick her lips.

"That's all right," she said, instead of "Oh, wow, that would be awesome!" "I was just joking. I could never afford anything of yours, anyway. Better not to tempt myself."

It was on the tip of his tongue to tell her he'd gift her with a piece while she was there. He'd never done anything of the sort before, never even been tempted. Yet suddenly he didn't want to just imagine her covered in his family's fine jewelry, he wanted to literally cover her with it. Throw it at her feet like a humble servant making an offering to the gods. Diamonds, emeralds, opals, sapphires… Whatever she wanted. As much as she wanted.

He wasn't sure exactly when he'd become such a weak-kneed sycophant. He'd certainly never given women jewelry before; at least not easily or as willy-nilly as he was envisioning doing with Jessica.

To be honest, he wasn't sure he liked these feelings and the lack of control she seemed to evoke. It was the number one reason he thought he should probably call it a night and get as far away as possible from this woman.

That would be the smart thing to do, for certain.

So why didn't he?

Desire? Lust? Sheer stupidity?

But rather than thank her for coming and seeing her to the door, he held out his hand, indicating that she should give him her wineglass. When she did, he set it aside, then held out his hand again, this time inviting her to take it. He was equal parts surprised and relieved when she did so without a hint of reservation that he could detect.

Her fingers were cool and delicate. For a moment he savored the simple touch, not letting himself ruin it by imagining more just yet.

Then he gave her a tug, urging her to the edge of the chaise. A second tug pulled her to her feet.

She came into his arms as though she was tied to him and he was drawing on the string that bound them. Another step and she was pressed to his chest the way he'd wished she could be earlier.

Her blouse was silky against his palms and the front of his own dress shirt, her breasts rubbing just enough to give him ideas and get the blood pumping hot and thick to his groin once again. He held her there, enjoying the feel of her, stroking his hands up and down the line of her spine.

To his great delight she didn't pull away, but sank into him even more, her breath blowing out on a soft sigh.

With one hand at the small of her back, he brought the other up the length of her arm and the side of her throat until he cupped her jaw, his thumb brushing along the baby-soft curve of her cheek.

"I want to kiss you," he told her in a low, graveled voice, "but I'm afraid you'll think I'm moving too fast."

Afraid he was moving too fast and that he would scare her

off. Afraid that this overwhelming need he felt for her wasn't normal, wasn't the typical interest he felt when he was in the mood for a one-night stand.

"Did you notice my hair?" Jessica asked in little more than a murmur, reaching up to finger a few strands of blue.

His brows knit. What did her hair have to do with anything?

Still, he answered, "Yes."

"And my ears? My brow?" She flicked her wrist at both.

"Yes," he said again, more confused than ever.

"These are not the piercings and hairstyle choices of a girl who scares easily."

For a second, he didn't move, didn't dare breathe while her words sank in. Then a slow smile spread across his face.

"No," he murmured, even as his head lowered toward hers. "I guess they aren't."

Five

The minute Alex's lips touched hers, she was lost.

She knew this was a mistake. Everything was, from the moment she'd stepped into his suite tonight, to letting her guard down over wine and a moonlit stroll onto the secluded balcony. Maybe even before that, when she'd recognized him and not gone running, or when she'd agreed to her cousin's ridiculous scheme.

It hadn't been easy to sit still and pretend she didn't know who he was, but it *had* been somewhat enlightening to listen to him talk about himself and his business. Knowing what she did about him—namely that he'd stolen a portion of the company out from under her family—she would have expected him to be proud, arrogant, boastful.

Instead, he'd been humble, speaking highly of Bajoran Designs, but not taking any of the credit for the company's success for himself.

She thought that might have been when her head had

started to go fuzzy and stars had formed in her eyes. Her skin had been flushed with heat, too, but that was nothing new; that was just part of the attraction that had flared to life as soon as she'd walked into his arms.

She shouldn't be kissing him…or rather, allowing him to kiss her. It was a worse idea than agreeing to dinner with him, but she just couldn't seem to help herself.

The entire time they'd been talking, all she'd wanted was to cross the balcony and lay a hand on his chest. To see if it felt as hot and hard as it looked. And then to touch his mouth with her own to see if he tasted as delectable as she imagined.

The good news was, his chest *did* feel as hot and hard as she'd thought it would. Better, even, pressed up against her breasts and her belly.

And his lips were as delicious as she'd expected. Warm and soft but with a firmness that spoke of power and total self-confidence. He also tasted of the lush wine and food they'd shared earlier.

The *bad* news was that his chest felt exactly as she'd imagined, his mouth tasted even better, and instead of allaying her curiosity, it only made her want more.

With a groan she leaned farther into him, letting his heat and strong arms surround her, letting the passion sweep her away.

It was just a kiss, just one night, and he had no idea who she really was. What could it hurt to surrender to whatever this was igniting between them and just let go?

She didn't let her mind wander past that, didn't let her brain actually consider all the things that really could go wrong. She didn't want to think about it, didn't want to slow down—or worse, stop. For once she wanted to let go, be wild, be free and not worry about the consequences.

Besides, it wasn't as though anyone would ever find out. Erin would think she'd searched Alex's suite and come up with nothing, and Alex would think he'd gotten lucky with a near-anonymous hotel maid. No strings, no ties, no awkward morning after.

His mouth possessed her, but she certainly didn't mind. If anything, her moan, the melt of her body, her meeting his tongue swipe for swipe and thrust for thrust told him exactly how much she liked it.

Liked it? Loved it and was eager for more.

Not bothering to breathe—who needed oxygen?—Jessica wrapped her arms around Alex's neck, running her fingers through the hair at his nape and hanging on for dear life.

It was Alex's turn to groan. He hugged her tight and she felt his arousal standing proud, leaving no doubt that he was just as turned on as she was, just as carried away on this wave of uncontrollable lust.

Thank goodness. She would hate to be coiled in a haze of desire, only to discover he'd been after nothing more than a quick kiss.

But she needn't have worried. He was all but sucking her tonsils down his throat. And then his hands went to her waist, her hips, her thighs a second before he scooped her into his arms.

They broke apart, only because the change of position forced it, and it turned out people really did need oxygen eventually. They both gasped for breath as he carried her across the balcony and through the French doors, his long strides eating up the thickly carpeted floor all the way to the bedroom.

Once there, he set her on the end of the wide, king-size bed with more gentleness than she would have managed if their roles had been reversed. Standing over her, he stared into her eyes, his own crystal-blue ones blazing like hot ice.

With both hands, he cupped her face, tipping her head

back a fraction of an inch. Then he leaned in and kissed her softly, almost reverently.

Jessica's eyes slid closed, letting the sensation of his lips on hers wash over her, carrying her away.

A moment later, his mouth left her, but she felt his hands at her throat, his fingers trailing down the sides, over her collarbones and the slope of her chest. Goose bumps broke out on her skin as he grazed the insides of her breasts and started to unbutton her blouse.

She held her breath while he worked. This wasn't the first time a man had undressed her, but it was certainly the first time one had done it so slowly and had seemed to take such pleasure in the act. Either that or he was torturing her, but even the torture brought exquisite pleasure.

When he reached the last of the buttons, she straightened enough for him to tug the blouse from the waistband of her skirt. He flicked it over her shoulders and arms, then tossed it away completely.

Sitting there in her skirt and bra, Jessica suddenly realized she didn't have to be so passive. As much as she was enjoying his seductive treatment, she wanted to be in on the action. And, yes—if she was soon going to be naked in front of him, then she wanted to see him out of his clothes, too.

While he went for the zipper at the back of her skirt, she went for his belt buckle. He sucked air through his teeth, and she was delighted to see his nostrils flare, his jaw tic.

After undoing his belt, she got to work on his fly. She slid the tab down so slowly, each individual snick of the zipper's teeth echoed through the room. He was just as deliberate unzipping her skirt.

He pulled her to her feet by the elbows, tugging her against his chest again while he slipped the skirt past her hips. At the same time, he kicked off his shoes, letting her push his pants down so that both items of clothing fell to the floor together.

He set her back on the bed, then stepped out of the pants and kicked their clothes out of the way, unbuttoning his shirt and shrugging out of it all with urgent efficiency. Standing before her totally naked, Alex stared down at her with fire in his eyes and a set to his tall frame that told her without words that there was no turning back now. No escape.

As though she'd even want to. If she hadn't been sitting already, Jessica was pretty sure she would have melted into a steaming puddle on the floor. Her knees were jelly, her stomach doing somersaults worthy of an Olympic gold medal.

Her mouth felt as if it was filled with sand, and she licked her lips, swallowing in an attempt to bring some moisture back before the dehydration went to her head and sent her into a dead faint.

His gaze zeroed in on that tiny gesture, and she could have sworn she saw smoke spiraling out of his ears. He took a single, purposeful step toward her, bringing himself flush with the foot of the bed. Leaning in, he towered over her, fists flat on the mattress on either side of her hips.

"Scoot up," he told her in a low voice.

Even though her bones felt like rubber, she put her hands under her and did as he'd ordered, slowing moving back across the mattress toward the head of the bed. He followed her every inch of the way. Hovering over her, crawling with her, plucking the heels off her feet and pitching them over his shoulder as they went. She stopped when she reached the pillows, letting her head sink into one of the feather-stuffed cushions, still covered by the spread she'd tucked around them that morning.

"You're overdressed," Alex murmured a moment before he tucked his thumbs into the waistband of her barely there satin-and-lace panties and drew them down her legs. She helped him by kicking them off, then lifted up so he could unclasp and remove her bra.

For several long seconds he drank her in, his gaze so intense, she could hardly breathe. Just when she was about to hide her breasts self-consciously with her arms, Alex reached around her, loosening the bed's comforter and dragging it down, uncovering the pillows and sliding the slick fabric under her body until they were resting only on cool, freshly laundered sheets.

Once he was happy with the state of the bed, he lowered himself down on top of her. From chest to ankle he covered her like a blanket, the heat of his skin warming her and the hairs on his legs and chest tickling in all the right places.

He offered her a small, confident smile, and she couldn't resist rubbing against him, loving every single seductive sensation. Then she looped her arms around his shoulders and met him for a long, deep, soul-rattling kiss.

Alex ate at her mouth like he was enjoying their succulent dinner all over again. And she licked back as though she had moved on to the most decadent of desserts.

Alex's hands skimmed her body, up and down, all around, learning her shape and form and sweet spots. Her breasts swelled at his touch, and he rewarded them with added attention, squeezing, caressing, teasing until her nipples tightened into pebble-hard buds.

Tracing his mouth over her brows, her closed eyelids, the line of her jaw, he made his way down to suckle those pert tips, making her moan and wriggle beneath him.

She let her knees fall open, pulling him farther into the cradle of her thighs. He came more than willingly, settling against her, rubbing in all the right places.

Soon they were panting, writhing, clawing each other like wild animals. With a strangled groan, Alex grasped her waist, sitting back as he tugged her up to straddle his hips. Her arms tightened around him, her nails raking his skin.

The flats of his hands swept up either side of her spine,

sliding under her hair to cup the back of her skull. His fingers massaged, then dug in as he captured her mouth.

Long minutes ticked by while the only sounds in the room were their mingled breaths, their bodies moving together and the staccato interruption of deep growls and desperate moans.

Even though she was perched inches higher than Alex, he was definitely driving their passion. Which was fine, since he was really, *really* good at it. But she didn't want to be just a passenger on this bus, passively riding along wherever he decided to take them.

She wanted to *drive,* baby, and show him that a resort cleaning lady could blow his socks off just as easily as some silver-spoon socialite strumpet. Better, even, since she didn't give a flip about messing up her hair.

Bracing her legs on either side of him, she gripped his shoulders and pushed, toppling him backward and coming to rest over him with a satisfied smirk on her face. He returned her smile with a grin of his own, letting her know he was just as game for this position as any other.

"A take charge kind of woman," he said, running his hands along her torso until they cupped her breasts. His thumbs teased the undersides, coming just close enough to her nipples to make her bite her bottom lip in longing. "I like it."

Well, then, he should *love* her. She'd been taking charge of her life for as long as she could remember—to her parents' continued consternation. Even before it had become a necessity, Jessica had been more headstrong than was probably wise. Lord knew, it had gotten her into trouble on more than one occasion. She only hoped tonight wouldn't prove to be the biggest mistake of them all.

"So you're in charge," Alex told her, breaking into her fractured thoughts. His thumbs were growing bolder, finally brushing the very tips of her oversensitized breasts, causing them to grow almost painfully tight. "What's next?"

That pesky act-before-you-think gene had backfired on her again. Because her liberal, uninhibited streak seemed to have abandoned her, along with all the strength in her limbs. She no longer wanted to tower over him, but thought she would be better off sinking into the bedclothes in a pile of boneless flesh and nerve endings. That's what Alex's touch did to her—turned her to mindless, quivering mush.

But she needn't have worried. Alex might *say* he liked a strong-willed, take-charge woman—at least in bed—but he had no problem taking the reins when necessary. Abandoning her breasts, he splayed his palms at her waist and down her hips. Raising her slightly, he centered her over his burgeoning erection, brushing lightly between her folds with just the tip.

Jessica sucked in a breath, and Alex bared his teeth, nostrils flaring. Taking her hands, he wrapped them firmly around his hardened length. He was hot to the touch, soft velvet over tempered steel and throbbing beneath her fingers.

"Take me," he told her through gritted teeth. "Show me what you want, how you want it."

How could she resist? He was like a holiday buffet and she was a very hungry reveler.

Angling her hips just so, she brought him flush with her center. Then slowly…slowly, slowly, slowly…she sank down. Inch by inch he filled her, and the feeling was exquisite. To him, too, she guessed, judging by his long, low moan of satisfaction. His eyes fluttered closed, his hands clutched at her hips and beneath her rear, his thighs were as tense as iron beams.

She, however, was loose, almost liquid. Warmth spread through her veins, filled her belly, and surrounded him with moisture where they were connected. His body jerked, driving him higher inside of her, causing her internal muscles to spasm in response.

Though he was still breathing heavily, still holding himself gallantly in check, he smiled up at her, blue eyes flashing with devilish intent.

Oh, my. How had she resisted him for so long? Granted, their "relationship" had pretty much moved at the speed of light as it was. But gazing down at him now, knowing that he was not only movie-star handsome, but oozed sophistication and charm from every pore, she wondered how she hadn't fallen at his feet the very first day—first moment—they'd met. How every woman he came in contact with didn't simply drop to the nearest surface flat on her back like an upturned beetle.

That was the power he possessed—at least over her. He had the power not only to seduce her with barely a whisper, but wipe every ounce of sense straight out of her head.

What they were doing here tonight, in this room, in this bed, had nothing to do with good judgment and everything to do with pure, raw, primal instinct and desire.

Tossing her head from side to side, she shook her hair back over her shoulders and wriggled atop him to find just the right position. Alex growled, fingers digging into her flesh, and tensed even more between her thighs.

"Don't do that unless you're ready to relinquish control," he warned in something akin to a hiss, "because I'm about two seconds from rolling you over and finishing this, whether you like it or not."

A shiver rolled down her spine at his deep-throated threat. Oh, she suspected she would like that very much, indeed. She was tempted to say *yes, please* and let him do just that.

But staying in charge—at least for a while longer—was the only way she knew she'd be able to look herself in the mirror tomorrow. She wanted no doubts, no cracks in the story she might tell herself that would allow her to alter facts. She didn't want to wake up with enough doubts to convince herself that he'd taken advantage of her.

No, she wanted to be sure that if guilt was going to set in, it would rest squarely on her own shoulders. And that if anyone—especially anyone in her family, such as Erin—ever found out, she wouldn't give them further reason to paint Alexander Bajoran as a bad guy.

Running her tongue across her lip—slowly…from one side to the other…first the top…then the bottom—she watched his pupils dilate and his chest hitch with his ragged breathing.

"Poor baby," she murmured in her best sex kitten voice. "Am I being too rough on you?"

On the word *rough,* she flexed the inner walls of her feminine channel, squeezing him like a vise.

He moaned.

"Making this too…*hard?*"

She flexed again, this time coming up on her knees so that the friction, the rasping of their flesh drew sparks, sending currents of electricity outward to shock them both.

He groaned, snarled, muttered a colorful oath. And Jessica grinned at the knowledge that if their social circumstances were reversed—if they'd been doing this five years ago while her family still had control of their company—she could probably have gotten *him* to sign his company over to *her.*

That feeling of superiority, though, was short-lived. While he lifted off the bed and she continued to cant her hips back and forth in a slow, methodical motion, Alex reached for her breast again with one hand. To rub and squeeze and caress. He tweaked her nipples, making her shudder. Then, when it was her turn to let her eyes slide closed, he dropped his other hand between her legs and found the secret, swollen bud sure to send her spiraling out of control.

She moaned, biting her tongue until she thought she might draw blood, as ecstasy built to an almost unbearable pressure inside of her.

Alex stared at Jessica, fighting his own need to moan, pos-

sibly even whimper. Had he ever seen a woman so beautiful? Ever met anyone quite like Jessica Madison? He'd never
gone to bed with one, of that he was certain.

He couldn't explain his overwhelming attraction to her,
but he was sure as hell grateful for it—as well as her mu-
tual enthusiasm. If she'd turned him down out there on the
balcony, walked away after only a single too-brief kiss, he
suspected he'd have spent the rest of the night taking out his
frustrations by trying to punch a hole in one of the suite's
walls with his forehead.

But she hadn't turned him down. She'd turned him *on,*
then stuck around to do something about it.

Her skin was alabaster silk, running like water under his
fingertips. Her mouth was equally soft: warm and inviting
and sweeter than anything he'd ever tasted.

And the rest of her... He didn't think words had yet been
invented to describe the rest of her. How she moved with him
and around him. How she welcomed him and made him want
to cherish her and ravish her both at the same time. How her
hazel eyes turned dark and liquid when she looked at him.
They were so wide and inviting, he thought he could drown
in them without a single regret.

Those weren't exactly the thoughts he wanted to be thinking about a one-night stand, but they were there all the same.

And then he couldn't think at all because she was moving on him like sin itself. Long, sure strokes that drove him
deeper. Made his jaw lock and his eyes roll back in his head.

He clutched her hips tight enough to leave bruises and had
to make a concerted effort to loosen his hold before he did.
Not that Jessica seemed to notice. Her straight white teeth
were locked on her lower lip...her lashes trembled like butterfly wings as she struggled to keep her eyes open while
passion coaxed them closed...and her pace never faltered as
she undulated above him.

His own hips rose and fell with her movements, meeting her stroke for stroke, thrusting as deeply as possible and trying for more. Her hands flexed and curled on his chest until her nails dug into the muscles like claws and then released as she reached up to cup her breasts.

The sight of those slender fingers with their neatly trimmed but unmanicured nails curving over her soft, cushiony flesh, touching herself, bringing herself added pleasure, nearly sent him over the edge. Then she tweaked her nipples, arched her spine, and threw her head back on a rich-as-hundred-year-old-scotch moan, and he knew he was a goner.

In one sharp, fast motion, he flipped her to her back, drawing a yelp of surprise from those pink, swollen, delectable lips. Rising over her, he shifted her legs to his waist, encouraged when she linked them together at the base of his spine, heels digging in.

"Hold on, sweetheart." The endearment slipped past his lips before he could stop it, but he couldn't say he regretted it, not when her grip tightened around him, both inside and out.

"Yes," she gasped when he began to pound into her. Long, sure strokes, as deep as he could go to bring them both to the keenest, highest peak of satisfaction.

He moved faster, thrusting in time with her rapid-fire murmurs of *yesyesyesyesyes* until the world tilted, an invisible surf crashed in his ears and everything washed away to nothing except the woman beneath him and the startling, intense, overwhelming pleasure rocketing through him like a meteor crashing to earth.

When he came down, Jessica was breathing rapidly against him, her body splayed on the mattress in proverbial rag-doll fashion.

Well, wasn't he a heel. He'd enjoyed himself to the nth degree, but hadn't bothered to make sure she'd reached her completion first. So much for being a gentleman.

Then she lifted her gaze to his, arms going around his neck while her fingers combed through his hair near the nape. And she smiled.

"Better than dessert," she said just above a whisper.

Blowing out a relieved breath, he returned her grin before leaning in for a soft, lingering kiss. "Who says we can't have both?"

Six

Jessica had been right about the resort's desserts—they were delicious.

So how scary was it that she hadn't enjoyed that indulgence nearly as much as getting naked and rolling around with Alex?

Three times.

After that first amazing encounter, they'd only made it to the bathroom for a quick potty break before somehow ending up back in bed, getting sweaty all over again.

An hour after that, Alex had regained enough strength to reach for the phone and call for room service. She'd told him it wasn't necessary, that she wasn't even particularly hungry anymore. At least not for food.

But he'd insisted. The dishes had been preordered, so the kitchen was simply waiting for his call to send them up. Besides, he'd said, no dinner date was complete without dessert.

She thought heart-stopping, pulse-pounding, coma-inducing sex probably qualified as a decent substitute.

The fruits and pastries, crèmes and sauces that he'd spooned and then hand-fed her had been pretty yummy, too, though. She'd especially enjoyed the bits he'd eaten off her bare skin, and then let her lick off his.

Which had led to that third and final incredible experience that had started on the sitting room sofa...and somehow ended on the very desk she'd snooped through earlier.

Afterward he'd picked her up and carried her back to bed. Good thing, since she'd been doing her best impression of a jellyfish by that point.

She'd drifted off, tucked snuggly against Alex's solid warmth, his strong arm holding her close. And for a while she'd let herself pretend.

That it meant something.

That what they'd shared had a longer shelf life than expired milk.

That she wasn't deceiving him and he hadn't ruined her family.

But all too soon she came awake, reality slapping her hard across the face. Careful not to disturb him, she'd slipped from the bed, from his arms, and gathered her clothes, dressing as quickly and quietly as possible.

Tiptoeing from the bedroom, she moved through the sitting room, praying she could find her purse and get out before Alex noticed she was missing. Then she saw his briefcase, lying open on the coffee table. Frozen midstride, she stood staring at it, battling with herself over what to do next.

Should she turn around and leave, as she'd planned, ignoring the blatant invitation to snoop just a little more? Or should she peek, check to see if there was anything even remotely incriminating inside?

She felt like a dieter standing over a plate of fresh-baked chocolate chip cookies. Tempted. So very tempted.

With a quick glance toward the open bedroom door, she decided to risk it. Rushing forward, she put her clutch down beside the case and started riffling through the papers and manila folders.

It was too dark to see much, her eyes adjusting as best they could to the bit of moonlight shining through the French doors leading to the balcony.

As far as she could tell, it was more of what she'd found in the nightstand. Interoffice memos, contract notations, design sketches. Nothing worthy of fueling Erin's proposed plan of corporate espionage.

Then, at the very bottom of the case, she spotted one final packet. Not a plain manila folder, but a darker manila envelope stamped with giant red block letters she couldn't have missed, even if the room had been pitch-black: CONFIDENTIAL

Jessica's heart stopped. It was sealed. Well, tied closed with a thin red string, at least. But it was obviously private, not meant to be viewed by anyone but Alex and other authorized Bajoran Designs personnel.

Sparing another glimpse toward the bedroom, she took a deep breath and hurried to untie the stringed closure.

She didn't know what she'd been expecting...a treasure map or stack of secret security codes, maybe. Or maybe that was just her vivid imagination, replaying various scenes from her favorite action-adventure movies in her head while she pretended to be a poor man's Indiana Jones.

But what she found was no more surprising than anything else she'd stumbled upon so far. A stack of papers labeled Proposed Princess Line, with sketches of a dozen or so fresh designs included. They were for earrings, necklaces and rings, all in matching sets with similar design elements.

Obviously these were suggested pieces for a new line Bajoran Designs intended to launch in the near future. Likely
a multimillion-dollar business venture.

Jessica couldn't have said what possessed her, but before
she even realized what she was doing, she set the envelope
under her clutch and replaced the other papers and folders
inside the briefcase, making sure to leave it open exactly as
she'd found it.

She was tired and maybe not thinking straight. But she
would take the proposed designs with her to study more carefully in the safety of her apartment, and decide then whether
or not to show them to her cousin.

With luck she could sneak them back into Alex's briefcase in the morning when she cleaned his room, long before
he even noticed they were gone.

Pushing to her feet, she grabbed her purse and the envelope and rushed to the door, careful not to make a sound as
she slipped out of Alex's suite, leaving him sleeping peace-
fully and hopefully none the wiser.

Seven

One Year Later

Alexander made his way down the hall toward his office with his nose buried in the company's latest financials. Not bad for a year when the country's economy was pretty much in the toilet, but he suspected they would have done better if someone else hadn't gotten the scoop on their Princess Line.

A deep scowl marred his brow. It had taken him a while to figure out, but now he knew exactly who was responsible for that little betrayal, too.

He was digging into his anger, mentally working up a good head of steam, when a peculiar sound caught his attention. Pausing midstride, he tilted his head to listen. Heard it again.

The unfamiliar noise seemed to be coming from the conference room he'd just passed. Backing up a few steps, he glanced through the open doorway.

His arms, along with the papers he was holding, fell to his sides. He blinked. Shook his head and blinked again.

He knew what he was seeing, and yet there was a part of his brain that refused to function, that told him it couldn't be what he thought it was. Obviously he was imagining things... but did illusions usually come with full surround sound?

The noise he'd heard earlier came again. This time he identified it easily, mainly because the source of that sound was sitting right in front of him.

In the center of the long conference table that was normally filled with high-ranking Bajoran Designs' employees sat a white plastic crescent-shaped carrier. And in the carrier, lined with bright material covered in Noah's ark cartoon animals, sat a baby.

A baby.

In his boardroom.

While the child continued to kick his legs and coo, Alex double-checked to be sure the room was empty. It was. No mother or father or grandparent or nanny in sight.

Stepping out of the room, he looked in both directions up and down the hall. It was completely deserted.

Since this was the floor where his office was located, it tended to be quiet and not heavily trafficked. Just the way he liked it. The majority of Bajoran Designs' employees were stationed on other floors of the building.

But that didn't mean someone wasn't visiting, child in tow. He couldn't say he thought much of their parenting skills, considering they'd left what looked to be their months-old infant completely unattended on a tabletop.

"Rose!" he shouted down the hall toward his personal assistant's workstation. He couldn't see her from where he was standing, but knew she would be there. She always was. "Rose!"

"Where's the fire?" she asked in an exasperated voice, coming into sight as she headed his way.

He ignored her tone. Having worked together for years, they knew each other better than some husbands and wives. He might be demanding and short-tempered at times, but Rose was twenty years his senior and only let him get away with so much before putting her foot down.

Rather than responding to her question, he pointed a finger and asked one of his own. "What is *that?*"

Rose paused beside him in the doorway, blinked once and said, "It's a baby."

"I *know* it's a baby," he snapped. "What is it *doing* here?"

"Well, how should I know?" Rose replied, equally short. "*I* didn't put it there."

A beat passed while Alex ground his teeth and struggled to get his growing outrage under control.

This was getting him nowhere. His secretary might be a woman, but she apparently wasn't teeming with maternal instincts.

Fine. He would handle the situation himself.

Stalking forward, he turned the baby carrier slightly to face the child head-on. Cute kid. Alex couldn't say he—or she—was any more or less cute than any other baby he'd ever seen, but then, he didn't pay much attention to children one way or another. They were—in his opinion—smelly, drippy, noisy things, and he didn't know why anybody would want or purposely set out to have one of their own.

Which still didn't explain why somebody had left *this one* in his conference room.

The baby smiled and blew a tiny spit bubble as it kicked its feet, sending the carrier rocking slightly. That's when Alex noticed the piece of paper tucked beneath the safety strap holding the infant in place.

Careful not to touch the baby any more than necessary, he removed the paper, unfolded it and read.

Alex—
I know this will come as a shock, but Henry is your son. I'm sorry I didn't tell you about him before now, but please don't hold that against him.
As much as I love him, I can't keep him with me any longer. He deserves so much more than I can offer right now.
Please take care of him. And no matter how you feel about me, please tell him that I love him very much and never would have left him if I'd had a choice.

It was signed simply "Jessica."

Jessica. Madison? Mountain View Jessica Madison?

The timing was right, he would admit that much. And he hadn't forgotten a single thing about their encounter, despite the year that had passed since she'd sneaked out of his hotel room—his bed—in the middle of the night.

A muscle ticked in his jaw as he clamped his teeth together more tightly than nine out of ten dentists would probably recommend.

She'd left without a word, which was bad enough. But it wasn't until later, much later, that he'd discovered the proposed designs for his company's Princess Line were also missing.

It hadn't taken more than three seconds for him to realize she'd taken them. That she'd apparently been some kind of spy, either sent by a competing corporation or come on her own to ferret out Bajoran Designs secrets.

And she'd found herself a doozy, hadn't she? He might be CEO of the family business, but it had been none too comfortable standing in front of the Board of Directors and explaining that he'd lost the Princess Line prospectus. Not just lost them, but had them stolen out from under him by what he could only assume was the competition.

Not that he'd told them the whole truth. He hadn't wanted to admit that he'd let himself be seduced and then robbed. He'd also hoped to get to the bottom of the theft on his own before coming totally clean. Which is why he'd talked them out of taking legal action or filing an insurance claim.

But he'd seethed for months. And though no one had said anything to his face—no one would dare, unless they had a death wish as well as a desire to be on the unemployment line—he knew he'd lost a certain amount of respect from his colleagues.

He wasn't sure which bothered him more—that, the loss of revenue for the company or his apparent gullibility at the hands of a beautiful woman.

Now, just when he'd finally begun to get his impromptu affair with Jessica the Chambermaid-slash-Evil Seductress out of his system and memory banks enough to focus more fully on the theft itself, here she was again. Popping into his life and claiming he'd fathered her child.

Not a single fiber of his being told him he could believe the note in his hand. If it was even from Jessica...or the woman he'd known as Jessica. After all, he had no proof that was her real name. Or that she'd actually written this letter...or that this was really her child...or that this was really *his* child.

Even so, he found himself studying the infant's features. Was there any hint of himself there? Any hint of Jessica?

"Call security," he told Rose without bothering to look in her direction. "Tell them to search the building for anyone who doesn't belong—especially a lone woman."

A lone woman with a streak of wild blue in her blond hair and eyes the color of smoky quartz. He thought the words, but didn't speak them.

"I also want to see the video footage from this floor."

Wrapping his fingers firmly around the handle of the carrier, he lifted the child off the table and marched away, certain his orders would be followed to the letter.

"I'll be in my office."

What the *hell* was he supposed to do with a baby?

At the moment, he was pacing a hole in the carpet of his home office, bouncing the squealing, squalling infant against his chest and shoulder. He still wasn't convinced this was his son, but the evidence certainly did point in that direction.

Security had searched Bajoran Designs' entire building— including the floors and offices that had no affiliation with the company. Nothing.

Then they'd reviewed the security tapes from Alex's floor, as well as the building's main entrance. Sure enough, there had been a woman who rang all kinds of bells and whistles for him.

She'd been wearing sunglasses and a knit cap pulled down over her ears, the collar of her denim jacket flipped up to cover as much of her features as possible. But her attempts at anonymity couldn't conceal the blond curls peeking out from beneath the cap, the high cheekbones holding up the shades or those lips that reminded him of sinful, delightful things better shared in the dark of night.

So while he couldn't say with one hundred percent certainty that the woman on the security tapes—toting a baby carrier on the way in but not on the way out—was the Jessica he knew from Mountain View Lodge, it was sure as hell looking that way. Which meant this *could* be his child.

According to Rose's best nonmaternal guess, she pegged the infant to be three or four months old. And given that he'd spent the night with the child's alleged mother a year ago… Yeah, the timing was more right than he cared to contemplate.

The question was: What did he do now?

Rose had been no help whatsoever. She'd told him to get himself some diapers and formula, and then take the baby out of the office because his coos—which were headed much more toward fussing by that point—were getting on her nerves.

Not having a better game plan, he'd done just that. Called his driver and ordered him to stop at the nearest grocery store on the way home.

Normally, he'd have sent his housekeeper out for baby supplies—and he probably still would. But at that very moment, he'd somehow known that he shouldn't wait much longer to have food for this kid's belly and clean Pampers on his bottom. Babies, he was quickly learning, were both demanding and smelled none too fresh after a while.

Thank God a clerk had come to his aid and pointed out a dozen items she insisted he couldn't do without. He'd been in no position to argue, so he'd bought them all.

No matter how rich he was, however, he learned the hard way that he couldn't snap his fingers and get a nanny to appear on his doorstep within the hour. He'd tried—asked Mrs. Sheppard to call every nanny placement agency in the city and offer whatever it took to have someone at his estate that night. She'd run into nothing but one stone wall after another.

No one was available on such short notice, and even if they had been, the agencies insisted he had to go through the official hiring process, which included filling out applications and running credit and background checks. He'd gotten on the phone himself and tried to throw his weight around in a way he rarely did, but suspected that had simply bumped him to the bottom of their waiting lists.

In a growing series of things that were just not going in

his favor today, it turned out Mrs. Sheppard was no more maternal than Rose. The minute she'd spotted him walking through the door carrying a whimpering child, she'd scowled like a storm cloud and firmly informed him with more than a hint of her usual Irish lilt that she "didna do babies," hadn't signed on to care for children and wasn't paid well enough to start now.

He *paid* her well enough to care for every child who passed through the gates of Disneyland on a daily basis, but understood her point. Until today he "didn't do babies," either.

Maybe that's why all of the people in his employ were less willing to volunteer for child-care duty than he was. Having an aversion to infants himself, he'd apparently hired staff who felt the same.

Which had worked perfectly well up to now. Suddenly, though, he wished he'd surrounded himself with more of the ticking-biological-clock types. A few women who couldn't wait to take a crying baby off his hands and work whatever natural magic they possessed to restore peace and quiet to his universe.

Before running out for a few more things he thought he might need before morning, Mrs. Sheppard had at least helped him stumble his way through his first diaper change and bottle preparation. He'd gotten the baby—Henry…the child's name was Henry, so he'd better start remembering it—fed and thought he was in the clear.

Still in the little rocking seat with the handle that made for easier toting around, the baby had started to drift off, eyes growing heavy as his tiny mouth tugged at the bottle's nipple like…well, like something he had no business thinking in the presence of an infant. Especially if that infant turned out to be his son and the image in his head was of the child's mother.

And then, just a few minutes after he'd emptied the bottle of formula, Baby Henry had jerked awake and started screaming at the top of his lungs. Alex had rocked the baby seat…shushed him in a voice he'd never used before in his life…and tried every trick he could think of—which weren't many, he was frustrated to realize.

Finally, having run out of options, he'd lifted the child from the padded seat and tucked him against his chest.

Surprised by his own actions, he'd begun patting the baby's back and bouncing slightly as he crossed the room. Back and forth, back and forth, back and forth in an effort to soothe the bawling child.

He didn't know where any of this came from, but it seemed the natural thing to do. Not that it was working. The baby was sobbing so hard, his little chest was heaving and his breaths were coming in hiccuping gasps.

If this lasted much longer, Alex was going to dial 9-1-1. It was the only option he could think of, given that he had no nanny and no personal knowledge of child rearing. Especially if it meant the difference between being thought a fool for overreacting or letting the poor kid suffocate on his own tears.

He was headed for the phone, intent on doing just that, when the doorbell rang. Halting in his tracks, he took a second to wonder who it could be at this hour—he wasn't expecting anyone except Mrs. Sheppard, and she had her own key—before Henry gave another hitching sob, driving him to action. Whoever it was, he hoped to hell they knew something, *anything* about babies.

Please, God, let this be Mary Poppins, he thought as he stalked out of his office and across the gleaming parquet foyer.

Yanking the door open, he jerked to a stop, shock reverberating through his system.

The person standing on the other side of the threshold was better than Mary Poppins…it was the baby's mother.

Jessica.

Eight

Jessica's heart was pounding like the bass of a hard rock ballad in her chest, tears pouring down her face. Coming here hadn't been part of the plan. And the last thing she'd intended was to knock on the front door.

But she couldn't stand it anymore. Henry's sobs were tearing her apart, causing a deep, throbbing physical pain that couldn't be ignored one second longer.

She'd been crying since she'd sneaked into Alex's office and left her sweet little baby on his boardroom table. No choice, nowhere else to turn.

She'd done everything she could on her own, and finally realized that turning Henry over to his father was the only option left unless she wanted to raise her child in a homeless shelter.

But doing the right thing, the *only* thing, didn't mean she could just walk away. She'd left Henry with a note for Alex to discover, praying he would believe her words and accept the baby as his son. That he would love and care for him the way their son deserved.

Then she'd sneaked back out of the building, but had stood across the street, waiting and watching. And crying. Crying so hard, she'd been afraid of attracting unwanted attention.

When she'd spotted Alex coming out of the building to meet his car at the curb, baby carrier balanced at his hip, her pulse had spiked. She'd taken it as a good sign, though, that he'd had the baby with him. And that he hadn't called the police to turn her in as an unfit mother, as well as for child abandonment.

She hadn't known where he was going, though, and suddenly she'd *needed* to know. Not that she could afford to hail a cab, and she'd sold her own car months ago.

With no other options, she'd taken a chance, using public transportation, then walking the rest of the way to Alex's estate. A gorgeous, sprawling sandstone mansion on fifteen private, perfectly landscaped acres in an area she was well familiar with from her own time living in Seattle.

It was also gated, but she'd lucked out—huffing and puffing from the uphill climb, she'd reached the entrance to Alex's property just as someone else had been leaving. The car had pulled out, turning onto the main road, and Jessica had slipped through the iron gate as it was slowly swinging closed.

Then she'd rounded the house, looking in every window she could reach until she'd spotted Alex and Henry. Heart in her throat, she'd used a less-than-sturdy hedge as a stepping stool, standing on tiptoe to watch. Just…watch.

She'd wanted so badly to go inside and hold her baby. To take him back and tell Alex it had all been a horrible mistake. But even if she had…even if it *was*…her circumstances would be exactly the same.

No choice. She had no choice.

It was when Henry had started crying—sobbing, really—and had refused to be calmed, that she couldn't stand it any longer. She wanted her baby, and he obviously needed her.

So here she stood, face-to-face with the one man she'd had no intention of ever being face-to-face with again.

She didn't know what to say to him, so she didn't mince words. "Give him to me," she said, plucking the baby out of his grasp.

She wasn't the least bit familiar with the layout of the house, but she didn't particularly care. Moving across the foyer, she headed in the direction she thought would take her to Alex's spacious office den. The one she'd been hiding outside of for the past half hour, spying on her child and ex-lover.

Pulling off her knit cap and shrugging out of her jacket—one arm at a time while balancing Henry in the other—she tossed them aside, bringing the baby even closer to her chest, tucking him in and crooning. From the moment he heard her voice, he began to relax.

It took what seemed like forever for his cries to die down, but she continued to sway, hum, pat him on the back. She whispered in his ear, telling him in a low, singsong voice how much she loved him, how sorry she was for leaving, and that everything would be okay. She wasn't sure she believed it, but she promised all the same.

A long time later, his tiny body stopped shuddering and she knew he was sleeping, his face turned in to her neck, his warm breath fanning her skin.

It was the most amazing sensation, one she hadn't thought she'd get to experience again anytime soon…if ever. Her own chest grew tight, moisture gathering behind her closed eyelids.

As much as she was trying to absorb every precious moment, she knew she was also stalling. Because Alex was standing behind her. Watching and waiting and likely fuming with fury.

She couldn't hide behind the baby forever, though. Time to pay the piper.

On a sigh, followed by a deep, fortifying breath, Jessica turned.

She'd been right. Alex was standing only a few feet away, arms crossed, blue eyes as cold as a glacier glaring at her. That look cut through her, chilling her to the bone.

Swallowing hard, she kept her voice low to avoid waking the baby, hoping Alex would take the hint and do the same.

"I'm sorry," she told him. "I shouldn't have abandoned him like that."

Abandoned. God, that made her sound like such a bad mother. But it was the truth, wasn't it?

She expected him to jump on that, throw all kinds of nasty accusations at her—though in a subdued tone, she hoped.

Instead, he pinned her in place with a sharp, angry stare. "Is he mine?"

"Yes," she answered simply. Honestly. "His middle name is Alexander, for you. Henry was my grandfather's name."

Without responding to that bit of information, he asked, "Are you willing to take a blood test to prove it?"

It hurt to have him ask, but she wasn't surprised. She'd lied to him—so many times, about so much…things he didn't even know about yet, let alone the things he did.

"Yes," she murmured again.

That seemed to give him pause. Had he expected her to refuse?

She wasn't exactly perched soundly on the higher ground, here. She had no room to complain and no right to be offended. If there were hoops he wanted her to jump through, and punishments he wanted to dole out, she had no choice but to acquiesce.

"I'll make an appointment first thing in the morning."

She nodded, though she knew he neither needed nor was waiting for her to agree.

"You'll stay here tonight," he continued, his tone brooking no argument. "In fact, you'll stay here until I know what's going on and have decided what to do about it."

As uncomfortable a prospect as that was, she was oddly okay with it. It wasn't as if she had anywhere else to go. Even after leaving Henry at Alex's office, her only plan had been to look for work here in Seattle or catch a bus back to Portland and try to find something there, but she suspected she probably would have ended up sleeping in the bus terminal instead. Provided Alex didn't intend to lock her in a dungeon somewhere in this giant house of his, it might be nice to sleep in a real bed for a change.

When she offered no resistance to his demands, he tipped his head and moved toward the door. "Follow me." He didn't look back, assuming—or rather, *knowing*—she would do exactly as he said.

Still holding a sleeping Henry, she trailed him out of the office, across the cavernous foyer and up a wide, carpeted stairwell to the second floor. He led her down a long hallway lined with what she could only assume was priceless artwork and credenzas topped with fresh-cut flowers in crystal and Ming-style vases.

Stopping suddenly, he pushed open one of the doors and stood aside for her to pass. It was a beautiful, professionally decorated guest room, complete with queen-size four-poster canopy bed and private bath. Done in varying shades of sage-green, it was unisex; not too masculine or too feminine.

"If you try to leave," Alex said from behind her, "I'll stop you. If you try to take my child from me—if he really is my child—I'll have both the police and my attorneys on you faster than you can blink."

She had no doubt he was rich enough, powerful enough and bitter enough to carry through with the threat. While she was broke, powerless and too exhausted to walk much farther, let alone attempt to run away.

Turning to face him, she continued to rub the baby's back. "I'm not going anywhere, Alex. I handled this badly, and for that, I apologize. This isn't how you should have found out you're a father. So whatever you need me to do…within reason," she added with a raised brow, "well, I figure I owe you one."

His raised brow told her he thought she owed him more than just one. And maybe he was right. But her response seemed to reassure him. Some of the tension went out of his shoulders and the lines bracketing his mouth lessened a fraction.

"Tell me what you need for him."

His eyes darted to Henry and she *thought* she saw a hint of softness there. Although she might have imagined it.

She had next to nothing. By the time she'd decided leaving Henry with Alex was her last resort, she'd been out of formula and down to her last diaper. If she hadn't, she probably wouldn't have been able to go through with it.

She could have gone to her parents, but that was still a can of worms she was trying to avoid opening. And the guilt of not alerting Alex to the fact that he was a father had started to eat at her, so she'd decided that he was a better "last resort."

"Everything," she said dejectedly.

"Make a list," he told her. "My housekeeper is picking up a few things right now. I'll try to catch her and have her get whatever else you need while she's out."

Jessica nodded, expecting him to go…unless he intended to pull up a chair and stand guard at the door all night. Instead, he remained rooted to the spot, his features drawn in contemplation.

"Will this be all right for him?" he finally asked. His arms swept out to encompass the room. "I don't have a crib or anything else...nursery-ish."

She offered a small smile. As angry as he was, he was still concerned about his son's safety and comfort. She found that endearing. And it gave her hope that his resentment would one day give way to understanding.

"We'll be fine," she assured him. "Henry can sleep in the bed with me, and I'll use pillows around the edges to keep him from rolling off."

He considered that for a moment, then said, "I'll make arrangements for someone to come by tomorrow and baby proof the place. Make a list for that, too—whatever you and Henry will need for an extended stay, and whatever needs to be done to keep him safe."

She wasn't sure what he meant by that. How *extended* a stay did he have in mind?

But now wasn't the time to question him. She was on thin enough ice as it was.

"We still have to talk," he informed her. "But you look tired, and I know he is. It can wait until tomorrow."

With that, he turned on his heel and walked out, closing the door behind him.

Jessica let out a breath, wishing it was one of relief. Instead, it was only...a short reprieve. As she set about readying the room, herself and the baby for bed, she felt as though a noose was hanging over her head.

Because as bad as today had been...tomorrow promised to be even worse.

Jessica didn't know what time it was when she finally came awake the next morning. Henry had had her up a few times during the night, needing to be changed or fed or simply lulled back to sleep. But she suspected yesterday's stress level had impacted him, as well, because he'd slept like a stone the rest of the time.

Stretching, she glanced beside her to find him awake and smiling around the pacifier in his mouth. His legs were kicking, and when he saw her looking down at him, he waved his arms, too.

"Good morning, sweetheart," she greeted him, unable to resist leaning over and kissing his soft cheek. He made a happy sound from deep in his belly, and she took a minute to blow raspberries on his tummy through his thin cotton T-shirt until he giggled.

Laughing in return, she scooped him up and finally looked at the clock. Ten-thirty. Later than she normally woke, but not quite as late as she'd expected, given the bright sunlight peeking through the drawn floor-to-ceiling curtains. As she started moving around, using the restroom and changing the baby, she heard noises from outside the bedroom door.

Last night, before she'd gone to bed, Alex's housekeeper had arrived with several large fabric totes bulging with baby items. Formula, bottles, pacifiers, toys, onesies, baby lotion, baby shampoo, baby powder…everything. More than Jessica would need to get through just the next few days. And now it sounded as though Alex had a construction crew in the house, building a nursery—or possibly an entire day care center—to his exact specifications.

With Henry at her hip, she opened the door only to find the hallway filled with oversize boxes and shopping bags. She stood rooted to the spot for a minute, stunned and confused.

Noises were coming from next door, and before she could decide which direction to turn—left toward the sounds of the pounding or right toward the stairs—Alex appeared. He strolled down the hall with two men on his heels who were carrying a large, flat cardboard box between them.

"In there," Alex instructed, pointing to the room where all

the building noises were coming from. He waited for them to pass, then waved her ahead of him.

They paused in the doorway of the room beside hers, where several men were busy putting furniture together and attaching shelving to the walls.

"What's all this?" she asked, though she could certainly guess. The half-assembled crib and changing table in the corner were dead giveaways.

"I'm putting a nursery in between our two rooms. That way we'll both be close to the baby in case he needs us during the night."

Jessica swallowed, not quite sure how to respond. Should she be more concerned that Alex's room was apparently only two doors down from where she'd spent last night...or that he seemed to believe she and Henry would be here long enough for a separate nursery to be necessary?

She owed him answers, and, of course, knew that he would want to spend time with his son now that he was aware of Henry's existence, but that didn't mean she—or the baby—were going to stick around forever.

Before she could decide how to respond, he continued.

"I've called Practically Perfect Au Pairs, the premiere nanny agency in the city. They'll be sending potential nannies out over the next few days to be interviewed. You can be there, if you like."

This time she wasn't at a loss for words. Her spine went straight and tight as outrage coursed through her system.

"Henry doesn't *need* a nanny. I'm his mother. I can care for him just fine by myself."

"As evidenced by the fact that you left him in the boardroom of my office building, with a note begging me to take him in," he replied, deadpan.

Jessica's chest squeezed. He was right, and they both knew it. But she'd changed her mind. She was here now, and damned if she'd let him foist her child off on some complete stranger.

"That was yesterday," she told him. "Today, I'm perfectly capable of watching out for my own child. I don't *need* a nanny," she stressed again.

She expected an argument. Worse, she expected him to toss more "unfit mother" accusations at her. Instead, he shrugged one shoulder encased in the fine silk-wool blend of a tailored dark blue suit.

"Humor me," he said in a tone that could only be described as wholly polite. "This is all rather new to me, and I'd feel better having a trained professional on hand for those times when you or I can't be with Henry."

Again the thought crossed her mind that she probably wouldn't be staying with him for long. Certainly not long enough to hire extra staff.

But what she asked him was, "Why wouldn't I be with him?" Her back was still stiff as a rod, her voice carrying more than a hint of wariness.

"We have a lot of ground to cover. You may need a nap after the grilling I plan to give you."

Her eyes widened at that, and suspicion gave way to fear.

"You missed breakfast," he added, jumping so easily from one topic to another that her head started to spin. "But I'm sure Mrs. Sheppard can see that you're fed."

"Oh, that's all right. I don't want to be a both—"

Alex took her elbow, forcibly turning her toward the other end of the house and leading her in that direction.

"Feed the baby," he told her. "Then get yourself something to eat. After that, we'll talk."

He said "we'll talk," but what Jessica heard was, "Let the inquisition begin."

Nine

Alex thought he deserved a damn Academy Award for his performance so far. Every second that he'd been with Jessica, he'd wanted to shake her. Every word that he'd spoken in calm, even tones, he'd wanted to shout at the top of his lungs. It had taken every ounce of control he possessed to hold a normal, mundane conversation with her rather than demand answers. Right there, right now, regardless of how many witnesses might hear.

But he'd bitten his tongue, fisted his hands so tightly he'd nearly drawn blood. Reminded himself that in most situations, one got further by keeping a cool, level head than losing one's temper and raging like a maniac.

As hard as it was to resist turning the full force of his fury on her, he told himself that would only frighten her and possibly cause her to run off again. This time taking *his son* with her.

Oh, there were going to be DNA tests to prove—or disprove—that claim. In addition to the nannies who would be dropping by on and off over the next several days, he had a doctor scheduled to stop in and conduct a paternity test as quickly as possible.

But until he knew for sure, he was going on the assumption that he *was* the child's father. Better safe than sorry, and if he was, he wanted to get a jump on being a dad.

He'd already missed… He didn't know how long. He did know, though, that he'd missed the entire pregnancy, the birth and any number of firsts. First feeding, first diaper change, first time being awakened in the middle of the night and rocking Henry back to sleep.

Alex clenched his teeth until they ached. One more thing to hold against Jessica. The list was getting pretty long.

Biding his time, he led her downstairs to the kitchen and asked Mrs. Sheppard to see to it that Jessica and the baby were both taken care of. Then he'd returned to the foyer to oversee the rest of the baby preparations.

He'd waited thirty minutes. Thirty-two to be exact, before returning to the kitchen, ready to get some answers to the questions burning a hole in his gut.

Walking into the room, he stopped short, taken aback by the sight before him.

Jessica sat at the table of the eat-in nook near the windows, a half-eaten plate of scrambled eggs and toast in front of her. She alternated between taking a bite of her own meal and slipping a spoonful of goopy gray cereal into the baby's mouth. He was perched on her thigh, nestled and in the crook of her arm.

"Why isn't he in the high chair?" Alex asked, his voice reverberating through the room more loudly than he'd intended, startling both Jessica and Henry. He'd ordered the expensive piece of infant furniture, though, so his son should darn well be using it.

Dipping the tiny spoon back into the baby goop, she said, "He's only three months old. He's not quite ready to sit up on his own yet."

Well, there was one question answered. Henry was three months old. The math worked.

He also made a mental note to buy some baby books. He didn't want to learn from Jessica or anyone else what his child could or couldn't do, or what he needed.

Feeling suddenly uncomfortable and slightly self-conscious, he cleared his throat. "When you're finished, come to my office. It's time to get down to business."

As she crossed the front of the house toward Alex's den, Jessica felt for all the world as if she'd been called to the principal's office. Her feet were lead weights and her heart was even heavier. Henry at her hip, in comparison, was light as a feather.

He was also happy today. She shouldn't have been quite so delighted about it, but from the moment she'd arrived last night and plucked him from Alex's arms, Henry had been relaxed and content. Something to be said for her mothering skills, she hoped, as well as their strong mommy/baby bond.

On the heels of that thought, though, came a wave of guilt. She'd had nine months of pregnancy and the three months since Henry was born to bond with him, while Alex had had only yesterday. And that hardly counted, since she'd sprung the baby on him with no warning and hadn't even stuck around to explain.

Which was why she was letting him get away with the strong-arm tactics. He was angry—with good reason. And she was guilty—for bad reasons.

The door was open when she arrived. Alex was seated behind his desk, another man—older and balding—sat in one of the guest armchairs with his back to her.

Alex spotted her almost the moment she stepped inside and stood to greet her.

"Come in," he said, rounding the desk as the other man also got to his feet.

"This is Dr. Crandall," he introduced them, closing the door behind her with a soft click. "Dr. Crandall, this is the young woman I was telling you about."

To Jessica, he added, "Dr. Crandall is here for the paternity test."

Having her integrity called into question stung, but in Alex's shoes she would have insisted on the very same thing. So she extended her arm and shook the doctor's hand.

"Nice to meet you, Doctor."

"You, too, my dear," he said, smiling gently. "And I don't want you to worry about a thing. This is a relatively painless procedure. Just a quick cheek swab, and I should have the results back from the lab by the middle of next week."

"I appreciate that, thank you."

The idea of having Henry's blood drawn hadn't appealed. He'd survived worse, of course, but that still didn't make it a fun prospect.

"Dr. Crandall assures me that the cheek swab tests are just as accurate as blood tests," Alex put in. "The only reason we'd have to have blood drawn later is if the initial tests come back as inconclusive or problematic."

Jessica nodded. "Whatever you need."

Ten minutes later, Alex was walking the doctor to the door, DNA samples labeled and tucked safely into his medical bag. She stood in the doorway of Alex's office, watching as he shook the physician's hand, then ducking back inside before Alex returned.

When he arrived, she was sitting in one of the leather guest chairs, bouncing a giggling Henry on one knee.

Alex stood for a moment, simply watching them. The

woman who'd seared some of the most passionate memories of his life into his brain, and the child they'd most likely made together.

His chest contracted. Without a doubt, he was furious. She'd used him, stolen from him, betrayed him and lied to him. Yet part of him wanted to cross the room, drop to one knee and wrap his arms around them, holding them close and cherishing them the way a family should be cherished.

He wondered what would have happened if his relationship with Jessica had played out differently. If she hadn't spent the night with him simply to steal company secrets. If she'd stuck around instead of running off before the sun rose the next morning so they could share breakfast, get to know each other better, perhaps agree to keep seeing one another.

Alex wasn't a man of fickle emotions, so when he'd awakened that morning after making love with her, looking forward to making love to her again…and possibly again…he'd known he'd found something special. Or thought so, at least. Reality had proven to be quite different.

But deep down, he knew the possibility of a good, old-fashioned romance had existed. They might have dated, shared a short engagement and walked down the aisle before deciding to start a family. Baby Henry would still have been part of the big picture, just a little further down the road.

Fate had a way of turning things upside down, though, then sitting back for a good chuckle at the expense of the humans who had been played with like marionettes.

Which meant he was now faced with fatherhood first and…he didn't know what else second.

Clearing his throat, he strode across the room, returning to his seat behind the desk. It was awkward to put such cold, professional distance between himself and the mother of his child, but he felt comfortable there, and if it intimidated Jessica at all, kept her on the level, then it was the right position to take.

"I think I'm going to need a quick rundown of events," he told her, careful to keep his tone level and unaccusatory. "Why did you take off in the middle of the night? And if Henry is my son, why didn't you contact me when you found out you were pregnant?"

He watched her eyes, saw the pulse in her throat jump as she swallowed.

"It was a one-night stand. I didn't think you'd want me to still be there in the morning," she murmured. "And then when I went back the next day to clean your room, you were gone."

"My business in Portland wrapped up a few days early, and I was needed back here in Seattle. I wanted to ask about you," he admitted—albeit against his better judgment, "or at least leave a note, but was afraid it might get you in trouble."

He very intentionally didn't mention the missing Princess Line prospectus. It was a subject that definitely needed to be discussed, but not now. Not until he knew for certain whether or not Henry was his son.

For the time being, the child and his possible unexpected fatherhood trumped everything else.

She nodded somewhat ruefully. "It probably would have gotten me fired."

Just as he'd suspected. "I called a while later, but whoever I talked to claimed there was no one by the name of Jessica Madison working at Mountain View. And that the only Jessica they'd had on staff had quit the week before."

He'd considered digging deeper, perhaps hiring a private investigator to track her down. But then he'd realized how that would look: desperate. Especially since he hadn't yet hired a P.I. to look into the theft. If their one night together hadn't meant enough to her to make her stick around, then he'd look pretty pathetic chasing after her like a lovelorn pup.

So he'd put her and what he still considered a spectacular intimate experience behind him. Or tried, at any rate. And he'd succeeded at putting her out of his everyday thoughts, if not his late-night, private ones.

"You must have called soon after I discovered I was pregnant," she said.

His mouth turned down in a frown. "You quit because of that?"

A strange look passed over her features, and it took a second for her to reply.

"I had to. It wouldn't have been long until I was unable to keep up with the workload, and the chemicals we used to clean wouldn't have been good for the baby. Besides, the owners of the resort weren't too fond of unwed mothers being on the payroll. They thought it tarnished the resort's pristine reputation and would have come up with a reason to let me go before long."

Alex made a mental note never to stay at Mountain View Lodge again. If anything, single and expectant mothers needed their jobs more than other employees. And considering some of the behavior that often took place at those types of high-scale resorts—adultery topping the list—he didn't think the owners had a lot of room to point fingers.

Getting back to the subject at hand, he said, "Why didn't you tell me when you found out? You knew who I was and where to find me."

It wasn't always easy to get in touch with him—Rose was an excellent guard dog—but if Jessica had left her name and at least a hint of what she needed to talk to him about, he would have returned her call. Hell, he would have relished the chance to see her again—for more reasons than one.

He didn't know how he would have handled the news of her unexpected pregnancy. Probably much the same as he was handling the news of Henry's existence now—with a fair dose of skepticism and trepidation. He liked to think he would have done the right thing, though, once he'd established the veracity of her claim. Much as he was trying to do now.

He was playing it smart, getting medical proof before accepting parental responsibility, but if Henry turned out to be his, he would do more than put a crib in one of the extra guest rooms and make sure his name was on the child's birth certificate. He would be laying full claim, taking whatever steps were necessary to be sure his son stayed with him. Whether Jessica liked it or not.

Why didn't you tell me when you found out you were pregnant?

It was the question Jessica had been dreading ever since she'd made the decision *not* to tell him.

It had been the wrong decision. Or at the very least, the wrong thing to do. There had been so many factors to consider, though, and she'd been so very frightened and alone.

To Alex, however, she said simply, "I didn't think you'd want to know. Most men wouldn't."

A muscle ticked in his jaw, and she got the distinct impression he was grinding his molars together to keep from doing—or saying—something violent.

"I'm not most men," he said slowly and very deliberately, almost as though each word was a statement unto itself. "I would have stepped up to the plate. And I most certainly would have wanted to know I'd fathered a child."

"I'm sorry."

Jessica didn't know what else to say, not without saying far too much. He was angry enough with her already; she didn't think telling him she was a Taylor and that she'd been poking around his hotel room looking for company secrets would do much to improve his mood.

So she kept her mouth shut, knowing he would find out eventually but hoping he would hate her a little less by then.

Ignoring her apology, both physically and verbally, he went on. "If you didn't want me to know about Henry, why did you dump him at my office yesterday?"

She flinched at his less-than-flattering description of her actions, even though that's exactly what she'd done—in his eyes and in her own.

"I didn't feel I had a choice," she told him quietly. "It's been rough being out of work and trying to care for a baby all by myself. I can't find a job until I put Henry in day care, and I can't afford day care until I get a job."

"Don't you have family to turn to? Parents? Relatives who could help you out?"

The short answer was no. The long answer would mean admitting she was a Taylor, and that rather than telling her family she was pregnant by Alexander Bajoran, she'd chosen to run away. Disappear and live one step up from on the streets.

She'd thought so many times about going home and telling her parents everything. But she hadn't wanted to see the disappointment on their faces when they found out who the father of her baby was. Even if she refused to tell them, she was afraid her mother would eventually wear her down and drag the truth out of her.

And if she'd managed to hold out against her mother's badgering, she'd been very much afraid her cousin would come along later and figure it out.

Because Erin knew what she'd been up to in Alex's room at the resort. And she knew that Jessica hadn't been dating anyone around that time. She'd have done the math in her head, become suspicious and started badgering Jessica until she confessed everything. Then Erin would tell Jessica's folks for sure, damn her meddling hide. Her cousin was the impetus behind all of this, yet Jessica was the one to suffer the consequences.

To Alex she said carefully, "No one who could help me out, no."

He considered that for a moment, the tension in his jaw easing slightly. "You should have come to me sooner. *Come* to me," he emphasized. "In person rather than sneaking around like a cat burglar."

"At least I left something instead of stealing something," she quipped in an attempt at levity.

"I'm not sure the authorities would see it that way," he replied with a withering glance that immediately wiped the lopsided smile from her face.

Before the adrenaline from his veiled threat made it into her bloodstream, however, he added, "You were actually pretty good at getting in and out of the building without being seen. How did you manage that?"

"Just lucky, I guess."

If *luck* included practically growing up there while her family was still part of the business, and knowing not only where all the security cameras and blind spots were, but also how the building's security functioned. Or how it *had* functioned, anyway. She'd taken a chance and hoped not much had changed in the past few years.

Alex's eyes narrowed, and she could see the questions swirling there, knew the interrogation wasn't even close to being over. And while he'd certainly earned the right to some answers, she didn't know how much longer she would be able to get away with partial ones and half-truths.

Then as though heaven actually heard her silent pleas, she was saved by the bell. Literally.

From the front of the house the doorbell rang. They heard footsteps, followed by muted voices, and then more footsteps. A minute later there was a soft knock at the office door.

"Come in," Alex called.

Mrs. Sheppard poked her head in. "One of the applicants from Practically Perfect Au Pairs is here," she said.

"Give us two minutes, then show her in," Alex instructed. "Bring us a tray of coffee and hot tea, as well. Thank you."

The housekeeper nodded, pulling the door closed behind her.

"This is only the first interview of many," Alex told Jessica. "Would you like to take Henry off to do something else, or would you like to stay?"

Another woman interviewing for the privilege of taking care of her son when she wasn't readily available? Oh, there was no way she'd leave that decision to anyone else. Not even her baby's father.

Ten

By the end of the day, they'd interviewed half a dozen nannies. They ranged in age from eighteen to probably forty-five or so; college-age girls needing a job and a place to stay while they attended school, to lifelong caregivers. Each of them came with a resumé and the stamp of approval from either Practically Perfect Au Pairs or one of the other professional nanny placement services Alex had contacted.

As nice as most of the people were, though, Jessica found herself balking at the idea of Alex hiring any of them. Credentials, references and background checks aside, none of them seemed quite good enough to be left alone with her child.

She stood in the foyer, waiting while Alex saw the last of the potential nannies out. Shutting the door behind him, he turned to face her.

"So…any possibilities?" he asked, his footfalls echoing on the parquet floor as he crossed to her.

She shrugged a shoulder, not saying anything.

One corner of his mouth quirked up in a half grin. A sexy half grin, she was troubled to note.

Damn him for being so attractive, even when he hated her. And damn herself for still *finding* him attractive when she had so very much to lose at his hands.

"Come on," he cajoled, raising a hand to rub one of Henry's cheeks with the side of his thumb before letting it drop... and stroking her arm with his cupped palm all the way down. The touch made her shiver as goose bumps broke out along her flesh.

"There has to be someone you liked at least a little. You can't be with Henry 24/7, and every child needs a babysitter at some point. So if you had to pick, who would it be?"

Taking a deep breath, she thought back to each of the interviews, the details playing through her memory. One jumped out over all the others.

"Wendy."

His gaze narrowed. "Why?"

"She was friendly and smart," Jessica told him. "And she engaged Henry almost as soon as she walked in. Spoke to him, smiled at him, played with him, split her attention evenly between the three of us. The others seemed more concerned with remaining professional and impressing you."

A beat passed while he digested that. Then he offered a curt nod. "I thought exactly the same thing."

"Really?" Jessica asked, more than a little surprised.

Taking her elbow, he turned her toward the stairs, leading her to the second floor.

"Absolutely. I may not know much about babies, but I do know that a nanny will be spending ninety percent of her time with Henry. Which means that whoever we hire should be more concerned with impressing him, not me."

He smiled at Henry while he spoke, earning himself a giggle and kick, which only made Alex smile wider.

Tweaking the baby's bare toes as they strolled down the hall, he said, "Besides, I noticed the same things you did. She was really quite good with him. I especially liked that she cleaned his toy giraffe with an antibacterial wipe from her purse before handing it back to him after it fell on the floor. All without a hitch in her conversation with us."

"Me, too," Jessica admitted. Actually, she'd loved that part of the interview. Even Jessica's first instinct would have been to simply take her chances that the floor wasn't that dirty, or maybe run the toy under some water if she was near a faucet. The fact that Wendy had come so well prepared before she'd even been hired definitely earned her bonus points.

"So we'll put her at the top of the list," Alex said. "There are still a few more potentials to meet with tomorrow, and then we can decide. But I think we should strike that Donna woman from the pool entirely. She was downright frightening."

Jessica chuckled, even as a shudder stole down her spine. "Definitely. She should be running a Russian prison, not caring for small children and infants."

Alex gave a short bark of laughter. "Maybe I'll mention that to the agency when they ask how the interviews went."

Jessica's eyes widened. "Don't you dare!" she exclaimed, slapping him playfully on the chest with the back of her hand.

She stopped in her tracks, both shocked and horrified at what she'd done. Dear God, what was she thinking? She was joking with him as if they were old friends. Never mind that he held her future in his hands and could decide to punish her in a million alarming ways at the drop of a hat.

She swallowed past the lump in her throat and forced her gaze up to his, an apology on the tip of her tongue. But his expression kept it from going any further.

Rather than looking annoyed or upset, his features were taut, his eyes blazing with something she hadn't seen since their time at the resort. It made her heart skip a beat and sent heat rushing through her system.

Or maybe she was imagining things. Maybe that blaze in his eyes really was annoyance, and she'd amused herself right into a boatload of trouble.

Chest tight, she licked her dry lips and wondered if she could distract him with a change of subject.

"What are we doing up here, by the way?"

For a moment, he continued to stare with that same barely controlled intensity. Then he pulled back just a fraction and gestured behind her.

"The nursery is ready," he said, leading her in that direction. "I thought you might like to see it."

The general decor of the room was the same as it had been before. Pale yellow walls, lacy white curtains at the windows and gleaming hardwood floors. But any original pieces of furniture had been replaced with top-of-the-line baby items.

A spacious oak half-circle crib rested against one wall, a large changing table and storage unit along another, and in the corner sat a beautiful rocking chair she'd be willing to bet was hand carved.

"What do you think?" Alex asked from just over her shoulder.

"It's lovely," she told him. Like something out of *House Beautiful* or *Babies Born with Silver Spoons in Their Mouths*. She was almost afraid to touch anything for fear she'd leave a smudge on the pristine interior. "I can't believe you had all of this done in only one day."

"Getting things done is easy when you have money and know the right people."

A fact she knew quite well from the good old days before Alex had destroyed her family.

"If there's anything else you or the baby need, anything you'd like to change, just say so," he continued. "I want everything to be perfect, and I'm afraid you're my only source of information at the moment where Henry is concerned."

He said it without a hint of censure. At least none that she could detect. But the guilt and underlying threat were there all the same.

"Why are you doing this?" she asked softly. Shifting Henry from one arm to the other, she turned to face Alex more fully. "You don't even know for sure that Henry is yours."

She did, of course, but she'd assumed that was the point of the paternity test they'd taken that afternoon.

Alex shrugged. "Better safe than sorry."

A very simple, off-the-cuff answer, but she suspected there was more to it than that.

"You're going to make us stay, aren't you?" she asked barely above a whisper.

"For the time being," he said without hesitation.

Then, surprising her yet again, he reached out and slid his hands beneath Henry's arms, lifting him out of her grasp and into his own.

For a split second, Jessica held her breath and nearly tried to tug the baby back. She had to remind herself that Alex *was* Henry's father. He *did* have a right to hold him, if he wanted to.

As distant as he'd been up to now, he didn't seem the least bit nervous about it. There was no hesitation, no pause while he considered the best way to position Henry against his thousand-dollar suit.

He was a natural. Either that, or he'd learned on the job during last night's screaming fit. Still, she couldn't resist stretching out a hand to smooth the baby's shirt down his back, making certain everything was just right and he was okay.

It was odd not holding her own baby, not having him almost surgically attached to her side when she was the only person who'd held him for any length of time since he was born. She didn't know what to do with her arms.

Letting them drop to her sides, she dug her hands into the front pockets of her jeans and told herself to leave them there, even though the urge was to fidget like crazy.

As hard as it was to admit, she made herself mumble, "You're really good at that."

"I've been watching you," he said, his gaze meeting and locking with hers. "I figured I should probably get the hang of it if I'm going to be responsible for this little guy from now on."

There it was again, the hint of a threat—or maybe just a reminder—that if Henry was his, Alex intended to exercise his full parental rights.

On the one hand, Jessica was impressed and sort of proud of him for that. A lot of men wouldn't have been the least bit pleased to discover they might have a child they hadn't known anything about.

On the other, she was scared almost spitless at what it might mean for her and Henry. What if Alex tried to take her son away from her? What if he wanted to keep Henry here with him, under his roof, but informed Jessica she was no longer welcome?

Jessica would fight—of course she would. But she already knew her chances were slim to none of winning any kind of battle against a man like Alex, let alone a custody one. Not given his money and influence and her total lack of either, not to mention her past actions and behavior where he was concerned.

Not for the first time she wanted to kick herself for bringing Alex into their lives. She hadn't had a choice; rationally, she knew that. And even more rationally, she knew he had the right to know about and *know* his own child.

But being here, disclosing Henry's existence to Alex, changed everything. It turned their world upside down and shook it like a snow globe.

To make matters worse, Jessica was afraid Henry was already showing signs of being a Daddy's Boy. He was leaning into Alex, completely trusting, completely content. One of his tiny hands was wrapped around Alex's silk tie, likely wrinkling it beyond repair, while his cheek rested on Alex's shoulder, his bow of a mouth working around his pacifier, his fine, light brown lashes fluttering toward sleep.

"He's getting tired," she told Alex, even as her heart cramped slightly at the sight. Until now she'd been the only one to see him get sleepy and doze off. She'd been the only one those miniature fingers had clung to.

"He missed his afternoon nap because of the interviews. We should probably give him a bottle and put him down for a while. If we don't, he's likely to get extremely cranky and keep us both up half the night."

"Only half?"

There was a twinkle of amusement in Alex's blue eyes. One Jessica couldn't help but respond to with a small smile of her own.

"If we're lucky."

Alex nodded. "Why don't you go downstairs for a bottle. I'll stay here with him. While you're down there, tell Mrs. Sheppard we'll be ready for dinner in thirty minutes. You'll join me, I hope."

That caught her off guard. "You're giving me a choice?"

"Of course."

"Would that choice happen to be eat a four-course meal

downstairs with you or enjoy a lovely serving of bread and water alone in my room?"

He chuckled. "My home isn't a prison, and you're not a prisoner."

"Are you sure?" It was a pointed question, one that had her holding her breath while she waited for the answer.

"After the way you've been living, I'd think staying here would almost be a vacation. Why don't you just enjoy it."

As responses went, it wasn't exactly a *You're free to leave anytime you like.* Although he did have a point; staying in this beautiful mansion was a far cry from worrying about where she was going to sleep that night or where her next meal might come from.

And yet she felt just as trapped as she would if he put her in her room and turned the key in the lock on the way out.

"You can't honestly refuse me this," he said when the silence between them had stretched on for several long seconds. "If Henry is my son, as you claim, I've missed the past three months of his life. The *only* three months of his life. I just want to spend some time with him, make up for a bit of that."

When all else fails, throw out a guilt bomb, she thought. And it hit its mark dead center. How could she possibly deny him time with his newly discovered son? Besides, it wasn't as though staying in a million-dollar house on a multimillion-dollar estate was going to be a hardship. Not physically, anyway.

Mentally, there was no telling yet what the toll would be. But she owed him at least this much.

Tipping her head, she kept her thoughts to herself, but let him know he'd won her over by saying, "I guess I'll go down for his bottle, then, and tell Mrs. Sheppard we're almost ready for dinner."

She patted Henry's tiny back, then stepped around them

and headed for the door. Just as she reached it, his voice stopped her.

"You can request bread and water, if your heart is set on it."

Her lips pursed as she fought a grin, but *his* chuckle of amusement followed her halfway down the hall.

Despite the beautiful new nursery just next door, Jessica couldn't bring herself to put Henry down in there for the entire night. He napped in the expensive new crib after his bottle and while Jessica and Alex ate dinner. But even though she left him there as she showered, changed into pajamas and got ready for bed, she hadn't been under the covers for ten whole minutes before leaping back up and marching next door to get him.

She hoped Alex hadn't gone into the nursery during the night to discover what she'd done. Or if he had, that he wouldn't say anything. She didn't feel like explaining her mild case of separation anxiety or the nagging worry that if she didn't have the baby in her sights at all times, Alex might take Henry away from her, hide him from her and never give him back.

Despite those very real concerns, however, Jessica had to admit that Alex had been perfectly pleasant at dinner. She'd been afraid to go down to the dining room with him, afraid to sit across the table from him—just the two of them alone in an almost cavernous room.

She'd expected more of the third degree. Inquisition, Part Two—only this time without the interruption of nanny interviews.

To her surprise and immense relief, he hadn't brought up even one uncomfortable topic of conversation. He'd asked about the baby. A few not-too-personal questions about her pregnancy. Even about where she'd been and what she'd done to support herself before Henry was born. And he'd spoken a bit about how he'd spent that time himself—mostly changes or new developments at Bajoran Designs.

It had actually been almost enjoyable, and she'd flashed back more than once to the only other meal they'd ever shared—that night at the resort. The night she'd let herself be led by her heart and her raging hormones instead of her head. The night Henry was conceived, though neither of them had had a clue about that at the time.

By the time dessert had been served—a simple but delicious fruit tart—he could have asked for her social security number and internet passwords...well, when she'd had use for internet passwords...and she probably would have turned them over as easily as she'd give someone the time of day. She was that comfortable, that lulled into a false sense of security.

But he hadn't. He'd remained a perfect gentleman, seeing her out of the dining room, then asking if she would be all right going back to the nursery and her room on her own while he went to his office to catch up on a bit of work.

It was the ideal opportunity to escape and put some distance between them. That should have made her happy, right? Just being this close to him, under the same roof, was dangerous with a capital *D*.

But she couldn't help feeling just a little disappointed. That what had turned out to be a lovely dinner had come to an end... That her memories of the last time they'd eaten together had been stirred up, warming her, yet leaving her somewhat frustrated by the fact that *this* meal wouldn't be ending the same way.... And possibly even that he wouldn't be accompanying her upstairs to check on Henry and say good-night.

Why she would want Alexander Bajoran to wish her a good-night, she had no idea. It was craziness to even imagine it. If anything she needed him to spend *less* time with her, watch her *less* closely.

In that, her prayers were answered, because he hadn't knocked on her door in the middle of the night to demand she return Henry to the nursery. He wasn't even waiting outside in the hall when she awoke the next morning and stepped out to begin the day.

Jessica did go to the nursery then, changing Henry's diaper and putting him into one of the matching baby-boy outfits Alex had had delivered the day before. He hadn't only ordered items for the baby, either, but had bought a good deal of stuff for her, as well. New clothes and toiletries; even a stack of puzzle books for her bedside table. Ostensibly in case she grew bored—something that rarely happened while caring for a three-month-old infant. Most nights she was asleep before her head hit the pillow.

But Alex's kindness hadn't gone unnoticed.

Henry was his son, a son he had every intention of laying claim to if those paternity tests came back with his name on them. So purchasing things for the boy was to be expected. Maybe not to the extent Alex had gone—"starting small" obviously wasn't a term that existed in his vocabulary—but buying diapers and formula and a few new pieces of clothing was completely within the realm of understanding.

He had absolutely *no* reason to feel the least bit generous toward her, however. He could have stripped the guest room of every creature comfort and left her to wear the same clothes she'd arrived in for the entire stay, and she would have considered it fair punishment for her deceptions.

But he was a bigger man—a kinder, more considerate man—than she could have anticipated. She only wondered how long it would last once he had the confirmation that Henry really was his son. Would he shower her with roses or take back everything and send her packing?

Hitching Henry higher in her arms, she strolled down the carpeted hallway and wide set of stairs, taking a right on her way to the kitchen. It was early yet, with the sun just beginning to cast purplish light through the windows as she passed.

But Henry was an early riser, especially when he was hungry. So she'd get him some cereal and juice, and make sure he was happy before looking for Alex and finding out what was on the agenda for the day. Likely more nanny interviews and questions from his long list of continued demands.

Half an hour later, she was sitting in the breakfast nook with Henry in his baby seat, his face and bib covered in splots of sticky and drying cereal. Mrs. Sheppard bustled around the center island, readying items for the meal she was about to prepare while Henry kicked his feet and sent the plastic seat rocking on the tabletop with every bite.

Jessica couldn't help grinning at her child's antics. He was so darn cute when he was happy and his belly was full. He was also extra adorable in the little choo-choo train overalls Alex had provided. He probably hadn't picked them out specifically, but whoever he'd put in charge of buying baby clothes had done an excellent job.

Raising a tightly closed fist into the air, Henry suddenly let out a squeal and jerked so hard, his seat scooted a good inch across the table. Jessica jumped, dropping the tiny Elmo spoon full of cereal and grabbing the seat before it could move any closer to the edge. Then she turned her head slightly to see what had gotten Henry so excited.

Alex stood only inches away, dressed in a charcoal suit and electric-blue tie that made his eyes pop like sapphires. He looked as though he'd just stepped off the pages of a men's fashion magazine. Or was maybe on the way to a photo shoot for one.

"Jeez, you scared me," she told him. Then she turned

back to Henry, picking up the fallen spoon and wiping up the spilled cereal with a damp cloth she had nearby.

When he didn't respond, and the awkward silence stretched from seconds into minutes, she craned her neck in his direction again. That's when she noticed the hard glint in his narrowed eyes and the still line of his mouth.

She swallowed and took a breath. "What's wrong?"

She'd never seen an expression like that on the face of anyone who wasn't there either to chew her out or tell her somebody had died. And with Alex she was betting on getting chewed out. What was it this time? she wondered.

"We need to talk," he told her simply, his voice sharp as a razor blade.

Uh-oh.

She looked back at Henry, her hand still on his carrier. His food-smeared smile was wide, his feet continuing to dance.

"Mrs. Sheppard," Alex intoned. "Can you please watch the baby while I have a word with Jessica?"

The housekeeper didn't seem thrilled with the prospect of babysitting duty, but dried her hands on a dish towel and crossed to the table, plucking the small plastic spoon from Jessica's fingers. Taking that as a sign that she didn't have much choice in the matter, Jessica relinquished the spoon and her seat, reluctantly following Alex from the kitchen.

Wordlessly, they walked to his office, where he waited for her to enter ahead of him, then shut the door behind them with a solid click of finality.

Much like the day before, she expected him to move behind his desk, and for both of them to sit down before he said whatever it was he had to say. Instead, he remained near the closed door, legs apart and arms crossing his chest in what could only be described as an aggressive stance.

"You're a Taylor," he blurted without preamble.

Her heart stuttered in her chest. "Excuse me?"

His eyes went to slits, a muscle ticking on one side of his jaw.

"Don't play dumb with me," he bit out. "Your name isn't Jessica Madison. It's Jessica Madison *Taylor*."

Eleven

The blood drained from Jessica's face. She felt it flush down her neck and through her body all the way to her toes, leaving her dizzy and light-headed.

Afraid she might actually faint, she took a step back, relieved when she bumped into one of the armchairs standing in front of his wide desk. She leaned her weight against it, reaching behind to dig her nails into the supple leather to help hold her upright and in place.

Licking her lips, she swallowed past the overwhelming drumbeat of her heart. Barely above a whisper, her voice grated out the only thought spiraling through her mind. "How did you find out?"

A flash of anger filled his expression. "DNA isn't the only thing I had tested. A friend on the police force ran your fingerprints for me, and they came back as Jessica Madison Taylor. No criminal record, I'm pleased to say, but it turns out you aren't at all who you claim to be. Your prints showed up as a former employee of both Mountain View and Bajoran Designs."

Well, not Bajoran Designs so much as Taylor Fine Jewels, when it existed. Still, she didn't know what to say. Shock that he'd found her out reverberated through every bone and nerve ending.

She certainly hadn't expected to be called out quite so soon. She'd actually been hoping she could find a time and place and way to tell him on her own. Eventually, when she couldn't keep it under wraps any longer.

"So what was your plan, exactly?" Alex asked, bitterness seeping into every syllable. "Seduce me for company secrets so you could sell them to the highest bidder? Or was the goal all along to get pregnant so you could blackmail me later with an heir?"

What little blood had worked its way back to her brain seeped out just as quickly. Her breath came in tiny, shallow gasps as her chest tightened and she swayed on her feet.

"What are you talking about?" she said, her jaw clenched. Partly because she was angry and partly because she was literally shaking. Her arms, her legs, her teeth. Every inch of her was quaking with the effort to hold back the maelstrom of emotions raging through her like a tidal wave. "I didn't get pregnant *on purpose*. And I didn't sell anything to anyone."

Alex didn't look as though he believed her.

"But I didn't get lucky with just a single, uninhibited chambermaid, did I? You're the daughter of Donald Taylor, granddaughter of *Henry* Taylor, both of whom used to be in partnership with Bajoran Designs. Aren't you?"

A beat passed before she answered. "Yes."

"And you just happened to be at the resort, cleaning *my* room."

She raised a brow, her grip on the chair at her back loosening as she began to regain some of her equilibrium.

"Actually, yes."

Doubt filled his stony features and was evident in his snort of derision.

"Call Mountain View. Give them my real name, and they'll tell you I was employed there long before you checked in. And the suite where you stayed was part of my regular rounds."

"Lucky for you that I landed there, then, wasn't it?"

"I wouldn't use the word *lucky,* no."

The day Alex had checked in to the resort was the beginning of her life's downward spiral. Except for Henry. He may have been unexpected, tossing her headfirst in a direction she wasn't ready to travel, but he was also the single greatest gift she'd ever been given.

"It was the perfect opportunity for you to take part in a bit of corporate espionage, though, hmm?"

Her pulse skipped in her veins. Wasn't that the exact term she'd used when Erin had first concocted her appalling plan? Of that, at least, she *was* guilty.

"I suppose you could say that, yes," she admitted. She wasn't proud of it, but the jig was obviously up, and she didn't intend to lie or deny any of it any longer.

"I recognized you the minute I saw you," she told him. "My family was devastated when you cut them off from Bajoran Designs and drove them out of business. I was okay with it, believe it or not. I might have ended up as merely a hotel maid, but I was happy and making enough of an income to live on. Unfortunately, the rest of my family didn't handle things quite as well."

Taking a deep breath, she released the rest of her hold on the armchair and moved on stiff legs to perch at the very edge of its overstuffed cushion. She was no longer facing Alex, cowering beneath his withering glare, but she didn't need to. His angry judgment filled the room like poison gas.

"When I mentioned to my cousin that you were staying at the resort, she convinced me to poke around your room. No excuses," she put in quickly, putting up a hand to hold off whatever his next verbal assault might be. "It was a stupid idea and I was wrong to ever agree to it, but I did. She wanted me to look for something that would hurt you—or rather, hurt Bajoran Designs. Something that could be used against you or put Taylor Fine Jewels back in operation."

"The design specs for the Princess Line," he said, his voice sharp as tacks.

Her head snapped up. So he knew she'd taken them. She'd kind of hoped she wouldn't have to confess that. But…

"Yes. I'm sorry about that."

"You seduced me to get them, and then sold the proposed designs to our competition."

The accusation struck her like a two-by-four. Her brows knit and she shook her head.

"No. No," she insisted. "I took them, but I didn't sell them. I never did anything with them."

"But you don't deny seducing me to get your hands on them," he tossed back with heavy sarcasm.

Spine straight, she lifted her chin and held his icy gaze. "Of course I do. I'm not a prostitute. I don't use my body to obtain information or anything else."

In for a penny, in for a pound, she thought before forging ahead. "I slept with you because I wanted to, and for no other reason. I'm also pretty sure *you* seduced me, not the other way around."

"I wouldn't be so certain of that," he muttered.

Stalking across the room, he rounded his desk and took a seat in front of the laptop set up there for his regular use. He tapped a few keys, waited a moment then turned the computer a hundred and eighty degrees so she could see the screen.

"Seduction aside, how do you explain this?" he asked.

She studied the images in front of her, growing colder by the second.

"I don't understand," she murmured.

Sliding forward, she looked even closer, narrowing her eyes, trying to figure out what was going on, how this had happened.

It had been months since she'd seen the original designs for the Princess Line, but she remembered them in acute detail. She'd even redesigned portions of them mentally and sketched changes in the margins of numerous pieces of paper that had passed through her hands since she'd taken them from his briefcase.

Nearly the *exact* designs from that folder were on the screen in front of her now, though, in rich, eye-popping color.

"What is this?" Swinging her gaze to Alex, she frowned. "Did Ignacio Jewelers buy the line concept from you? They needed work, but you shouldn't have given them up. They were perfect for Bajoran Designs."

His eyes turned to chips of blue glass, his fingers curling until the knuckles went white. "What kind of game are you playing, Jessica? I already know who you really are. I know what you were doing in my suite that night. You can stop with the lies."

"I'm not lying about anything," she said, growing more confused by the moment. "What are you talking about?"

"What are *you* talking about?" he demanded. "You know damn well you stole those designs from my briefcase that night after we slept together and sold them to Ignacio. I assume as part of your plot for revenge. Though why the hell you would have it in for me or my family's company, I'll never know."

Closing her eyes, Jessica shook her head and rubbed a spot near her temple where a headache was forming at record speed.

"No. This is…this is insane."

Opening her eyes again, she met his gaze head-on. "I told you I made a mistake in taking those designs. But I never did anything with them. I tried to return them the very next day, but you were already gone. Do you really think that if I'd sold them, I would be here now? That line of jewelry was worth millions. Even with a baby to care for, I couldn't have gone through that kind of money in under a year."

"I don't think you did," Alex told her. "I think you decided that showing up with a baby and telling me he's mine is all part of your plan to get even more money out of the Bajorans."

Tears prickled behind Jessica's lashes. "I'm sorry that I lied to you and betrayed your trust by taking those sketches," she said, struggling to keep her voice even and unwavering. "But no matter what you think of me, Henry *is* your son. I'm here because of him, *not* because I want anything from you. And I don't know what happened with that line," she rushed to add. "I don't know how Ignacio Jewelers got hold of it, but…I'll find out. Or at least I'll try."

Alex watched the myriad emotions playing over Jessica's delicate features. She looked truly distraught. Guilty and confused and hurt by his rapid-fire accusations.

It was no less than she deserved, of course, he thought to himself, clenching his jaw and refusing to be swayed by the moisture gathering in her eyes.

He wasn't sure what angered him most—the fact that she'd stolen the plans for one of his company's million-dollar ventures, or that she'd slept with him to get them.

That night might have been a one-night stand, but it sure as hell hadn't been meaningless. Not to him. Now he felt like a first class fool for ever thinking there was more between them than simply sex.

Crossing his arms in an attempt to rein in his temper, he arched a brow. "How, exactly, do you intend to do that?"

He could see the wheels in her head turning, desperately searching for a solution, a way out of the fix she was in.

Finally, she took a deep breath, her expression filling with resolve. "I left the proposal with the rest of my things when I stored them at my parents' house before leaving town. It should still be there."

"And who's to say you didn't simply make a copy before selling it out from under me?"

"I—" She screeched to a halt, blinking in confusion. "Why would I do that? I'd have no reason to keep a copy once I sold it for millions and millions of dollars to keep me in the wonderful lifestyle to which I've become so accustomed."

For having started out on a stammer, she ended with more than a fair note of snark. He had to bite the inside of his lip to keep from laughing aloud at her spunk.

Not for the first time, he was impressed by her resilience. She was in trouble, here. With his power and money, he could squash her like a bug if he so desired. Yet she was standing in front of him with her chin out and her "dare me" attitude wrapped around her like a shawl.

It also got him thinking. She was challenging him, and no one in their right mind would do that—not in this manner, about something so vital—unless they could back it up. Would they?

"So your assertion is that if the file is still there, hidden amongst your other belongings, then you couldn't have betrayed me and my family's company by selling it, is that it?"

"Yes."

"How do you intend to prove that?"

She took a deep breath, causing her breasts to rise beneath the lightweight material of her daffodil-yellow top. He wondered if it was one he'd had delivered for her, or if she'd brought it stuffed in that ridiculously small knapsack she'd been carrying when she'd arrived.

"I guess I'll have to go home and dig it out." A beat passed as she narrowed her gaze on him and pursed her lips. "Would you believe me if I did?"

Another challenge. Damned if he didn't like that about her. Not enough to give her a free pass, but the benefit of a doubt was a possibility.

"I'd consider it," he said carefully, not ready to promise anything he wouldn't later be willing to deliver.

"Well, that's encouraging," she mumbled half under her breath. Shaking her head, she straightened and looked him in the eye. "Tell me what you want me to do. Should I go to Portland and look for the file, or would you prefer to continue hating me for wrongs you *think* I committed?"

"Oh, you've committed plenty of wrongs, with or without the sale of that design line to our competitors," he reminded her even as he battled a grin.

She was guilty of so much, but she didn't let that hold her back one bit when it came to sticking up for herself. Arguing business with his contemporaries was definitely never this exhilarating.

Then again, no one at Bajoran Designs was as attractive or compelling as Jessica, and he'd never had quite as much to lose —or gain—if he suffered a defeat at their hands.

"We'll go together," he told her. "We can take the corporate jet. Be down there and back in a matter of hours."

Sucking her bottom lip between her teeth, she worried it for a moment, her face reflecting sudden alarm.

"What?" he asked. "Change your mind already? Decide to confess and put an end to the charade before we waste any more time or a load of jet fuel on a wild-goose chase?"

"You're an arrogant ass, do you know that?"

His brows rose. So much for the effectiveness of his harsh features and intimidating demeanor.

"If you must know," she continued sharply, "my parents don't know about Henry."

The shock must have shown in his expression because she flushed crimson and shifted guiltily in her chair.

"I know. I know how terrible that sounds," she admitted, tucking her hair behind one ear and running her fingertips through to the ends. "I'm a horrible daughter. It will crush them when they find out I've been lying and keeping a grand-child from them all this time."

"Then why did you?"

She cast him a glance meant to singe him on the spot. "Can you just hear that conversation? 'Hey, Mom and Dad, I know this will disappoint you, but I'm pregnant from a one-night stand. Oh, but that's not the best part. The *best* part is that the baby's father is our family's arch nemesis, Alexander Bajoran, the man who single-handedly ruined Taylor Fine Jewels and destroyed our lives. Surprise!'"

"Archenemy is a bit strong, don't you think?" he asked with an arched brow.

She gave a snort of derision. "Not amongst the Taylor clan. Your name might as well be Lucifer Bajoran, as far as they're concerned."

Which seemed to be an awfully harsh sentiment to have for a former business associate who hadn't had much at all to do with the split between their families. All of that had taken place quite literally before his time. Alex had been working at Bajoran Designs, of course, but hadn't taken over as CEO until well after the Taylors' departure.

He frowned to himself. Perhaps there was more to the story than he knew, more that he *should* know. He made a mental note to look into it when he got back to the Bajoran Designs offices. Out of curiosity, if nothing else.

"Then what do you propose?" he asked, focusing instead on the matter of visiting Portland so they could retrieve the Princess Line proposal. If it was even still where she claimed it was.

"If we go on Sunday, my parents will be at my aunt's house for brunch. They're usually gone three or four hours, so we should be able to get in and out before they get home."

He thought about that for a minute. "You're really going to sneak into town without letting your parents know you were there? After not seeing them in almost a year?"

Her chest shuddered as she took in a deep, unsteady breath. "If I have to, yes. I told you I was a terrible daughter," she added when he tipped his head quizzically. "I need to tell them, I know that. And I will. Soon. I just…I need time to work up to it, and frankly, I can only deal with one major crisis at a time. At the moment, *you* are the main crisis I'm dealing with."

"Then the sooner we get to the bottom of some very important facts, the better."

"Agreed."

"In that case, let me know exactly what time we need to be at your parents' house, and I'll make all of the arrangements for the trip, including someone to stay here with Henry."

He expected an argument over that, but all she did was nod. Apparently she, too, saw the wisdom in not dragging an infant along on a mission one step up from breaking and entering.

Twelve

"I don't understand. They were right here."

Jessica hoped her voice didn't reflect the panic beating in her chest and at her pulse points.

They were at her parents' home in Portland. A lovely two-story brick house at the end of cul-de-sac in a modest development.

The flight down had been uneventful, and only uncomfortable because Jessica didn't like being alone in such close quarters with Alex. If "alone" included a pilot in the cockpit and one very discreet flight attendant who made herself scarce between serving drinks and asking Mr. Bajoran if there was anything else he required. And if the private plane could be described as "close quarters." It wasn't as large as his mansion, but it wasn't exactly a broom closet, either.

She'd blamed her antsiness on a mild fear of flying and being away from Henry. Only one of those factors actually bothered her, but Alex didn't need to know that. And the sooner they found the folder and got back to Seattle, the better.

Back to her baby, who was probably even now being rocked to sleep by Wendy the nanny. She liked Wendy well enough; she was actually the nanny Jessica would have hired if it had been her choice alone. But that didn't mean she was keen on another woman caring for her child when she should be there with him instead.

The garage attached to her parents' home was large enough for two midsize cars—one of which was currently absent—and all of her belongings from when she'd had to clear out her apartment. Thankfully she didn't own much by way of material possessions.

Even so, she'd gone through everything. *Everything* because the folder with the Princess Line designs inside wasn't where she was almost positive she'd left it. She specifically remembered tucking it away with some of her other important papers and legal documents. Not only for safekeeping, but because she knew it would blend in and wasn't likely to be noticed if anyone snooped through her things.

She couldn't imagine her parents going through her stuff.

Her mother would be like a dog with a bone about the paternity of her first grandchild, but they weren't the nosy sort otherwise. For heaven's sake, she'd quit her job, given up her apartment and taken off for parts unknown, all on a whim, and they hadn't asked a single question. As far as they were concerned, she was traveling, sowing the female equivalent of wild oats and would call if she needed them. Otherwise they assumed no news was good news.

"Maybe they were never there to begin with, and this is just part of your elaborate ruse to convince me they were," Alex said from two or three feet behind her. He'd been standing there, hovering less than patiently while she searched.

"You'd like that, wouldn't you?" she retorted without turning around. She was still on her knees, digging through the same banker's box for the third time in thirty minutes. "One more nail to drive into my coffin. One more reason you'll give the courts to convince them I'm an unfit mother—a *criminal,* even—and that you deserve full custody of Henry."

Frustrated, angry and increasingly frightened he would do just that, she climbed to her feet, brushing off the knees of her jeans.

Facing him, she said, "Well, that isn't going to happen. I'm not lying, and this isn't a ruse. They were *there,* dammit, and I'm going to find out why they aren't anymore."

Big talk when she had no idea how to go about it. But she couldn't let Alex see her uncertainty, not when there was so much at stake.

Think. Think. Think.

Her erratic pulse suddenly slowed, and she realized she *wasn't* the only person who had known about the Princess Line proposal. She'd told her cousin. Shown her the designs, even.

Not to use them against Alex, but to prove she *had* poked around his room the way she'd promised, and also because she'd simply loved the designs. The artist in her had been impressed and unable to resist sharing them with someone she'd thought would appreciate their beauty and intricacy as much as she did. With a few notations on how she would improve upon them, if she could.

That's what they had discussed the morning she'd shown Erin the design sketches. *Not* how they could best go about selling them out from under Bajoran Designs. She would never have done that, regardless of what Alex might think.

As much as she wasn't looking forward to what she had to do, it needed to be done. She owed it to Alex, and at this point, to Henry and herself, too.

"Can I borrow your cell phone?" she asked.

Alex's eyes widened a fraction, the blue of the irises stormy and nearly gray. Whether due to mistrust or the dull light in the interior of the garage, she wasn't sure.

Without a word, he reached into the inside pocket of his suit jacket and removed his phone, handing it over.

Dialing by memory, she waited through three rings for her cousin to answer.

"Erin, it's Jessica." It was strange having this conversation in front of Alex, especially considering what she was about to say, but it wasn't as though she had much choice.

"Erin, this is important," she bit out, cutting into her cousin's fluffy, drawn-out greeting. Once Erin quieted, she said, "What did you do with the design folder I stole from Alexander Bajoran?"

Lord, it hurt to use that word—*stole.* But she'd taken it without permission, so she had to call it what it was.

"What do you mean?" her cousin asked. Too innocently. Even through the phone line, she could tell Erin was feigning naïveté.

"Don't play dumb with me, Erin. I mean it. This is important. I need you to tell me *right now* what you did with the Princess Line designs. I put them with my things in Mom and Dad's garage, but they're missing, and *you* are the only other person who even knew they existed."

Silence filled the space between them for several long seconds. Jessica didn't look at Alex. She couldn't. Instead, she pressed her fingers to the bridge of her nose and prayed she wouldn't break down in front of him, no matter how close to tears she felt.

Finally, in a tone of complete entitlement, her cousin said, "I sold them."

Jessica's heart sank. "Oh, Erin," she groaned, "tell me you didn't. *Please* tell me you didn't really do that."

"Of course I did," Erin replied without a hint of apology.

"That was the plan from the very beginning, after all. To stick it to those Bajoran bastards."

Despite her best efforts, tears leaked from Jessica's lashes. "No, it wasn't," she told her cousin, voice cracking. "That was never the plan. I *never* agreed to anything even close to that."

"Why else were you poking around the man's room, then?" Erin asked haughtily. As though she had any right to be offended.

"Because I was an idiot," Jessica snapped. "And because you convinced me I needed to do something to avenge the family against the evil Bajorans. Which is the most ridiculous idea in history and the stupidest thing I've ever done."

Taking a deep, shuddering breath, she dropped her hand from her face and turned away from Alex. She couldn't bear to look at him or have him look at her, at least directly, while she was making such a soul-shattering confession.

"You had no right to go through my things, Erin. No more right to take that proposal from me than I had to take it from Alex." Her voice was ragged, and she was skating close to the very edge of hysteria. "You have no idea what you've done, Erin."

"Oh, what did I do?" her cousin retorted, snottier than Jessica had ever heard her. "Get a little revenge against a corporate tycoon who used his money and influence to put our family out of business? Make some well-deserved money of my own while screwing the Bajorans out of another couple million they *didn't* deserve? So what."

"No," Jessica murmured, forcing herself to speak past the lump in her throat. "What you've done is betray my trust. Worse, you've done irreparable damage to my life. My reputation. My *son's* life. I can't forgive you for this, Erin. Not ever."

She clicked the button to end the call just as her voice

broke and her lungs started to fight against her efforts to draw in fresh oxygen.

How could Erin have done this to her? She'd convinced Jessica to do the wrong thing, true. And Jessica took full responsibility for having actually done the snooping and taking of the papers.

But she hadn't truly planned to do anything with them. Had fully intended to put them back, and suffered months of guilt when she hadn't been able to. She'd almost traveled all the way to Seattle to return them in person, but had been too afraid Alex would call the police and have her arrested.

That, in fact, had been one of her greatest fears about returning to Seattle with Henry. She'd been beyond lucky that he'd put their son first and not called the authorities on her the moment she stepped into his house.

"Are you all right?"

He spoke softly, his tone kinder than she would have expected given the circumstances. In fact, he hadn't sounded quite so nice since that night at the resort when he'd been intent on getting her into bed. Or according to him, open to allowing her to seduce him.

His hand touched her shoulder. Lightly, almost comfortingly.

Fresh moisture glazed her vision. How could he be so understanding *now* when the evidence was clearly stacked against her? He should be furious. Sharp and accusing, just like before.

"Jessica?" he prompted again.

She shook her head. "I am definitely not all right," she told him with a watery laugh.

Turning back to the stacks and boxes of her things, she started replacing lids and putting everything back in order. It was busywork, something to keep her hands occupied so she wouldn't sit down right in the middle of the hard concrete garage floor and sob uncontrollably.

"I guess that's it," she threw over her shoulder in Alex's general direction. "You win. Erin took the proposal and sold the designs to Ignacio, just like you thought I had. So there's no way to prove my innocence. No way to convince you I'm not the lying, thieving bitch you accused me of being."

"I don't remember using the term *bitch*."

Sliding the last cardboard box onto a short pile of other boxes, she turned to face him. Calmer now, more composed. Resigned.

"I'm pretty sure it was implied," she said, emotionless now.

"No, but perhaps it was inferred," he replied.

Moving toward her, he stopped mere inches away. She still couldn't bring herself to meet his eyes, so she stared at a spot on his blue-and-black-striped tie instead.

"I should probably apologize for that," he continued, surprising her enough that she lifted her head. "I might have been a bit more critical of your actions than was warranted."

Jessica's mouth didn't actually fall open in a big wide O, but she was certainly shocked enough that it should have.

He was apologizing? To her? But she didn't deserve it. She may not have been guilty of *exactly* what he'd accused her of, but she'd undoubtedly put it all in motion.

She hadn't set out to seduce him or to get pregnant, but both had happened because she'd been poking her nose where it didn't belong.

And she hadn't sold the designs for the Princess Line to a competing company, but she had taken them and shown them to her cousin, who'd done just that.

Cocking her head, she studied him through narrowed eyes. "Did I accidentally drop one of those boxes on your head?"

she asked him. And then, "Who are you and what have you done with Alexander Bajoran?"

She was too upset and emotionally wrung dry to mean it as a joke, but one corner of his mouth lifted nonetheless.

"I heard both sides of the conversation. Enough to get the general idea, anyway, and to accept that it was, indeed, your cousin who sold the line proposal to Ignacio Jewelers. Which isn't to say you don't still carry some of the responsibility," he added with a note of severity he wasn't sure he felt.

"What are you saying?" Jessica asked, justifiably suspicious. "That you just…forgive me? Absolve me of guilt for everything I've done since we first met?"

"I wouldn't go quite that far," he replied dryly. "But I'd be a hypocrite—as well as a heel—if I held you responsible for something you didn't technically do. I'll talk to our attorneys, see if there's anything we can do about your cousin's spin at corporate espionage."

He paused to gauge her reaction to that, expecting anything from a heated defense of her family member to hysterical tears and begging for leniency. Instead, her full lips pulled into a taut line and her shoulders went back a fraction.

"I'm sorry," he said, "but we have to at least look into it. Losing those plans cost us millions of dollars."

"No, of course," she responded quickly. "What Erin did was wrong. What *I* did was wrong, but I never would have taken it as far as she did. She made her bed…I guess she'll have to lie in it."

"Strange as it might sound," Alex told her, "I actually believe you."

And he did. Not only because of what he'd heard with his own two ears, but because if she'd made a dime off the Princess Line prospectus, she would have shown at least a modicum of guilt. Or been dancing like a spider on a hot plate trying to wiggle her way out of trouble.

He even had to wonder about his assertion that she'd seduced him that night back at Mountain View to get her hands on company secrets. If that were true, she wouldn't have wasted a moment now trying to seduce him into letting her transgressions slide.

But she wasn't fast-talking, and she didn't have her hand down his pants. More's the pity on the latter. She'd simply admitted her part in the whole ordeal, all but assuming the position and waiting for the cops to slap on cuffs.

That was not the behavior of a liar, a cheat or—quite frankly—a gold digger. The verdict was still out on Henry and her purpose in leaving the baby in his boardroom. But since she'd been telling the truth about the majority of charges he'd leveled against her…well, there was a fair chance she was telling the truth about the rest.

Clearing his throat, he stuffed his hands in the front pockets of his slacks to keep from doing something stupid like reaching out to touch her. And not to console her.

He wanted to brush the lock of loose blond hair dusting her cheek back behind her ear. Maybe slide his hand the rest of the way to her nape, thread his fingers into the soft curls there, tug her an inch or two closer….

And from there his thoughts took a decidedly hazardous turn. Better to keep his hands to himself before he risked complicating matters even more than they were already.

"Just because I believe you about your cousin doesn't mean you're off the hook," he told her in a voice that came out rougher than he would have liked.

That roughness wasn't caused by anger but by the fact that he was suddenly noticing the bounce of her blond curls— sans the blue streak of a year ago. The alabaster smoothness of her pale skin. The rosy swell of her lush, feminine lips. And the slight dusting of gray beneath the hazel brown of her eyes, attesting to the stress she'd been under for…he suspected months now.

He hadn't exactly helped alleviate that stress, either, had he? No, he'd added to it in every possible way from the moment she'd walked into his home.

With good reason, he'd thought at the time. But not such good reason now that he knew she wasn't quite the conniving witch he'd made her out to be.

"At the very least," he intoned, "I'd say you owe me one."

She stared at him with eyes gone dull with wariness. "Owe you one…what?"

Rather than answer that question directly, he shrugged a shoulder and finally reached out to take her hand. "I've got something in mind. In the meantime I think we should get out of here. The jet is waiting, and your parents will probably be back soon."

With more familiarity than he thought she realized she was showing, she grabbed his wrist and turned it to glance at the face of his watch.

"You're right, we should go."

She didn't look any happier about leaving than she had when they'd arrived.

"I'm sorry we didn't find what we came here for," she muttered softly as they headed for the garage's service door.

"That's okay." He let her pass first, then followed, closing and locking the door behind them. "I know just how you'll make it up to me."

Thirteen

Though she asked a handful of times on the flight home exactly how Alex expected her to "make it up to him," he wouldn't give her so much as a hint of his plans. Rather than put her out of her misery, he merely smiled a cruel and wicked smile and let her squirm.

Hmph. He was probably enjoying her suffering. He probably didn't have a single clue yet what he was going to ask of her as so-called "repayment"—he just liked having her dangle like a little worm at the end of his hook.

And there was nothing she could do about it. She was at his mercy.

Hunched in the plush leather window seat, the sound of engines roaring in the background, she tried to hold on to her indignation and put on a full pout. The only problem was, she'd never been much of the pouting type. She also knew she deserved a bit of payback for what she'd done to Alex, both the intentional and the unintentional.

That didn't mean she was going to let him walk all over her. If he said he wanted her to assassinate the president or be his sex slave for a month, she'd know he was a crazy person and wasn't as interested in compensation as simply using and abusing her. But if he just wanted her to eat a little crow, she would do her best to sprinkle it with seasoning and choke it down.

Twenty minutes later the plane landed, and Alex accompanied her onto the tarmac and straight to the shiny black Lexus waiting for them. A private airstrip employee opened the passenger-side door, waiting for her to slide inside before rounding the hood and handing the keys to Alex.

They rode in silence until Jessica realized they weren't headed for Alex's estate. At first she thought she just wasn't familiar enough with the area. And then that he was taking a shortcut…except that it turned out to be a long cut. She remembered the route they'd taken from the house to the airport, and this wasn't the reverse of that.

"Where are we going?" she finally asked, finding her voice for the first time in more than an hour.

"You'll see," was all he said, strong fingers wrapped around the steering wheel.

She didn't sigh, at least not aloud. But she did sit up straighter, fiddling with the safety strap crossing her chest while she studied each of the street signs and storefronts as they passed.

Before long, he slowed, easing effortlessly into a parking space in front of a shop called Hot Couture. Sliding out of the car, he came around, opened her door and pulled her up by the hand.

She began to ask again where they were going, but bit down on her tongue before she started to sound like a broken record. He led her across the wide sidewalk and inside the upscale boutique.

Okay, she had to say something. "What are we doing here?"

Everywhere she looked, headless size-zero mannequins were draped in costly bolts of silk, satin, sequins and a dozen other expensive materials she couldn't begin to identify. She'd been away from this sort of extravagance for too long...and hadn't cared for it all that much when she'd been expected to wear gowns like these on a regular basis.

"This is Step One of your penance," he told her as they were approached by a saleswoman who looked as though she'd had her facial features lifted one too many times. Her eyes were a tad too wide, her brows a tad too high, her lips a tad too pursed.

"Good afternoon," she greeted them, focusing her attention much more firmly on Alex than on Jessica. With good reason—Alex looked like every one of the million-plus dollars he was worth, while Jessica was dressed in a pair of worn jeans and a stylish but nondesigner top. They were Daddy Warbucks and Little Orphan Annie...Richard Gere and Julia Roberts...the Prince and the Pauperette.

She rubbed her palms nervously on the legs of her jeans. "This isn't necessary, Alex," she murmured so that only he could hear.

At full volume, he replied, "Yes, it is." Then to the other woman, "We need a gown for a very important gala fundraiser. Shoes and handbag, as well."

The woman looked positively giddy at the prospect of a large commission.

"Alex..." Jessica began.

"I'll take care of the jewelry," he said over the beginning of her protests.

"What kind of fundraiser?" she asked, wanting to know at least that much before she began trying on a year's worth of dresses in the next couple of hours.

"Sparkling Diamonds," he said, naming the well-known charitable organization founded and run by Washington State's most notable jewelers. Since its inception only a few years ago, Sparkling Diamonds had raised hundreds of thousands of dollars to support a variety of worthwhile causes, from childhood cancer to local animal shelters.

"Tuesday night's benefit is being sponsored solely by Bajoran Designs. Some of Seattle's deepest pockets will be there, and we want to rake in as much as possible for this year's literacy campaign. I was planning to go stag, but now that you're here and—as we established—owe me one," he tacked on with an uncharacteristic wink, "you can be my plus-one."

Jessica wasn't entirely sure how she felt about that. Getting dressed up and going to a swanky party with Alex? Hanging on his arm all night with a smile on her face while they mingled with people who might recognize her as a Taylor Fine Jewels Taylor? Oh, the rumor mills would be rife with chatter after that. Word might even get back to her parents.

She thought she might prefer to undergo an extra hot bikini wax. But then, she didn't have much of a choice, did she? And after her conversation with Erin, the cat was pretty much out of the bag, anyway.

"Literacy is important," she said by way of answer.

"Yes," he agreed, rare amusement glittering in his too-blue eyes, "it is. The event is also a chance to show off a few of the company's latest designs. Ones we've been unveiling instead of the Princess Line."

There it was. Knife inserted and twisted forty degrees clockwise. It pinched, just as he'd known it would.

"You'll be wearing the most significant pieces. Yellow gold and diamonds, so they'll go with almost anything."

Turning his attention back to the saleslady, he said, "I want her to look absolutely stunning. Find a dress that showcases her natural beauty."

Inside her chest, Jessica's heart fluttered, heat unfurling just below the surface of her skin. If she weren't fully aware of the situation and where each of them stood, it would be all too easy to be flattered by that comment. After all, Alex was a very charming man. Isn't that how she'd ended up in bed with him in the first place?

But he wasn't trying to be charming. He wanted her dressed up and pretty to impress donors at his charity event. She was sorely out of practice, but that was something she could definitely do.

"Yes, sir," the woman replied, money signs glowing in her eyes along with her wide smile.

Jessica followed her silently to the rear of the store, listening with only half an ear to the older woman's cheerful chatter. Leaving Jessica in the changing room to strip, she went in search of gowns that would meet Alex's high standards.

An hour later, Jessica felt like a quick-change artist. She was tired and out of sorts, and just wanted to get home to see Henry.

She'd tried on so many dresses, she couldn't remember them all. After viewing the first few, even Alex had seemed to lose interest. He'd made low, noncommittal noises, then told her he trusted her to make a final decision before wandering off to talk on his cell phone.

Another six or eight gowns later, Jessica was pretty sure she'd found one that would pass muster. It was hard to be sure how anything would look with the jewelry he had in mind, since she hadn't actually seen the pieces for herself, but he'd described them briefly and she did her best to imagine them with each of the gowns she modeled.

She needed just the right color, just the right neckline. Just enough sparkle to shine, but not *out*shine the jewelry itself.

She'd forgotten how stressful the whole socialite thing could be. There was a reason she hadn't missed it. Much.

It didn't help, either, that her performance needed to be perfect this time. It wasn't just a public appearance or a high-priced fundraiser. It was one of her only options for redemption with Alex and getting into his good graces. There was still so much he could hold against her. So many ways he could punish her, if he so desired.

Licking her dry lips, she finished putting on her street clothes, then carried the gown she'd decided on—albeit uncertainly—out of the dressing room.

"We'll take this one," she told the sales lady.

"Excellent choice," the woman agreed, taking the gown and carrying it to the counter.

Jessica was pretty sure she'd have said the same thing about a gunny sack, as long as Alex was willing to pay a high four figures for it.

A few minutes, later she had shoes and a matching clutch, all of it wrapped up with tissue paper in pretty boutique boxes, ready to go. When the sales woman recited the total, Jessica's eyes just about bugged out of her head and her throat started to close.

It was almost as though she was having an allergic re-action to spending so much money for *one* night out on the town. She had half a notion to tell Alex that if everybody who planned to attend the fundraiser would simply donate the amount they would have spent on getting dressed up for the evening, they wouldn't need to hold the event at all.

It had been a long time since she'd poured money like that into anything that couldn't be eaten, driven or lived in, but the outrageous total wouldn't make a man like Alex so much as blink.

As though to prove her point, he seemed to appear out

of nowhere, passing his platinum card to the clerk over her shoulder.

The sales woman flashed a delighted grin. Thirty seconds later, Alex and Jessica were headed back to the car, expensive packages in tow.

"You found something you like, I take it?" he said once they were on the road again, finally on their way to his estate.

A knot of eager anticipation tightened in her stomach. She couldn't wait to get there and see her baby. They'd only been gone a day—not even a full day, really—but she wasn't used to being away from him. She'd missed him and wanted to see how he'd fared with the nanny Alex had hired—possibly on a permanent basis.

"Yes," she responded, trying to keep her mind focused on the conversation rather than the fact that Alex was driving the speed limit. He could have gone a *few* miles over without risking a ticket, for heaven's sake.

"I hope it's all right. It was hard to pick something to go with the jewelry you have in mind when I couldn't actually try them on together."

"I'm sure they'll be fine. The fundraiser starts at eight. Dinner will be served around nine-fifteen. Can you be ready to leave by seven?"

"Of course." It wasn't as though she had anything else to do or anywhere else to be aside from wandering around Alex's enormous house and spending time with Henry. She could be ready by seven o'clock *tonight,* if he needed her to be.

And in a way, she wished they were attending the charity function tonight. At least then it would be over and she wouldn't have to spend the next day and a half dreading the evening to come.

Alex stood in his den, one hand braced against the mantle of the carved marble fireplace, the other slowly swirling the ice cubes in his glass of scotch. He studied the empty hearth, lost in thought.

Jessica would be down soon to leave for the Sparkling Diamonds fundraiser. How the evening would proceed wasn't at the forefront of his mind, but Jessica certainly was.

After discovering that she wasn't the mastermind behind the theft of the Princess Line designs, he'd begun to wonder what else he might have been wrong about where she was concerned. Could she be telling the truth about everything?

She wasn't one hundred percent innocent, that was for sure. But for each wrongdoing he knew about or had accused her of, she'd come clean.

So what if she was also telling the truth about Henry being his son? He hoped she was, actually. It was a can of worms just waiting to be opened, but having Jessica and the baby under his roof had turned out to be a unique and surprisingly enjoyable experience.

He was just as attracted to Jessica now as he had been the first time he saw her. No matter what had happened in the year since, he still wanted her. His mouth still went dry the minute she walked into the room. His fingers still itched to stroke her skin and peel the clothes off her warm, pliant body.

And the baby...well, he'd been more than a little put off at first, but now he had to admit he was quite smitten. It was hard as hell to wear a mask of indifference, waiting to find out *for sure* whether or not Henry was his son. Not when he spent every day wanting to shed his suit and get down on the floor to tickle the baby's belly, dangle brightly colored plastic keys or play hide-and-seek behind his own hands just to hear the little boy giggle.

Then at night he lay in his big king-size bed imagining Jessica down the hall, sleeping alone. More than once he'd nearly tossed back the covers and marched over to join her...

or drag her back to sleep with him. Not that he had any intention of letting her fall asleep.

Pushing away from the fireplace, he crossed to his desk, setting aside his drink to flip open the file he'd read once before. He needed time to digest the information inside, figure out exactly what to do about it. But even as he rolled it over in his head, he looked the papers over again and was just as stunned and sickened as he'd been when he'd first seen them.

Jessica had mentioned that her cousin blamed him for the Taylors being driven out of business with Bajoran Designs. To his knowledge the decision had been mutually arrived at by the individual heads of each company. At the time that had been Jessica's father as CEO and her uncle—Erin's father, as it turned out—as CFO on the Taylor Fine Jewels side, and Alex's father as CEO and Alex's uncle as CFO on the Bajoran Designs side.

Both companies had been started separately by brothers—Alex's and Jessica's grandfathers and great-uncles. Then they'd joined together because all four brothers had met, formed a strong bond of friendship and thought Fate was trying to tell them something. And it had been a wonderful, very lucrative partnership for many years.

As far as Alex knew, the Taylors had simply decided to go back to being a separate business. His father had assured him the split was amicable and that everything had been taken care of before he'd retired and Alex had taken his place.

Of course what Alex and his family had learned only *after* his father had stepped down, and a few months before his death, was that the elder Bajoran's memory had started to slip. From the moment Alex had taken over the role of CEO, he'd been putting out small fires that his father had unintentionally set ablaze.

This, though…this wasn't a small fire, it was a damn inferno.

Oh, nothing that would harm Bajoran Designs. On the contrary, Bajoran Designs had come out miles upon miles above Taylor Fine Jewels.

But that made Alex far from happy. The bottom line was not more important to him than honor, integrity and proper business ethics. He didn't feel good about the fact that they'd apparently forced the Taylors out of the partnership and probably screwed them out of millions in profits.

The question now became *who* was responsible for that turn of events. It wasn't his father. The man might not be here to defend himself or even question, but Alex knew in his bones that his father would never have done something like that. Not to a business partner, and especially not to one he also considered a friend.

He highly doubted it had been his uncle, either. The two brothers were cut from the same cloth—honest and trustworthy to a fault.

The company investigators he'd put on the case had turned up these initial records fairly quickly, but they hadn't yet tracked down the name of the person who had put this ball in motion. He expected the information to come through any day now, and then he would have to deal with it.

But that was business. Jessica was personal, and he wasn't quite sure what to do about her or the way this information impacted her, as well as the rest of her family.

At the very least an apology was in order, even though he'd awakened that morning thinking she still owed him one.

A soft tap at his office door had him straightening up, closing the file and slipping it into one of the desk drawers for safekeeping. Then, clearing his throat, he called, "Come in."

Mrs. Sheppard poked her head in and said, "Miss Taylor asked me to tell you she's ready and waiting in the foyer."

"Thank you."

The nanny—who was turning out to be an excellent

choice, despite Jessica's original protests—was already upstairs with Henry, and his driver had been sitting outside in
the limo for the past half hour. Grabbing the jewelry box he'd
brought home with him that afternoon and the lightweight
camel hair coat he'd had special ordered for Jessica for this
evening, he headed toward the front of the house, his footsteps echoing in the cavernous emptiness.

He saw just the back of her head over one of the main
stairwell's newel posts as he rounded the corner. Then, as
he drew closer, she heard his approach, turned and took a
step in his direction.

His heart lurched, slamming against his rib cage hard
enough to bruise, and he faltered slightly, nearly tripping
over his own two feet.

This was why he'd had to walk away at the boutique on
Sunday. He'd waited while she'd changed into two different
gowns, then stepped out of the dressing room looking like a
supermodel hitting the end of a Paris runway…or an angel
dropped straight from Heaven.

His heart had thudded then, too, threatening to burst right
out of his chest, and other parts of his body had jumped to
attention. Whether it was a white spaghetti strap sheath or
long-sleeved red number, she'd made everything she put on
look like a million bucks.

He'd had to feign indifference and use phone calls as an
excuse to escape before he'd done something phenomenally
stupid, like giving the saleslady a hundred dollars to take off
and lock the door behind her so he could push Jessica into
the changing room and make love to her right up against the
wall. He'd broken into a cold sweat just thinking about it.

And that was before she'd landed on *the* dress, added ac-
cessories and done her hair and makeup to match. She was
so beautiful, she literally took his breath away. His lungs
burned from a lack of oxygen, but he couldn't have cared less.

The dress she'd chosen was a sapphire-blue that leaned toward turquoise and made the hazel of her eyes positively pop. It would have clashed horribly with the rebellious near-navy blue stripe that used to be in her hair. Her now all-blond tresses were swept up from her nape, held in place by invisible pins to leave her shoulders and the column of her long neck bare.

The gown was classically understated. A strapless, slightly curved bodice hugging the swell of her breasts…a wide swath of sparkling rhinestones circling the high waist…and yards of flowing blue fabric falling to the floor, with a sexy slit running all the way up to reveal a mouthwatering expanse of long, sleek leg when she moved.

Though she'd balked, Alex had finally convinced her to go into town for a quick mani-pedi. The pampering had done her good, and he'd been sure to spin the suggestion as part of the payback for her lies and thievery. And now her freshly painted toes peeked out of the strappy, diamond-studded heels that poked out from beneath the hem of the gown.

Alex didn't know how long he'd been standing there, drooling like a dog over a particularly juicy steak, but it must have been a while because Jessica's eyes narrowed in concern and she glanced down the line of her own body, checking for flaws. Of which there were absolutely none.

"What's wrong?" she asked, returning her gaze to his. "Don't you like the dress? I told you I shouldn't be the one to choose. It's *your* fundraiser, you should have—"

He cut her off midrant. "The dress is fine. More than fine," he said, grateful his voice came out only a shade rusty and choked.

Her chest rose as she inhaled a relieved breath, drawing his attention to all that lovely pale skin and the shadow of her cleavage. He couldn't decide if he was delighted or annoyed that he now got to decorate it with some of the shining jewels from Bajoran Designs' most recent unveiling.

He knew they would look amazing on her, even if she outshone them just a bit. But on the downside, draping her neck with shimmering diamonds would drag everyone else's eye to something he preferred to keep to himself.

"Do you have the jewelry you want me to wear?" she asked, seeming to read his mind.

He held out the large leather case, embossed in gold with the Bajoran Designs logo. Flipping open the lid, he let her see what lay on the blanket of black velvet inside.

"Oh," she breathed, reaching out red-tipped fingers to touch the necklace's center gem. "They're beautiful."

And yet they paled in comparison to the woman standing in front of him.

Tossing the coat he'd gotten for her over the banister, he set the jewelry box on the flat top of the newel. "Here, let me put them on you."

He started with the bracelet, slipping it on her wrist, and then the oversize dinner ring on the middle finger of her opposite hand. Her ears, normally glittering with multiple studs and tiny hoops, were completely bare, leaving room for his earrings and his earrings alone. Since he didn't want to hurt her, poking around trying to get the fish hooks into the proper holes, he handed the three-inch dangle earrings to her and let her insert them on her own.

"Spin around," he told her, reaching for the pièce de résistance.

Lifting the necklace up and over her head, he waited for her to arrange it in just the right spot before fastening the latch at the back of her neck. He let his fingers linger on her smooth skin, lightly stroking the tendons that ran from nape to shoulders, down to the delicate jut of her collarbones and then back up to cup her shoulders, stroking all the way down the length of her arms.

Circling one wrist, he lightly tugged her around to face him once again. The diamonds at her throat and ears twinkled in the light of the giant chandelier far overhead. But his gaze wasn't locked on the priceless set of jewels that were supposed to be the focal point of tonight's event. Instead, he was struck mute by the brilliant facets of Jessica herself.

Her fingers fluttered up to touch the netted V-shape of the necklace crossing her chest. Even without seeing them ahead of time, she'd chosen the most ideal gown possible to display the jewelry he'd intended to have her wear.

"Would you be offended if I said this set is much prettier than most of the pieces in the Princess Line?" she asked.

He gave a low chuckle. Leave it to Jessica to speak her mind, even when she thought she was in the doghouse.

"It better be. We really had to scramble to make up for that loss. We needed something to release in its place that would make just as much of a splash. Or so we hoped."

She tugged one corner of her lower lip, glossy with red lipstick, between her teeth. "Are you trying to make me feel worse about that than I already do?"

"Actually, no. I wouldn't give up this moment, seeing you in this dress wearing these particular pieces, for anything in the world."

She blinked at him, eyes round with disbelief. He was a little surprised that the words had come from his own mouth, but he wasn't sorry. After all, it was the absolute truth.

Another absolute truth was that if he'd had a choice in the matter, he'd say to hell with the Sparkling Diamonds fundraiser, scoop Jessica into his arms and carry her upstairs to his bed where she belonged. Or where he wanted her, at any rate. Almost more than his next breath.

His hand tightened on her wrist and he had to make a concerted effort to lighten his grip before he hurt her. Or followed through on his baser instincts.

"We should go," he murmured reluctantly. Lifting his free hand, he brushed the back of his knuckles along her cheek to her ear, pretending to straighten an earring.

She gave a small nod, but didn't look any more eager to move than he was.

"Here," he said, reaching for the ladies' camel hair coat. He was glad now that he'd chosen to order one in black. It went beautifully with her gown, but would have gone with a dress of any other color, as well.

He held it for her and she turned to slip her arms into the sleeves. Pulling the front closed, she lightly knotted the belt at her waist then took his elbow when he offered.

Crossing the polished parquet floor and stepping outside to climb into the waiting limousine, Alex let himself imagine, just for a moment, that this was real. That Jessica was his and that going out with her for a night on the town was the most normal thing in the world.

As would be coming home late, crawling into the same bed together and making love until dawn.

Fourteen

Two hours into the fundraiser, Jessica was ready to go home. Not because it wasn't enjoyable, but simply because she'd forgotten how exhausting events like this could be.

Once the thousand-dollar-a-plate dinner had been served and consumed, it was all about mingling. Rubbing elbows, making polite conversation, promoting your company and raising money for the cause du jour.

To his credit, Alex was a pro at it. There must have been close to two hundred people in attendance, but he acted as though each person he talked to was the *only* person in the room. He was charming and handsome, and positively oozed self-confidence.

Everyone they met was treated to the same suave greeting, which included introductions, questions about the other person's family and/or business, and then idle chitchat until Alex found an opening to bring up both a reference to Bajoran Designs and a request for a healthy donation. Jessica didn't know who was in charge of collecting checks, but she would be willing to bet his or her head was spinning in delight by now.

She was also relieved that even though Alex was introducing her by her real name, and she was sure most of the guests recognized her for exactly who she was, nobody seemed to be giving her curious looks or talking behind their hands about a Taylor returning to the fold on the arm of a Bajoran.

That wasn't to say the grapevine wouldn't be ripe with fresh rumors by morning, but at least no one was making an issue of it this evening.

Breaking away from the latest group of smiling faces, Alex put a hand at the small of her back and led her on their continued circuit of the room.

In addition to key Bajoran Designs executives and board members wearing the latest pieces of jewelry to show off, there were blown-up full-color signboards on easels arranged throughout the large ballroom featuring other Bajoran designs. It was an enticing display. Jessica had noticed more than one woman already decked out in her weight's worth of gold and jewels admiring what Jessica suspected would be her—or more likely, her husband's—next acquisition.

And for some reason she was inordinately pleased. She loved the jewelry business, loved the sparkle of priceless gems and the intricacies of the designs themselves. Hadn't realized just how much she'd missed it, actually. And even though she and her family were no longer involved in it the way they'd once been, she still wanted Alex's company to be successful.

Alex slowed his step when he noticed her studying one of the extraneous designs more closely than the others photographed on a background of bright pink satin.

"Do you like it?" he asked softly.

"Of course. Your company does very nice work."

"Very nice?" he replied.

When she tipped her head in his direction, she saw that one dark brow was notched higher than the other.

"Shouldn't you be swooning and dreaming of the day you can wear that necklace around your own neck?"

She gave a low chuckle. She was already wearing a lovely necklace from Bajoran Designs worth probably twice as much as the one in the oversize photo. Not that either of them would be very practical in her day-to-day life unless she sold them for things like food and diapers.

To Alex she said, "You forget that I used to be around jewelry like this all the time. After a while it loses a bit of its allure."

He leaned down to whisper in her ear. "Shh. Don't let anyone hear you say that or we'll lose customers."

She laughed again. "Sorry," she returned in an equally low, equally conspiratorial voice.

"So why were you studying this one so intently?"

Shrugging a bare shoulder, she turned back to it. "There are just a few things I would have done differently, that's all."

It took a second for Alex to reply. Then he asked, "Like what?"

She worried her bottom lip for a moment, not sure she should say anything. Then with a sigh, she decided she probably couldn't get into any more trouble with him than she already was.

"The metalwork is a bit heavy-handed," she said, pointing to the spots she was talking about. "These stones don't need that thick a setting. If the gold were a bit thinner, more of the emeralds would show and the whole thing would have more sparkle to it."

One beat passed, then two.

"What else?" he asked.

"I might have gone with more slope to the design." She ran

her finger over the outline of the piece to illustrate her point. "This is very boxy, whereas more curvature would lay better against a woman's chest and be more appealing to the eye."

This time, more than a couple of beats passed in silence. She'd counted well past ten and begun to sweat before she twisted slightly to face him.

His expression was inscrutable. The only thing she could tell was that his eyes had gone dark and he was studying her as though he expected her to burst into flames at any moment. And she just might, if her embarrassment grew much hotter.

She opened her mouth to apologize, backpedal as much as possible, but he cut her off.

"How do you know so much about this stuff?"

Caught off guard, she rolled her eyes and said the first thing that popped into her head. "Hello? Jessica Taylor, Taylor Fine Jewels. I told you, I grew up around all of this. Before my family and your family went their separate ways, I was in line to start designing for the company on an official basis. But even before then, my father let me offer suggestions on existing design specs."

She turned toward the crowd, watching until she spotted just the right example. "See that woman standing over there in the too-short red dress?"

Alex followed her line of sight. "I don't think it's too short."

With a snort, Jessica murmured to herself, "Of course you don't." He probably didn't think the dress was too tight for the woman's build, either, considering how much of her breasts were popping out.

Then to him she said, "The earrings and necklace she's wearing are mine. Marquise-cut diamonds in a white gold setting, with a lone ruby as the main focal point. My father made me work with one of the company's design teams, but only to be sure everything was done correctly. Otherwise, he told them to give me free reign."

Jessica could feel that she was smiling from ear to ear, but she couldn't help it. Perfecting and designing those pieces, working at her family's company and having her father show so much faith in her had been one of the happiest times of her life. She'd so been looking forward to doing that every day. Not just on a whim or trial basis, but as a career.

For the first time, she realized she shouldn't have given up on that dream so easily. She'd been so busy starting a new life that she'd lost sight of those goals. Even if it had been in another city, for another company, she should have found a way to continue designing.

Once again the stretch of silence from Alex brought her head around. His sharp blue gaze made her pulse skitter and sent a shiver rippling under her skin.

"The only other time I've ever seen you smile like that is when you're playing with Henry," he told her, his tone so low and intense, her chest grew too tight for her lungs to draw in a breath. "Why didn't I know about any of this before?"

Jessica blinked, her fingers curling into the palm of one hand and around the rhinestone-studded satin clutch in the other. He was moving too fast for her, jumping from business to personal, personal to business, too quickly for her to keep up. Not with the conversation, but with the feelings he was stirring inside of her and with what she *thought* he might be conveying with his suddenly severe expression.

Was the heat of his gaze banked passion or tightly controlled anger? She couldn't tell for sure, but from the arousal coiling low in her belly, she found herself hoping it was the former. As dangerous as that thought was.

Licking her dry lips and swallowing until she thought she could manage clear and normal speech, she said, "I guess my father never told anyone. Maybe he was waiting to see how I performed and whether my pieces actually sold before taking steps to hire me into the company officially."

Reaching out, he brushed a tendril of hair away from her face, letting the backs of his fingers skim her cheek. Sparks of electricity went off in her bloodstream at the contact, raising goose bumps over every inch of her flesh.

"We didn't manufacture very many of that design," he said softly, the words barely penetrating her hormone-addled brain. "But they sold very, very well."

She blinked, pleasure flooding her at his admission.

"I even remember commenting that we needed to put out more pieces like that on a larger scale, but I never thought to ask for more from the actual designer. I simply assumed they were the result of a design team's efforts."

"If you're saying all of this just to be nice or to butter me up for something, please don't tell me the truth yet," she murmured, letting her eyes slide closed on the riot of sensations washing through her. "Let me savor this feeling just a while longer."

Eyes still closed, she smelled Alex moving closer a second before she felt his warm breath fan her face. His aftershave was an intoxicating mix of spicy citrus and sandalwood that she remembered intimately from their single night together. Now, as she had then, she inhaled deeply, wanting to absorb his scent and carry it with her from that moment on.

His mouth pressed against hers. Soft, but firm. Passionate, but not at all inappropriate given their current location and how large an audience they might be attracting.

He pulled away long before she was ready, leaving her cold and lonely. Her eyes fluttered open and she almost moaned with disappointment.

Still standing close enough to draw undue attention, he whispered quietly, "I meant every word. Although I do have a question for you that you might think I *was* buttering you up for."

His thumbs stroked the pulse points at her wrists, which she was sure were pounding harder than a jackhammer.

"For the record, I wasn't. You can say no, even though I sincerely hope you'll say yes."

Yes. Yes, yes, yes! She didn't even know what the question was yet, but the word raced through her mind, anyway, rapidly multiplying like furry little bunnies. She almost didn't care what he asked— Will you marry me? Will you sneak into the ladies' room and let me take you against the vanity? Would you like brown sugar on your oatmeal?—she wanted to say yes.

Her voice cracked as she made herself say, "All right. What is it?"

So many words. And she sounded so reasonable, when inside she was flailing around like a passenger on a tilt-a-whirl.

"Will you come home with me?"

Some fragment of her brain thought that was a silly question.

"I have to," she told him. "You're making me stay with you until the paternity results come back."

His lips curved in a patient smile. "No," he said softly. "You know what I mean. Let me take you home, to my bed. Spend the night with me the way I've been wanting you to since you came."

She nearly wept. Inside she actually whimpered. If he only knew how hard it had been to lie in bed all those nights, alone, knowing he was only two doors away. She'd thought about him, fantasized about him, even cursed him. And then, once she'd fallen asleep, she'd dreamed about him.

"What about your fundraiser?" she asked, needing to buy a little time for her heart to slow its frantic gallop and her mind to be sure—really, really sure—she could deal with the consequences of her answer.

"There are others here who can see it through to the end. And if we don't get out of here soon, it's possible they'll be in for more of an evening than they bargained for. We're talking full-out, triple-X public displays of affection right here in the middle of the ballroom."

He emphasized his point by pressing against her, letting her feel the full state of his arousal through his tuxedo slacks and the fall of her gown. She leaned into him, reveling in his palpable desire for her. Though her response wasn't nearly as noticeable, it was just as intense, just as overwhelming.

She also wasn't sure she'd mind if he threw her down on the nearest banquet table and had his wicked way with her, but it might turn into a public relations nightmare for his people.

"Then maybe it would be best if we left," she murmured.

She felt his chest hitch as he sucked in a breath.

"Is that a yes?" he asked, his voice sounding like sandpaper on stone.

"Yes," she answered easily. "It's definitely a yes."

She wanted to laugh at the endearing, lopsided grin he beamed at her. And then they were moving. He spun her around, keeping her in front of him as he steered her across the room, making excuses and lining up others to oversee the rest of the fundraiser in his place. Depending on who he spoke to, he blamed their premature exit either on *his* early meeting schedule the next morning or *her* phantom headache.

Finally they were in his limo, pulling away from the hotel portico and racing toward his estate.

As soon as the chauffeur had closed the door behind them, Alex was on her, devouring her mouth, running his hand up and down her leg through the slit in her gown, anchoring her to him with an arm around her back.

Her fingers were in his hair, loving the silky texture and holding him in place while her tongue tangled with his. The plush leather of the wide seat cushioned them and brushed against the bare skin of her shoulders and back, making her realize they'd left the benefit without a thought for the coats they'd checked at the beginning of the evening or the chill in the late-night air.

Breaking the kiss, Alex panted for breath, his hands never pausing in their rabid exploration of her body through the sleek material of her gown.

"I want to take you right here," he grated, "so I'll never again be able to ride in this car without thinking of you."

Her heart did a little flip. "Then what are you waiting for?" she asked in a soft voice. Thankfully the privacy window was up—and she hoped soundproof.

His teeth clicked together, a muscle throbbing in his jaw. "Not enough time," he bit out. "But soon. Believe me—very soon."

With that, he pulled away, tugging her down to lie almost flat along the wide seat.

"What are you—?" she started to ask, but his hands were beneath her skirt, finding the elastic waistband of her panties.

In one swift, flawless motion, he had them down her legs and off. Then he was pushing aside the folds of the dress, leaving her naked from the belly button down except for the diamond-studded heels strapped to her feet.

Sliding to the limousine floor, he knelt there, a wolfish grin slashing his face and flashing straight white teeth. His hands at her hips tugged her forward, then gently parted her knees.

A quiver of anticipation rushed over her, pooling low in her belly. "Alex—" she whispered in a halfhearted protest, but it was already too late.

Lowering his head, he brushed kisses along the insides of

both thighs, leading upward until he reached her mound and pressed one there, as well. His lips moved over her, nuzzling the sensitive flesh and burrowing between her damp folds swollen with arousal.

He tortured her with long, slow strokes of his tongue that made her back arch and her nails dig into the leather seat cushions. She whimpered, writhed, panted for breath. Alex merely hummed his approval and redoubled his efforts to drive her out of her mind.

He licked and nibbled, flicked and suckled until Jessica wanted to scream. She was pretty sure *that* sound wouldn't remain on this side of the privacy window, however, so she squeezed her eyes shut and bit her lips until she tasted blood.

A second later, the limousine started uphill, rolling them together even tighter and pressing Alex more fully between her legs. His lips and tongue and fingers hit just the right spot with just the right amount of pressure to make her shatter, her insides coming apart in sharp, mind-blowing spasms of pleasure.

When she regained consciousness—because she truly believed she might have fainted from pure physical delight—Alex was hovering over her, smiling like a cat who'd just figured out how to unlock the birdcage. Her legs were demurely draped across his lap, her dress rearranged to cover them.

"We're home," he said quietly, leaning in to brush his fingers through her hair, which she was pretty sure was a tangled mess by now, no longer pinned in the lovely swept-up twist she'd fought so hard to get right only hours before.

With his help, she sat up, struggling to get her bearings and stop her cheeks from flushing bright red with awkwardness. It didn't help that the front of Alex's pants were noticeably tented by the bulge of his erection.

Spotting the direction of her gaze, he chuckled, shifting

slightly to alleviate the pressure behind his zipper. Then he reached down and plucked a scrap of sheer blue fabric from the car floor.

She held out her hand, expecting him to return the lost article of clothing. Instead, he dangled it from one finger, continuing to grin.

"Alex, those are my underwear," she said on a harsh whisper. Not that anyone else was around to hear. "Give them back."

"Nope."

She made a grab for them, but he slipped them into the pocket of his tuxedo jacket before she even got close. Sliding across the seat, he opened the door and stepped out, reaching a hand back to help her out.

"Come on. Let's go inside before Javier asks what all that screaming was about."

Fifteen

"Oh, no," Jessica groaned in utter mortification.

Taking his hand, she followed him to the house as fast as she could, making a concerted effort not to look around for fear she'd make eye contact with Alex's driver and die of humiliation right there on the front drive.

Once inside, he slammed the door shut, then spun her around to press her back flat to the thick wooden panel. His body boxed her in, arms braced on either side of her head, chest and hips and upper thighs pressing against her like a big, warm, heavy blanket.

His mouth crashed down on hers, stealing her breath and reviving every sensual, red-blooded nerve ending in her body, even the ones she'd thought had gotten their fair dose of pleasure for the night. She gripped the lapels of his jacket, hanging on for dear life while their tongues mated and their lips clashed hard enough to bruise.

One minute she was standing upright, pressed to the front

door. The next she was biting off a yelp of surprise as he swept an arm behind her knees, placed another at her back and yanked her off her feet.

Reluctantly, he pulled his mouth from hers and turned to march up the stairs. He carried her as though she weighed no more than Henry, but still she could feel his heart pounding beneath the layers of tuxedo jacket and dress shirt.

She kept one hand flattened there on his chest, the other toying with the short strands of hair at his nape. All the while she pressed light butterfly kisses to his cheek, his jawline, his ear, the corner of his eye, the pulse at his neck.

He growled low in his throat. She gave a long purr in response.

Stopping in the middle of the hallway, he gave a sigh that had her lifting her head. They were standing only a few feet away from the nursery door, which was slightly ajar.

"As much as it pains me," he said, "I don't want you to blame me later for not letting you see Henry before we go to bed. Especially since I intend to keep you there for a very long time. Do you want to run in and check on him?"

Her body might be humming, her blood so hot it was close to boiling her alive, but she was still a mother, and she really did want to see the baby one last time before Alex made her forget her own name.

"Would you mind?" she asked, lips twisted in apology.

He made a face. One that told her he didn't want to waste even a second on anything but getting her naked and between the sheets. But just as she'd always known, he was a good man. A kind, generous, sometimes selfless man.

Without a word, he slowly lowered her to the floor until she was standing none too steadily on her own two, three-inch-heeled feet. Keeping a hand at the small of her back, he walked with her to the nursery door.

Pushing it open, she tiptoed inside. Wendy was sitting

in the rocking chair in one corner, reading beneath the low wattage of the only lamp in the room. She lifted her head and smiled when she saw them.

"How was he tonight?" Jessica whispered, continuing over to the crib. Henry was on his back on the zoo animal sheets, covered almost to his chin by a lightweight baby blanket.

"He was an absolute angel," the nanny said, moving to Jessica's side. "We played most of the evening. I read him a story and gave him a bottle around eight. He's been sleeping ever since."

"That's great," Jessica replied, even though she was a little disappointed he wasn't still awake so she could wish him good-night. Doing the next best thing, she kissed the tips of two fingers then touched them to his tiny cheek. His mouth moved as though starting to smile—or more likely to give an extra suck of his pacifier—and warmth washed through her.

Straightening away from the side of the crib, Jessica thanked Wendy. "You can go to bed now," she told her. "I'm sure he'll be fine for a few more hours, at least."

The nanny nodded and moved back to the rocker to gather her things.

Standing close, having looked into the crib at Henry himself, Alex said, "Keep the monitor with you, if you would, please. We'll be available if you need us for anything, of course, but we'd prefer not to be disturbed tonight, if at all possible."

Jessica was sure that his hand at her waist and the high color riding her cheekbones left nothing to the nanny's imagination.

But she nodded without blinking an eye. "Of course. Not a problem, sir."

"Thank you," Alex murmured, applying pressure to Jessica's waist to get her moving toward the door.

"Thank you," Jessica said again, casting one last glance

over her shoulder at both the nanny and what she could see
of the baby through the slats of the crib. "Good night."

And then she was back in the hall, being hustled next
door to Alex's bedroom. She laughed at his speed and single-
minded determination as he shoved her inside, catching a
quick glimpse of dark wood, a masculine color palette and
sprawling space before he closed the door, shutting out the
light from the hall and locking them in near darkness.

As soon as they were alone, he was on her like a bird of
prey, holding her face in both of his hands while he kissed her
and kissed her and kissed her, turning her round and round
and round as he walked her in circles farther into the room.

"Wait," she breathed between tiny nips and full-bodied
thrusts of his tongue. "Turn on the lights. I want to see your
room."

"Later."

"But…"

"Later," he growled.

She started to smile in amusement, but then his hands
skimmed up the length of her spine, found the miniscule tab
of the gown's zipper and slid it all the way down. The bil-
lowy, strapless blue material fell away from her breasts and
dropped to the floor in a soft whoosh.

Since the dress didn't allow for a bra, and her panties were
currently tucked in the pocket of Alex's jacket, the action left
her completely naked but for her strappy stilettos and all four
pieces of priceless Bajoran jewelry. Cool air washed over her,
cooling the diamonds against her skin, raising gooseflesh
and pebbling her nipples.

Or maybe it was the anticipation of making love with Alex
again after what seemed like forever.

He stepped back, his eagle eyes roaming over her nude-
but-bejeweled form from head to toe. Though how he could
see much of anything in the dark, she didn't know. Only the

faint glow of moonlight shone through the sheer curtains at the windows.

Not that the lack of illumination seemed to bother him. Not letting it slow him down one tiny bit, he shrugged out of his tuxedo jacket and started to undo his tie, collar and cuff links.

One by one, items were discarded, the buttons at the front of his starched white shirt slipped through their holes. Slowly, the hard planes of his chest came into view. Shadows of them, at any rate.

Heart rapping, she closed the scrap of distance between them, covering his hands at the waist of his slacks. His movements stilled and she pushed his hands away entirely.

He let them fall to his sides, giving up so easily. Yet she could feel the tension emanating from his body, in the steel-cable rigidity of his stance and every tightly held muscle.

His chest rose and fell in sharp cadence as she tugged the tails of his shirt out of the waistband of his pants. Pushing the fabric open and off over his shoulders, she let her palms run the full expanse of his wide masculine chest.

Just as she remembered from so long ago, it was broad and smooth, throwing off heat like a furnace. A light sprinkling of hair tickled her fingertips while she explored his flat abdomen; the rise of his pectorals with their rough, peaked centers; the hard jut of his collarbones and the curve of his strong shoulders.

The white material floated to the floor, and she returned her hands to the front of his pants. Sliding them open, she lowered the zipper past his straining erection while he sucked in a harsh breath and held it. She let her knuckles brush along his length through his black silk boxers.

Muttering a curse, he kicked out of his shoes, stripped the slacks and underwear down his muscular legs, and dragged her away from the entire pile of their shed clothing. He walked them over to the large four-poster bed, lifting her onto the end of the high mattress.

He moved in for a kiss, tipping her chin up and cupping her face in both hands. His thumbs gently brushed the line of her jaw while he drank from her mouth. She parted her knees, making room for him in the cradle of her thighs, and he pressed close, brushing every part of her with every part of him.

Her nails dug into the meat at the sides of his waist, then she brought her legs up to hitch her knees over his hips. He groaned, the sound filling her mouth as he leaned into her even more.

A second later she found herself lifted by her buttocks and tossed several inches closer to the center of the bed. Alex came with her, landing on top of her even as she bounced lightly, the glossy satin coverlet cool at her back.

While she wrapped her legs more firmly around him, he buried his face in her neck and began trailing kisses down her throat, tracing the lines of the necklace until it gave way to the bare flesh of her chest and one plump breast. He pressed his mouth dead center, then started to lick and nip all around.

Beneath him, Jessica arched, moaned, writhed. And Alex reveled in every ripple, every soft whimper of sound.

He'd wanted to drape her in his jewels, and now he had. And she was just as glorious as he'd known she would be in nothing but what he'd borrowed from the company safe.

He could hardly believe he actually had her in his bed again.

Different bed. Different city and state. Different year. Maybe even two different people…different than they'd been the first time around, anyway.

But so much was the same. The instant spark between them that quickly turned into a five-alarm fire. The uncontrollable desire he felt for her almost every minute of every day. Her hot, liquid response to his touch.

She humbled him and made him feel like a superhero all at once. And it was quite possible she'd given him a son. An heir. Another Bajoran to someday take over the family business.

That thought made him want to put her up on a pedestal and treat her like a queen. Surround her in swaths of cotton and bubble wrap, and keep her safe for the rest of their lives.

But for now, with her warm and willing beneath him, he most wanted to drive her to the brink and then straight over the edge into mind-bending bliss.

If only he could hold back his own climax long enough to get her there. And the way her legs were wrapped around his hips, her damp heat brushing him in all the right places, was making that more and more impossible.

Her stiff nipple abraded his tongue as he swiped at it over and over again. Around it, her dusky rose flesh puckered and tightened.

With a groan, he moved to her other breast and did the same. Her hands stroked his bare back, his shoulders, through his hair and along his scalp. Her nails scraped and dug and clawed.

Between her legs her warmth beckoned. He burrowed closer, locking his jaw to keep from moaning aloud. Continuing to toy with her nipples and the sensitive area surrounding them, he trailed his hands down her sides, over her hips and the mound of her femininity. She gasped as his fingers found her, and he captured the sound with his mouth.

For long languorous minutes, he explored her feminine core. The soft folds, swollen channel and tight, sensitive bud, all slick with tantalizing moisture.

"Alex, please," she whimpered against his lips, her pelvis rising upward, straining for the pleasure he was so cruelly withholding.

As much as he wanted to keep playing, keep touching and stroking and teasing her for hours on end, he didn't have all that much restraint left, either. Not after a year of celibacy since their last time together and the torturous session in the limousine.

Sliding more closely against her, he let her wet heat engulf him as he slowly pressed forward. He gritted his teeth while she took him inch by inch, her chest hitching beneath him in an effort to continue taking in oxygen. His own lungs burned just like hers, every muscle bunching tight.

"I remember this, you know," he grated, nostrils flaring and mind racing while he tried desperately to distract himself from the incredible sensations threatening to make him come apart at the seams.

She made a sound low in her throat. Part agreement, part desperation.

"I never forgot," he told her, "even though I tried hard to do just that."

Jessica's breath blew out on a shuddering sigh. "Alex?"

"Hmm?"

"Let's talk later, okay?"

She panted the words, her nails curling into his shoulder blades and making him shudder from the top of his scalp to the soles of his feet.

He chuckled. "Okay."

Grasping her about the waist, he yanked her toward him as he thrust, driving himself to the hilt. She gasped, and Alex ground his teeth to keep from doing the same.

Rolling them both to their sides, he held her there, moving inside of her, kissing her while temperatures rose, sensations built and the air filled with the sounds of heavy breathing and needy mewls. Jessica's hands on his body licked like flames. Tiny flicks of pleasure that shot straight to his center.

They rocked together on the soft, wide mattress. Side to side. Forward and back. Tongues mingled while bodies meshed, slowly becoming one. Her hips rose to meet his every thrust, her breasts rubbing his chest.

"Alex," she whispered, pulling her mouth from his to suck in a heartfelt breath. "Please."

She didn't need to beg. He was right there with her, desperate and so close to going over, his bones ached.

Clasping her smooth, bare buttocks, he tugged her closer, then rolled them again so that she was on her back and he was above her, covering her like a blanket. Faster and faster they moved until she was clenching around him and he was straining not to explode.

Which would have been a lot easier if she weren't grabbing at his hair and murmuring, "Yes, yes, please, yes," over and over again in his ear.

"Jessica," he bit out, not sure how much longer he could hold out.

"Alex," she returned with equal urgency. "Alex, please. Now."

"Yes," he agreed, forcing the word past his locked jaw. "Now."

And then he was breaking apart with Jessica spasming around him, her cries of delight filling the room and echoing in his ears.

Sixteen

Jessica stretched and rolled to her opposite side, surprised to find herself alone in the wide king-size bed. All through the night, Alex hadn't let her get more than half an inch from him except to run to the bathroom or peek in on Henry.

He'd wrapped his arms around her, tugged her snug against his long solid frame and held her while they slept. Then he'd woken her with kisses and the light caress of his hands on her skin to make love to her again. And once she'd awakened him the same way.

As nights went, it had been just about perfect.

Finding herself alone with the midmorning sunlight shining through the curtains put a bit of a damper on that perfection, though. It made her wonder if the entire evening had been as wonderful as she remembered. If the feelings she'd felt for Alex and *thought* he might return were real.

Insecurities flooding her, she slipped from the bed, pulling the rumpled coverlet along to tuck over her breasts, letting it trail behind her like a long train. She gathered her dress and shoes and other personal items from the seat of a chair where Alex had apparently collected them from the floor. Checking the hall, she tiptoed to her room and dressed in something other than an evening gown and three-inch heels.

With her hair pulled back in a loose ponytail and her body encased in comfortable cotton and denim, she headed for Henry's nursery only to find the crib empty. Far from being worried, she simply assumed he was with the nanny.

Making her way downstairs, Jessica checked Alex's office first, wanting to see him again, even though she wasn't entirely sure how he would respond to her in the bright light of day. But the room was empty, the door standing wide open and Alex's chair pushed back from his desk.

Turning toward the other side of the house, she trailed along to the kitchen, deciding that even if she didn't find Alex or Wendy and Henry there, she could at least grab a bite of breakfast.

As soon as she stepped into the deluxe gargantuan room, she heard the sounds of her son's giggles over the gentle din of pots and pans, spoons and spatulas. Alex sat in the breakfast nook before the wide bank of tall windows with Henry balanced on one strong thigh.

He was dressed more casually than she'd ever seen him in a pair of simple tan slacks and a white dress shirt open at the collar. Henry had a bib tucked under his chin, and there were small dishes of assorted baby foods on the table in front of them. Alex was obviously attempting to feed him, but he must have been teasing too much because Henry couldn't stop laughing and wiggling around.

Slipping her fingers into the front pockets of her jeans, Jessica strolled to the table. She was a little nervous after what she and Alex had shared last night, but happy, too, to see him so friendly and comfortable with the baby.

"What are you two up to?" she asked in a near singsong voice, sliding onto the bench seat across the table from them.

Raising his head, Alex shot her a wide grin, a spoonful of orange goop—peaches, she assumed—hanging from his free hand.

"Just letting you sleep a little longer," he replied. "And getting to know my son a bit better."

He said it so easily, so casually that she almost didn't catch his meaning. Then the words sank in and her eyes snapped to his.

Her sharp gaze must have been questioning enough, because he gave an almost imperceptible nod. "The doctor called this morning. The test results are positive—Henry is most definitely mine."

Jessica almost couldn't hear for the sound of her heart pounding in her ears. She'd never doubted Henry's paternity, of course—she *knew* Alex was the father for the simple fact that there'd been no other men in her life at the time of his conception...as well as long before and after. But she'd nearly forgotten Alex's doubts, and that DNA results were what they'd both been waiting around for.

Taking a moment to mentally slow her rampant pulse, she swallowed and then cocked both her head and a single brow. "Am I allowed to say *I told you so?* Because I *did* tell you so."

To her surprise, he chuckled, a genuine smile breaking out across his normally stern features. "Yes, you did." His smile slipping a couple of notches, he added, "I hope you know I wanted to believe you. I wanted it to be true, I just... I had to be sure."

His heavy-lidded eyes were storm-cloud blue and almost— she could have sworn—apologetic. She did understand. Alex alone was worth millions of dollars, his family as a group likely worth hundreds of millions. For all she knew, dozens of women had shown up on his doorstep claiming he was the father of their children.

Her own father had run off many a young man he suspected was more interested in the Taylor fortune than in her. It had made dating in high school an adolescent nightmare.

"So what do we do now?" she asked quietly.

Before Alex could answer, Mrs. Sheppard appeared at her elbow, sliding a plate of scrambled eggs and toast in front of her. She added a glass of orange juice and then disappeared again to the other side of the room, well out of earshot.

"Are you going to eat?" Alex asked after she'd sat there a few long minutes staring at the meal but making no move to touch it.

Taking a deep breath, she picked up her fork and stabbed at the eggs but turned her true attention to him instead.

"I'm a little distracted right now," she told him.

"For good reason, I suppose," he said, inclining his head and taking a moment to feed Henry another spoonful of pureed baby breakfast.

"I need to run into the office for a while this morning, but was hoping you'd meet me there later. Do you think you could do that—and bring Henry with you?"

"A-all right," she stuttered, confused by his nonchalance and focus on a topic unrelated to the recent discovery that he was, indeed, Henry's father. "But what about—"

Pushing to his feet, he carried Henry over to her and deposited the baby into her arms instead. Henry giggled, kicked and wiggled until she got him arranged on her own lap. Alex moved the jars of baby food to her side of the table and handed her the tiny peach-caked spoon.

"Just meet me at my office in a couple of hours, okay? Around one o'clock."

He leaned down and pressed a kiss to the crown of her head, ruffling the top of Henry's at the same time.

"Trust me," he added.

Calmly, competently, completely at ease while her insides were jumping around like seltzer water.

Two hours later, almost on the dot, Jessica walked into the Bajoran Designs office building. She wasn't sneaking around this time, hoping to get in and out without being spotted by security. Instead, Alex had made sure a car and driver were available to bring her into the city and drop her off at the front door.

She'd also changed from jeans and casual top to a short burgundy wraparound dress, and put Henry into a long-sleeve shirt covered in cute yellow ducks with a pair of brown corduroy overalls. She didn't know what Alex's intentions were for asking her to come to his office with the baby, but she wanted to be prepared. And knowing she looked good helped to boost her self-confidence.

At least that's what she told herself as she made her way up to the twelfth floor in the main elevator. The doors slid open and she stepped out.

She was a little surprised to find the reception desk and hallway completely empty on a Wednesday afternoon. Not even a receptionist behind the main desk. If the place had been this deserted when she'd left Henry on Alex's boardroom table, she wouldn't have had nearly as much trouble sneaking in and out or been half as nervous about getting caught.

Since Henry's carrier—with Henry strapped safely inside—was getting heavy, she set him on the low coffee table in the waiting area, wondering if she should stay here or go in search of Alex.

Before she could decide for sure, a door opened at the end of the long hallway and voices filtered out. A minute later Alex stepped into view, standing aside while several other men, also dressed in expensive, conservative suits, filed out. The last man exited the room, flanked by two security officers.

He wasn't handcuffed. In fact, they weren't touching him at all. But it was clear they were escorting him, and he looked none too happy about it.

Jessica stayed where she was, watching as the group of men made their way to the elevators, waited for the car to arrive and stepped on. The second elevator carried the angry man and the two security guards to the lobby.

After both sets of doors slid closed, she turned her head to find Alex striding toward her, a warm smile softening the strong lines of his face. From the moment he'd issued the invitation, she hadn't known what to expect. That look encouraged her, made her think they might be here for something other than bad news.

"You came," he said, leaning in to press a light kiss to her mouth. He stroked a hand down her bare arm to thread his fingers with hers at the same time he patted Henry's leg and sent the carrier rocking back and forth.

"You asked us to," Jessica replied carefully, not quite sure what else to say.

"And you trusted me enough to do it, even though I didn't tell you why I wanted you here."

He seemed infinitely pleased by that fact, and she found herself returning his near grin.

"I have a surprise for you," he said. "But first we need to talk."

"All right."

He gestured for her to take a seat on the low leather sofa, then sat down beside her. Their knees brushed, and he reached for her other hand so that he held both of hers in both of his, resting on his upper thigh.

Inside her chest, her heart bounced against her ribs, her

diaphragm tightening with nerves. She had no idea what he was going to say, but she felt like a teenager about to be reprimanded for missing curfew.

"I looked into the problem you mentioned about your family," he told her. When her brows came together in a frown, he clarified. "The belief that Taylor Fine Jewels was forced out of partnership with Bajoran Designs."

She understood what he was talking about, but was no less confused.

"It turns out you were right. For the record," he was quick to point out, "I knew nothing about it. All of that was over and done with before I took over the position of CEO, and behind my father's back. But my cousin George apparently decided he could rise higher and bring in more money for the Bajorans if our two families were no longer in business together."

Jessica's eyes widened. She wasn't all that stunned by Alex's pronouncement, considering she'd known the truth all along. Maybe not the details—about his cousin being the impetus for her family's ruin—but she'd certainly known the rest.

What surprised her was that Alex had listened to her and looked into her claims rather than automatically taking his family's side and dismissing her as crazy or scorned.

"Thank you," she said with a small hitch in her voice.

Knowing what Alex had done—that he'd discovered the truth and was man enough to admit it—suddenly meant the world to her.

It was so much more than she would have expected of anyone...but especially Alex.

"Don't thank me," he said with a shake of his head. "Not when I owe you an apology. What my cousin did was wrong and is what started all the bad blood."

Jessica gave a watery chuckle. "It seems we both have evil cousins hiding in the branches of our family trees. What I did to you back in Portland thanks to *my* cousin was wrong and unfair to you, as well. If you can forgive me for that, I think I can forgive you for something you had absolutely nothing to do with."

Lifting a hand to his lips, he kissed her fingers. "I forgive you," he murmured in a tone so resolved she could never doubt his sincerity.

"I forgave you long ago," he continued, "though I'm not sure I realized it until recently. But I owe you—and your family—more than that."

She started to shake her head. "You don't owe me—" she began, but he cut her off with a smile and the pad of one index finger pressed to her lips.

"It's already done, so just sit there for a minute and let me tell you how I'm making this right."

She swallowed hard, taken aback by his determination on the subject. But she did as he asked, sitting back and giving a short nod to let him finish.

"The man you saw being led out by security…that was my cousin George. The others were board members who came in for an emergency shareholders meeting. Once I explained to them what George had done and showed them definitive proof, they agreed to his immediate termination."

His lips twisted at her shocked gasp. "He only went quietly under threat of having criminal charges leveled against him."

"I can't believe you would fire your own cousin," she whispered.

Alex scowled. "He's lucky I didn't throttle him. I might yet. But that doesn't do much to help your family, so I want you to know that I intend to approach them about going into business with us once again."

Jessica's lungs hitched, her pulse skipping a beat. "Oh, Alex," she breathed.

"Do you think it's something they'll go for?"

"There may be hard feelings at first," she said with a laugh. "The Taylors can certainly be stubborn at times. But once they've had a chance to consider your offer and realize it's genuine, I think they'll be delighted."

On a burst of pure gladness she bounced off the sofa cushion and threw herself against Alex's chest, hugging him tight. "You really are a wonderful man, Alexander Bajoran. Thank you."

His arms wrapped around her, squeezing her back. He cleared his throat before speaking, but even then his voice was rough.

"You're welcome. There's more, though," he said, giving her one last embrace before setting her away from him and taking her hands again.

His chest swelled as he took a deep breath. This next part was delicate. She was either going to be thrilled with him and throw herself into his arms again, or she was going to be furious and possibly slap him a good one.

"Your parents are here," he announced quickly—almost too quickly, like tearing off a bandage. He saw the question in her eyes, the incomprehension on her face.

"What? Why are they… What?"

Mouth dry and pulse racing, Alex tightened his grip on her fingers. "I'm hoping you'll consider sticking around Seattle for a while longer, preferably staying with me so that we can see if this…*thing* between us is as real and as strong as it feels. And in order to do that, your parents need to know where you are—and that they have a grandson."

He'd crossed the line in contacting Jessica's parents behind her back and without her permission, but he hadn't known how else to get all of their problems ironed out and taken care of in one fell swoop. And for some reason it was important to him to get everything out in the open and dealt with *right now*.

There had been too many secrets, too many lies already. Starting years ago with his cousin's slimy, despicable actions toward her family on behalf of his, to as early as this morning when the doctor had called and announced that he *was* indeed Henry's biological father.

That phone call had both elated and disgraced him.

Elated him because he couldn't imagine anything that would make him happier than knowing Henry was his. Especially after last night when he'd pretty much decided he didn't care one way or the other.

Being with Jessica again, in and out of bed, had reignited the same powerful feelings he'd felt for her a year ago, and he'd known he wanted to keep her in his life. Jessica and Henry both, regardless of DNA.

But the test results had shamed him, too, because they reminded him that he'd doubted Jessica to begin with. Doubted her word, doubted her integrity, let pride and suspicions cloud what his heart and gut had been trying to tell him.

Hadn't he known as soon as he'd seen her again that he was in love with her? Hadn't he known the minute she'd told him Henry was his son that she'd been telling the truth?

She'd made some bad decisions, but he had some making up to do, that was for sure. And today's business was a step in that direction.

Still clutching Jessica's hands in his lap, he stroked her long slim fingers distractedly.

"I told them everything. Explained how we met last year, how you tried to steal company secrets to avenge the wrong that had been done to your family. And I told them about Henry."

With each word he uttered, Jessica's eyes grew wider, her expression panicked while the color leeched from her skin. On his lap her hands started to quiver.

"I'm sorry," he told her quickly. "I know it was probably

your place to tell them about the baby and why you disappeared on them, but I didn't want them to feel ambushed once
they arrived. And I sort of hoped that having time to think
during the flight—" he'd sent his own jet to pick them up
"—would help them absorb the turn of events more easily."

"Oh, God," Jessica groaned, dropping her head to rest on
their clasped hands. She was breathing fast and shallow…
he hoped *not* on the verge of hyperventilating.

"Oh, God, oh, God. What did they say?" she asked in a
muffled voice. "Were they angry? Do they hate me? Did my
mother cry? I can't handle it when my mother cries. Oh, they
must be *so* upset and disappointed in me."

Her hysterics were enough to make him chuckle, but he
very wisely held back. Instead, he freed a hand to rub his
wide palm up and down the line of her spine.

"Your mother did cry," he said, remembering his meeting
with them in his office before he'd crossed the hall to deal
with his cousin and the board.

"But I'm pretty sure they were happy tears. She's delighted
to have a grandson, and can't wait to see him. They're eager
to see you again, too, though your father did admit that if
you'd shown up pregnant with my child, they probably would
have been none too pleased. Realizing how they likely would
have reacted to the news helped them to understand why
you've stayed away these past months, I think."

Taking a deep, shuddering breath, Jessica raised her head
and met his gaze. Her eyes were damp and worried.

"Do you really think so?"

He gave her a reassuring smile. "I do. Your parents are
very nice people," he added. "I liked them, and am looking
forward to working with them if they agree to partner with
Bajoran Designs again."

The anxiety in her features seemed to fade as she reached

up to stroke his cheek. "You're something else, you know that?"

Alex quirked a brow. "In a good way or a bad way?"

"Oh, a very good way. I might even go so far as to say amazing, but I don't want you to get an inflated opinion of yourself. Or more of one, at any rate," she teased.

Then she sobered again. "I mean it, Alex. What you've done, all of it, it's…wonderful. And you didn't have to. You didn't have to do any of it. I'd have told my parents everything eventually. And what happened between our families, with the company… It was so long ago, and you had nothing to do with it. You could have let it all go on just as it has been."

"No," he said with a sharp shake of his head and the beginning of a scowl, "I couldn't. I don't want either of us to go into this relationship with baggage."

Jessica licked her lips, eyes darting to the side before returning to his.

"Relationship?" she asked in little more than a whisper.

"Yes." His tone was low, serious. Because this was possibly the most serious, important conversation of his life.

"I meant what I said," he continued, being sure to hold her gaze. "I want you to stay. Move in with me officially, as more than just a temporary guest. I'd really like to see if we can make this work. As a couple. As a family."

For several tense seconds she didn't respond. Except to blink, her thick lashes fluttering over wide eyes.

She was silent for so long, Alex nearly squirmed. Maybe this had been a bad idea. Maybe he was pushing for too much too soon.

As usual he'd forged ahead with his own plans, his own desires, expecting everyone and everything to fall into place just as he wanted it. After all, wasn't that how it had been his entire life?

This was so much more important than anything else

had ever been, though. And it wasn't only about what he wanted—it was about what Jessica wanted, and what was best for both her and Henry.

His ideal would be for them to stay with him. He didn't know if they were ready for forever just yet, but he certainly wouldn't mind if they moved in that direction.

If Jessica wanted something different, however, if her ideal was something else entirely, then he would have to accept that. He would still be in Henry's life, there was no doubt about that. And he didn't think Jessica would ever try to keep him out of it.

When the near-static buzz of intense silence became oddly uncomfortable, Alex cleared his throat and made a concerted effort to loosen his grip on Jessica's fingers. As romantic and sweeping as he'd hoped his actions and this gesture would be, it was a lot to digest. He couldn't blame her for being wary and needing time to consider her options.

"It's all right if you're not ready for something like that," he told her. He kept his tone even, devoid of the disappointment churning in his gut. "I shouldn't have sprung everything on you quite so quickly. I understand if you need time to think it through. And maybe last night was just one of those things. It didn't have to mean anything—"

The pads of two fingers pressed to his lips stopped him midsentence.

"It meant something," she said, barely above a whisper. "And I don't need time to decide anything. Yes—Henry and I would love to move in with you. Your house—mausoleum that it is—" she added with a grin "—is starting to feel like home already. I'm just…surprised you're asking. I'm shocked by all of this," she admitted, leaning slightly away from him and sweeping her arms out to encompass the waiting area and beyond.

Turning back to him, her eyes were warm, her expression

open and inviting. It made his heart swell and his own blood heat to a healthy temperature as it pumped through his veins.

"But, Alex," she began, her voice quietly controlled, "are you sure about this? You were so unconvinced of Henry's paternity, so suspicious of me. I didn't think you felt...*that way* about me."

She wasn't trying to make him feel like a heel, but he did. And if he'd ever needed confirmation that she was one of the most honest, genuine women he'd ever met—*not* a gold digger after his or his family's fortune—her cautious protests would have done it.

With a grin he felt straight to his bones, he brought her knuckles to his lips and kissed them gently. "Maybe I wasn't convincing enough last night."

"Oh, you were plenty convincing. But that's just sex, Alex. What you're talking about is...more. At least if you're saying what I think you're saying."

"I am," he told her. No hesitation, no mincing words. "It was definitely more than just sex between us. Last night and a year ago—I think you know that. From the moment we met," he murmured, alternately brushing the tops of her fingers and the underside of her wrists, "there was something between us. I'm just asking now for a chance to make it work. To see if we have a future together."

A short, shaky laugh rolled up from her throat. "I'd like that. More than you can imagine."

Yanking her to her feet, he held her close and kissed her until they were both gasping for breath.

"I'd like to take you home right now and celebrate properly," he told her, hands tangled in the hair at either side of her head while he cradled her face. "But your parents are still waiting in my office, no doubt growing more agitated by the minute. I know they're eager to see you...not to mention meet their grandson for the first time."

She inhaled deeply, then let the air slip from her lungs in a quavering sigh. "Will you come with us? I don't want to do this alone."

Rubbing his thumb along the full swell of her lower lip, he smiled gently. "You don't ever have to be alone again."

Epilogue

One Year Later...

The ballroom was brimming with guests dressed in tuxedos and designer gowns. Their voices were a loud din, interspersed by laughter and the clinking of glasses.

Beside her, Alex smiled and nodded as an associate droned on about his recent vacation in Milan, while the butterflies in Jessica's stomach fluttered violently enough to break through and fly away.

She tried to pay attention, really she did. And her cheeks hurt from trying to keep such a pleasant smile on her face. Inside, though, she was shaking, her fingers cold and stiff around her flute of champagne.

Apparently noticing her silent distress, Alex wrapped up his conversation with the couple before them and took her elbow to lead her several feet away. There weren't many quiet corners in the overflowing ballroom, but he managed to find one.

"You look like you're going to pass out," he remarked, clearly amused. His hands moved up and down her bare arms, rubbing warmth back into them along with a semblance of normalcy.

"Take a deep breath," he commanded. "Now slow and easy. Relax. You're the guest of honor tonight...you should be walking on air."

She followed his instructions, *tried* to relax and was relieved to feel her pulse slow by at least a couple of beats per minute.

"What if they hate it? What if you lose money? What if they hate *me* and start hating Bajoran Designs? You know the rumor is that I trapped you for revenge, and blackmailed you into bringing my family back into the company."

He had the nerve to chuckle, which earned him a less-than-ladylike scowl.

"Only a few very shallow, catty and jealous people think that. Everyone else—everyone who counts, at any rate—thinks you're delightful and knows how lucky I am that you and your family gave me a second chance."

Continuing in her downward spiral of unladylike behavior, she snorted with disbelief.

Alex lifted a hand to her face, brushing his knuckles lightly along one cheek and into her hair, which was currently loose around her shoulders, streaks of cotton-candy-pink spiraling through the otherwise blond curls.

Another bit of ammunition the gossips relished using against her, but she liked it and Alex claimed it was "hot."

"It's true," he told her. "Just as it's true that you're magnificently talented, and your True Love Line is going to be hugely successful."

Dropping her head to his chest, she inhaled the spicy masculine scent of his cologne and fought not to cry. "I just don't want to embarrass you or make anyone at your company mad for taking a chance on me."

Thumbs beneath her jawline, he raised her gaze to his. "First, you could never embarrass me. And second, it's not *my* company. Not anymore. It's *our* company, which means you have just as much say in what takes place there as I do. Besides, everyone at Bajoran Designs knows incredible natural talent when they see it. Giving you your own line was, as they say, a no-brainer."

That brought a smile to her face, the first honest one of the evening.

"Your family is here," Alex continued. "My family is here. Even Henry is here."

He cast a glance over his shoulder to where their fifteen-month-old son—the only child in attendance—was perched on his grandmother's hip in his adorable miniature tuxedo. He was starting to pull himself up and toddle around now, eager to learn to walk so he could become even more independent and keep up with the adults in his life. Until he managed that, however, he spent his time alternately napping, charming the world or getting into trouble as only a rambunctious toddler could.

But she and Alex both adored him more each day. Even the days they fell into bed utterly exhausted from chasing him around Alex's sprawling estate.

She'd been surprised, actually, when Alex had insisted they bring the baby along tonight, despite the fact that it was well past Henry's bedtime and they were inviting public crankiness by keeping him awake. But Alex had wanted—in his words—his "entire family" there for the debut of Jessica's True Love Line. A gesture that had both touched her and filled her with added anxiety.

"All to show how proud they are and how much they support you."

Chest finally beginning to loosen, she gave a peaceful sigh. "You're better than a full body massage, do you know that?"

Alex made a low, contented sound at the back of his throat. "I'll remind you that you said that—later, when we get home."

Leaning into him, she let his warmth and love surround her, calm her, remind her why she'd been inspired to name her debut jewelry line True Love to begin with. The wisdom of that decision was only underscored when he pressed a kiss to her brow.

"At the risk of sending you into a near faint again," he murmured against her skin, "I have one more thing I need to discuss with you before we unveil your designs."

A shimmer of tension rolled through her, but nowhere near the level of moments before.

Reaching into his pocket, Alex drew out a small velvet jewelry box with the Bajoran Designs logo stamped on the outside.

"We've been together a year now. Living together, raising Henry, loving each other like a real family. And I, at least, think it's working."

Popping open the lid of the box, he held it out to her. Inside was the most beautiful, sparkling diamond engagement ring she'd ever seen. Her heart lurched and the air stuck in her lungs.

"So how about we make it official?" he asked. "I love you, Jessica. I have almost since the moment we met, even if I didn't quite realize it. You getting pregnant with Henry that first night together was the greatest miracle of my life, because it brought you back to me when I might have lost you otherwise."

Moisture prickled Jessica's eyes as emotion filled her with a wave of unadulterated joy, tightening her chest.

"Oh, Alex," she breathed. "I love you, too. And I'm so glad you saw Henry and me as a blessing rather than a burden."

He tugged her close once again, framing her face with both hands, placing a hard kiss on her lips this time. When he spoke, he had to clear his throat, and even then his voice was rough and deeper than normal.

"The only burden you or Henry could ever cause me is making me hold this ring much longer. Will you marry me, Jessica? Be my wife, my lover, my partner both at home and at the office, and the mother of not just the child we already have, but any others who might come along?"

It was the easiest question she'd ever had to answer.

"Oh, yes." A tear slipped down her cheek, and she couldn't have cared less that it might mar her perfectly applied makeup.

He took the ring from its nest of velvet and slipped it on her left hand. The stone, roughly the size of a dime, glittered in the light of the room. She turned her hand one way, then another, taking pleasure in every facet and detail that caught her eye.

"It's beautiful, Alex, thank you."

It was also huge and quite heavy. She would need a little red wagon to cart it around with her all day, every day.

"I designed it myself," he told her, chuckling when she shot him a surprised look. "I may not be as talented as you, but I knew what I wanted. I also know what you like."

Taking her hand, he slid the ring back off her finger. "I know you think it's too big, too ostentatious, even though secretly, you adore how large and showy it is."

Well, he had her there. Didn't every woman want an engagement ring the size of a compact car to show off and use to impress their friends?

"Which is why it's actually two rings that come together to form one."

He wiggled things around with a little click, and suddenly he held a piece in each hand. They were both gorgeous and still quite remarkable, while also being a bit more manageable.

"You can choose which to wear on a regular basis, or switch back and forth, if you like. And when you want to flaunt your wealth or show off just how much your husband adores you, you can put them together and cause temporary blind spells everywhere you go."

She laughed, amazed at his ingenuity and how much thought he'd put into it when he could have pulled any ring from the Bajoran Designs collection instead, and she wouldn't have known the difference.

"I'm *very* impressed," she admitted as he clicked the two bands into place and slipped all umpteen carats back on her finger.

Going on tiptoe, she wrapped her arms around his neck and pressed a soft kiss to his waiting lips. "I also love it. And I love you. Coming to Seattle was the best decision I ever made, even if we got off to a slightly rocky start."

His own arms came up to circle her waist, holding her close while he nibbled lightly at the corners of her mouth and jaw.

"Ah, but don't you know that the rockiest paths sometimes lead to the very best destinations?"

With a perfectly contented sigh, she leaned back to stare deep into his crystal-clear sapphire eyes.

"Yes, I guess I do," she whispered as everything else faded away, leaving them the only two people in the world, let alone the crowded ballroom. "Because my rocky path led me to you."

* * * * *

LET'S TALK
Romance

For exclusive extracts, competitions
and special offers, find us online:

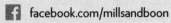 facebook.com/millsandboon

@MillsandBoon

@MillsandBoonUK

Get in touch on 01413 063232

For all the latest titles coming soon, visit
millsandboon.co.uk/nextmonth

MILLS & BOON

MODERN

Power and Passion

Prepare to be swept off your feet by sophisticated, sexy and seductive heroes, in some of the world's most glamourous and romantic locations, where power and passion collide.

Eight Modern stories published every month, find them all

millsandboon.co.uk/Modern

MILLS & BOON
Desire

Indulge in secrets and scandal, intense drama and plenty of sizzling hot action with powerful and passionate heroes who have it all: wealth, status, good looks… everything but the right woman.

P. ♀